Gordon

Sensuous Seduction

"I want to be with you, Christopher," Katie whispered. "I love you."

With a groan, he took her in his arms. "You're so tempting, Katie. But . . ."

"Christopher," her voice was throaty and her whole body was on fire with longing, "we have to . . ."

Moving a little away from him, she began to unbutton the bodice of her gown. Christopher watched hopelessly for a moment, then surrendered to the desire that flamed within him. He loved her and he could wait no longer to have her. In a surge of blazing passion, he guided her to their makeshift bed.

Katie was lost in the splendor of his embrace as Christopher caressed her flawless flesh in long, smooth strokes that traced her from shoulder to thigh. She moaned in anticipation. It felt so right being with him. Molding her hips to his, she wrapped a slender bare leg around his still-clad thighs and moved eagerly against him.

"Is it always this perfect?" she gasped as he pulled her even closer to his lean strength.

"Between us, it will be," he said, his voice like velvet. "Always."

MORE CAPTIVATING ROMANCE FROM ZEBRA

FORBIDDEN FIRES (1295, $3.50)
by Bobbi Smith

When Ellyn Douglas rescued the handsome Union officer from the raging river, she had no choice but to surrender to the sensuous stranger as he pulled her against his hard muscular body. Forgetting they were enemies in a senseless war, they were destined to share a life of unbridled ecstasy and glorious love!

WANTON SPLENDOR (1461, $3.50)
by Bobbi Smith

Kathleen had every intention of keeping her distance from Christopher Fletcher. But in the midst of a devastating hurricane, she crept into his arms. As she felt the heat of his lean body pressed against hers, she wondered breathlessly what it would be like to kiss those cynical lips—to turn that cool arrogance to fiery passion!

LOVE'S ELUSIVE FLAME (1267, $3.75)
by Phoebe Conn

Enraptured by his ardent kisses and tantalizing caresses, golden-haired Flame had found the man of her dreams in the handsome rogue Joaquin. But if he wanted her completely she would have to be his only woman—and he had always been taken women whenever he wanted, and not one had ever refused him or pretended to try!

ECSTASY'S PARADISE (1460, $3.75)
by Phoebe Conn

Meeting the woman he was to escort to her future husband, sea captain Phillip Bradford was astounded. The Swedish beauty was the woman of his dreams, his fantasy come true. But how could he deliver her to another man's bed when he wanted her to warm his own?

Available wherever paperbacks are sold, or order direct from the Publisher. Send cover price plus 50¢ per copy for mailing and handling to Zebra Books, 475 Park Avenue South, New York, N.Y. 10016. DO NOT SEND CASH.

Wanton Splendor

by Bobbi Smith

ZEBRA BOOKS
KENSINGTON PUBLISHING CORP.

ZEBRA BOOKS

are published by

Kensington Publishing Corp.
475 Park Avenue South
New York, N.Y. 10016

First printing: October 1984

Printed in the United States of America

This book is dedicated to so many wonderful people that I can't possibly list them all. You were there when we needed you and your help will never be forgotten. Thanks.

A special note of thanks to Mrs. Pamela Arcenceaux of the New Orleans Historic Collection.

And a very special note of thanks to Dianne and Bill without whose phone, food, and friendship I wouldn't be quite as sane as I am right now!

Prologue

The Reason

Late summer, 1855

In the gaming room of the Bird of Paradise saloon, a strained silence reigned as the onlookers crowded around the main table to watch the poker game in progress. The air was stale with the scent of old cigars and too-sweet perfume but no one noticed as all attention was riveted on the scenario being acted out before them.

"Damn!" The tense mood was fractured by James Williams's muttered oath. "I'm out," he proclaimed in disgust, throwing his cards face down on the table.

An expectant hush fell over the crowd again as they waited to see who would be the next to fold in this high stakes game. That dubious honor fell to young Edward Courtois who followed his friend James's wise example and dropped out before it got too expensive even for his well-lined pockets.

It grew quiet again. Only two players remained, Andre Montard, a local planter's son, and a Northerner,

Christopher Fletcher, who was in town for a visit and was staying with Williams.

The pot had grown to over $12,000 and everyone waited anxiously to see what the Yankee would do next. Sentiment was with the stranger for he had proven himself to be a true gentleman, while Andre . . . well, he was his father's son—arrogant, loud, and often openly cruel.

"I'll raise you $1,000," Christopher Fletcher spoke, his tone indifferent.

Christopher had had enough of the game and of Montard. All evening he had successfully managed to ignore Andre's crude manner. But now, he was forced to contend with him and Christopher found the situation quite taxing. The man was a bore. Smiling to himself, he watched Andre across the green felt-topped table. The man was nervous. More confident than ever, he smiled serenely.

"Andre? Your bet." Tapping the ashes from his cheroot, Christopher met his gaze evenly.

Andre Montard looked at the self-confident Yankee pig sitting at the table with him with carefully concealed disgust. Anger filled him as he realized that this stranger had bested him in front of his friends. Glancing down at his cards, he knew there was no chance he could win. He had only a pair of jacks and an ace, not quite a winning hand. Trying to appear nonchalant, but not succeeding, Andre threw in his hand.

"I'm afraid I'm out too."

A surprised gasp ran through the crowd at the Creole's sudden capitulation. The visitor had just won over $12,000!

Christopher continued to stare at Andre for a long moment. Then slowly folding his hand, he added his cards to the confused stack on the table. A second later, when Andre would have turned his cards over,

8

Christopher quickly grabbed his wrist.

"You only see my hand if you pay." His voice was quiet and deadly.

Andre blanched. "I've paid enough!" he complained, eyeing the small fortune Christopher had just won, largely at his expense.

"Not quite. It would have cost you another $2,000 to see my cards and you didn't want to chance it." Christopher spoke quietly.

Livid with frustrated fury, Andre contemplated challenging this Northerner to a duel. It was only the memory of an earlier conversation that held him quiet. According to rumor, Fletcher was a crack shot and Andre was overly fond of living. Not that he would forget this moment. No, he would remember what had happened here tonight. But for now, it seemed sensible to excuse himself as quickly as possible. Rising from the table, he bid them all a curt goodnight and hurriedly left the saloon.

James and Edward looked at Christopher triumphantly, "We knew you would do it!"

Christopher smiled broadly at them as he pocketed his winnings. "You had doubts?"

"None at all!" Edward reassured him.

"What were you holding, anyway?" James asked, now that the crowd had wandered away.

Christopher's grin was almost mischievous as he flipped over the five cards.

"You're joking! A pair of eights?"

"That's wonderful!"

Laughing heartily, they clapped him on the back.

"The rest of the evening is on me," Christopher offered and James and Edward accepted eagerly as they followed him to the bar, anxious to relax now that the card playing was over.

* * *

It was daybreak the tinge of gold on the eastern horizon bringing an end to the stifling blackness that New Orleans called night. A predawn silence hung heavily in the humid air — as if the city were holding its breath in anticipation of another sweltering day.

The three drunken revelers, however, took little notice of the oppressive heat or the brightening of the sky as they bid a fond yet boisterous goodnight to the ladies of the establishment. Echoes of their laughter rumbled through the still, silent streets as they made their merry, unsteady way to the waiting carriage.

"Let's head home, Andy," James Williams called to his driver as he climbed inside ahead of his friends.

"What a night!" Edward declared as he collapsed heavily on the seat next to James.

"Especially the last game. Eh, Chris?" James smiled wickedly as Christopher joined them in the carriage.

Christopher, who somehow managed to appear half-way sober, grinned at his drunken companions. "That last hand certainly was profitable."

"I'll say!" Edward agreed enthusiastically. "Where did you learn to play cards so well?"

"Around," Christopher answered absently.

"Well, Andre Montard sure was upset," James added. "I don't think he's ever been beaten that badly before."

Christopher shrugged his broad shoulders indifferently. "If he can't afford to lose, he shouldn't play," his clipped Northern accent a definite contrast to his cohorts' melodic drawl.

The conversation lagged then as the carriage jolted forward on the familiar trip to the Williams's home.

Gazing out the window, Christopher watched the passing buildings with little interest; his expression solemn. It was happening to him again, he realized,

10

and after only three weeks. He had hoped his visit with James and Edward would still his restlessness and it had, for a little while. But now, somehow, the endless nights of drinking, card-playing and wenching were taking on a repetitive sameness. No matter how high the stakes or how beautiful the women, he found little to amuse him. Christopher felt jaded and very weary of it all.

Sighing inaudibly, he reflected on his life. Things had always been easy for him, too easy. As the only son of a wealthy Philadelphia couple, he had been pampered and spoiled. He'd grown to adulthood expecting and receiving only the best that life could offer. It wasn't until he was away at the university that he'd discovered the first real challenge of his life — gambling. For Christopher, the desire to win was overwhelming; he had to be the best. He played cards with a vengeance, matching wits with the best, until he'd perfected his skill to a fine art. But the glamor had worn off after a while. He didn't gamble because he needed funds and there had been little sport in taking money from his inexperienced fellow classmates. So, turning his attention back to his studies, he had finished school and returned home to Philadelphia, where he'd been welcomed into that very closed society with open arms. After all, he was a Fletcher.

Darkly handsome and self-assured to the point of arrogance, Christopher had enjoyed to the hilt his new status as the most sought-after bachelor in town. Even now the memory of those marriage-minded mamas and maidens could make him smile. True, there had been pretty ones among the available young women, but not one had caught his eye. And so he'd played with them all, yet promised them nothing. In the end, frustrated in their attempt to maneuver him into the happy state of wedlock, they gave up one by one and married, in his opinion, a far less worthy quarry.

It seemed to him, now though, that the wanderlust that plagued him had begun after his parents were killed in a tragic carriage accident some four years ago. Suddenly at twenty-two, he'd found himself footloose, fancy-free and the sole beneficiary of the Fletcher family fortune. After a suitable period of mourning, he'd left the family business in the hands of trusted advisors and had toured Europe, partaking of all the delights those cultured countries had to offer. It was there that he'd met Edward and James who were on their Grand Tour. They'd forged an immediate friendship and had finished their travels together. Upon returning to America, they'd gone their separate ways but somehow managed to keep in touch.

Now, here he was with his friends in a very exciting Southern city and he was bored. Even the lucrative win from that Montard fool this evening hadn't improved his spirits. Dismissing his thoughts, Christopher turned his attention back to Edward and James and he almost laughed out loud. In spite of the bumpy ride, the hard seat and the now bright sunlight, James had managed to fall asleep. Edward, however, was busily staring out the window, watching the streets of New Orleans come to life.

"Damn! I'm not ready to call it a night!" Edward insisted, turning to Christopher.

"I think we should call it a day," Christopher said ruefully. "I could use some sleep."

"No. We can sleep anytime. Let's celebrate!" Edward shook James unceremoniously. "Wake up! We're going to celebrate!"

"Celebrate what?" James asked wearily, straightening up almost painfully from his cramped position. "I believe we've already toasted every occasion for the next ten years."

12

"Well, we have to do something," Edward argued. "We just can't go home."

"Ed," James was losing his patience. "I don't know about you, but I'm exhausted."

"I'm afraid I've had enough for one night, too," Christopher said, knowing that unless he was firmly dissuaded, Edward would conjure up some obscure event for them to attend.

"I've got it!" Edward shouted excitedly, ignoring James as he flinched. Hanging out the window, he shouted a change of instructions to Andy.

"What are you up to now?" James asked irritably. "You know Christopher and I are both tired."

"Don't you remember what Andre said?" Edward remarked in exasperation.

"Andre said a lot of things and most of it was pure —" James started.

"I know, I know, but don't you remember his telling us about the auction today? That big buck who's been giving them so much trouble up at Greenwood is going to be sold this morning!"

"Do you mean Joel?" James frowned in concentration as he tried to recall the conversation.

"That's his name! What do you say? Shall we go?"

"I would like to see him. . . . I wonder if he's as bad as Andre said?"

"I've learned to take everything Montard says less than seriously, but why would Joel, after a lifetime of faithful service turn on his master and try to run away?"

"I don't know." James was truly puzzled.

"Maybe he wanted to be free," Christopher put in.

"Some slaves, possibly, but Joel has been with the Montards all of his life."

"But you know, James, over the years I've heard things — bad things about the Montards . . ."

"You're right . . ." James nodded in agreement.

"How about it, Christopher? Have you ever been to an auction?"

"No," Christopher answered flatly. The idea of buying and selling human beings was abhorrent to him.

"Well, try it with us this once," Edward encouraged. "Who knows, you might enjoy it. Some of those black wenches are damned attractive and, lord knows, you've got enough money to buy any one that would catch your eye." Edward smiled at Christopher admiringly.

It was in his mind to refuse. After the night he'd just passed, Christopher had no desire to witness the horrors of a slave auction. But Edward and James persisted, regaling him with the intimate details of what transpired there. Finally, only in an effort to shut them up, Christopher agreed to go. He felt cold inside after he'd made the decision, but he didn't want to insult his gracious hosts, who until this time had asked nothing of him.

It surprised Christopher to find himself reacting so strangely to the thought of witnessing an auction. After all, slavery was a way of life here. Hadn't he been waited on by slaves ever since his arrival? It hadn't bothered him before . . . so why now? Dragging his thoughts back to what his friends were saying, he caught the end of the conversation.

"It's agreed then. We'll stop at the townhouse so we can clean up a bit and then head downtown about nine," Edward stated.

"Fine." Christopher found himself swept along in their plans and he was grateful when the carriage pulled to a stop in front of the Williams's home. He needed time to think things through, so he could view the slave sale with studied aloofness instead of the revulsion he now felt. Christopher prided himself on being in control of his emotions and he fully intended to be unaffected during the auction.

In another part of town, the dawning of the new day brought only terror. Crowded into the dark confines of a windowless shanty, the slaves who were to be sold this forenoon awaited their fate in fearful silence. The night had passed slowly. Each minute had seemed an hour, as the suffocating heat had held them paralyzed. Only the droning of the ever-present mosquitoes and the occasional cry of a babe in arms broke the deathly stillness.

From his vantage point in the corner opposite the door, Joel watched the sun rise. His expression was bleak as he realized that the hour of the auction would soon be upon him. Sleep had been impossible as the turmoil of his emotions had kept him fully awake. Shifting painfully, he cursed under his breath as the chains that bound him, neck, hand, and foot, rattled loudly. All eyes turned toward him in the dim light, but Joel looked away, his humiliation too great. Never before in all of his twenty some odd years had he been in chains. And yet, here he was, the only one in the room who'd been beaten and bound. Joel could feel the others looking at him, but he didn't speak. He hadn't spoken since he'd been thrown in here half-conscious yesterday afternoon and he didn't intend to start now.

A sudden tenseness settled over the room as the gate to the pen that surrounded the shack clanged open and the bellowing of the guards drew nearer.

"Get off your lazy asses!" the guard gruffly commanded as he pounded on the outside wall. "And get out here where we can see you!"

The blacks looked at each other nervously and then,

afraid of the cruelty of the guards, they scurried out the door. They had seen what had happened to Joel the day before.

The brightness of the morning sun was blinding as they poured forth from the haven of the little cabin. Joel almost thought it amusing. What good did it do to act the perfect slave for these men? These guards were poor white trash who couldn't afford to buy an expensive slave.

Slowly, Joel got to his feet. The severe flogging he'd been dealt the day before left him dizzy and weak and he swayed momentarily. Concentrating solely on walking, he staggered toward the door taking care not to trip over the short length of chain that hobbled him.

Moving outside into the small fenced yard, Joel waited, silently watching the guards with undisguised hatred. He had had no quarrel with whites before, but now he was filled with righteous anger. In the past seven days his whole life had been destroyed . . . all because of Andre Montard and his father Emil. The pain ran deep as Joel thought of the long years he'd spent working for them. He had been a loyal, faithful servant and had worked his way up to the respected position of head groomsman in the Montard's well-stocked stables. True, he had longed for freedom, but he'd seen what fate had befallen the other slaves who'd been foolish enough to try to revolt against the master. So, Joel played his role and reaped what few benefits he could.

The Montard family was not known for their generosity or their kindness. Extremely wealthy, they worried little about the welfare of their slaves, for after all, they could be easily replaced.

Joel himself had never experienced the Montards' cruelty until this past week. A week in which he had to stand helplessly by while Dee, his wife, had been made the sexual plaything of the younger Montard. In desperation, they had fled the plantation with their child, but their freedom had been short-lived. Hunted down by the patrollers and their dogs, they'd been dragged back to a gloating Andre. He'd ordered Dee and the baby taken to the quarters, while he had personally whipped Joel. And, in order to insure no further interference, Andre had instructed the overseer to have Joel sold downriver.

Now, here he stood, his back a mass of seeping sores, waiting for the auction to begin. A surge of pride swelled within him. He had nothing to be ashamed of. Lifting his head, he met the eyes of the nearest guard without fear.

"Who you lookin' at, boy?" the short, wiry man challenged.

"Nuthin'," the tone of Joel's deep voice was flat as he looked at the filthy little man with open contempt.

The guard's face turned red at the insult and he lashed out with his whip, the stinging leather drawing blood as it cut Joel across the side of the face.

"Keep yore eyes down, nigger!" he ordered and strutted like a bantam rooster in front of the big, bound black. "I hope the man who buys you beats some sense into yore thick skull."

He would have continued to taunt Joel, but another guard called him away as a crowd of well-dressed buyers gathered by the fence to view the "merchandise." Joel eyed the eager group of potential bidders with nothing short of disgust. He straightened his shoulders as best he could and tried to ignore the comments of the white men. It was only when one of the guards and a customer took a young girl into the shack for "a closer inspection" that Joel made a move. He knew by the leering faces and the snide remarks what was about to happen to her, but before he could reach

17

them to help, the vicious guard stopped him.

"Stop where you are, boy," he sneered, unrolling his whip for effect. "That gentleman wanted a look at what he might buy. You jes' stand back and mind yore own business."

Had Joel been free of his bonds, he would have taken the whip from the little man and used it on him. But as it was, he was helpless to aid anyone . . . even himself. Frustrated and furious, he moved back, the clanking of his chains once again drawing all attention to him.

"See, folks. This big buck ain't near as mean as you heard tell," the guard smiled as he walked triumphantly away.

Joel's hate-glazed eyes followed him to the fence where three young men had stopped to watch.

"Is that buck Montard's?"

"Yes, suh. That's him all right. Montard's slave," he answered. Then noting their interest, he confided, "Looks meaner than he really is."

"If he's not dangerous, why is he chained?" Christopher put forth the question in earnest. He'd been there just long enough to see Joel's reaction to the young slave girl being taken into the seclusion of the hut. James and Edward had not noticed Joel's protectiveness, but Christopher had. Across the width of the pen, his eyes met Joel's in understanding and he knew what he had to do.

"I can tell by the sound of you that you ain't from around here," the guard spoke smugly and spit a wad of tobacco juice out the side of his mouth to emphasize his opinion of Northerners. "So I'll explain all this to you real careful. That buck's a runaway, so his master had him sent down here to be sold. I don't know why anyone would want him, though, 'cause he ain't no damn good."

18

"He looks like a healthy specimen, except of course where you've beaten him . . ." Christopher took note of Joel's powerful shoulders, now sagging slightly in pain.

"Damn fool black deserved it. He ran away. They oughta do more than flog 'em. They oughta—"

"Never mind. I get the idea . . ." Christopher cut him off and somehow managed to maintain an expression of complete indifference. Turning away from Joel, he spoke to James and Edward. "I've seen enough. Let's go."

"Aren't there any you want to look at more closely?" Edward asked almost eagerly.

"No." Christopher was certain. "Where does the actual auction take place?"

"Over here." Edward led them off.

Their voices faded as they moved toward the block to await the beginning of the sale, leaving Joel puzzled by the question that the Yankee had asked.

It was near noon and high overhead the sun continued to beat down relentlessly. As the morning wore on, the crowd had increased and at times the bidding had grown quite spirited. Strong young field hands were bringing top dollar—some as much as $3,000—and women of breeding age were selling well too. Wells, the auctioneer, was having such a good day that he held Joel back, knowing that a troublemaker never went for much.

Alone in the pen, sweat glistening on his bare, tortured torso, Joel waited. He was last and he had expected as much. The guards had been enjoying themselves at his expense, taunting him with the knowledge that he'd probably bring in less money than the little pickaninny who'd just been sold away from her mama. Joel gritted his teeth as he remembered the anguish of the mother begging her new master to buy her young daughter. But the master had had no use for a child and had roughly booted the mother aside, instructing his overseer to take charge of the screaming woman. Joel realized that Dee would probably have behaved the same way if someone had sold their son away from them. Anger blazed anew within him. He knew that he would never see his wife and child again unless he could somehow break free. Surveying the pen for what must have been the hundredth time, Joel realized it was all but hopeless. There was no way to escape; guards were everywhere. Resignedly, he turned his attention back to the auctioneer who was finally instructing one of the men to bring him out.

"At last!" James murmured to Edward and Christopher as the guard prodded Joel from the enclosure. "I wonder why they waited so long?"

"They always save the low bidders until last," Edward responded. "Who'd want to buy him anyway?"

Christopher remained steadfastly silent as he watched Joel, awkward in his bonds, climb the few stairs and stand on the block. He admired the way the slave stood proudly before the bidders, ignoring the ribald comments and the racial slurs.

"What's he really worth?" Christopher asked casually.

"If he hadn't run away and had a reputation as a good, hard worker, he'd be worth about $2,000 or $3,000. As it is . . . he'll be lucky to go for half that," Edward answered.

"No one wants to buy trouble," James added.

Christopher nodded his understanding and fell silent as the bidding was opened.

"What am I offered for this strong, healthy male?

I've been told that he's a potent stud and is experienced in handling horses," Wells shouted. "Let's open the bidding at $1,500."

Silence reigned and Wells searched the sea of faces before him for an interested party. He had had great hopes of getting more than usual for this one because of his size . . . chains or not. Quickly recognizing his error, he dropped the opening bid.

"Let's make it $1,000 then. Do I have any takers?"

"I'll give you $750," a gruff voice called from the back. "No runaway is worth more than that."

"I've got $750! Do I hear $800?" Wells bellowed. When it grew quiet again, he spoke, "Surely you realize what a prime piece of flesh this buck is. Look at the size of his shoulders . . . Turn around, boy."

Joel glared up at the auctioneer and didn't move. He was through trying to please these men.

The auctioneer was aghast when the slave didn't move on command.

"I rescind my bid!" the lone bidder shouted. "He must be deaf and dumb, too!"

"Turn him around," Wells ordered and the guards moved menacingly toward Joel.

Christopher almost felt Joel's desperation and he spoke out for the first time that day. "I bid $4,000 for him."

A hush fell over the crowd.

"You what?" James and Edward chorused in shocked surprise.

Coolly, Christopher glanced at his friends, "I believe I've just bid on a slave."

"I realize that, but why?" Edward pushed for some explanation but Christopher only smiled slightly and turned his attention back to the auctioneer.

"I don't need to see any more of him," he informed Wells. "So there's no need for them." He indicated the advancing guards.

Wells stared at Christopher, momentarily dumbfounded, and then as an afterthought waved the men away from Joel.

"Suh, did you say $4,000?" the auctioneer questioned.

"I did," Christopher confirmed, ignoring the consternation of his companions.

"Are there any other bids?" he asked quickly. Then banging his gavel, "Sold to the Northern gentleman for $4,000."

Joel remained expressionless through the whole exchange, but his mind was racing. What manner of white man was this who would pay so much for him when he could have gotten him so cheaply?

Christopher approached the block and stood before Joel. His eyes met and challenged the slave's, but Joel looked away, startled by the perceptiveness in his new owner's gaze. Abruptly, Christopher turned and moved off to speak to Wells.

"I'm Christopher Fletcher and I'm staying at the Williams's home. Have him delivered there at three this afternoon. I'll arrange payment for you then."

"That'll be jes' fine, suh." Wells could hardly believe his good fortune.

"And Wells . . ."

"Yes, suh?"

"Just be certain that there are no new marks on him. Is that understood?" Christopher's bearing was arrogant and the intimidated auctioneer nodded hurriedly. "Also, strike those chains. There will be no need for them now."

"But, suh! He might try to run . . ."

"Do as I say, is that clear?"

"Yes, suh."

"Fine. Until this afternoon, then."

And as Christopher strode confidently away, Wells glared at his back, muttering, "Damn fool Yankee!" under his breath.

James and Edward were astonished by their friend's surprise bid and were still trying to make sense of it when he rejoined them.

"But why, Chris?" James questioned.

"Because I wanted to." His answer was as cryptic as his bid.

"You could have had him for less than a thousand. Why in the world did you pay $4,000 for him?" Edward was at a loss to understand.

Christopher sighed, "I don't really know why. I just know that the man deserved better than the fate Montard had arranged for him. Besides, it's a matter of pride."

"Pride?" They were confused. "Whose?"

Glancing at his friends he was jolted by their naiveté. All their lives they'd been taught the "Great Southern Myth": that the white race was superior and that by putting the "wild blacks" into bondage they had civilized them. And sadly, Christopher thought, they believed it. Edward and James gave little credence to any other way of life. Their methods for dealing with their world worked, so why change. The thought that blacks might have feelings never occurred to them. To them, the slaves were only property, much like horseflesh. As long as they did what they were supposed to do things went smoothly. But let them get out of line and . . .

"Never mind . . ." Christopher dismissed the thought and smiled cordially. "Let's go back to the house."

"What about him?" Edward gestured toward Joel who still stood on the block.

"They're going to bring him out late this afternoon," he answered easily. "Let's go get something cool to drink, the heat is really getting terrible."

Following Christopher's lead back to the waiting carriage, Edward and James looked at each other in bewilderment. They had always known that Christopher could be unpredictable, for he had proven that often enough during their "Tour." Realizing that there was really no way to understand him, they gave up trying and set about enjoying the rest of the day.

The full moon was struggling to be free of the tenacious grasp of the fading storm and all was still. The heat wave that had been broiling the city by both day and night had finally broken. Standing alone at the open French doors in the Williams's study, Christopher watched as the last of the lightning played itself out in the distance. All that remained were mere wisps of clouds that gave the moon a muted, softly hazy appearance as they skimmed before it borne onward by the cool, damp breeze.

Rubbing his neck in a weary motion, Christopher moved to the liquor cabinet to freshen his drink. James and Edward had gone out for the evening leaving him alone to enjoy the solitude. It gave him time to think—and that was something he hadn't done much of the last few months. The endless, purposeless carousing had made him weary and he was glad for this time of peace and quiet.

Lounging in a leather wing chair, newly refilled bourbon in hand, he reflected on his interview with Joel that afternoon. It hadn't gone well; the black man had been sullen and uncommunicative. Taking a stiff drink, Christopher wondered how to break through the "master-slave" mentality. Joel had been born and raised on the Montard Plantation. How could he convince this man that he was not going to abuse him?

Christopher knew without a doubt that it was going to be a long hard struggle overcoming what Montard had done to him.

Stretching his long legs out before him, Christopher sighed deeply and rested back against the cool, smooth leather. He found it very relaxing to sit alone in the dim light of this study. An easy feeling of languor stole over him and for a moment he allowed himself the ecstasy of closing his eyes.

The sudden banging at the study door brought Christopher to his feet.

"Master Christopher!" the loud voice of Elroy, James's most trusted servant, sounded in the hall. "Master Christopher, please. It's important!"

Hurrying to the door, Christopher threw it open to confront the distraught slave.

"Elroy, what is it?" he was confused; how long had he been asleep? "What's wrong?"

"It's your new nigger, suh!"

"What about Joel? Is he all right?"

"No, suh . . . He done run away and been caught already. Dey's outside. Hurry," Elroy rushed ahead of Christopher to lead the way.

Christopher followed, still trying to make some sense out of the situation.

"How long was he missing?" he questioned.

"I doan know, suh. I jes' went out to the quarters and dey was tellin' me dat he was gone. Dat's when I heard the horses . . . Dey already done dragged the fool back here!"

Stepping out onto the front veranda, Christopher was confronted immediately by three white men on horseback. They stared smugly up at him.

"This here your buck?"

"I can't see him. Bring him closer so I can get a look at him." Picking up a lantern, Christopher moved to

25

the steps to get a better look at the black man whom they were leading by a rope around his neck.

Christopher stared at Joel's defeated face for a moment in mute surprise, but quickly masked the emotion.

"Yes. This is my trusted servant. Why have you accosted him?" he demanded.

"Don't you know niggers have to have papers if they're going to be out on the streets at night?"

"I'm new here and I didn't realize . . ." Christopher lied. "I've only been in town for a short time."

"Oh." They sounded skeptical.

"You haven't injured him in any way, have you?" He took the offensive, hoping to distract them.

"No, sir."

"Then untie that rope and let me get him inside. I can see that he didn't have time to take care of the business I sent him on," Christopher complained.

"Yes, sir. If you're sure . . ."

"I'm positive," he insisted. Then to Elroy, "Take Joel inside and fix him some dinner. I'll join you shortly."

Thus dismissed, Elroy led a tired, frightened Joel off to the kitchen.

"Now, gentlemen," Christopher turned his attention back to the three unsavory characters before him. "I appreciate that you were doing your job and in the future I will make certain that my slaves carry papers with them at all times when they are out without me."

They grunted in disgust at his pretty speech and rode off, disappointed that they hadn't received something more tangible for their efforts.

Christopher entered the kitchen quietly and stood there just inside the doorway watching Joel wolf down the hot food that Elroy had just set before him.

"Hungry, are you?" His voice was soft, but there

26

was a steely quality to it and Joel quickly looked up. "Answer me."

"Yes, suh. Ah's hungry," Joel forced the confession.

"Then eat. We'll talk when you're finished." Then turning to Elroy, "You may go. I'll take care of things from here."

"Yes, suh." Elroy was decidedly upset with this crazy Northerner. What he had just done outside was unheard of in the South. This white man had lied to protect a slave. Shaking his head and muttering to himself, he headed off once again to the quarters to get some sleep.

Christopher didn't speak the whole time Joel was eating. He merely sat patiently at the table with him and waited.

"Ah's done," Joel admitted grudgingly, pushing his plate away. He knew he owed a show of respect for this new owner of his who had just rescued him from another flogging.

"Good." Christopher paused, taking time to phrase his thoughts correctly. "I think you should tell me where you were going tonight."

Joel looked nervously about the room. "Ah was goin' home."

"Home? To Montard's plantation?"

"Yes, suh. To Greenwood."

"But for God's sake man, why? That fool just beat you within an inch of your life and you want to go back?!"

"Yes, suh. Ah cain't leave Dee and Jebediah behind . . ." his voice was fierce, yet anguished.

"Dee? Jebediah? Who are they?"

"My family . . . my wife and son . . ." Joel fought to control the desperation that gripped him.

Finally, Christopher was beginning to understand, "So Andre sold you downriver away from your wife?"

27

"Yes, suh."

"But that still doesn't explain why you ran away from Greenwood originally."

"No, suh."

"Well, why Joel?" Christopher persisted. "You were willing to leave Greenwood then, why not now?"

"Ah had Dee and the baby with me. We was running from Montard." Joel shook with the force of his emotions. "He took a liking to Dee and she couldn't stand him touchin' her and all . . ."

"Montard took your wife?" He was outraged.

Joel nodded, his misery clearly evident.

"Where is Dee now?" Christopher was pensive.

"Still at Greenwood."

There was a long pause as Christopher debated his choices.

"Joel, I want you to go back to the quarters and stay there until morning. Will you do that?"

Joel searched his new owner's face for a long moment.

"Yes, suh. Ah'll stay there."

"Good. I'll see you some time tomorrow morning."

Joel nodded and left the room, thoroughly confused.

After watching Joel leave, Christopher returned to the study for another drink. He knew he had some serious planning to do.

Christopher stood, hands clasped behind his back, admiring the painting hanging above the fireplace in the parlor of the Montards' New Orleans home.

"Mr. Andre will be with you shortly," the butler spoke from the hallway door.

"Thank you," Christopher responded turning around. "Please inform your master that I appreciate his seeing me on such short notice."

"Yes, suh."

When the servant had discreetly disappeared in search of Montard, Christopher moved to the front window to watch the idle flow of the midmorning traffic. It had been a difficult decision to come to Andre with his request, but he could think of no other way to achieve his goal quickly. His goal being to purchase Dee and the child.

"Mr. Fletcher? To what do I owe this dubious honor?" Andre's remarks were snide and he eyed Christopher warily, recognizing a worthy adversary.

Christopher returned the regard. There was something about this swarthy little man that he didn't like. He couldn't pinpoint it—it was just an instinctive distrust and he always followed his instincts.

"Mr. Montard," Christopher spoke cordially. "I won't take much of your time. I have come with a business offer for you."

"Oh?" Andre was not impressed. "What can I do for you?"

Christopher ignored Andre's rudeness at not offering him a seat and came straight to the point.

"I have come to make you an offer on some property you own."

"Oh, really?"

"Yes. There's a slave woman on your Greenwood plantation—Dee, I believe her name is. Anyway, I would like to buy her from you."

Andre looked at him oddly, "Dee?" How had this Yankee found out about his new mistress?

"Yes. And I am prepared to make you a very generous offer for her and her son."

"I'm sorry, Fletcher. She's not for sale."

"Name your price, Montard. I intend to have her."

"Like I said," Andre's voice was cold and cutting. "She's mine and she's not for sale. I'm sure you can find your own way out. You will excuse me, won't you?"

Without a backward glance, Montard strode from the room.

Thwarted in his honest attempt, Christopher left quietly. He had known before he'd come how Andre would react to his offer, especially if Dee was his current mistress. But he had wanted to try, if for no other reason than to prove to Joel that he'd done everything possible.

So it was that he arrived back at the Williams's home, wondering how to get Dee and Jebediah away from Andre. Joel was waiting for him and listened dejectedly while Christopher explained what had happened.

"He wouldn't sell her to me, Joel. I'm sorry."

Joel knew he couldn't give up. "Ah have to get her out . . ."

"Joel there's just no way. Not without getting yourself killed. We'll think of something, but you'll have to be patient."

For the first time Christopher saw a glimmer of hope and trust in the huge black man's eyes. "Ah'll try."

"Good. I don't know how, right now, but we will get them out of there. Trust me."

They looked at each other very seriously for a moment; Christopher offering understanding and a friendship that Joel could scarcely understand and yet Joel in turn offering his trust for the first time to a white man — a man he'd known only a few hours.

One

The Meeting

Late Spring, 1856

Aboard a steamer on the Mississippi, heading South . . .

Kathleen Kingsford, Katie to all her family and friends, made her way slowly down the promenade deck of the riverboat. Though she appeared to be enjoying herself on her mid-morning stroll, in truth, her emotions were as turbulent as a late summer storm. She was miserable. Had she been of a meeker constitution, she probably would have been in her cabin crying. But Katie had never been one for tears; she found direct action to be much more effective in gaining control of a situation.

And so, here she was, walking nonchalantly along, looking for her brother and once she got her hands on him . . . It was bad enough that he'd gone to the card game with Emil Montard last night, leaving her alone to fend off the unwanted advances of his son, Andre, but missing their breakfast date had added insult to injury.

Katie did not want to be here. She longed to be back with her father at the railroad construction camp enjoying life, not all gussied up in these new clothes on this gilded steamboat heading for Kingsford House. Where had her father gotten the idea that she needed to be presented to society? She felt no need for balls and parties. She had been happy where she was. Katie loved the wilderness and the gruff, good-natured acceptance of the men she'd grown up around. Why, she could ride and shoot with the best of them, and curse pretty well, too, although she was trying to refrain now that she was in "polite society."

Pausing at the rail, she tilted her face to the sun wanting to feel its soothing warmth, but the protective brim of her fashionable bonnet foiled her efforts. Oh, how she hated these hats! Katie knew some people considered them pretty, but she found them utterly ridiculous. What possible reason could one have for wearing all these flowers and bows on one's head? Just because fashion dictated it didn't mean it was comfortable. Her basic maverick nature urged her to untie the blooming monstrosity and give it a good heave overboard. She certainly wouldn't miss it, no matter how perfectly it matched her dress. Looking down at the delicate blue sprigged material of her new daygown, Katie almost snorted in disgust. She was used to practical clothes — split riding skirts and the like, not these confining, breath-stealing garments which pushed parts of her anatomy where they weren't supposed to be.

Shaking her head in mute denial, she started down the deck once again hoping to find her errant younger brother. They were supposed to be taking this trip together and yet he had spent very little time with her, leaving her mostly at the mercy of Andre Montard. Katie fought to keep from shuddering. She didn't know why, but something about the man repelled her. Oh, he was handsome enough in a smooth sort of way, possessing the typical Creole dark good looks, but Katie always judged a person by their eyes and Andre had the shiftiest eyes she'd ever encountered.

Nodding a greeting to one of the other passengers, she caught sight of Andre heading in her direction and she almost stamped her foot in frustration. The man was everywhere!

"Miss Kingsford, what a pleasure," Andre greeted her, his gaze devouring her trim figure and lingering just a little too long on the firm upthrust of her breasts.

"Good morning, Mr. Montard." She forced a smile and turned back to the railing to avoid his probing eyes.

"May I say you're looking quite lovely this morning. Your bonnet is very becoming." He tried to charm her.

With that remark, Katie nearly laughed, "Thank you." And this time her smile was real.

"May I join you?"

"Of course. In fact, you might be able to help me. I'm looking for my brother."

"Well, maybe if we circle the deck we'll run into him." Andre offered her his arm and Katie was forced to accept his gallantry.

"Fine."

Andre felt pleased indeed as he escorted her down the promenade deck. Perhaps at last he was making some progress with her. She had been most discouraging these past few days, refusing all of his advances. But Andre's interest had been piqued even more by Katie's reluctance. He was not accustomed to being rejected; women usually pursued him! Glancing down at her as she strolled gracefully by his side, Andre knew that she'd be worth whatever effort it took to win her. Engaging her in conversation, he expounded on the pleasures of living on a Louisiana plantation, hoping to impress her with his family's wealth. He was going to have her and he would do whatever was necessary to achieve that goal.

* * *

Though it was morning, no one in the close confines of the crowded, smoke-filled private cabin aboard the steamer took notice. Nerves were stretched taut as what had begun as a friendly game of cards last night turned into a major confrontation. Just when the mood changed, they weren't sure, but change it had. And now the remaining two players faced each other across the wide expanse of the green felt tabletop, their expressions equally determined and equally confident.

Christopher Fletcher lit up a new cheroot, his eyes narrowing as he studied his opponent, Emil Montard. All evening Montard had huddled over his cards, his manner nervous and uncertain. But now, he appeared almost relaxed as he sat easily back in his chair. Instinct told Christopher that he was holding a good hand, a very good hand. Glancing down at his own cards, Christopher controlled the urge to smile with some difficulty. Things couldn't have worked out better if he'd planned it. Who would have guessed that the elder Montard would be so eager to engage in a night of serious gambling? And now he had him right where he wanted him . . . in a high stakes showdown hand.

Christopher was relieved that Andre Montard had chosen not to join his father this night. With a concerted effort Christopher and Joel had managed so far to avoid running into him on the boat and they wanted to keep it that way.

"Montard?" Christopher spoke sharply, knowing that he'd given the older man ample time to study his cards. "Your bet."

Emil looked over his hand one more time and fought to keep the smirk off his face. He had the damn Yankee now! A full house! He'd been waiting all evening for his luck to change and finally it had. He was going to win,

34

just like he always did. Montards never lost!

Meeting Christopher's gaze, Emil's tone was triumphant. "I'll match your bet and raise you $2,000."

There was a collective gasp from the onlookers and Mark Kingsford moved closer to the table to get a better view. He found it hard to believe that these were the same two men who only a few hours before had been playing seemingly for the fun of it. There was something deadly earnest about this hand . . . the stakes were so high.

Mark had been forced to drop out early in the game after Fletcher had cleaned him out rather handily. Fletcher was good, too good as far as Mark was concerned, and a big win by Montard would help to even the score.

Mark and his sister Katie had met Emil Montard and his son Andre their first day on board. Having discovered that the Montards were neighbors of their Uncle Isaac's in Louisiana, their plantations sharing a common boundary, they had spent the better part of the voyage in their company. Andre had been immediately taken with Katie's slender blond beauty and had been pleased to find out that she and Mark would be staying with their Uncle Isaac and Aunt Suzanne at Kingsford House.

And so, when Emil had been invited to join in the card game, he'd brought Mark along, too. Andre had declined to play, preferring to spend as much time as possible with Katie.

At the thought of Katie, Mark pulled out his pocket-watch to check the time, for he had promised to meet her for breakfast at eight. Much to his disgust, he found it was already after ten and knew that there would be hell to pay when he finally met her. She'd be furious and with good reason.

Mark almost decided to leave so he could go look for

Katie in order to apologize, but the temptation to see the game through to the end was overpowering, especially if Emil had a chance to beat Fletcher. Mark wanted to see him lose.

The sound of Fletcher's voice drew Mark's full attention back to the table and he forced all thoughts of his sister from his mind for the time being. He would face Katie's wrath later. Right now, this game was more important.

Mark watched intently as Christopher Fletcher responded to Emil's bet. Displaying no emotion, he regarded his adversary evenly. After a long, silent minute and without even looking at his own cards, Christopher pushed all of his money to the center of the table.

"I call."

For a moment, Emil was apprehensive, but a quick glance at the full house he held renewed his flagging confidence.

"How much?" Emil indicated the large stack of greenbacks.

"As near as I can figure, about $20,000." Christopher waited almost indulgently for his opponent to respond. His quiet, stoic manner revealing none of the excitement burning within him.

Counting what money he had in front of him, Emil came up sadly lacking, his earlier repeated losses to this man having stripped him of his ready cash.

"I find I am short on cash right now."

Christopher leaned forward to rake in the pot.

"Wait!" Emil spoke quickly. "Would a piece of prime land be acceptable to you?"

"I have no desire to be a farmer, Montard," Christopher sneered arrogantly, idly tapping the ashes from his cigar onto the floor.

A murmur ran through the crowd as Emil paled at the implied insult. "Suh. The owner of Greenwood

36

would never be considered a farmer."

"What is Greenwood?"

"A very profitable, working, sugar plantation."

"A plantation?" Christopher quirked an eyebrow.

"Yes. Five thousand prime acres. It's on the Mississippi just a little south of Baton Rouge."

"I have no use for land. Is there a house on it?"

"My home is there . . . sixteen rooms in excellent repair."

Christopher nodded, pausing to think, "All that land with no one to work it . . . What about slaves?" he pressed.

"They would be included, the livestock, too . . ." Emil bit out, eager to lay down his winning hand and put an end to this humiliating scene. "The value of Greenwood far exceeds your paltry $20,000," he concluded contemptuously.

"Maybe so, if you want it . . ." Christopher hedged, wanting absolute control of the game.

Again the onlookers muttered their surprise at Fletcher's insolence. Why, Emil Montard was a powerful figure in Louisiana . . . you just didn't toy with him.

"Just why are you so eager to bet this 'Greenwood'? If it's as valuable as you say."

Emil started, totally shaken by this fool's arrogance. "I wish to stay in the game. If you are not interested in my wager, then say so!" he sputtered, indignant in his outrage.

Christopher held up his hand to stop Emil's tirade. "As long as the slaves are included, all right."

"Agreed." Emil brought his hot, Creole temper under control with obvious effort. Never had he been treated so insolently before! He would get enjoyment out of taking this man's money.

Quickly writing out a note offering Greenwood as his

37

bet, Emil tossed the paper on top of the cash. Then, slowly, pompously, he spread out his cards to the approving murmurs of the group gathered around the table.

Smiling, Emil looked up at Christopher, "Full house."

Christopher noted the three nines and pair of queens and remained quiet, watching as Emil smugly grabbed for the winnings.

"But I'm holding two pair," Christopher offered offhandedly.

"So?" Emil continued to pull in the dollars.

"Maybe you'd better have a look."

Christopher carefully laid out four jacks and a king and took a moment to enjoy Emil's stunned disbelief.

"I believe the hand is mine."

Picking up the deed to Greenwood, Christopher carefully folded it and slipped it into his vest pocket, while Emil looked at him aghast.

"Four of a kind?"

"That's right," he answered, standing to pull on his coat after gathering his winnings. "And now, if you'll excuse me? Gentlemen, it's been a pleasure."

Bowing slightly to the speechless Montard, he nodded to the others and quit the cabin.

As the door closed behind Christopher, all eyes turned back to Emil. But Montard was a man of quick wit and he recovered enough to smile at those around him.

"Mr. Montard . . ." Mark broke the strained silence, wanting to sympathize with him, but a cutting look from Emil strangled the words before he could speak them. "May I buy you a drink, sir?"

"A fine idea," Emil consented. "I feel the need for something potent."

Donning his jacket, he led the way from the room,

38

anxious to be gone from there.

They were comfortably ensconced at the bar, drinks in hand before either ventured to speak again.

"Was he cheating?" Mark voiced the thought that had been bothering him all night.

Emil stared thoughtfully at his drink for a long moment. "No, my friend. I think not."

"Then how?"

Emil leveled a cold-eyed stare on the younger, more inexperienced man. "He was very good, Mark."

"But how can you be so sure? He won everything."

Emil shrugged. "You will learn the difference in time."

Mark, viewing his losses through an alcohol clouded mind, shook his head in confusion, "You're so calm . . ."

"Looks can be deceiving," Emil advised. "You would do well to learn the same control."

Mark blanched at the reprimand and fell respectfully silent.

"I will be sorry to lose Greenwood. It's a most successful plantation," Emil finally revealed.

"And Andre? How will he take the news?" Mark inquired. "Just last evening he was boasting of your home . . ."

"He loves Greenwood. He grew up there . . . it was to be his." Emil downed his drink. "But Greenwood is not my only property. We shall just move into our New Orleans townhouse until I can arrange for one of my other houses to be readied for us."

"You own other plantations?" Mark was impressed.

"Only three now that I've lost Greenwood." Emil smiled reassuringly. "Don't worry, Mark. I will get Greenwood back. Montards never lose. Now, if you will excuse me . . . I think sleep is in order. Good day."

Mark watched the older man as he left the bar, leaving him alone with the bartender, a big burly man named Jake. After getting his bourbon refilled, Mark drank deeply of the golden liquid.

"Little early for such heavy drinkin', don't you think?" Jake questioned the young man.

"Actually, it's a little late," Mark mumbled, still feeling the sting of his own losses and Emil's reprimand. More control, hah! More action, that's what was needed.

"Late?"

"I haven't been to bed yet."

"Oh," Jake nodded knowingly. "You were in the poker game?"

"Yeah. I made it through a few hands."

Jake smiled. "Yep, that Fletcher fella is good."

"He wouldn't last an hour where I came from," Mark stated emphatically, his words slurring as the liquor he'd consumed began to take effect. "Why in the railroad camps they gamble for gold . . ."

Mark was used to the untamed land and people who followed the railroad, not Southern gentlemen and smooth-talking, well-dressed gamblers.

"Where ya headed?" Jake asked, making conversation.

"Kingsford House, south of Baton Rouge. Do you know it?"

"Sure. It's a pretty place and right on the river."

Mark nodded. "That's what I've heard, but I haven't been there before. It's my uncle's. My sister and I are stopping for a visit before I go on to school in New Orleans in a few weeks."

"Well enjoy yourself while you're there. I've heard these planters know how to live the good life." Jake refilled Mark's glass again. "So who won the final hand of the game?"

"Fletcher did. Made quite a haul, too. He won Montard's plantation, Greenwood."

Jake hooted with laughter. "I'll say Fletcher made a haul! Greenwood is one fancy place. But Montard didn't seem too upset by it all."

Mark shrugged. "If he couldn't afford to lose, he wouldn't have been playing."

"That's true enough."

Mark was quiet as he tossed off his drink. Noting the time once again, he wondered if Katie was looking for him. He had no doubt that she was furious with him and with that thought he hurriedly headed out of the bar, his gait unsteady. The sooner he found her and apologized the better, for when Katie Kingsford was angry, she was a woman to be reckoned with.

Joel was smiling widely as he accompanied Christopher on their way to the grand salon.

"How soon will we be there?" he asked, his long-awaited dream about to come true.

"We're about two days out of New Orleans, so we'll go there first and get everything in order. That should give Montard plenty of time to move out," Christopher explained. "The way it looks I think we can be back at Greenwood by early next week."

A relieved "Good" was Joel's only comment; he'd waited this long to be reunited with his family, he could wait a few more days.

As they were about to enter the salon, the door flew open and a very drunk Mark Kingsford emerged and stood swaying before them.

"Kingsford," Christopher greeted him as he attempted to enter.

"You!" Kingsford exclaimed.

Christopher glanced sideways at Joel, giving him a well-understood grimace.

41

"We were about to get breakfast. Would you care to join us?" Christopher tried to divert Mark, knowing that he was quite drunk.

"Eat? With you? You tinhorn gambler! Why, where I come from, you wouldn't last an hour!"

"Then, if you'll excuse us . . ." Christopher started to move around Mark, but he was not about to give quarter.

"Who's this? Your bodyguard?" he taunted, eyeing Joel's massive size. "I suppose you need a bodyguard, the way you play."

Christopher stiffened; as much as he wanted to avoid any unpleasantness, Kingsford was getting to him. "Joel, I suppose we could skip breakfast today. What do you say?"

"Yes, sir," Joel answered and they turned to go.

"You're yellow, Fletcher!" and Mark swung at him.

At the defiant gibe, Christopher turned to confront Mark and barely missed his vicious right hook. In an effort meant only for self-defense, he countered with a swift powerful uppercut. When the blow connected full force with Mark's unprotected chin, his legs buckled and he collapsed, out cold, on the deck.

Katie was nodding benignly to some inane remark of Andre's as they walked slowly along. There had been no sign of Mark and she'd been forced to endure Andre's self-centered chatter, faking an interest she truly didn't feel. Stifling a yawn, she was about to invent a good excuse to return to her cabin when the raucous call "Fight!" interrupted Andre's monologue.

"Where?" Katie demanded, instantly alert. She hadn't had any excitement in her life for weeks.

"Down there," he answered with little interest, pointing down the deck. "Probably just some rowdy low-lifes. Come, we'll go on back. You don't want to be exposed to that."

But Katie eagerly pressed forward even against Andre's restraining hand. The gathering crowd parted just enough to allow her a quick glimpse of the combatants and she couldn't believe her eyes!

"Brawling is so common," Andre was condemning when Katie's excited words cut him off.

"Oh my God! It's my brother!" Glaring up at Andre she pulled free of his restricting grip.

"You shouldn't go . . ." he began.

But Katie was already running toward the altercation, cursing all the while the billowing hoop skirts that made fast movement virtually impossible. Mark might need her help, she rationalized even though he hadn't lost a fight in years. Breaking through the crowd, she arrived just in time to see the stranger land a punishing blow and Mark drop to the deck unconscious.

Kate took the final steps slowly, her movements almost stalking in nature. During her charge down the deck, her hat had fallen off and her hair had come unbound giving her the appearance of a lioness as she moved sleekly, her tawny sun-streaked mane a glory as it tumbled in rich vibrant waves down her back.

Christopher was amazed to look up and find a beautiful woman approaching. Where had she come from? And who were the rest of these people who'd gathered around? Wiping his hands on his pants, he straightened his jacket and adjusted his cuffs. Then turning to the gaggle of nosy passengers, he spoke.

"You can break it up now." His tone was chastising as he glared at the group. Then directing his attention to Katie as she drew nearer, he ordered again, "Go on folks. The excitement's all over."

"I wouldn't bet on that," she seethed as her fist came out of nowhere and landed a sharp punch to Christopher's left eye.

Katie lunged at him again but lost her balance as her

43

legs got tangled in the profusion of her skirts. Twisting, she fell awkwardly, only to be saved from the humiliation of landing on the deck by the strong arm of her adversary.

"Let me go, you . . . you!" she raged, fighting to be free as the big man held her immobile against him.

Loud guffaws of laughter surrounded them and even Joel had a hard time keeping a straight face. Suddenly aware of all the attention she'd attracted, Katie blushed furiously and, ceasing her struggles, she glowered up at her tormentor.

"Release me now, you ass," she hissed through gritted teeth. "You're giving these people a damn sideshow!"

"Me?" Christopher chuckled, despite his throbbing eye. Never before in his life had he been bested by a female. "You're done fighting me?"

Katie nodded, too angry to speak. At her acquiescence, Christopher let her go and immediately put his hand to his tender swelling eye.

"I always thought you fought women off, not fought with them," Joel joked.

Katie, who'd knelt beside Mark, couldn't resist the urge to speak up. Turning a frosty-eyed glare on Christopher, she spoke cuttingly. "I can't imagine why any woman would want you."

"Shut up, Joel," Christopher ordered when his companion began laughing again, not wanting to chide this woman who had a tongue as vicious as her right hook.

"Sorry," Joel managed as he took a closer look at Christopher's eye. "We had better get something on this right away."

Mark, meanwhile, was slowly coming around, "Katie? What . . . "

"Miss Kingsford! Are you all right?" Andre exclaimed as he joined them, too stunned by what had just happened to say any more. He looked quickly from Katie to Mark before Fletcher's words froze him.

"Andre Montard, I believe?" Christopher spoke sardonically and he frowned as he wondered what the connection was between his blond nemesis and Andre.

"Fletcher? Joel?" Andre swelled with indignation at the sight of his former slave. Why the black was actually well-dressed!

"You remember my manservant, Joel, don't you Montard?" Christopher said drily.

Katie, sensing more trouble brewing, wanted only to get some help for Mark.

"Andre, please." She called him by his first name to distract him. "Mark's been injured. Can you help me get him back to my cabin?"

"Your husband's more drunk than hurt, lady," Christopher said coldly, resenting somehow her familiarity with Montard.

"He's my brother, not my husband!" she returned sarcastically, turning her back on Christopher as she tried to help a reeling Mark to his feet.

When Andre finally got an arm around him they started off to her cabin without a backward glance, supporting a staggering Mark between them.

As they disappeared through a cabin door, Joel looked at Christopher and smiled.

"What are you grinning about?" Christopher snapped.

"That woman and your eye," Joel answered bluntly. "She was somethin'. I ain't never seen a white woman quite like her before."

"Well, quit worrying about Miss Kingsford and get me a beefsteak for my eye." In mid-thought his tone changed as if he suddenly saw the entire incident in a new light. "She did pack a good punch." He smiled broadly and then quickly grimaced in pain. "Ouch!

Damn it, get me a steak. I'll meet you back in the cabin."

"Right away."

And with one last quizzical look toward her cabin, Christopher headed off to his own.

"How was your morning?" Emil asked Andre when he had joined him in their stateroom.

"Fine until the fight," Andre told him sourly.

"Fight? What fight?"

"Mark Kingsford got into it with Christopher Fletcher. Got himself knocked out for his trouble, too. And then Katie got involved."

"Kingsford and Fletcher and his sister?" Emil was surprised. "That damn hard-headed young idiot . . . what did his sister do?"

"When she saw Fletcher hit Mark, she went after him . . ."

Emil looked at his son in astonishment. "The girl attacked him? No lady would . . ."

Andre nodded, "I found it very hard to believe, too, but she even managed to hit him before he stopped her."

"Couldn't you control her and save you both such an embarrassing scene?"

"She was too fast." Andre shrugged, not wanting to discuss Katie's bizarre behavior. "Do you have any idea what Mark would be doing arguing with Fletcher?"

"He lost a good deal of money to him in the poker game last night and he was upset about it. I told him after the game that Fletcher was clean, but I guess he didn't believe me."

"How did you fare?"

"Not well. I lost quite a bit. But I'll get it back," Emil informed him smoothly.

Andre smiled confidently at his father. "Of that I have no doubt. How bad was it?"

"All my ready cash and Greenwood," Emil answered bluntly.

"Greenwood?" Andre glanced at his father, stunned. "Fletcher has Greenwood?"

"He won it in the final hand. I thought I had him with a full house, but he held four of a kind."

"Damn!" Andre was furious. "Did everything go with it?"

"Slaves, livestock and all," Emil confirmed. "It was the only way he'd accept it as a wager."

"I can imagine. Why, he knew what he was doing all the time!"

"Why do you say that?"

"Last year he wanted to buy Dee from me."

"Dee?"

"That's right."

"You refused the offer?"

"Of course. She's mine. All mine!" Andre nodded. "I should have known, though, that Fletcher wouldn't give up."

"So," Emil stated softly, yet his tone was stern. "This is the second time he has outmaneuvered us?"

At Andre's affirmative answer, Emil vowed, "This is the last time."

Two

The Attraction

"Who was that man and why were you fighting?" Katie demanded much later as she applied a cold compress to Mark's puffy, discolored jaw. Getting rid of Andre and sobering Mark up had robbed her of her usual good nature and her temper was short. Standing with her hands on her hips, her hair in disarray, Katie awaited a straight answer from her brother, who was being extremely evasive.

Mark looked up at his sister sheepishly. "His name is Christopher Fletcher."

"That doesn't tell me a thing," she snapped. "I want the whole story and I want it now! Do you realize what a scene I caused out there?"

"You really let him have it?" Mark's eyes were twinkling.

"Yes, I did." She didn't waver from her purpose, despite his attempts to sidetrack her. "Now what was that all about?"

"I'd had one too many and I got mad."

"But just what did this Fletcher do to make you so angry?"

"I lost quite a lot to him in the poker game," Mark finally admitted.

"And you picked the fight?"

"Yes."

Katie groaned, "Were you cheated in any way?"

"No," Mark admitted grudgingly, and Katie lost her temper.

"You could have gotten yourself killed! You're lucky that he didn't challenge you to a duel!" The more she thought about it, the angrier she got. "And I made a complete fool out of myself, thinking that he . . . Get out of here! Go on!"

"But Katie . . ."

"Don't 'But Katie' me! I have no patience with overgrown little boys!"

Mark stood up and headed for the door. "See you later?"

"No. You didn't worry about me earlier, so don't be concerned now." Scowling, she ushered him from her cabin.

When Mark was outside, Katie closed the door behind him with marked emphasis. Her frustration was great as she sat down heavily on her bed. She knew what she had to do, but it wasn't going to be easy. She had to apologize to Fletcher. She had made a bad mistake. And although she was never afraid to admit when she was wrong, there were times when it was a trifle embarrassing . . . like now. Sighing deeply, Katie roused herself enough to set things right.

Lying stretched out on his bunk in the darkened cabin, Christopher pressed the cold raw meat on his sore eye. Considering how ridiculous the whole situation was, he couldn't decide whether to swear or laugh. Taking a drink of the whiskey Joel had brought him, Christopher cursed loudly when a knock sounded at the stateroom door.

49

"Who is it?" he growled, thinking it Joel and not wanting to get up.

The voice which answered was muffled and indistinguishable and so with great effort he hauled himself off the bed, tossed the bloody steak on the small bedside table and threw open the door.

"What the hell do you want?" he barked before even looking to see who was there.

"Oh!" Surprised by his abrupt appearance, Katie was momentarily speechless. "Your eye . . ." she finally blurted out and then blushed guiltily. It was swollen and bruised a vivid shade of purplish-blue.

"Yes, it's attractive, isn't it?"

"I—I, um . . ." Having never blackened a stranger's eye before, she wasn't quite sure how to handle this confrontation.

"Miss Kingsford, is there something I can do for you or did you just come to survey your handiwork?"

"No—I mean—"

"Won't you come in?"

"No, I can't . . . I mean it wouldn't be suitable. I just—uh—I just came to apologize."

Christopher looked at her in amazement. "You came to apologize?"

Passersby were watching them and Christopher was suddenly irritated at their obvious interest.

"Yes, I . . ."

"Since you won't come in, why don't I come out?"

Katie nodded, "Fine."

"Give me just a minute and I'll be right with you."

"All right," she agreed and walking to the railing, she waited for him to join her.

"Miss Kingsford," Christopher greeted a few moments later when he met her at the rail.

"Mr. Fletcher," She acknowledged.

There was something about this man that made her wary. Staring up at him, Katie tried to analyze why she

50

felt so strangely. There was no doubt that he was classically handsome. His eyes were dark and expressive, his nose straight, his chin determined, yet his mouth was mobile with good humor. Yes, he was definitely good-looking, but while she'd been around attractive men before, none of them had possessed this overwhelming sense of presence. Katie knew instinctively that Christopher Fletcher was a very capable, self-confident man. And that knowledge put her on edge.

"I owe you an apology, Mr. Fletcher." She spoke stoutheartedly, wanting to deal with him in a straightforward manner.

"Christopher, please," his voice was soft, almost coaxing.

"Mr. Fletcher," she restated emphatically, irritated that he was speaking down to her, much as Andre had been these past few days. Didn't these men realize that women were intelligent too? Keeping her tone deliberately haughty, she went on, "I was under the impression earlier today that you had hit Mark without provocation. And that was why I . . ."

"Why you attacked me?" he mocked, aggravated by her refusal to use his first name.

"Yes," she paused, meeting his derisive gaze evenly. "But I just found out from my brother that the whole incident was his fault . . . that he swung at you first." Katie waited to see his reaction, but Christopher maintained his indifferent expression. "So, I apologize for hitting you and causing such an outrageous scene. I should have known better." Katie was glad to end the conversation.

"What's your first name?" Christopher asked, as he leaned against the railing.

Katie looked up at him, annoyed by the question. What did her name have to do with her apology?

"Kathleen," she finally responded, not wanting to get into a verbal battle. Now that she had finished, all she

51

wanted to do was leave.

"Pretty. Very pretty. It suits you."

"Thank you," she replied curtly, knowing what he was up to. He was just like Andre, she decided, and she wanted no part of his smooth talk. "And now, if you'll excuse me . . ." Katie turned to walk away.

"Not so fast, Kathleen." He emphasized her name. "I'm afraid you owe me more than an apology, my dear," he continued and Katie stiffened.

"I do?"

"Um," Christopher nodded. "You see, I'll be wearing your brand for quite a while." He indicated his injured eye.

Katie swallowed nervously, not knowing what he was leading up to. "Oh." She certainly didn't want to be cornered by the likes of him.

"So, to even the score . . . first, you'll have to call me Christopher and second, have dinner with me tonight." He relaxed, smiling widely at her obvious relief.

"Dinner?" Katie had expected much worse from him.

"Did you have other plans?" he questioned quickly, thinking immediately of her easy familiarity with Andre.

"No . . ."

"Good. I'll come by for you at seven."

"But your eye . . ."

"There's not much more to be done for it. I'll just have to suffer," Christopher grinned.

Katie was relieved to finally realize that he was teasing her and she flashed him a warm smile.

Christopher stared, suddenly struck by the warmth of her natural beauty. She was attractive no matter what, but when she smiled, Kathleen Kingsford was devastating. She was definitely different from any woman he'd ever known before.

"Shall I escort you back to your cabin?" he offered.

"No," she declined. "There's really no need."

"Until this evening, then, Kathleen." He excused himself and went back to his stateroom.

Katie stood watching until the cabin door closed behind him. Christopher Fletcher was an enigma. According to her brother, he was a gambler; according to Andre's grumblings, he was a scoundrel; and yet, neither description fit the man she had just spoken with. She half-smiled to herself. Apologizing to Christopher Fletcher hadn't been too difficult. True, there had been a few awkward moments, but he had seemed to view the whole incident with careless disregard. Why, if it had been Andre Montard she'd hit . . . Well, Katie didn't want to think about that. Katie's smile widened as she realized that for the first time since she'd left home she was enjoying herself. Lord knows, this trip had been boring up until now, maybe this gambler/scoundrel would liven things up a little bit. Quite pleased with herself for having taken matters into her own hands, Katie headed back to her room, almost looking forward to dressing up for the evening ahead.

Joel eyed Christopher with open curiosity as he reentered their cabin. "Where've you been? I'd have thought with that eye you'd be holed up here."

"No, I've been to the barbershop," Christopher replied, shedding his coat, tie and shirt.

"The barbershop? What for?"

"I have a dinner engagement tonight and I didn't trust myself with a razor and only one good eye." He rubbed his chin ruefully.

"So who you goin' to dinner with?"

"Who else? Kathleen Kingsford."

"You mean that little gal who—"

"The same." Christopher grinned as he poured warm water from the white ceramic pitcher into the matching bowl and began to wash.

"How'd you manage that? She didn't seem none too fond of you this mornin'."

"She came around," he responded with his usual arrogance where women were concerned. Then seeing Joel's doubtful expression he amended, "She came around to apologize this afternoon for hitting me."

"You're foolin'?"

"No. In all seriousness, she did apologize and I asked her to dinner tonight; she agreed."

Joel gave a low whistle, "That's one woman I ain't never gonna understand."

"She is intriguing." Christopher paused as quick thoughts of Katie spun through his mind—Katie defending her brother, Katie stumbling over her apology and then the warm smile she'd bestowed on him. Yes, she was intriguing and damned attractive, too. Setting his mind to the business of getting ready, Christopher hurriedly finished washing and changed into evening clothes.

Just as he was about to leave, he stopped and started to rummage through the pockets of the jacket he'd worn that day.

"What are you looking for? Did you lose somethin'?"

"No, wait a minute . . . Ah, here it is." He pulled a small black packet from the breast pocket of the coat.

"What's that?" Joel was really curious now.

"The latest in evening wear for losers of fist fights." Slipping it on quickly, but carefully, Christopher faced his friend, the eyepatch in place. "Well, what do you think?"

"I don't blame you one bit. Your eye is ugly," Joel laughed. "Oh—Chris?"

"What?"

"Be careful you don't make her mad . . ."

Christopher gave Joel a one-eyed glare and left the cabin.

Lying back on his bunk, Joel smiled broadly. He had never seen Christopher in such good spirits. The past year had been a long and tedious one for them. Joel grimaced as he thought of all the time they had wasted sparring with each other. Though Christopher had freed him as soon as they'd gone North, Joel still had not believed in him completely. It was only with the passing of time that he'd come to realize that Christopher was a man of his word. When he had finally been able to trust him, they had forged an enduring friendship that had helped to strengthen their purpose. Now, they both knew what had to be done and they were prepared to do it. The fact that Christopher now owned Greenwood only made their task that much less complicated.

Joel supposed that it was the sense of having so smoothly accomplished such an important part of their plan that had lightened Christopher's mood. But then again, the prospect of an evening with a woman as pretty as Kathleen Kingsford could definitely improve any man's outlook. Silently, Joel wished his friend well. Somehow, he felt with this particular lady, Christopher Fletcher might just have met his match.

Straightening her skirts for what seemed like the hundreth time, Katie stood in the middle of her cabin awaiting Christopher's arrival. It amazed her that she was actually excited about this dinner.

Swirling around, she took a quick glance to double check her appearance in the small mirror that hung over the washstand. She supposed she was ready. With her hair pinned up, dressed in her best dinner dress, she felt confident that she looked nice. Katie was totally unaware that the simple hairstyle and sleek unadorned gown transformed her from Mark's sister to Miss Katie Kingsford, a rare and precious beauty. Katie only knew that tonight she was glad to have Christopher Fletcher as a diversion. He certainly had beautiful eyes, she mused, from what she could see of them anyway. She was smiling at the thought when his knock came at her door.

"Good evening, Katie," Christopher greeted her, his

gaze skimming over her, memorizing the vision she made in the mellow softness of the lamplight. "You look beautiful."

"Good evening, Mr. . . . Christopher," she smiled as she caught herself. She gave a small gasp as she looked up at him; over his battered eye he wore a wicked looking black patch.

"A patch?"

"I thought it makes me look dashing. What do you think?" he grinned.

"Well, ah, it's certainly different," she hedged.

"Believe me, I look better this way. You pack quite a punch," he chuckled.

Katie blushed at his mocking words. "Does it still hurt?"

"I can take it," he confided. "Just next time warn me so I can duck."

"There won't be a next time."

"You're sure?" his tone was bantering.

"Positive," she assured him, remembering her promise to her father to behave in a lady-like manner.

"Good." Then changing the topic, he asked, "Are you ready?"

"If you are."

"You might need a wrap on deck. The dampness of the night air can be chilling," he advised, and Katie got her best shawl from her trunk.

As she came back to him, Christopher took it from her and spread it gently across her shoulders. Even through the material, Katie could feel the heat of his touch and she shivered, stepping quickly from him.

Christopher led the way out onto the deck, wondering at her shyness.

"Kathleen," he began, but she interrupted him.

"Before you say another word, there is something you have to know." Katie sounded determined and Christopher looked concerned.

"What is it?"

Grinning at his momentary look of discomfort, she explained, "Everyone calls me Katie."

"Katie?" he tested.

"Katie," she answered.

"All right, Katie. Are you hungry?"

"I'm starving."

Christopher was amused by her candid answer. He couldn't ever remember getting such an honest response from a lady before.

"Well, this boat is renowned for its chef. I think you'll enjoy dinner." He held the door for her and they entered the grand salon together.

What had occurred on deck earlier that day was now common knowledge and the other diners watched them with open curiosity. Christopher suddenly had the unbidden urge to protect Katie from any more gossip. Smiling and nodding to those who were staring, he forced them to look away. With a guiding hand at Katie's back, he directed her to a table and held her chair for her.

"Thank you." Katie had been so intent on walking correctly in her hoop skirt that she had not noticed the others' interest in their arrival.

Looking up at Christopher, she was surprised to find him scowling blackly.

"Is something wrong?" Katie glanced about her but could see no reason for him to be upset.

"No," he replied, quickly masking the irritation he felt. "Shall we order?" he suggested as a waiter approached.

"Fine," she answered, wondering what she had done to upset him.

After the waiter had taken their orders, he moved away and Katie was left alone with Christopher. Feeling a little awkward, Katie was not quite sure what to talk to him about.

"Are you from New Orleans?" she finally ventured.

"No. Philadelphia, originally," he told her. "But I haven't lived there for years."

"Have you been travelling?"

"Yes. Europe . . . New Orleans . . . St. Louis."

"You must be very good at what you do, if you can afford to travel so extensively."

Christopher was puzzled for a moment by her statement and then realized that Katie knew nothing about him, save that he was a gambler.

Giving her a lazy half-smile, he replied, "I like to think that I am." He paused, "Are you from New Orleans?"

"No!" she answered almost too quickly. "I don't think I'm from anywhere in particular."

"Oh?"

"My father's with the Pacific Railroad. He's a survey engineer," she told him proudly.

"You follow the tracks?" Christopher was amazed; he had heard of the rough life in the railroad camps.

Katie nodded. "He's working in southern Missouri now."

"And you enjoy that life?" Christopher was clearly mystified by what he'd discovered.

"Of course," she bristled, thinking that he was being critical of their lifestyle.

"Now, don't get all prickly," Christopher cajoled, sensing her anger and understanding it. "Joel warned me not to get you mad again . . ."

She couldn't control the smile that teased her lips, "It's just that you sounded so condemning . . ."

"No, Katie, not at all. In fact, I'm fascinated. Will you tell me about it?"

Katie eyed him warily and then relaxed. "I'm sorry. But Andre reacted so strangely when I told him . . ."

"Don't ever compare me to Andre Montard," Christopher told her seriously. Then lightening his tone, he continued, "Now tell me what it's like, living in a railroad construction camp."

"It's wonderful," Katie told him enthusiastically, her

beauty made even more radiant by her eagerness to talk about her home. "The country is open and free. And so are the people. We work hard, but there's time to enjoy life, too."

"Does your father actually build the railroad?"

"No. He does the survey work. He always rides out ahead to set the line."

"How far ahead of the rails does he work?"

"It depends on the terrain. Usually, he's gone for a week or so at a time."

"How does your mother like it?"

"My mother's dead."

"I'm sorry."

"So am I, but she died a long time ago."

"So, you and Mark are alone in camp most of the time?"

"Yes, and I think that probably is why Father made me go on this trip with Mark." She sounded so disgusted that he looked at her quizzically.

"You didn't want to come?" He was surprised. Most of the women of Christopher's acquaintance would have loved a chance to visit New Orleans.

"No. I'd much rather be back in camp. But with Mark going away to school this fall, Father was worried about leaving me alone."

"I can appreciate his concern for you. You'd be unprotected." Christopher studied her, knowing that she would be a temptation to any man . . . and to lonely men working on the tracks . . . well, how could they resist her?

"That's ridiculous. I can take care of myself. I always have," Katie informed him.

Not wanting to mar their evening with an argument over the merits of her ability to protect herself—he'd already discovered firsthand that she was no simpering miss when it came to decisive forceful action—Christopher dropped the subject.

"So, why are you going to New Orleans?" Katie realized that she'd told him practically her whole life story and yet she knew very little about him.

"I have some business to attend to," he answered vaguely, not used to discussing his personal affairs.

"Well, perhaps we'll see each other again," she said politely.

"No doubt, since Greenwood and Kingsford House border each other."

"Greenwood?"

"Your brother didn't tell you?"

"Tell me what?"

"That I won Greenwood from Emil Montard in the poker game this morning."

Katie was stunned at the news and yet excited to find that Christopher would be near during her stay with her uncle. "I'll bet they're upset about that."

Christopher had no sympathy for the Montards and answered coldly, "He chose to bet it."

"That's true enough," she agreed and then fell silent as the first course of their meal was served.

Andre Montard was in the saloon when he happened to glance out into the grand salon and caught sight of Katie dining with Fletcher. Rage shook him. It was hard enough to deal with the loss of Greenwood but Katie was his. He wanted her and he planned to have her. Why just that morning she had called him Andre! Surely that was a sign that her affections were warming to him. Andre didn't know how Fletcher had managed to insinuate himself into Katie's life, but he was going to see it ended as soon as possible. Surely her brother didn't know that she was dining with Fletcher. Perhaps, he could locate Mark Kingsford and let him know what was going on. Hurrying from the bar, Andre went in search of Mark, thinking mistakenly that the young man could exert some control over his errant sister.

* * *

Their dinner was sumptuous, each delicacy perfectly prepared. And they both ate their fill; Katie being unencumbered by the rules of Southern society, much to Christopher's delight. He had grudgingly come to admire Katie as the meal had progressed. Her conversation was witty and intelligent and, despite the fact that she knew him only as a gambler, she was not critical or judgmental.

She was unlike any woman he'd ever encountered before. Women had always wanted only one of two things from him: Money and/or marriage. Their entire approach had been to flirt with him and try to entice him to their beds, hoping by sampling their charms that he would either fall madly in love with them or get them pregnant, whichever came first. During all his years, he had carefully avoided entangling himself too deeply with virginal women, knowing how awkward things could become. Yet, here he was courting a young beauty who not only appealed to him physically but stimulated him mentally, as well. He frowned at the thought, but then realized that Katie was a far cry from the society debutantes he'd known in Philadelphia.

Katie, sensing that he was pondering something serious, looked at him questioningly.

"Christopher? Is something wrong?"

"No. Nothing. Would you like to take a walk on deck?" He was tired of the crowded, bustling dining room and wanted to get away, to spend some time alone with this thoroughly delightful, unpredictable woman.

"I'd love to."

Helping her up from her chair, he led her from the room. As they stepped out into the chilling dampness of the night air, Katie remembered her shawl.

"I'm afraid I left my wrap inside."

"Wait here," he told her gallantly. "I'll get it."

As Christopher disappeared back inside, Katie moved to stand at the rail.

"Here she is now." Katie recognized Mark's voice and looked up.

"Good evening, Mark," she began and then caught sight of Andre with him. "Andre," Katie acknowledged barely concealing her dislike.

"Is it true?" Mark demanded heatedly.

"Is what true?" She had no idea what he was talking about.

"Did you have dinner with Fletcher?"

Katie's eyes narrowed as she glanced from Andre to Mark. "So what if I did?" she countered.

"The man's a card-shark!" Mark started, but Katie interrupted.

"He is not! You admitted yourself that you weren't cheated!"

"That's beside the point."

"He's no good, Katie," Andre put in.

"Katie! How could you?" Mark said. Fletcher had just humiliated him and now his own sister was going out with him.

"I'll tell you how I could, Mark Kingsford." She glared at him, her hands on her hips. "After you told me what really happened I was so embarrassed that I went to see him to apologize."

"You went to see him to apologize?" Mark was dumbfounded. "Katie, it wasn't your place!"

"You may have started the whole ordeal, but I definitely finished it!" she declared.

"But Katie . . ." Mark and Andre argued. "Fletcher is . . ."

"I have your shawl." Christopher's voice was deep and mellow as he rejoined her. "Good evening Mark, Andre."

Christopher automatically knew what they were trying to do and he could barely restrain the anger that flared to life within him. He wanted to throttle these two.

"Fletcher," their voices were strangled.

"Katie, if you're ready?" Christopher took her elbow,

steering her away.

At his firm, guiding touch a totally foreign thrill shot through Katie and suddenly her nerves were jangled. Between Mark's warnings and her own body's reactions, Katie was confused. Her instincts told her to trust Christopher, but still . . .

"Yes, I'm ready," she managed and didn't look back as they left Mark and Andre behind.

When they were far enough away, Katie smiled up at Christopher.

"Thank you."

"For what?"

"Rescuing me from my brother and Andre."

"My pleasure. I take it you don't care for Andre?"

"No . . ." she hesitated about telling him the truth, but finally decided to follow her innate feelings. "No, I don't. There's just something about him . . ."

"How do you judge people, Katie?" Christopher was interested. Women he had known in the past would have been attracted to Montard's wealth and repelled by his own "profession." But then, Katie was different.

"Honestly?" At his nod, she replied, "By their eyes."

"Their eyes?"

"Yes. I can tell a lot by what's mirrored there. And in Andre's case, he has the shiftiest eyes I've ever seen."

Christopher couldn't stifle a chuckle. "And what about me?"

"In your case." She met his one-eyed gaze evenly. "I'm sure my estimation of your character will be only half correct."

He laughed loudly as her quick-witted answer broke the web of restraint that had bound him all night. He liked her . . . why deny it?

"I wonder what your determination of my character will be when I finally have both eyes in working order?"

"That you're twice as bad!" she retorted.

And with lightened spirits, they strolled around the

deck.

Mark and Andre exchanged frustrated glances as Katie and Christopher disappeared down the deck. Making their way inside they entered the saloon together in silence.

"Why didn't you do something?" Andre demanded arrogantly.

"What could I do?"

"Forbid her to see him!"

Mark looked at Andre incredulously, "Forbid her? Andre, whether you're aware of it yet or not, Katie always does what she pleases."

"She's only a woman, Mark and as her brother, you have an obligation to control her. You should protect her. How can you stand by and allow her to ruin her life?" Andre replied heatedly.

"I hardly think one dinner and a walk around the deck are going to harm her."

"Once she is my wife, she won't have such a free run of things." He was furious.

"Your wife?" Mark was surprised. "Have you proposed?"

"Not yet, but I intend to make her mine."

"Katie does have some say in the matter, you know," he stated, suddenly disliking this hot-tempered, egotistical man.

"We shall see," Andre concluded stalking away from Mark in an indignant huff.

The night was magical, illuminated only by the soft beams of the half-moon and a dusting of twinkling stars. Standing at the stern, protected from view by the fantail Katie stared out in wonder at the silver-coated darkness. High on a bluff, a white, pillared plantation house stood sentinel over the river. And all was quiet, save for the rhythmic splashing of the paddlewheel.

"It's a beautiful night." Katie's eyes sparkled as she spoke in muted tones.

"Yes, it is." Christopher stood next to her, enjoying the peace of the moment.

A northbound steamer passed them, churning white froth on the black satin of the river, its decks alight with a profusion of flickering lamps.

Sighing, Katie faced Christopher and smiled, "Thank you for dinner. I have to admit this is the most fun I've had on this whole trip."

"You really didn't want to make this trip, did you?"

"No."

"Why? Most women would love to have the opportunity to see New Orleans."

"I don't need dresses and parties every night to make me happy. And besides . . ." Katie almost gave away too much.

Christopher wasn't letting her off that easily. "And besides what?"

"Nothing." Her answer was sullen as she tried to avoid his question.

"Katie?" he coaxed.

She looked up at him in the semi-darkness and her heart skipped a beat. There was something so overpowering about this man — his dark good looks, his easy manner, his engaging smile — His effect on her was devastating and Katie gave in to her desire to trust him. Gambler-rogue-ne'er-do-well . . . no matter what Mark and Andre said he was, Katie didn't care. She was following her instincts — she liked Christopher Fletcher.

"Well, it's just that I feel like Father's putting me on display . . . like an auction block or something . . ."

"I don't understand."

"I know what Father thinks. He thinks by having me presented to society, I'll find a 'suitable husband'." She sounded thoroughly disgusted at the prospect.

"You don't want one?" Christopher was delighted by

her open response. And if Katie was telling the truth then she would be the only woman he'd ever met who hadn't had matrimony foremost in her thoughts.

"No. I don't want to get married. At least, not yet."

"Is there someone you care for back home?" Jealousy flared but he refused to acknowledge it to himself.

"I have a lot of friends in camp but no one special." She regarded him from beneath lowered lashes, not realizing how naturally seductive her expression was.

"You know, you are the first woman I've ever known who wasn't totally obsessed in her quest for the most beautiful gown to wear to the biggest ball in order to catch the richest husband." Christopher spoke his thoughts hoping what he said really was true.

Katie was startled by his reference to her as a woman. She had always been Katie the daughter or Katie the big sister. The prospect of discovering who Katie the "woman" was, intrigued her.

"You look concerned about something," Christopher broke through her thoughts.

Looking up at him, her expression one of consternation, "I've never thought of myself as a woman before."

"You haven't?" Now it was his turn to be amazed. How could any female, as pretty as Katie, be unaware of her own loveliness?

"No, but it's certainly an interesting thought."

"How old are you?"

"I'm eighteen. I'll be nineteen in October," she answered as their eyes met and locked; hers unguarded yet bemused, his penetrating yet not threatening in any way.

"You are a rarity, Katie Kingsford."

"Why do you say that?" The words were mechanical, murmured without conscious thought, as her whole being was drawn to the warmth of his dark-eyed gaze.

"You're fresh . . . unspoiled . . ." Christopher caressed her cheek sensuously with gentle fingertips.

Katie drew a sharp breath at the feelings his one small

touch evoked. Who was this man, that he could move her as no one ever had before, awakening within her heart a need as old as time itself? Struggling with this new emotion that surged through her, Katie fought for equilibrium — for time to decipher the strange yet thrilling desire to know this man as she had known no other.

"Ah, Katie." Christopher spoke softly, his voice gruff with the control he was exerting over himself. "You're so special."

Bending to her, there in their dark, secluded place on deck, he kissed her gently, savoring the sweet intimacy of their first embrace. For a long breathless moment, all the world stood still, as Katie was lost in the joy of exploring her own desire.

As he ended the kiss and drew away from her slightly, Christopher read all the confusion of her emotions in her face. He wanted to move from her — to give her time, but her arms slipped about his neck as she yearningly whispered, "Christopher . . ."

He knew she was to be treasured, but the sound of his name on her lips urged him on. Clasping Katie to him, his mouth slanted heatedly across hers, parting her lips and plundering her inner sweetness for the first time.

Katie was mildly shocked by Christopher's deepening of the kiss, but the pleasurable sensations it aroused soon overcame her timidity. Pressing closer, she kissed him back, in no way embarrassed by her eagerness to be near him.

Surprised and pleased by Katie's reaction, Christopher longed to carry her off and have his way with her.

Katie was lost in the sultry splendor of Christopher's kiss. An ache was growing deep with her for this man. He had set her afire and she knew instinctively that he would be the only one who could release her from the heat of her need. Fleetingly, she thought . . . so this is what it means to be a woman . . . this wonderful sense of loving and being loved. She wanted Christopher. It didn't matter what people said about him . . .

And then, all thoughts flew from her mind as she gave in to the desire that pulsed ever stronger within her and in her inexperience she arched invitingly against him.

Christopher wanted to touch her, to caress the enticing swell of her firm, young breasts, to strip away the layers of her restrictive clothes and savor the beauty that he knew was her. And he surrendered to the urgings of his natural drives, when Katie offered herself so freely to him. Thus encouraged, his hands began their restless exploration of her, stroking her back and shoulders before moving to cup the tempting fullness of her bosom.

Katie stiffened at the strange feelings that the boldness of his touch stirred within her. Gently but firmly she removed his hand from her breast and guided it to a less intimate spot at her waist.

Pressing his lips to her throat, he inhaled the heady scent of her as his hands moved slowly upward over her ribcage intent on capturing the sweetness of his prey. When at last they rested beneath her breasts, he kissed her deeply and ran his thumbs sensuously over their peaks.

"Don't!"

The shooting thrill of his touch set her blood racing and startled her with its intensity. Attracted to him as she was, she knew that she had to stop. Kissing him was one thing but these further intimacies . . .

"Don't?" Christopher stepped back to look at her questioningly. When Katie refused to meet his gaze, he moved to take her in his arms again. "Katie . . ."

"Wait a minute, Christopher," she put him off, as she tried to come to terms with her feelings . . . feelings that were new and almost frightening to her.

"What kind of a game are you playing?"

"Game?"

"You know you like it . . ." He started to pull her to him. He knew she was a virgin, but he also figured as untamed as Katie was, that she had had some experience with men.

"Christopher Fletcher, let me go or I'll . . ."

"You'll what? Hit me again?" he sneered, his amorous feelings dying painfully. Frustrated and not understanding her, he mocked, "Why don't you grow up, Katie?"

Katie glared at him, "Grow up? I may not be as experienced as the women you're accustomed to, but where I come from the men know how to treat a lady."

"Lady? Did you forget you just blackened my eye this morning? And you're the one who agreed to come on deck with me. What did you think we were going to do? Look at the water?"

His hateful words cut her to the quick and Katie blinked furiously, trying to control her angry tears.

"Let's get you back to your cabin, where you'll be safe," he ridiculed, his frustration venting itself in his cruel, taunting jibes.

Katie shook off his hand as he tried to take her elbow.

"Don't touch me, you arrogant . . ." she began.

But Christopher silenced her with his sarcastic, "Yes, my dear? What were you about to say?"

"Oh, you . . ."

Turning her back on him, she stormed off down the deck cursing under her breath and mentally chiding herself for having trusted him. He was just like Andre. Locating her cabin, she entered and slammed the door behind her.

Christopher watched her go, wondering what had happened. She had been so responsive and then stopped so suddenly. Katie had given him every indication that she would welcome his advances and yet, she rejected him outright . . . Christopher shook his head. Maybe she wasn't so different from the other women after all. Her teasing encouragement was to tempt a man into trying and then her cold refusal was designed to keep him off-balance, so he never knew where he stood.

Well, he decided, he had had enough of Katie Kingsford tonight to last him quite a while. He had too many other, more important things to worry about. He didn't have the time to concern himself with her quicksilver moods. Trying to dismiss all thoughts of her, he strode off down the deck intent on finding some diversion in the saloon.

Katie paced her room, trying to understand what had just occurred. Now that her anger had faded, confusion reigned supreme. Was Christopher right? Had she been too bold? She bit her lip as she realized how her behavior might have appeared to someone who didn't know her. She had openly gone to a stranger's cabin . . . had accepted his invitation to dinner and then gone naively for a stroll in the moonlight.

Disgusted with herself, she flopped down on her bed. No wonder he'd thought she was less than virtuous. Katie shook her head at her own stupidity. He had every right to be angry with her. Her thoughts a jumble, Katie curled up on her side and hugged her pillow to her. She'd bungled the whole thing. She sighed deeply, wondering if she'd ever see him again.

Her eyes were drooping with fatigue when someone pounded loudly on her cabin door. Katie flew from the bed, all thoughts of sleep forgotten. It had to be Christopher! He had come back to apologize . . .

When Katie threw open the door, she was thoroughly disappointed to see Mark standing there, his expression thunderous.

"Mark . . . What do you want?"

"I want to talk to you." He walked past her into the cabin.

Katie watched him for a moment and then closed the door behind him.

"About what?"

"About Christopher Fletcher."

"I don't really think we have anything to say."

70

"Yes, we do. You've embarrassed me, Katie," Mark commented, remembering Andre's critical remarks.

"Embarrassed you? You've got a lot of nerve accusing me when you're the one who started the fist fight this morning."

"That was bad enough, I know. But then you went and apologized!"

"Damn right, I did," she defended herself. "I had made a fool out of myself. All because of you!"

"But Katie, he humiliated me . . ."

"It was your own fault. You're the one who got drunk and . . ."

"I've given up the hard stuff . . ."

"That's beside the point. Your best bet would be to apologize to him yourself. You were wrong, you know."

Mark looked uncomfortable. "I know. But still, Katie, he's just a riverboat gambler . . ."

Katie gave him a silencing look. "I don't care what he does for a living. You owe him an apology."

"All right. I'll do it." He gave in to her logic.

"When?"

"The next time I see him."

Katie nodded her satisfaction and then ushered him out of her stateroom. "Good. Now, let me get some sleep."

Andre Montard downed his drink in a vicious motion, barely containing his fury. While he had been outraged earlier in the evening, now, after what he'd just witnessed, he felt murderous. Why hadn't that Mark Kingsford listened to him? He had warned him not to let Katie go on deck with Fletcher, but the damned fool had paid him no mind. And now Fletcher was probably bedding the wench! He had seen them on deck, kissing passionately. Why the little whore had rebuffed him at every turn and yet this very night, she was allowing Christopher Fletcher to do the very things to her that he, Andre, longed to do!

71

Andre tried to calm down, but visions of Katie naked in Fletcher's arms assaulted him and he gritted his teeth in impotent rage at the thought of the Yankee being the first to penetrate her sweet, untouched flesh.

Picking up his glass, which the bartender had automatically refilled, Andre turned his back to the bar and glanced about the room just as Christopher entered in search of a diversion from his thoughts of Katie. It didn't occur to Andre that it had only been ten minutes since he'd seen Katie and Fletcher in the embrace and that they could hardly have consummated anything in that amount of time. All he knew was that Christopher Fletcher had once again bested him. And this time it was with the woman he wanted to marry. Jealousy burned uncontrolled within him. He would deal with Fletcher tonight and then tomorrow, he would see to Katie. Draining his drink, he slammed the empty glass down on the bar and left the saloon.

Christopher watched as Andre left, anger evident in his every move. Idly he wondered if Andre's anger was because of his father's loss of Greenwood. Shrugging, he dismissed all thoughts of the Montards and turned his attention to his bourbon and the card game at the corner table.

As he entered the saloon, Mark spotted Christopher at the bar. Girding himself for the upcoming conversation, he approached him hesitantly.

"Good evening, Fletcher," Mark greeted before ordering a beer from the bartender.

"Kingsford," Christopher returned.

"I want to talk with you for a moment, if you have the time."

Christopher looked at him levelly, trying to judge his intent. Sensing no malice in his manner, he agreed, "Do you want to sit at a table?"

"Yes."

They walked silently to a table in the rear of the room

and sat down across from each other.

"Well?" Christopher urged him to speak.

"I want to apologize for my behavior this morning."

"You, too?" He almost laughed out loud.

"I'm serious," Mark frowned at the other man's off-hand remark.

"Apology accepted," Christopher replied wearily and Mark looked at him oddly. "Frankly, Mark, I'd like to forget the entire incident."

"Well, uh, fine. I feel the same way . . ."

"Good, it's settled. We'll speak of it no more."

"All right. Thank you." Mark stood, offering Christopher his hand and they shook hands companionably.

It was the early morning hours when Christopher finally made his way back to his cabin. He had won at the poker tables again tonight and though the pot was large, it meant very little to him. He had gone out on deck after the final game to smoke one last cheroot before retiring and was about to unlock his cabin door when the unseen assailant struck him from behind. Christopher fell heavily against the portal and slid unceremoniously to the deck, the wound on the back of his head bleeding profusely.

Joel heard the crash and jumped from his bed to throw open the door, just as the attacker was rifling Christopher's pockets. When Joel appeared, uncertain as to what was going on, the unknown man fled, quickly disappearing in the darkness.

"Christopher?" Joel rolled his groaning friend over. "Wait a minute," he instructed, hurrying back inside for a towel to press on the bloody wound. He returned quickly, applying pressure to stop the bleeding as Christopher sat up groggily on the deck.

"Who the hell hit me?" he growled, struggling to get to his feet with Joel's help.

"I couldn't see him, he ran as soon as I opened the door," Joel told him as he helped him inside their cabin.

"Damn! He got my money, too." Christopher checked his pockets in vain. "I just left the tables . . ."

"Well, whoever it was must have known that you'd won," Joel deduced, examining the wound on Christopher's head.

"Ouch! You ham-handed . . ."

"Shut up and let me take a good look." Joel ignored his complaints.

"First a black eye and now this!"

Joel chuckled, "The bleeding's stopped. You ain't pretty anymore, but you'll live."

"Thanks," Christopher grumbled sarcastically as he stripped off his bloodied coat.

When he'd washed off the worst of the gore, he collapsed wearily on his bunk, "I'm not leaving this cabin tomorrow under any circumstances. Tie me to the bed if you have to, but don't let me loose. I seem to have developed a talent for self-destruction."

Covering his eyes with a forearm, he ignored Joel's smothered laughter.

"Aren't you going to report this to the captain?"

"Ask me in the morning. Right now my head is pounding so hard that it hurts to think!"

In respect to Christopher's headache, Joel didn't answer, but he wondered at the wisdom of waiting to report the robbery. Whoever it was who had attacked Christopher must have watched him and followed him for some time. How else would he have known about the money? There was a chance to catch him now, but by morning— Irritated at having missed his chance at the thief, Joel settled down and tried to get back to sleep. This had been one long day.

Katie Kingsford sat in the grand salon feeling very frustrated and very trapped. There had been no sign of Christopher all day and she longed to see him so she could try to straighten out the misunderstanding between

74

them. But instead, here she was dining with her brother and Andre, who somehow, had managed to invite himself to join them. She was paying little attention to their conversation, hoping that they would ignore her. But as luck would have it, Andre directed all of his comments to her and drew her reluctantly into their small talk.

Andre's glittering dark eyes studied Katie's every feature. The sun-streaked loveliness of her honey-blond hair fascinated him as he imagined it loose and flowing about her in all of its wanton splendor. He had only seen it down once—yesterday morning after the fight—and the unrestrained glory of her thick, golden tresses had haunted him ever since. Though her fair complexion appeared creamy in the soft lamplight of the diningroom, Andre knew that in the brightness of day, she was not as pale as was fashionable. Perhaps if he could convince her to stay out of the sun for a few weeks, her skin color would fade to a more delicate hue. Andre had to admit that he found Katie's green-eyed gaze unnerving. Sometimes, he felt she had the power to see right through him, although he quickly dismissed such notions as ridiculous. She was a lovely woman . . . her nose was small and refined, her mouth was expressive with an unawakened sensuality that Andre ached to arouse. And despite the primness of her gown, he was well aware of the round, fullness of her breasts and the trimness of her tiny waist. Yes, he still wanted her, Andre acknowledged. He would forgive her her indiscretion with Fletcher. In fact, he would overlook anything that might deter him from his goal to have Katie Kingsford for his own.

Andre only regretted that he hadn't had time enough last night to get rid of Fletcher permanently. But when he'd heard Joel coming to the stateroom door, he knew he had to get away. Luckily, the money had been easy to grab, giving the whole attack the look of a planned robbery.

"I believe I'll retire to my cabin now," Katie was saying

and Andre took advantage of the opportunity.

"Allow me to escort you back," he offered gallantly and again Katie was a victim of circumstance.

"It's not necessary." She tried to beg off.

"I would be honored," he insisted, and there was no way for her to get Mark's attention without causing a scene.

"Thank you." She was not at all pleased with the prospect of being alone with him. She had been acutely aware of his scrutiny during dinner and it had left her feeling somehow unclean.

Andre held the door for her, not missing the chance to slip an arm about her waist as he guided her through. Once outside, though, Katie moved away from the heat of his hand upon her back.

"You know we'll be at Greenwood and Kingsford House tomorrow morning."

"Yes, I'm looking forward to it," she half-lied . . . anything was preferable to spending time with him.

"I'm sure Suzanne and Isaac will be delighted to have you."

"I've never met Aunt Suzanne. What's she like?" Katie wanted to keep their conversation as impersonal as possible.

"Suzanne is a very beautiful woman. Your uncle was most fortunate when she agreed to marry him."

"My uncle is also a very attractive, wealthy man," Katie defended the man she had only met twice in her life. "Perhaps Suzanne is lucky that Uncle Isaac married her."

"I didn't mean to offend you, but Isaac Kingsford is more than twice her age."

Katie pondered that. She had known that her uncle had remarried, but no one had told her that his new wife was young. For some reason, she had been expecting a matronly woman, someone closer in age to her uncle's 55 years.

"I'm glad you told me. I didn't know Suzanne was

young."

"You were expecting a matronly aunt?" At her nod, Andre laughed. "Suzanne is definitely not matronly."

"Oh." His tone made Katie uneasy.

"Enough about her." He changed the topic, taking Katie's arm and directing her to the rail. "Tell me what you plan to do while you're here."

"A little of everything, I suppose," she responded noncommittally.

"I would like to spend as much time as possible with you during these next weeks," he told her earnestly.

"Why, I'm very flattered and I'm sure we'll be seeing a lot of each other." Katie was deliberately evasive.

"Good." His approach was quick and slick as he pulled her tightly to him and kissed her passionately.

Katie was stunned by his unexpected embrace and stood for a moment unmoving in his arms. When the shock wore off, she was furious. How dare he! And in full view on deck! Katie wanted to gag as Andre's tongue pillaged her mouth. Struggling against his chest, she was disgusted by his roaming hands and devouring kiss. It was only with the greatest effort that she finally managed to remove his probing fingers from her breast.

"Mr. Montard!" she ordered when he broke off the kiss. "Unhand me!"

"You play the part well, my sweet," Andre told her, his words slurred with his passion. Her kiss had been every bit as exciting as he'd imagined. "One more . . ."he murmured, capturing her lips once again in a wet, sloppy kiss.

Katie had no doubts now about Christopher's embrace. There was absolutely no comparison. She realized that fighting Andre was useless, for even though he was a small man, he had great strength. So freezing herself, she allowed him no response at all. And when his tongue attempted to enter her mouth again, she bit him viciously. Katie was delighted when he abruptly let her go.

77

"You . . ." Andre's fist clenched.

"*You*, Mr. Montard, will one day learn that I mean what I say!" Turning away quickly, she stormed off to her cabin, leaving a frustrated Andre behind to nurse his bruised ego and very sore tongue.

Three

The Setting

The morning had passed slowly for Suzanne Kingsford as she went about her myriad duties as mistress of Kingsford House. Sometimes, she found the role of Isaac Kingsford's wife a bit too restrictive.

"Patsy," she instructed the black girl who accompanied her, "bring me a cool drink. I'll be on the gallery."

"Yes, ma'am."

Suzanne moved gracefully out onto the wide porch. Even in her ordinary daygown she was a strikingly beautiful mature woman. Her raven black hair was pulled back into a soft chignon emphasizing the perfect bone structure of her face and her tip-tilted dark eyes gave her an almost gypsyish appearance. Her mouth was full, her lips naturally red and tempting. Careful protection of her skin had helped her maintain the pale complexion so valued by southern women. For an older, married woman, her figure was still firm and attractive. Having never had children, she had had no trouble staying slim. Her breasts were full, her waist small, her hips gently rounded.

Standing in the shade of the gallery, she was the epitome

of southern grace. She had been raised in beauty and gentility to become a great lady and in her own opinion, she had succeeded. But having already accomplished at age twenty-six the major goal of her life, Suzanne felt something was lacking. All of her days had taken on a tedious sameness. The weekends of parties and balls were all she had to look forward to and even those had become routine . . . the same people, mouthing the same platitudes . . .

Oh, how she longed for the freedom of her lost youth! She mourned the carefree years she had wasted so light-heartedly. If she had only known . . . But at the time Isaac had seemed to be the answer to her prayers. His age hadn't mattered, he had been rich and handsome and he'd wanted her. Who could resist such a man? Certainly not she. He had swept her away on a cloud of romance and they were married before she really had time to think about it. Not that she would have decided differently, for the prestige of being Mrs. Isaac Kingsford was worth any sacrifice . . . or so she'd thought—then.

Now, Suzanne wasn't so sure. After eight years of a passionless marriage, she was bored. In the beginning, it hadn't been this way. Isaac had been eager to claim her virginal body as his own and on their wedding night, he had introduced her to the joys of shared connubial bliss with expertise and enthusiasm. But as soon as the novelty of having a young, willing wife had worn off, he had returned to his first real love . . . his quadroon mistress Cherie and their son Denis, whom he kept in considerable comfort in a house on Rampart St. in New Orleans.

Suzanne hadn't found out about them right away for she'd been too innocent and too naive to suspect. But as the weeks passed and Isaac failed to return to her bed, Suzanne had become concerned. She had accidentally discovered the truth of their existence by overhearing a conversation between Lucille the cook and Roscoe, Isaac's manservant.

80

Shattered, she'd taken to her bed for the better part of a week, all to no avail because Isaac never came home. Finally, her pride had gotten the better of her and she'd been forced to fight back. When Isaac sent word of his imminent return to the plantation, Suzanne had made certain that everything was perfect for him in hopes that he would be more inclined to make love to her and stay with her at Kingsford House. But all her eager efforts came to naught and, after being so rejected, she'd lost her temper, and confronted him with her knowledge of his illicit affairs.

Isaac had been mildly surprised by her discovery, but was left unmoved by her childish tirade. He had informed her that he wanted no children from their union for he did not want the perfection of her body marred by childbirth. She was to be his companion when he was there, his hostess whenever he entertained, and she was always to look her best. If Suzanne did these things for him, he would give her anything she desired to keep her happy. What he did when he was not with her was, in his opinion, none of her business.

Suzanne had loved him passionately in the early years but the passion had died when she realized that she meant no more than a bauble to him. He treated her now with a kind of warm-hearted indulgence, much as he would have a favored child.

Though the desire she'd felt for him had faded, the need for physical intimacy had not. So, as the years had passed, Suzanne had discretely begun to take lovers. Men who could take what she offered and not demand more.

Sighing, she sat down on one of the high-backed rockers that graced the gallery. It had been so long now since she'd been with a man . . . Maybe . . . just maybe, when Isaac returned the next night she would be able to entice him to her bed. The thought of strong arms holding her once again warmed her and leaning back, she closed her eyes letting the peace of the morning flow over her. She hoped that the mellow sounds of the plantation would soothe her discontented soul.

Patsy reappeared and ever sensitive to the mood of her beautiful mistress, she quietly left the tall, iced glass of sweetened lemonade on the table by her side.

"Thank you, Patsy," Suzanne spoke without opening her eyes, giving credence to the belief that she knew everything that happened at Kingsford House whether she witnessed it or not.

Patsy scurried away, leaving Suzanne, once again, alone to think.

She realized logically enough that there was no point in feeling sorry for herself. She had everything most women wanted — money, a beautiful home on the river and a handsome husband. And if that husband was less than faithful . . . well, a lady dealt with it as best she could. Suzanne couldn't help but think, though, that a normal marriage with Isaac would have been more satisfying than the life she had now: a life with many lovers but little real intimacy.

Looking back, she supposed that the months last year she had shared with Andre Montard had been the best of her life. He had been an aggressive lover who had not been afraid to dominate her . . . something she secretly enjoyed. Isaac left her so much to her own devices that she found a masterful, forceful man most sexually stimulating.

A flash of heat surged through her at the memory of Andre's wildly erotic lovemaking. He had taught her more in their short time together than Isaac had in all their years as man and wife. A wildfire of coiling desire spread through her loins as she thought of his arousing touch and his uncanny ability to know just what she needed to achieve satisfaction.

Suppressing a shudder of excitement, she knew now what she must do. She had to find a new lover . . . a man who would be a challenge for her. She found it titillating to imagine what he would be like and where she would meet him. Lost in her daydreams, her passion grew. With great frustration she realized that there would be no release this day from the yearnings that plagued her.

Rising from her seat, intent on getting on with her work, she was about to re-enter the house when the whistle of a steamer pulling in at the Kingsford Landing drew her attention. She first thought that perhaps Isaac was returning early from his trip, but she knew it couldn't be him for his meeting wasn't until the next morning. Finally, she remembered . . . it had to be Isaac's niece and nephew from Missouri. He had told her that his brother's children were coming for a visit and she had had both guest rooms prepared for over a week now in anticipation of their arrival.

Glad for the diversion, she called for the carriage to be brought around. Having some young children in the house would definitely be a change and she had secretly looked forward to it.

Having packed their clothes much earlier in the morning, Katie and Mark waited on deck for their first look at Kingsford House. The morning was warm and sunny and they had both enjoyed a comfortable stroll on deck before pausing by the rail to watch the passing landscape.

"Good morning, Mark, Katie," Emile Montard's voice broke through their reverie as he and Andre joined them. "Waiting for your first glimpse of Kingsford House?"

"Good morning, Emil, Andre. Yes, from what I understand, we should be there soon."

"We'll probably dock in about fifteen minutes," Andre told them.

Katie stifled a groan. The last person in the world she wanted to see was Andre Montard.

"Good morning, Katie." Andre spoke intimately and Katie wished she could run screaming from his slimy presence.

"Mr. Montard," she answered coldly.

"I'd like to apologize for last night." He talked so only she could hear him.

Katie gave him a chilling look. "I would hope so, Mr. Montard. Now, if you'll excuse me, I have to see to some things in my cabin. Good day." Turning to Mark, she said, "I'm going to my stateroom for a few minutes. I'll meet you back here."

"Fine," Mark replied absently, as he listened intently to something Emil was saying.

Andre watched her walk away, admiring the jaunty sway of her hips and wondering if she would be as exciting in bed as he expected her to be. One day, very soon, he was going to find out.

Katie entered her cabin and slammed the door behind her. Ugh! Why did Andre Montard have to show up and ruin an otherwise enjoyable morning? Sitting down on her bed and leaning forward, she rested her elbows on her knees and her chin on her hands. Her expression was thunderous. Why couldn't it have been Christopher she'd run into? But there had been no sign of him and Katie felt that he was deliberately avoiding her after their evening together had ended on such a strained note. Disappointed that she hadn't had the opportunity to talk with Christopher, she stood and glanced around the room, making sure that all her possessions were packed and ready to go. Leaving her cabin, she headed slowly to meet Mark, hoping that Andre was not there. But as luck would have it, Andre was there, involved in a deep conversation with her brother.

"He was robbed?" Mark was saying when at last Katie joined them.

"Last night . . . he was on his way back to his stateroom when someone attacked him from behind."

"Was Fletcher badly injured?"

At the mention of Christopher's name, Katie came to full attention.

"What happened? Has Christopher been hurt?"

"He was robbed," Mark informed her.

Andre scowled at Katie's interest in Christopher

Fletcher and her use of his Christian name. It was a damned shame that he hadn't had the time to throw Fletcher overboard as he'd planned.

"On board? Was he injured?" her concern was very real.

"Hit over the head, I think," Andre answered her coldly.

"It's true that I didn't see him on deck at all yesterday . . ." Mark was pensive. "I hope he wasn't hurt seriously."

"Thank you for your concern, Mark, but as you can see, I'm fine." The sound of Christopher's voice was a balm on Katie's nerves.

Turning to face him, unable to disguise her delight at seeing him and finding him safe, Katie smiled brightly.

"I'm so glad you're all right," she told him, touching his arm in an open friendly gesture that surprised Christopher. "Mr. Montard was just telling us that you were robbed?"

"Yes, I was," he told them coolly. "The thief got away but he left me with a sizeable headache."

Andre smirked to himself. The fool was lucky to be alive. Being forced to observe Katie and Fletcher grated on Andre, but there was little he could do. He knew now that after the way she'd reacted to him last night, he would have to go more easily with her. She needed to be coaxed and tamed, not dominated as was his usual method. Andre decided as he watched her, that since she was so special, he would change just for her. He would treat her tenderly, with control, and woo her gently. But the sight of her touching Fletcher so casually filled him with a rage to kill. Gritting his teeth, he managed a polite smile and made his apologies.

"If you'll excuse me. I also have packing to do. Mark, I'll see you again," he spoke cordially. Then bending over Katie's hand, "My dear, I trust I'll see you soon." Nodding abruptly to Christopher, he left.

"Look!" Mark interrupted as the steamer rounded a bend in the river and Kingsford House was suddenly visible in a distance framed by massive oak trees hung heavily

85

with Spanish moss.

Set back a half mile from the landing amidst the emerald green, perfectly manicured lawns, the gleaming white three story house was a testimony to the evident wealth of its owner. Massive Corinthian columns circled the home, supporting a wide second floor gallery whose balustrade was trimmed in intricate wrought iron scrollwork. Twin garconierres flanked the main structure as did a dovecote and a kitchen house.

Katie and Mark exchanged bemused looks.

"I knew Uncle Isaac was rich, but I never dreamed that he was this rich!" Mark declared.

"I know." Katie, too was awestruck.

"So that's Kingsford House." Christopher looked at the mansion appreciatively. "It's as impressive as everyone said."

Katie and Mark nodded in agreement. "We'd better get on down to the main deck." Mark took Katie's arm. "We'll be seeing a lot of you once you settle in at Greenwood, won't we? How soon are you planning to take possession?"

"Joel and I have business in New Orleans first, so it will probably be early next week before we can get back."

"Well, be sure to look us up." Mark shook hands with Christopher.

"Of course," he replied distantly. "Katie. I hope you enjoy your stay."

He did not take her hand and she felt angry at his indifference. She glared at him and was about to speak when Captain Lindell joined them.

"If you're ready, Miss Kingsford, Mr. Kingsford?" he directed them to the companionway.

"Goodbye, Christopher." Katie spoke up, at last drawing his attention, her eyes revealing her regret at their parting.

"Goodbye, Katie." Christopher was suddenly tempted to say more, but held his tongue. The memory of her refusal was still vivid in his mind. "Mark."

Christopher watched them until they had disembarked and the boat was reversing back out to midstream. He was more than a little aggravated with himself. He had sworn all day yesterday that he would steer clear of Katie Kingsford and yet he had almost weakened from that purpose. She was a beautiful woman and he cursed her for rejecting him.

Heading into the grand salon for breakfast, he was even more determined to deny his desire for her.

Suzanne waited in the carriage at the landing as the plank of the big steamer was lowered. She watched eagerly, but could see no sign of any youngsters. She was frowning in concentration when a young man and woman left the boat and made their way to her.

"Aunt Suzanne?" Katie questioned, noticing the woman's consternation. "I'm Katie and this is Mark."

Quickly regaining her composure, Suzanne smiled warmly. "You are hardly the 'children' I'd expected. Welcome to Kingsford House."

Climbing down from the vehicle with the help of her driver, Suzanne embraced them both.

"Uncle Isaac didn't tell you about us?" Mark was curious.

"He only said that his younger brother's children were coming for a visit. I just assumed you'd be . . . children." Laughing, she ushered them into the carriage. "Let's go up to the house so you can relax."

The driver loaded their bags and then they were off, following the much-used path to Kingsford House's main entrance. Suzanne took the time to study Katie and Mark. What a shock! They were certainly a far cry from what she'd been expecting. Mark was tall and lean, his features tanned and rugged. He looked more mature than his seventeen years. And the girl! Katie Kingsford was pretty . . . too pretty as far as Suzanne was concerned. She had no desire to spend her time nursemaiding Katie through the upcoming social season. Disguising her thoughts, Suzanne engaged them in small talk, telling them Isaac would be gone for one more day on business and asking them about their trip. She was pleased to discover that they'd already met Emil and Andre Montard.

"I'm glad. They're our nearest neighbors and very good friends," Suzanne was saying as they climbed down from the carriage.

After directing the servants as to where to put Katie's and Mark's belongings, she led them indoors. Bidding them to take a seat in the front parlor, she sent Patsy to the kitchen for light refreshments.

"So, how were Emil and Andre?" she asked, as she sat down across from them.

"Not so well toward the end," Katie put in.

"Really?" Suzanne raised an eyebrow at the younger woman's statement.

"What Katie means is that Emil had a run of bad luck at the poker tables."

"How bad?" Suzanne was curious.

"Well, you're going to have a new neighbor next week; Emil lost Greenwood."

"He gambled Greenwood away?" Suzanne was horrified. "But it's one of the most profitable plantations in the state!"

"So I was given to understand," Mark replied. "But he lost it fair and square. I watched the whole thing."

"Who won it?"

"A man named Christopher Fletcher," Mark supplied.

"Christopher Fletcher," Suzanne tried out the name. "Was he honest?"

"Very."

Suzanne pondered this for a moment, "Well, it will certainly be different without the Montards in residence."

Patsy returned with the cool drinks and a plate of small sandwiches.

"Please, help yourself," Suzanne offered and Mark and Katie didn't hesitate to partake of the food.

"Kingsford House is gorgeous," Katie told Suzanne in between bites.

"Isaac has done his best to make it perfect," Suzanne told them with great pride. "I'll give you the grand tour after I show you your rooms and you rest a while."

"I'd love to see it. Mark and I have never stayed anywhere quite so—impressive before."

"I'll probably need a guide for at least a week," Mark joked.

Suzanne laughed lightly in agreement. "I know the feeling. When Isaac and I were first married, I was quite overwhelmed by the size of it, too. But don't worry, within a few days, you'll know it as well as I do now. Would you like to settle in?"

"Please."

Suzanne led them back into the main hall and then up the gently curving staircase.

"This will be your room, Mark." She directed him to the corner bedroom overlooking the garden.

It was large and airy with French doors on two sides opening onto the upstairs gallery. The furniture was heavy and ornate and most suitable for a man.

"It's wonderful, thank you." Mark was pleased to find that his things had already been unpacked and put away.

"I'm glad you like it. Take your time. If you find you need anything, just pull this." She indicated a silken cord behind the bed. "It calls a servant for you."

Mark nodded as Suzanne and Katie went back outside and closed the door behind them. Excitedly, he explored the room, searching through the armoire and testing the massive bed for softness before finally venturing out onto the gallery. The view of the gardens was breathtaking. The deep green of the foliage was highlighted by the riotous brightness of the blooming spring flowers. Going back inside, he stretched out on the comfort of the bed, knowing that with very little effort he could come to truly enjoy this life.

Katie meanwhile was being shown to a room at the front of the house. It, too, opened onto the gallery but its view was of the river.

"Do you like it?" Suzanne asked Katie as she moved silently about the room.

"It's lovely, thank you." She turned to smile at Suzanne.

"Good. Should you need anything, the pull is by your bed. I'll see you downstairs later."

When Suzanne had gone, Katie sank slowly down on the canopy bed. Perhaps this visit would turn out to be better than she'd expected. Suzanne was being so kind and thoughtful and soon, Christopher would be living near by . . .

Grateful for the time alone, Katie kicked off her shoes and started to undress. Stripping quickly, she shed all her undergarments save for her cotton chemise and lay down feeling free, at last. Closing her eyes, Katie tried to relax, but thoughts of Christopher kept intruding . . . his laugh . . . his promise to see her again . . . his kiss . . . Pulling the sheet up, she rolled over as memories of his embrace stirred feelings deep within her . . . feelings that she was finding more and more difficult to ignore. Maybe, once he was living at Greenwood they would see more of each other . . .

Andre stalked down the back path at Greenwood, frustrated and furious. He'd been trying to figure out how he could arrange to keep Dee for himself. Legally, she went with the plantation, but there had to be some way . . .

The small cabin he kept for her was secluded and private and he was grateful for that this day. He had no time for prying eyes and nosy darkies. Entering without pause, he found Dee sitting on the floor playing with her son, Jebediah.

"I thought I told you I never wanted to see you with that

brat." He looked with disgust at the black toddler she held close to her breast.

Andre found it hard to believe that a slave as light-skinned as Dee could have borne such a dark baby. It had been that damned nigger she had "married" . . . that damned Joel. He was a big buck and black as night, too.

"Get rid of him. *Now*," his voice was quiet but deadly and Dee hastened to take her son outside to one of the other women.

When she returned, Andre had already loosened his tie and discarded his jacket and had stretched out on the bed.

"Close the door and come here."

"Yes, suh," her voice was throaty and low as she approached him.

"Stand here by the bed, Dee," he ordered and she obeyed. "I don't ever want to see that child again. Do you understand me?"

Dee was clearly nervous; Jebediah was all she had left. "Yes, suh."

"I've told you before how I feel about it and I expect you to satisfy my wishes. If you don't . . ."

"Doan worry none, Mastah Andre. Ah'll leave him wid ol' Alice. He wouldna been here today, ceptin' I was lonely."

"You missed me?"

"Ah did," she lied, wanting to distract him from thoughts of her son.

"Show me how much." He grabbed her by her wrist and pulled her to her knees on the floor beside him. "Now."

Dee knew what he wanted. He had taught her from the beginning those things which pleasured him most and she had every intention of satisfying him completely. It was the only way she could insure the safety of her child.

Andre watched intently as Dee bent over him to loosen the rest of his clothes. It was a ritual in their coming together and he enjoyed the feeling of power it gave him to control her. Even though he was certain that she loved every minute of it, too.

Andre's body tensed with lustful desire at the thought of having her again. The business trip with his father had taken longer than expected and he was more than ready for the relief she would provide.

Dee ignored his watchful eyes as she stripped his clothes, gently, methodically from him. She was very much aware that for Andre this was the most erotic part of their joining. He liked her to wear her shift while she came to him so that she would concentrate only on his pleasure. When he was nude before her, she once again knelt at his side caressing his manhood to full erection before taking him within her mouth. There was no passion in Dee's ministrations as she thrilled Andre with her lips and tongue, only the need to keep him enamored with her.

Only when Andre was content did he forget about Jebediah. He had threatened to sell her son away from the plantation once and that had been the year before, right after he'd sold Joel; since then she had been frantic with fear. Dee knew that his warning was not to be taken lightly for he was a cold, vicious man who would do whatever he had to to achieve his own personal goal. And where she was concerned, his goal had been to make her his willing mistress. Dee realized sadly that he had accomplished what he had set out to do, for she was his mistress and for all outward appearances she was willing. It was only in the deepness of her soul that her hatred of him burned steadily, banked by his continued use of her body and his malice toward her child.

Andre's body grew taut as he felt his time draw near. With eager hands, he pulled Dee up beside him and entered her roughly, his thrusts deep and powerful. Dee wrapped her legs around him and moved expertly, carefully keeping the revulsion she truly felt from showing on her face. When at last he climaxed, he collapsed on top of her in complete satisfaction.

Looking down at the contented woman lying with him,

Andre's expression was one of satisfaction. He had taught her well, his golden-brown beauty, and he wondered idly if Katie could ever be as passionate as Dee. One thing for sure, he decided, bet or no bet, he would never give up Dee. Why, he wouldn't give her up even if Katie did become his bride. In no way could her blond coolness match Dee's torrid dark passion.

Dee's head rested on his chest, her skin glowing silkenly with a sheen of perspiration. Somehow, Andre's touch always made her feel dirty and she longed to bathe . . . to wash away all remembrances of his possession.

"Take off your shift and let me see all of you," he demanded, his voice once more thick with desire.

Sliding from the bed, she slipped the short shift over her head and stood perfectly still before him.

"You're lovely, Dee. Your body was made for this," he murmured, reaching out lazily to explore her intimately.

Dee closed her eyes as his hands had their way with her. Andre assumed that she was already weak with longing for him and rose from the bed to crush her to him.

"Want me do you?" he questioned mockingly as he squeezed her breast. "This time you'll have to wait. I intend to take my time with you now."

Dee shuddered as she thought of what she would have to endure during these next hours and she prayed that the time would pass quickly. She gasped in pain as his fingers probed between her legs and Andre chuckled.

"I know you're in a hurry, Dee. But this time, we're going to go real slow . . ." Andre's voice was husky in anticipation as he lowered her slowly to the bed.

Dee put her arms around him, hoping against hope that somehow she could excite him enough so that he would take her quickly and be done. But logically she knew what Andre was capable of and she doubted if he'd be finished with her much before the following morning. Resigning herself to her fate, she gave herself to him, knowing that submission was the price she had to pay.

Later that evening, Suzanne sat at the head of the dining room table, listening to Katie and Mark reminisce about their home. She found it thoroughly amazing that they had turned out to be so well-mannered, after having been raised in such a rough and tumble environment. In Mark's case, Suzanne admired it; in Katie's case, she resented it. She was irritated at the thought of having to introduce Katie into society. But she also knew that since Isaac expected her to do it, she would. She had already taken the liberty of having Patsy check their wardrobes and make note of everything they'd need for the coming months. Now, it was just a matter of taking them into New Orleans so they could get what they needed.

Picking up the conversation, she laughed appropriately at something Mark was saying and then spoke.

"The Fontaine Ball is coming up this Saturday. I hope you don't mind that I went ahead and ordered evening clothes for you both."

Katie looked at her in surprise, "But we have all new clothes."

"Yes, dear, and they're quite satisfactory, but you just don't have anything quite fancy enough for Renee Fontaine's debut ball."

"I don't?" Katie was a little skeptical.

"I had Patsy check while she was doing your unpacking."

"Oh." She wasn't quite sure what to say.

"Believe me, Katie," Suzanne confided condescendingly. "The Fontaine Ball is going to be the high point of the social season and, of course, you'll want to look your best."

Katie stiffened at the tone of the older woman's voice, "Of course."

"Will they be ready in time?" Mark asked, obviously excited about the prospect of attending such an important event.

"My seamstress will have Katie's gown delivered Saturday morning, so there will be time for a final fitting. Isaac's tailor should have your things here by tomorrow afternoon."

"Thank you." Mark was impressed not only with Suzanne's beauty but also her generosity.

Katie, on the other hand, was more than a little put out. She was unaccustomed to having her life managed so completely. Already this woman was picking out her clothes and planning her days. Resentment flared hotly. She'd expected to have some say in her activities during these next few months.

"We'll have a simply wonderful time Saturday evening," Suzanne was saying. "Isaac will be so proud of you."

"I hope so." Katie gave her a forced smile, noting a coldness in Suzanne's eyes that hadn't been there before.

"Don't worry, Katie. You'll look just fine. I sent instructions as to the color and style of your new gown so it will emphasize all your good points."

Suzanne secretly wished Katie was either uglier or fatter. As it was, her trim figure was perfectly proportioned and her beauty was fresh and natural. Suzanne knew that her own stately attractiveness would be dimmed when compared to Katie's youthful good looks. But, in frustration, she realized that there was nothing she could do about it. Her best bet would be to get the girl engaged and out of her way as soon as possible. So, with that purpose in mind, she knew what had to be done. With an all new, exquisite wardrobe, a change of hairstyle, a little practice flirting . . . why the child would be snapped up quickly by one of the younger, eligible men of the parish and then she could get on with her own life.

"I'm sure," Katie was responding.

Though earlier Katie had thought the trip might turn out to be fun, she was rapidly changing her mind. If tonight was any indication of how the rest of this visit was going to go, she was ready to pack up and head home now. Fancy new gowns and balls and debuts—Katie could hardly imagine what kind of creation Suzanne's seamstress was going to come up with and in a way she was afraid to find out. Emphasize her good points? Really! And while Katie hated the dresses she'd brought with her, she perversely resented Suzanne's implication that they weren't good enough. She had been independent and without female guidance for so long that Suzanne's determination to help her only served to make Katie indignant. She had come this far on her own and there was no need for Suzanne to concern herself.

"Are you sure Mark and I will be welcome?" Katie ventured.

Suzanne turned to look at Katie, her expression one of shocked disbelief. "But of course. You are Kingsfords. Your name alone guarantees you entry anywhere here in polite society."

"Oh." Katie was silenced by Suzanne's haughty reply and her instincts warned her to tread easily with this woman.

"I don't think you realize how fortunate you are that your uncle is Isaac Kingsford." Suzanne wanted to impress these two with Isaac's vast wealth and power so that they would be more aware of their social positions. "He is the richest man in the parish, possibly in the state."

Katie watched Suzanne as she spoke of her husband. And while money wasn't important to her, it seemed to be the measure that Suzanne used to gauge a person's true worth.

While Katie was busy trying to analyze the other woman's motives, Mark was rapidly falling under the spell of her charm. From her perfectly coiffed hair to the impeccable elegance of her dinner dress, Mark found Suzanne to be the very picture of Southern beauty and grace.

Feeling his rapt gaze upon her, Suzanne gave Mark a warm attentive smile and, with that one gesture, captured his inexperienced heart completely.

"Tell me more of this new neighbor we're getting. I'm

sure Isaac will want to know everything we can find out about him."

"He's a Northerner," Mark began.

"A Yankee?" Suzanne paled.

"A very nice Yankee," Katie put in and Suzanne looked at her sharply.

"I wouldn't be too quick to sing the praises of Yankees in this house, Katie Kingsford. The abolitionists have caused so much trouble for us . . ." she controlled her temper with an effort.

"I'm sure Fletcher is no abolitionist. He travels with his own black slave," Mark continued, hoping to calm her fears.

"Thank heavens for that." Suzanne was relieved.

"There was no planning to the bet . . . Montard needed more money in the final hand and Fletcher accepted his offer of Greenwood. That's all."

Suzanne nodded in understanding, "Well, it will be interesting to see how this Mr. Fletcher fits into our community."

Katie wanted to tell her that Christopher would do well anywhere . . . but she had felt the bite of Suzanne's disapproval earlier and was at a temporary loss as to how to deal with her. Obviously, straightforward discussions were not the answer.

Up until now, Katie had lived a very simple life: basic honesty and the acceptance of each person on his merit were the standards she had lived. But now, here, the rules were different and Katie would have to learn how to do things their way.

"And if nothing else," Suzanne went on. "It will certainly give us something to talk about at the Fontaine's."

Suzanne knew that Mark found her attractive. Eager once again to feel a man's adoration, she subtly flirted with him as the evening progressed, asking him personal questions and encouraging him to talk about himself . . . two ploys guaranteed to win any man's devotion.

Mark, innocent in the ways of sophisticated women, thought she was truly interested. And as the hours passed, he fell ever more deeply under her spell.

Katie took little notice of the web Suzanne was weaving around Mark. She was too busy enjoying his light-hearted banter.

An unbidden thought had come to Suzanne as she talked with Mark. What an interesting conquest he would make! And what a perfect opportunity she had to make that conquest. Why he'd be staying right here in her home — her husband's nephew . . . who would ever suspect? Pondering the possibility, she noted the powerful width of his chest and shoulders. He would be entertaining and she doubted that it would take much effort on her part to encourage him. Having never had an inexperienced lover before, Suzanne found the prospect of instructing him in the finer art of lovemaking quite stimulating.

Finally, realizing that it was getting late, she suggested that they call it a night.

"A good night's rest will do wonders for you and in the morning, if you like, we can go riding."

"I'd love to!" Katie came to life.

"Fine. Mark? You'll join us, won't you?"

"I wouldn't miss it."

"All right. Then plan on breakfast at 7:30 and our ride at eight. That way we'll be back before it gets too warm."

Agreeing to meet the next morning early, Katie and Mark went up to their rooms. Katie was surprised to find a young black woman waiting for her.

"Ah'm Lottie. Miz Suzanne says that Ah'm to be your personal maid while you're here."

"My maid?" Katie hadn't expected this.

"Yes, ma'am. Let me help you outta your dress." Lottie automatically started to help Katie disrobe.

"But . . ." A knock sounding at the door cut off her protest. "Come in."

Suzanne swept in, "Lottie, I'm so glad you're already up

here. Katie, Lottie has been fully trained as a ladies maid and she's yours for as long as you stay. She is just a marvel at styling hair . . . There's no one better."

The slave glowed under her mistress' compliment. "Thank you, Miz Suzanne."

"It's the truth, and you know it. Why I've had offer after offer for you," Suzanne told her smiling.

Katie was not yet used to the master/slave relationship and she observed the exchange in silence.

"So, if you need anything at all, dear, you just let Lottie know and she'll take care of it for you." Suzanne spoke with finality.

"I will," Katie answered, not knowing quite what it was Lottie was to help her with but not wanting to challenge Suzanne.

Then, with a quick goodnight, she was gone, leaving Katie and Lottie alone.

"I'm afraid, I'm not going to be very good at this, Lottie."

"Pardon?" The black woman was confused.

"I've never had a servant before," Katie confided. "I've always taken care of everything myself."

"You don't like me?" Lottie was clearly disturbed.

"I like you fine. I just don't know what to do with you," Katie smiled and Lottie relaxed.

"Doan worry, Miz Katie. Ah'll take care of you. Seems to me it was time you was pampered a bit."

Katie found it difficult to accept her aid. But later she did admit to herself that it was easier to undress with help.

After dismissing Lottie and settling into the wide comfort of the bed, Katie sighed with relief. It had been a very long day and she was glad that it had finally come to an end. And, as she drifted off to sleep, her last conscious thought was of a tall, dark-haired man with the look of a one-eyed pirate about him.

Four

A Seduction

The morning dawned brightly, but a low-hanging fog obscured the river and its banks, giving Kingsford House the appearance of a cloud kingdom, a magnificent palace set apart from the rest of the world.

Katie had been on the balcony since sun-up, patiently watching the plantation come to life and wondering if she would ever really belong in this kind of environment. She hadn't called Lottie to help her dress, for this morning there was no need. Today, she was going to be comfortable. She had put on her favorite split skirt, and along with her white blouse and riding boots, she was ready for anything.

Thoughts of Christopher crossed her mind as she stood on the second floor gallery. Katie realized that a sophisticated lady like Suzanne would have handled the encounter with him on the boat in a completely different manner . . . She would have enthralled Christopher while maintaining her virtue and still somehow managed to keep him interested. But, though Katie couldn't argue with the end result, using of such feminine wiles, she knew that that kind of game-playing was not for her. She had needed that night to learn how to deal with the new feelings he'd aroused. Christopher had not been willing to wait.

Leaning back against a column, Katie sighed as memories of his embrace swept through her. She shivered as she remembered the flame of desire his one touch had evoked. There could be no comparison between his exquisite caress and Andre's fumblings. She felt nothing but revulsion for Andre but Christopher . . . Katie wistfully hoped that she would get another chance to be with him. And when she did, she would make sure that she didn't bungle it. She would handle herself in a proper ladylike manner that even Suzanne wouldn't be able to find fault with. And then . . . well, then Christopher would know that she was a woman . . . in all ways.

Thinking of Suzanne, Katie grudgingly admitted to herself that she had managed to intimidate her last night with her perfect dress and impeccable manners. But after sleeping on it, she knew she would no longer be afraid to stand up to her, hostess or not. She had been off-balance yesterday. Her frustrated parting with Christopher and the necessity of making a good first impression had been worrying her, but today, she was Katie again. . . .

By seven o'clock, Katie could wait no longer. She was eager to be gone . . . to feel the wind and sun against her face once more. Escaping into the hall of the still-silent house, she went to get Mark out of bed. Without knocking, she entered his room and shook him unceremoniously, waking him from a deep sleep.

"Get up! It's already after seven!"

"Get up for what?" he grumbled, pulling the covers over his head.

"Because we're going riding!" she informed him,

yanking the blankets away.

Opening one eye to glare at the pesky woman-child who was his older sibling, Mark growled, "I think I'll pass up the ride today and just sleep this morning."

"Oh no you don't!" she laughed, tugging at him playfully. "C'mon, get up. I want to have some fun."

"I thought you enjoyed the trip downriver?"

"Are you really serious?" Katie was taken back by his observation.

"You had men courting you the whole time—Andre and then Christopher . . ."

"Have you ever known me to care about a man that way?"

Mark looked suitable chastened but added hopefully, "Well, no. But, Katie, maybe it's time you thought about it."

"Now you sound just like Father!" she charged, angry that everyone wanted to change her life. She had come in here in a good mood and now . . .

"But he's right, you know," Mark continued as he sat up on the edge of the bed. He was not afraid of Katie, even though at times she could cut him to the quick with a sharp word. Mark just couldn't understand her objection to getting married. "What's so terrible about settling down?"

"Nothing. Nothing at all. But Father needs me with him and I liked the life we were living . . ."

"You liked it because it was the only life you knew. And I can understand that. But instead of fighting this whole visit, why don't you look on it as a challenge—a game. You never were one to turn down a dare," he taunted.

Katie stared at him thoughtfully, "What kind of dare?"

"Like I dare you to try to enjoy life here. Surely it can't be hard for you to accept being waited on hand

102

and foot."

"Well . . ."

"Look, big sister, you know Father would love to have you with him, but he wants to give you every chance for happiness. Sure, you were content in camp, but that was only because you didn't know any other way of living. Try this for his sake and then go home. He'll welcome you with open arms."

"Do you really think so?"

"I'm sure."

"How do you know?"

Standing before him dressed in her riding clothes with hair tied back with only a ribbon, Katie looked very young and very confused. Getting up, Mark went to hug her.

"Because, Katie my love, he told me so."

Protected in his brotherly embrace, Katie took a minute to digest everything he had just told her. What did it matter if for a few months she let Suzanne take charge of everything? No one could force her to marry and when her visit was over, she could go home to her father once more.

"You're right."

"As usual," he countered, teasingly. Normally it was the other way around though, with Katie giving the advice. "Now, get out of here and let me get dressed."

"I'll go . . . now that I know you're awake."

"Well, maybe I'll just lie back down . . . it is still early," he started for the bed.

"Mark Kingsford!" she threatened.

"All right, you hard-hearted woman. I'll stay up, but if I fall asleep before dinner tonight, it's all your fault!"

Katie left his room smiling and made her way slowly downstairs, taking the time to admire the beauty of her uncle's home.

Suzanne had heard their voices and taking the time

to throw on a silken wrapper, she'd started down the hall to Mark's room. His door was ajar, but she knocked softly anyway.

"Mark? Katie?"

"I'll be right there," Mark answered, opening the door wide as he shrugged into a shirt.

The sight of Suzanne at the door to his bedroom, so scantily clad, teased his imagination and Mark fought off all thoughts of what could happen between them if she wasn't married to his uncle.

"Mark," she spoke a little breathlessly, pleased by the sight of his bare, muscular chest. His body had to be beautiful, she thought . . . "I thought I heard Katie."

"You did," he smiled. "She just got me up so we wouldn't be late for our riding date."

"Oh." She pulled her clinging robe more tightly about her and while the action was one of modesty, the calculated result was to perfectly outline her lush curves for him under a shimmering layer of silk. "I'd best get dressed then, too."

Turning, she walked back to her room, leaving Mark watching her hungrily.

It was almost an hour later when they finally rode away from the house. Suzanne had been stunned by Katie's insistence on riding astraddle and her choice of such mannish clothes. She had informed Katie pointedly that she had a position in society to uphold and she would be expected to live up to that. Katie had bristled at the criticism and had started to argue the point, when Mark's challenging look reminded her of her dare. Backing down, they had reached a compromise. Katie had agreed to ride sidesaddle whenever they were in public as long as she could ride astraddle whenever she was alone.

Suzanne hadn't been too thrilled with the whole situation but she'd handled it the best way she knew how.

At least, Katie wouldn't embarrass them in public with her uncouth behavior.

They rode down to the landing and then followed a river trail to the south, as Suzanne engaged Mark in conversation, trying her best to ignore Katie. The girl was a vexation to her spirit. But Katie took no notice of them, being totally absorbed in studying the countryside.

"Is this the road to Greenwood?" she finally asked, after they'd ridden quite a distance.

"It's right up ahead about half a mile." Suzanne pointed toward a tall grove of oaks in the distance. "Would you like to stop for a visit?"

"No," Katie said firmly. "I was just wondering where it was."

"We'll turn off here, then." Suzanne directed her horse down a narrow path that opened into a wide clearing.

Feeling free and uninhibited, Katie put her heels to her mount and flew past Suzanne and Mark. Leaning close over the horse's neck, she urged him on as the wind whipped at her face, tearing the ribbon from her hair. Laughter bubbled from her, as her spirits soared. And the sight of a low fence didn't deter them as Katie took the horse over it in a perfect jump.

Suzanne gasped in shock as Katie jumped the fence at full speed. She had had no idea that the girl was such an accomplished rider and the discovery didn't sit well with her. She had always considered herself to be quite good on horseback, but compared to Katie . . .

Redoubling her efforts to seduce Mark, she turned back to him irritated to find that he was smiling widely at his sister's wild ride. Sidling her mare closer to his mount, she touched his arm.

"Wherever did she learn to ride so — well?" she pretended interest.

"Father taught us both to ride almost before we could walk." Mark turned his full attention back to Suzanne.

"Well, he did an excellent job. You're both quite good."

Mark reined in his horse and paused to let his gaze sweep over Suzanne. She wore a tight-fitting riding habit that clung to her full breasts as sensuously as her robe had this morning and Mark had a difficult time controlling the desire he was beginning to feel for her. She was a magnificent woman. He hoped Uncle Isaac would return soon, so he could see them together and forget his fantasies of having her for his own.

Suzanne knew he was studying her and she thrust her breasts forward in unspoken invitation.

"I'm getting warm . . . Would you like to sit in the shade for a while?"

"Sounds wonderful," and he followed her to a glade where they could both watch Katie and let the horses cool down.

Picking a dry spot, Suzanne sat down gracefully and leaned back against a tree trunk. Taking off her bonnet, she set it aside as the dark mass of her hair tumbled free. Mark had been tying up his mount and when he turned to face her, heat surged through him. She had unbuttoned the top button of her bodice and was fanning herself gently. He had tried to picture her with her hair down, but the reality far surpassed his imaginings. She was exquisite.

Suzanne sensed his quandary and held out a hand to him. "Come. Sit with me," she invited and she drew him down beside her. "So tell me, Mark. How do you like staying at Kingsford House so far?"

"It's wonderful. You've been very kind." He held himself stiffly, fighting the need to have her.

"I like you Mark." She told him simply, resting her

head back against the tree and wetting her lips seductively.

Had Mark been more learned in the ways of women, he would have known what Suzanne was leading up to. But he was totally unaware that he was being seduced. He was ashamed of the incestuous desire he had for her and yet he was powerless before her, drawn to her like a moth to a flame. Mark was helpless to thwart her calculated scheme. Held captive by her smoldering look, he sat unmoving as she put a warm hand on his thigh, her fingers gently massaging the inner side of his leg.

"Why don't you relax?" she began.

In one last valiant effort to escape a situation he felt responsible for, Mark quickly stood up and started back to his horse.

"I think I'll ride with Katie for a while," he spoke brokenly. Mounting quickly, he spurred his steed to a gallop, needing to get away . . . to deny the sinful lust he felt for his uncle's wife.

Suzanne watched him ride off and smiled to herself. This was going to be more of a challenge than she'd thought . . . But she knew that the prize was worth the effort as she remembered the naked troubled yearning she'd just seen in his eyes. How powerful she'd feel when at last she had him! Casually tying up her hair, she put on her bonnet and then remembered to rebutton her dress. Within minutes, she had caught up with them and they all started back to Kingsford Hosue, ready to relax and enjoy a quiet noonday meal.

It was near dusk when Suzanne heard the sound of a steamer at the dock. After quickly arranging for a carriage to be sent to the landing, she hurried to her rooms to freshen up. Isaac was home and she needed to look her best. When she was satisfied with her appearance, she started back downstairs.

"What's all the excitement about?" Katie asked as she met Suzanne in the main floor hall.

"Isaac's home."

"Oh, good! I'll get Mark!" Racing on upstairs, Katie pounded on the door to her brother's room. "Come on! Uncle Isaac's boat just docked."

"I'll be right down," he called from behind the closed door.

"Hurry up!"

Lifting her skirts, Katie dashed down the steps and reached the front porch just as Isaac climbed down from the carriage. While Suzanne awaited him with regal restraint, Katie flushed from her run, launched herself into his arms as soon as he was on the gallery.

"Uncle Isaac! I'm so glad to see you!"

"Katie? My little Katie?" he hugged her and set her from him. "You're a beautiful young woman now."

"Thank you."

She twirled for him approvingly, not aware of Suzanne's seething jealousy.

"Welcome home, darling." Suzanne came forward to kiss his cheek. "How was your trip?"

"Successful. Very successful," he told her. Then turning his attention to Katie, he said, "But tell me, when did this scamp arrive and where's that good-for-nothing brother of yours?"

"Right here, Uncle Isaac." Mark came out onto the porch to shake hands.

Isaac was astounded that the young lad he'd last seen had grown into such a handsome man.

"You both look like your mother," he stated matter-of-factly after studying them for a moment. "Have you been here long?"

Taking Katie's arm, he led her indoors, leaving Mark to escort Suzanne.

"You look dashing tonight, Mark," she told him, her

108

nger with Isaac only making her all the more deter-
nined in her pursuit of Mark.

"Thanks." He didn't want to touch her, but there was
no way to avoid it as she brushed past him to enter the
house. The delicate scent of her perfume filled his head
and he bit back a groan of desire.

"Dinner is ready, if you'd like to eat," she was saying
as Mark followed her in.

"That sounds fine," Isaac responded absently as he
went to listen more closely to something Katie was telling him.

Suzanne silently fumed, but kept her dignity as she
led the way into the dining room. Isaac made a big display of seating his niece, laughing loudly at some remark she made, leaving Mark to seat his wife.

"Thank you, Mark." She gazed up at him adoringly
and held his eyes for a long moment.

Mark broke the eye contact and sat down nervously
as the servants brought in the meal.

"So, has my wife been treating you right, Mark?"
Isaac bellowed good-naturedly from his end of the
table.

"She's made us feel most at home, sir," Mark responded.

"Good, good. What's mine is yours. My dear, have
you made plans to take them to New Orleans for a
shopping spree yet?"

"We haven't had a chance to plan anything. I did,
however, order clothes for them for the Fontaine Ball
on Saturday."

"Fine. I'm sure you chose wisely."

"I sent detailed instructions as to what I wanted.
Mark's things arrived this afternoon and Katie's
ballgown will be here in the morning so there will be
time for a final fitting."

"As usual, you have taken care of everything," Isaac

complimented her. "I would love for our little Katie to outshine the Fontaine girl tomorrow night," he winked at Katie, who blushed.

"She'll look lovely. I chose a very simple design for her so she wouldn't be lost in all those frills and bows that are so popular right now."

"An excellent decision, my dear."

Katie resented Suzanne not telling her sooner about the style of her gown, but then she remembered her brother's words. Turning on her most charming manner, she smiled at her aunt.

"I'm sure the dress will be wonderful, Suzanne. Your taste in gowns is superb," Katie commented.

Suzanne's eyes widened at the unexpected compliment from Katie. "Thank you."

"You two should have a marvelous time when you finally do go shopping. Katie, Suzanne can spend money faster than any woman I know."

Though he was joking, Suzanne took his words to heart. What else did she have to do?

"Don't you believe a word," she replied, the smile on her lips not reaching her eyes. "He has so much money, he doesn't miss the little I spend."

"True enough," Isaac sat back, replete from the delicious dinner. "Mark, my boy, you've been quiet."

"Just listening," Mark laughed. "It was hard to get a word in edgewise."

"So you're ready for the university, are you?"

"Yes sir. I'll start classes in the fall."

"And you're studying to become an engineer like your father?"

"Yes sir."

"No need for the sir, Mark. Isaac will do. You are no longer a boy. You're a man now."

"Yes . . . Isaac."

"I tell you what. You go on and get your degree, but if

110

you decide later that you don't like the work, there's a partnership waiting for you here with me."

"You're serious?"

"Very. I have no children of my own and in a few years, I'll be needing somebody to help out." He grinned at Mark's dumbfounded expression. "I am getting old, you know."

"Hardly," Suzanne put in and he patted her fondly.

"Sweet of you to deny it, but it is the truth. One day I'll have to slow down and I'd like to have you with me when the time comes. Are you interested?"

"Very."

"Good. While you're here I'll familiarize you with some of the simpler aspects of my businesses. Then, if you want to become more involved you just let me know."

Mark was totally surprised by Isaac's offer. He knew that Isaac had always been fond of him, but he had had no idea that he'd cared this much.

The rest of the evening passed quietly as everyone retired early.

Suzanne and Isaac's bedrooms were connected by a comfortable sitting room and it was here that Suzanne stood a few minutes later, clad only in a sheer nightdress that revealed far more than it concealed. She was nervous. She knew that Isaac didn't like aggressive women, but the desires within her clamoured for release. And, he was her husband. Squaring her shoulders, she knocked softly at his door before entering.

"What is it?" Isaac asked, already in bed. "Is there something wrong?"

"No, Isaac. I just wanted to spend some time with you. I've missed you." She approached the bed with her usual grace, the gown swirling about her seductively.

"That's nice, dear. But I am tired tonight."

"But Isaac, it's . . . it's been so long . . . I need you."

111

Isaac's expression hardened at her blatant proposition. "Suzanne," he stated firmly. "You know how I feel about this. I don't see any need to discuss it any further."

"I know. But tonight . . ."

"Tonight is no different than any other night," he refused coldly.

Suzanne paled at his rejection. Maintaining her composure with an effort, she walked stiffly from the room determined not to let him see her frustration.

Closing Isaac's door quietly behind her, Suzanne walked straight to the small liquor cabinet that they kept in the sitting room and poured herself a liberal portion of brandy. After quickly downing the heady liquid, she paused to take a deep breath, cursing her own stupidity. Why had she bothered to try? She should have known what his answer was going to be . . .

Anger replaced her frustration and she returned to her own bedroom. Locking the door, she pulled off the gown and turned up the lamp. The image reflected in the full-length mirror was of a well-endowed mature woman. Her breasts were full and ripe, her hips nicely rounded. Suzanne turned sideways to critically survey her profile, but she could find no fault there either. Her stomach was flat and her buttocks trim unlike many women of her age whose figures had been lost bearing children. The fleeting image of Katie's slim, young body crossed her mind and once again Suzanne mentally compared herself to her niece. She dismissed the thought quickly though, for Katie was only a child. There really could be no comparison between them.

Turning the light back down, Suzanne opened the French door that led onto the upper gallery and felt the cool river breeze flow over her body, its gentle caressing touch stirring her heightened senses even more. Groaning out loud as the throbbing ache within her grew more demanding, she drew on the diaphanous gown and climbed into her solitary bed, in hopes that sleep would release her from the desires that plagued her.

The moon was low in the night sky and the chiming grandfather clock had struck two when Suzanne finally realized that her quest for sleep was useless. Slipping from her bed, she moved quietly out onto the gallery. Without conscious thought, Suzanne found herself standing at Mark's open doors, gazing into the darkness of his room. Her heart beat fast as she went inside after only a second's hesitation. She had to see him . . . be with him. He wanted her . . . she was certain of that. So it was only a matter of openly offering herself to him.

Dropping the gown from her shoulders, the soft material settled in a frothy pool at her feet. Stepping away from it, Suzanne went to stand by the bed. Mark was asleep, lying on his stomach. He was clad only in a nightshirt that did little to disguise the strong width of his shoulders. With his expression relaxed and unguarded, he looked young, but Suzanne knew that he was on the threshold of manhood. Drawn irresistibly closer, she reached out to smooth a tumbled lock of hair from his forehead. Emboldened by her success when he didn't awaken, Suzanne closed and locked the French doors. She came back to him then in total darkness, knowing it would be safer for them this way.

The bed was so large that she didn't disturb him when she climbed in with him. It was only as she bent to kiss him that he stirred and came awake.

Mark had tossed and turned for hours, it seemed, before he finally managed to fall into a troubled sleep. Visions of Suzanne had haunted him all night—Suzanne as she'd looked that morning clad only in her wrapper—Suzanne sitting on the grass inviting him to join her — Suzanne at dinner tonight looking so sophisticated and unattainable. He knew that nothing could ever come of his fantasies — after all, she was his aunt. But still that didn't keep him from desiring her. And desire her he did, until he was so exhausted from thinking about it that he'd drifted off . . . the dream of having her in his arms seeming almost real.

It was a featherlight touch on his shoulder that roused him just as Suzanne was about to kiss him.

"Mark . . ." she murmured softly, as her lips met his. "Kiss me, Mark."

His instincts clouded by sleep, Mark accepted the kiss of his vision passively, afraid to move lest he awake too soon. He wanted to enjoy this dream, so he lay still, unmoving as his wraith-like phantom deepened the kiss.

Suzanne was surprised when Mark made no sudden moves, but instead lay back in seeming indifference. She couldn't bear another rejection this night! She had to make him want her. Sliding full length against him she moved her hips erotically, teasing yet inviting at the same time. Unbuttoning his nightshirt, she pushed it from his shoulders and pressed her breasts intimately to his chest.

Mark came to the sudden realization that this was no dream when he felt the coolness of the night air on his bare back. Momentarily stunned, he drew back, trying to focus on her features in the shielding darkness of his room.

"Suzanne?" he managed, unsure of what else to say.

"Yes, Mark," her response was throaty and deep as the masculine hardness of his body thrilled her. It had been so long and he felt so good!

"What are you doing here?" Mark wasn't sure whether to get up and get away from the intimacy of her touch or to stay and fulfill his deepest desire.

"I came to love you, Mark. Make love to me — please. . ."

"But Isaac . . . ?"

"Please Mark," her mouth found his in a desperate kiss.

For a moment he struggled against this . . . but her plea was so convincing that he gave up trying to rationalize the situation. He had wanted her since the first time he'd seen her and he was going to have her. He would worry about betraying Isaac later.

"Suzanne." He worshipped her name as their lips parted and then met again in sightless accuracy.

At the touch of his mouth on hers, Suzanne groaned in primal passion. She became a creature commanded only by her desire as she guided Mark into the realm of the purely physical. Taken from the safety of his dreams to the wonder of reality, Mark's response was instinctive. Clutching her to him, they strained together.

Suzanne was ecstatic. She had worried that he would hesitate as he had that afternoon, but now, after breaking down his defenses, she had discovered him to be a natural, sensual man. She relished the feel of him as her hands explored his heavily muscled torso. Slipping from his grasp, she pushed Mark down on his back and straddled him, taking him deep within her. Suzanne could sense the shock and she gave a soft, triumphant laugh.

"Let me please you," she insisted when he would have pulled her down to him. "Just relax and enjoy."

Her voice was a provocative purr and Mark let the resistance he felt flow away. Her body was doing wondrous things to his and he shook with the force of emotion she was arousing. Suzanne's hands were everywhere, caressing and exploring, while she leaned forward to kiss him passionately. With her breasts barely grazing his chest, Suzanne ground her hips against him. Held throbbing yet motionless within the hot, molten center of her body, Mark felt the last vestige of his control evaporate when she moved so wantonly against him. He wanted to roll with her and plunge even deeper into the moist secrets of her, but Suzanne was controlling their encounter, giving him little time to think.

Sitting up straight, she arched her back as she rode him, savoring the sensations of possessing him fully. She was using him, draining him, and that knowledge made her orgasm all the more exciting when it came. But Mark, lost in the throes of his own climactic release, knew nothing of her thoughts and feelings. He only knew that this had been the most erotic moment of his life. And when at last she lay breathlessly on his chest his thoughts were filled with the wonder of their union.

Suzanne rested heavily on top of Mark, satisfied for the time being. She had reached her peak so quickly that she felt somehow cheated. Lovemaking was meant to be an art, not a race. After having been alone for so long, she hoped this encounter would be prolonged and enjoyable. But the fear of discovery nagged at her persistently.

"I want to see you," Mark reached for the lamp as they moved slightly apart.

"No. As long as we're together, we must remain in the darkness," she insisted. "You must respect my wishes in this matter or what we have ends right now."

Mark fell silent. He understood that she feared being found out, but he also knew that he wanted to see her; to watch her face as their bodies joined together. As he imagined making love to her in the light, he hardened again.

Suzanne, who had been stroking him lightly, delighted in the renewed, eager strength he displayed.

"We have all night, Mark," she whispered encouragingly.

"Yes. All night," Mark murmured, before losing himself in her exacting embrace once more.

Five

The Declaration

Wearing her new gown, Katie stood patiently on a small stool while Suzanne's seamstress carefully completed her alterations. Katie was glad now that she hadn't protested when Suzanne ordered the ballgown for her. For, as much as she hated to admit it, the dress was beautiful. Suzanne's taste in clothing, as in everything else, was impeccable.

Created of pale yellow satin, it was off the shoulder in style with a form-fitting bodice that revealed the fullness of her breasts in a provocative yet innocent manner. The skirts were flared, full and fluid, and set in back at the waist were matching yellow satin rosettes.

It had never occurred to Katie that she would ever care one way or the other about a dress, but it had been love at first sight for her when the seamstress had unpacked this one. She had no doubt that in this particular gown she would look her best and therefore make Uncle Isaac proud of her. She only regretted that Christopher wouldn't be at this ball to see her.

"All done, my dear," Marie the seamstress said. "All

we have to do is finish off a few seams and you'll be ready for tonight."

"Thank you, Marie," Katie stepped down carefully and slipped out of the costly creation. "I have to tell you, this is the first ballgown I've ever had and it's absolutely gorgeous."

"The gown is only a gown. It's you who makes it special, Miss Katie."

Katie smiled, "I hope I look nice tonight. I do so want to make a good impression for Uncle Isaac's sake."

"Don't worry," Marie confided. "There are only two other females around here who come close to your beauty. One is your aunt. I've never known a more elegant woman in my life."

"She is lovely," Katie agreed.

"And the other is Renee Fontaine."

"The girl whose ball I'm going to?"

Marie nodded. "She's not only pretty, she's nice. I like her a lot."

"Well, I hope I get to meet her tonight."

"I'm sure you will, Renee's a very friendly person." Picking up the gown with the greatest of care, Marie started from the room. "I'd best get to work on this. I'll have it ready in plenty of time."

"Thanks."

When Marie had gone, Katie dressed in her old riding clothes and went in search of Mark. After searching the rest of the house, she finally found him, sound asleep in his room.

"Mark! Get up and we'll go riding."

Mark's lack of sleep the night before left him with little enthusiasm for a late morning ride.

"Not today, Katie. I'm going to rest up for tonight."

"Tonight? What's so strenuous about tonight? You've been to dances before."

"I just want to sleep, Katie," he snapped. "Go on without me."

More than a little hurt by his refusal, she headed out of his room.

"And Katie," he called after her.

"Yes?" She brightened, hoping he'd changed his mind.

"From now on, knock before you come in here."

Startled by such an unusual request, she mumbled her reply and hurried outside, shutting the door behind her. What was wrong with him? He sure was acting strangely today. Knowing that there was no reasoning with him, she hurried on downstairs anxious to be gone on her ride.

Stepping from the warm scented water of the bath, Suzanne dried herself and with Patsy's help began to dress. She felt relaxed and content, her body satisfied yet more sensually aware than ever. Even the softness of her silky chemise against her skin held its own brand of eroticism for her this day. The memory of her pleasures from the night before brought a glow to her face that even Patsy remarked on.

"Ah doan think Ah've ever seen you lookin' so fine, Miz Suzanne," the servant admired her mistress' stunning good-looks.

"I don't think I've ever felt so fine, Patsy. But thank you. Do you think my dress is appropriate?"

"Mmm . . ." she nodded happily. "If you was a single lady, there wouldn't be any man safe tonight."

Suzanne, preening before the mirror, was forced to agree with her servant's assessment. She felt delightfully wicked and very sexy in her low-cut, full skirted gown of deep rose. And she couldn't wait to play her game of temptation with Mark again tonight. She was sure that he wasn't expecting it and that's what made it all the more appealing. Taking one last approving look at herself she started downstairs. Isaac would be waiting and

120

she needed to keep him happy.

Mark glanced at himself once more in the mirror over the fireplace in the study as he waited with Isaac for the women. He found it hard to believe that a simple change of clothes could so alter his appearance. He seemed quite the man-about-town in his fashionable dark suit and intricately embroidered vest. Flashing a smile at his reflection, Mark straightened his cuffs and turned away, satisfied that he looked his very best.

Strangely enough, he felt as confident as he looked, though earlier today, he had been reluctant to face Suzanne. He had been unsure as to how to act around her, but she had treated him with such cool nonchalance whenever they met, that Mark wondered if last night had really happened. As the day had passed he'd been grateful for her ability to remain unaffected, for it was only her indifference that had kept him at arm's length. He wanted her . . . desired her passionately . . . and the illicitness of their coming together only made it more exciting. The prospect of being near her all evening in the company of Isaac wore on him greatly. As much as he liked and respected his uncle, Mark did envy him his wife and he wondered why Suzanne had married him in the first place.

The door to the study was open and Mark glanced out into the hall just as Suzanne began her descent.

"Suzanne's ready," he told Isaac as he watched her, taking in every detail of her loveliness.

Gliding toward him, her eyes darkened with remembered passion as she noticed how handsome he looked, "Good evening, Mark."

"Good evening, Suzanne," he responded automatically, his gaze riveted on her breasts, so amply displayed. "You look lovely, as usual."

"Why, thank you." She brushed against him as she

121

went to greet her husband. "Isaac, you look very dashing tonight."

"Always the flatterer, my dear," he protested as he kissed her lightly. "I've never seen you look more beautiful. I'm pleased. But where is that Katie-girl of mine? She should have been down here by now."

Suzanne bristled at being so casually ignored, especially in favor of the younger Katie. So she took the time to talk with Mark, drawing him even further under her spell.

Katie couldn't decide whether she was nervous or excited. She only knew that she'd never before felt so feminine. When she'd returned from her ride, Lottie had been ready and waiting for her. Despite her initial grumblings, Katie had given in to Lottie's demands and the results had mystified her. She had been bathed, perfumed and powdered. Her hair had been combed up and away from her face and then allowed to tumble down in back in smooth, soft curls and Lottie had highlighted the style by weaving delicate yellow flowers in with the heavy golden coils. Her breasts, round and full, swelled temptingly above the décolletage of her gown and Lottie had had to lecture her twice about being embarrassed. The pastel paleness of the gown matched the sun-lightened streaks in her hair and the total effect was dazzling. From the carefully coiffed tresses to her new yellow slippers, Katie Kingsford was devastating.

"I'm ready," she greeted them as she entered the library and all eyes turned to her at once.

"Katie?" Mark couldn't believe his eyes.

"My dear, you are ravishing." Isaac came to kiss her cheek. "You are a woman now."

"Thank you." His compliment meant the world to her. "Suzanne, the dress is perfect."

"Yes, you chose wisely," Isaac added his approval. "Well, shall we be on our way?"

Ordering the carriage brought around, Isaac squired Katie from the room, leaving Suzanne to follow with Mark.

"Suzanne?" Mark offered her his arm and she placed her hand gently upon it, the contact lighting a fire in his blood. He had been waiting all day to be alone with her. He wanted to talk to her about what had passed between them in the dark last night.

Suzanne sensed that Mark had something to tell her, but she was giving him no opportunity to be maudlin about their encounter. She wanted to keep him totally off-balance so she could be in control. Smiling at him, her eyes wickedly taunting him, she started after Isaac and Katie and Mark was forced to hurry to stay by her side.

"Are you certain I'll be accepted?" Christopher asked Robert Adams.

"Of course. And even more so, now that you've won Greenwood," Robert confided confidently. "In fact, even if you hadn't shown up, I wager your name would have been bandied about more than anyone else's . . . with the exception of the Montards, of course," Robert paused. "You realize our plans couldn't be going any better, don't you?"

Christopher nodded. "Winning Greenwood was a godsend. No one's ever suspected . . ."

"No one, and we must never break confidence. You understand the significance of complete secrecy in this matter, don't you? There are lives at stake here and not only our own."

"I understand completely," Christopher answered solemnly as their carriage drew to a stop and the driver hopped down to open the door. "Are you familiar with the Kingsford family?"

"Isaac Kingsford is a personal friend of mine. He's a

very shrewd businessman and his wife Suzanne is one of the most gorgeous women I've ever had the pleasure to meet. They should be here tonight. Why do you ask?"

"I met his niece and nephew on the boat coming down."

Christopher made his statement conversationally, but a glimmer of anticipation lit his soul. Try as he might, he had been unable to forget his night of thrilling passion with Katie and as much as it irritated him, he still wanted her. Maybe if, Christopher decided, he saw her tonight, he would be able to get her out of his system once and for all . . . for surely Katie couldn't be as beautiful and desirable as his memory made her out to be.

"Good," Robert was saying, "then you've already made some headway toward being accepted. The Kingsfords are most influential. Come now and let me introduce you to our host, Roger Fontaine."

Katie's cheeks were flushed and her eyes were aglow as Isaac led her to the refreshment table after dancing with her. Carefully opening the delicate, spangled fan that Suzanne had insisted she carry, Katie fanned herself lightly.

"I never thought dancing was much fun before tonight," she told her uncle happily.

"So you are having a good time?" They had been at the ball for over an hour now and Katie hadn't missed a dance yet. Only Renee Fontaine, who was making her debut, had had more offers.

"I'm having a wonderful time. But what amazes me, Uncle Isaac, is that none of these men have noticed how badly I dance!"

Isaac chuckled. "My darling girl, they're too smitten with your charms to notice anything else. I'd venture to guess that you could step all over their feet and they'd still tell you that you were the best dancer here tonight."

Katie laughed. "Now I know what Mark meant when he told me to play the game."

"I don't understand."

Looking up at him, Katie knew that now she could tell him the truth.

"I didn't want to come on this trip, Uncle Isaac."

He was surprised. "Why not?"

"I just had the feeling that Father was trying to force me to marry. And believe me, I'm not in the least bit interested."

"Oh," Isaac acknowledged sagely. "Were you nervous about all these fancy parties?"

Katie nodded. "I just thought it was a waste of my time. I was happy where I was. I didn't want to change anything in my life."

"I don't think you've changed, Katie. I think you've grown. There's a difference, you know."

"There is? When I'm dressed like this I hardly know myself." Katie was confused.

"On the outside, maybe. But inside, where it counts, you're still Katie."

"Do you really think so?"

"I know so."

Katie gave him a warm, open smile, "I guess you're right. I've been so busy resisting the outside changes that I didn't think about anything else."

"So, relax. You'll always be you no matter how your hair is styled or what dress you're wearing."

"Isaac . . . Miss Kingsford." That dreaded voice interrupted their conversation and Katie turned to face Andre Montard.

"Good evening, Andre," Isaac greeted. "Join us, we were just having some punch."

"Mr. Montard." Katie said his name coldly, but there was no escaping his maneuvering this time.

"Maybe later. Right now, I'd like to dance with your niece, if you've no objections?"

"None at all. Katie?"

Out done once again by Andre's sly manipulations, she stifled the urge to run away screaming and reluctantly consented to the dance. Perhaps if she stepped on him a few times, he would hesitate before asking again.

Christopher had spent the best part of the evening with Robert in the gentlemen's study drinking their host's fine aged bourbon and discussing the merits of sugar cane over cotton as a base crop. Each time that he'd started to leave to go in search of Katie, he had been caught up in another conversation and many hours passed before he and Robert managed to get away. Finally, realizing that they had yet to make an appearance in the ballroom, they crossed the hall and stood in the doorway watching the dancers float gracefully around the floor.

"It's time I claimed my dance with Renee," Robert said as the music ended. "I trust you'll be all right?"

"I'll be fine, Robert. Don't worry."

When his friend had moved off, Christopher headed for the refreshment table where he'd caught sight of Mark talking with a very attractive woman.

Suzanne noted the approach of the handsome, dark-haired man immediately. He was a stranger and yet seemed to be coming straight toward her. She absently answered a question Mark posed, as she watched him draw nearer, hoping that for some reason he was going to single her out. To her amazement, the man greeted Mark like an old friend.

"Christopher?, I can't believe you're here," Mark told him as they shook hands.

"I'm staying with Robert Adams and Mr. Fontaine was gracious enough to include me in Robert's invitation." Christopher explained his unexpected appearance.

"Let me introduce you to my uncle's wife, Suzanne Kingsford. Suzanne this is Christopher Fletcher, your new neighbor."

Suzanne turned the full force of her wiles on Christopher as she smiled up at him.

"Mr. Fletcher, I've heard so many things about you. How nice to finally get to meet you."

"I'm pleased to meet you too, Mrs. Kingsford," Christopher charmed her. "Robert Adams has told me of your beauty and now I know he is a man of his word."

For the first time in years, Suzanne blushed, thrilled that this newcomer would find her attractive.

"Why thank you. You say Robert Adams is a friend of yours?"

"Yes. I'll be staying with him for the next few days until I take over Greenwood."

"Well, you must join us for dinner soon."

"I'd be delighted," he answered.

Mark was surprised by Suzanne's change of heart. Why just yesterday she'd been upset about Yankees and now she'd invited Christopher to dinner. He was finding her to be a very complex woman and he wondered if he would ever understand her.

"If you'll excuse me," Christopher said, "Robert looks like he needs me."

"Of course, I'll see you later," Mark told him.

"Mrs. Kingsford," Christopher nodded as he started to walk away.

"I hope we'll see you again soon, Mr. Fletcher," Suzanne said.

When Christopher had disappeared across the floor Suzanne took Mark's arm to get his attention. She wanted to learn all she could about this new man and Mark seemed to be the best source of information.

"Shall we dance?" she suggested.

Mark had been waiting all evening for some indication that she cared about him and his heart was light as he gazed down at her.

127

"My pleasure," he answered, taking her in his arms.

Suzanne managed to give him an encouraging smile and they moved out onto the floor.

"Christopher, I'd like you to meet Renee Fontaine, our hostess," Robert spoke as Christopher joined them.

Turning politely, he bowed over her hand, "Miss Fontaine. How nice to meet you."

Renee smiled warmly, "Welcome to L'Aimant. I hope you've been enjoying your evening with us.

"I have, thank you for including me." Christopher frankly admired the young dark-haired beauty.

"It's been our pleasure. Now, if you'll excuse me, I promised this next waltz to my father. Robert, Mr. Fletcher."

"Let me escort you to him, Renee," Robert offered and they moved away. "Christopher, I'll see you later."

Christopher's expression was inscrutable as he followed Renee and Robert's progress across the ballroom. Then as the crowd shifted, he glanced out into the center hall. There, looking even more lovely than he remembered, stood Katie, seemingly deep in conversation with Andre.

Christopher tensed as he observed them and his fists clenched as he noticed Andre staring pointedly at her cleavage. In that instant, Katie looked up and her eyes met his in mute appeal.

There were no second thoughts as he strode purposefully toward them. Christopher didn't know why he felt he had to rescue her from Andre and he didn't take the time to analyze it. He just knew that he couldn't stand to see the other man near her.

Despite her reluctance to accompany him, Andre had led Katie outside into the hall after their waltz. He needed to talk to her alone . . . to impress her with his decision to court her more slowly.

"Have you been enjoying your visit so far?" he questioned attentively, hoping to engage her in conversation.

"Suzanne and Uncle Isaac have been very kind," she responded flatly, knowing that she was stuck here with him until the music began again.

"They are very generous people," he agreed, his gaze fixed lasciviously on her bosom. "I didn't think it was possible but tonight you are even more lovely."

"Thank you." Katie was growing very uncomfortable as Andre openly ogled the low-cut neckline of her gown.

"Am I ever to be forgiven for my impetuous behavior on board the steamer our last night out?" her pleaded, greatly irritated at having to humble himself.

"Mr. Montard, I have already accepted your apology. I don't know what else you could possibly want from me." She turned slightly to obscure his line of vision.

As Katie glanced up, she caught sight of Christopher coming toward them and her heart skipped a bet. She didn't know what he was doing here, but she was overjoyed to see him.

"I want to . . ." But Andre didn't get a chance to finish for Christopher broke in on his declaration.

"Katie! Here you are. I've been looking for you."

"You have?" Katie couldn't hide her surprise at his statement.

"Fletcher!" Andre's voice was tinged with hatred and frustration.

"Good evening, Montard. I've come to claim Katie," his tone was possessive. "This is my dance, I believe."

"Yes," she agreed hastily. She wondered at Christopher's change in attitude but she was eager to be away from her unwanted suitor.

"Very well." Andre knew that he could do nothing but acquiesce gracefully. "Katie, we'll talk again later."

"Of course," she replied, hoping that "later" would never come.

"I'll see you on Tuesday at Greenwood, Andre."

"We are expecting you."

"Good, if you'll excuse us then?"

As the sweet, flowing strains of a waltz filtered out into the hall, Christopher led her back inside. Then sweeping her into his arms he guided her expertly out among the other dancers.

"You don't look much like a knight in shining armor, but you are one. Thank you," she told him earnestly.

Christopher grinned. "Glad to be of service. I may not have looked my part, but you definitely had the air of a damsel in distress."

"I know. He's a very subtle, very clever man and I don't trust him."

"I don't either."

"What are you doing here?" Katie asked impulsively changing the subject. "I thought you were going to be in New Orleans until next week."

"I thought sò, too. But my host, Robert Adams, was invited tonight, so he suggested that I come along with him. Robert thought it would be a good opportunity for me to meet some of my new neighbors."

"Well, I'm very glad you came." Her voice was husky with undisguised emotion. "I've wanted to talk to you . . . ever since that night on deck . . ."

Suddenly needing to be alone with her, Christopher danced them near the open French doors and then quickly led her out onto the gallery. The night was cool, dark and inviting as they stood together at the balustrade that overlooked L'Aimant's garden.

Christopher was confused. He'd decided to see her one more time in order to rid himself of his desire for her. Yet the sight of her with Andre had disturbed him and he had felt a great need to get her away from the other man's leering advances.

"Let's walk."

Katie hesitated, remembering the last time she'd gone

with him.

Christopher sensed her discomfort and remembering his own cutting words, he smiled sincerely at her, "This time we'll talk and if there is any water we will look at it."

Katie couldn't help but grin as his assurance relieved her misgivings, erasing the memory of their last encounter from her mind. She was where she had wanted to be . . . alone with Christopher and this time the outcome would be different.

"I'd like that."

The muted voices of other strolling couples came to them as they started down one of the shell-lined paths of the carefully landscaped garden. The black velvet sky was star-studded and the pale sliver of the moon hung low on the horizon.

"You wanted to talk?" Christopher reminded her, breaking the silence that had enveloped them.

"I was just trying to figure out where to begin," she explained, hesitating. "I'm not going to apologize for what I did that night. It's just that everything happened too fast for me. I wasn't sure how to handle it."

Christopher reached out to take her hand, "You don't have to explain . . ."

"Yes, I do. I've thought about this ever since that night and I want you to understand."

"I do, now." He looked at her seriously, recognizing her inexperience and cursing himself for having pushed her too hard that night.

"And I'm sorry for what I said. But it was the second time in one day that you'd bested me and I was angry and more than a little frustrated."

"And I had just heard all these terrible things about you from Andre and Mark and I wasn't sure what to think."

"Oh, my reputation . . ."

The night was heavy with the sweet scent of magnolia

blossoms as Katie and Christopher stopped walking and turned to look at each other. There, protected from view by the darkly shadowed foliage of the garden, their eyes met, openly acknowledging all the feelings they both were trying so hard to control. With a gentle hand, Christopher reached out to caress her cheek before drawing her nearer. Framing her face with his hands, his eyes roved over her features, committing to memory the perfection of her moonlit beauty before his mouth claimed hers in a passionate kiss that spoke more eloquently than words.

Katie moaned softly as the anticipation of his embrace became reality. His touch was as exciting as she'd remembered and she gloried in it. Encircling his waist with her arms, Katie leaned closer, wanting to know him more intimately.

Christopher drew back for a moment. He wanted more from Katie, much more, but he wouldn't take it. She had to offer. There would be no more scenes like their last time alone . . .

Bending to her, he pressed a tender-soft kiss at the corner of her mouth before exploring the sweetness of her throat. When she made no move to refuse him, he grew more aggressive. His hands moved to her shoulders, massaging there gently before slipping lower to cup her bodice.

Katie stiffened momentarily but then forced herself to relax. This was what she had wanted . . . what she had dreamed of . . .

The pressure of his hands beneath her bosom pushed her breasts upward until they swelled daringly over the décolletage. Unable to resist the temptation, Christopher kissed the exposed tops of the creamy, firm mounds.

Her eyes closed, Katie's head fell back as his mouth explored her. And, when he could wait no longer to taste the fullness of her breasts, he pushed the offending material lower to free the budding peaks.

Christopher paused to look at her . . . worshipping the smooth glory of her hard-tipped breasts with his eyes.

"You're perfect, Katie . . . Perfect . . ." His knowing fingers stroked each one teasingly, drawing patterns of fire around each nipple but never quite touching them.

"Oh, . . . please, Christopher . . ." Katie begged, wanting to feel his hot, moist mouth upon her.

Encouraged by her desire, he lifted her breast and drew the taut pink crest into his mouth, flicking it with his tongue as he sucked gently.

Katie's knees weakened at the pleasure from his intimate caress and she clutched at his shoulders for support.

Christopher was on fire with his need for her, yet knew that a garden path was no place for lovemaking. Though Katie whimpered, he drew away, covering her.

"Christopher? Don't stop . . ." Her eyes were wide with her confusion as her body throbbed with unfulfilled desire.

"We need to be alone, Katie. Really alone. I wouldn't want anyone to see us . . ."

Katie took his hand pressing it to her bosom. "Please."

Christopher turned with a groan, pulling her into his arms.

Dipping a hand within the low confines of her bodice, he caressed her eagerly as his mouth met hers in a kiss of mutual surrender . . . Katie surrendering to the overpowering attraction she felt for him and Christopher giving in to his desire to possess her completely.

Only the sound of footsteps crunching on the sea-shell strewn walkway drew his attention and he broke off the embrace.

"Darling," he muttered in frustration. "We've got

company."

Straightening her clothes, they were both breathless as they resumed their walk and it was only minutes before the other couple came upon them.

They exchanged polite greetings and continued on their separate ways down the maze of walkways.

The musical splashing of a fountain beckoned them onward and as they reached the center of the garden they came upon it, sparkling and bubbling in the moonlight. The crystal froth of the water enchanted them and they stood arm-in-arm mesmerized by the cascading display.

"This is paradise!" Katie spoke in hushed tones, her voice full of wonder.

"No," Christopher countered, taking her masterfully into his arms. "This is paradise," and he kissed her deeply.

When the kiss ended, he held her close to his heart savoring the serenity of the moment.

"Katie, look." Christopher had glanced up and had caught sight of a small white gazebo, some distance away, partly hidden by a copse of trees.

Anxious to be alone, they hurried to the summer-house hoping that it would provide them with the privacy they wanted so badly. Entering into the seclusion of the small airy building, they smiled in conspiracy.

"What do you think?" he asked, pleased with his discovery.

"I think you were right."

"I was? About what?"

Katie nodded, "This *is* paradise."

Moving to him, she put her arms around his waist and kissed him. Instinct took over as he crushed her to him, returning her kiss full measure.

Katie was breathless and this time there would be no interruptions. This was what she'd wanted . . . waited for. In that one moment of melding, the perfection of his embrace took her heart. As she stood in the middle of the deserted gazebo held tightly in his grasp, she knew without a doubt that she loved him.

Abandoning herself to his kiss, they strained together, wanting to share their desire. Christopher guided her to one of the low, built-in benches and drew her across his lap.

"You are so beautiful . . ." he murmured, as his mouth sought hers, reverently. "So beautiful . . ."

Thrilled by his touch, Katie melted against him. Looping her arms about his neck she offered herself to him in innocent ecstasy. She loved him.

Loosening her bodice, Christopher bared her breasts and caressed them eagerly. Katie trembled at the onslaught of emotion his lovemaking aroused and when his lips followed the path his fingers had forged, she arched in passionate surprise. Katie held his head to her as he suckled first one breast then the other. Her excitement mounted to a fever pitch and vaguely, she wondered how she could ever have stopped him that first night.

Christopher, sensing her rising desire, shifted their positions so that they lay side by side on the padded bench. Brushing her skirts aside, he stroked the tender flesh of her inner thighs and though his caress was gentle, Katie tensed at his touch.

"Don't be afraid, darling," Christopher kissed her tenderly. "Let me love all of you. I won't hurt you."

Drifting ever higher, his hand kept up its hypnotic massage until, at last, he found the center of her. Katie froze again at the foreign touch, but when he murmured encouragingly she opened her legs for him.

"You're perfect, Katie. All of you . . ."

Katie held Christopher close, relishing his nearness. As his mouth took hers in a passionate kiss his hand slipped between her thighs exploring her inner secrets for the first time.

135

"Easy, love," he spoke softly, gentling her with his words and hands.

Christopher continued his practiced caresses as Katie grew restless and her body urged her to seek release from his passionate torment. With skillful strokes, he stoked the flames of her desire until, finally, she climaxed. The pulsing waves of ecstasy shocked Katie and she lay still enjoying the sensual pleasure Christopher had brought her.

Looking up at him, her expression almost bewildered, she smiled, "I didn't know . . ."

"Ah, love, but we're not through yet." His voice was husky with passion.

Knowing that he'd satisfied her pleased him and Christopher was hard put to control his need for her. Rising above Katie he freed himself from his pants and easily moved between her legs.

Katie felt the hardness of his manhood pressing against her and she shifted her hips to accept him within her. There was no thought of right or wrong, only of passion and desire and fulfillment.

"I don't know what to do," she told him, worried that she wouldn't satisfy him.

"Relax for me, love," he instructed as he slowly began to enter the moist depths of her womanhood.

The sensation of being penetrated was so alien to her that, despite her initial determination to help him, she stiffened against him making his entry sharp and painful.

"Christopher!"

He felt her reluctance and withdrew for a moment.

"I'm sorry," she told him. "But it hurt."

Christopher smoothed her hair back from her face and smiled at her tenderly, "It's all right, Katie. It's all right."

The thought that he had caused her discomfort took

the edge off his lusty yearnings and he slowed his pace. Fondling her breasts, he kissed her and as he felt her tension begin to ebb, he grew more bold.

Christopher's insistent caresses demanded response from her and Katie was amazed to find herself responding again. He knew exactly where to touch her to bring her the greatest pleasure and when his mouth nuzzled at her breast, she couldn't control the urge to move against him.

Christopher smiled to himself as he felt her hips wriggle and slowly, with as little pressure as possible, he pressed himself into the hot velvet of her womanly sheath.

Katie was oblivious to all, save the tightening coil of desire growing within her once more, and, as Christopher's hands caressed her buttocks lifting her to him, she surged upward wanting to be nearer. Katie's eyes reflected her amazement as she impaled herself upon his rigid staff. Falling back, Katie lay unmoving on the cushioned bench, as she waited for the sharp pain to pass.

Deeply embedded inside her, Christopher rested, savoring the sensuous tightness of her body.

"Are you all right?" he murmured, kissing her softly.

Katie gradually became aware that the pain had lessened and only a tight, fullness remained . . . that and the sensation of totally belonging to this man. Smiling at him tremulously, she looped her arms around his neck.

"I'm fine," she assured him, pulling him down for a flaming kiss. "I've never been better."

Christopher groaned as she slid her hands down his back to his hips. The contact causing him to thrust against her involuntarily. Unable to stop, he began to move, their bodies merging and parting in love's rhythm. The sweetness of their union heightened his excitement and he shuddered in ecstasy as he emptied his loveseed deep within the heat of her.

Katie held Christopher to her, cherishing the knowledge that she'd pleased him. She had never dreamed that love could be so exciting or that a man could be so wonderful.

They rested, locked in a tight embrace, their hearts beating in unison.

It was long moments before reality intruded on them and Christopher was forced reluctantly to withdraw from her. Rising, he straightened his own clothes and then helped Katie to her feet. With Christopher's help she straightened her clothes and smoothed her hair back into place.

"How do I look?" she worried.

"You look more beautiful than ever," Christopher told her honestly as his gaze swept over her appreciatively.

But as he took her hand to lead her from the gazebo, she held back.

"Katie?"

"I love you, Christopher," she told him, going into the warmth of his embrace.

And Christopher tilted her face up to receive his heart-stopping kiss before they started back to the ball leaving their paradise behind.

Drink in hand, Andre stood in the study with Isaac, making general conversation. He realized that his plan to gently seduce Katie was not going to work as long as Fletcher was in the picture. So, with that in mind, he knew his only hope was to turn Isaac and Suzanne against the Yankee. For if they disapproved of him, they certainly wouldn't allow Katie to see him.

"You know, Isaac. This Fletcher fellow has a very unscrupulous reputation," he began and Isaac listened attentively to what he had to say.

Mark drank thirstily from his cup of punch as he watched Suzanne dance with Andre. There was something almost too familiar in the way he was holding her and Mark longed to tear her from his arms. Frustrated, he turned abruptly to refill his glass and accidentally bumped into one of the young ladies he'd met earlier in the evening.

"Miss La Zear . . ."

The petite Jacqueline La Zear smiled coquettishly at him. "Mr. Kingsford."

"I'm sorry if I hurt you."

"No. I'm fine. Did you want more punch?" She offered him a glass.

"Why don't we dance first?" he invited boldly.

"I'd be delighted," she accepted, glad that she'd finally managed to attract his attention. She'd been watching him all night and found him most handsome. "Please, call me Jacqui."

"I'm Mark, Jacqui," he said as they joined the others on the dance floor.

Andre moved easily about the room with Suzanne in his arms.

"So, what is your interest in telling me these things about Christopher Fletcher?" she asked shrewdly, knowing what Andre was up to but not completely understanding his motives.

Andre was not surprised by her insight. "You know me so well . . ."

"You're right."

"The truth?"

"The truth," she answered, not mincing words.

"I want your niece for myself. But she's too damned enamored with Fletcher . . . . Perhaps if you and Isaac should disapprove of him . . ."

"I see your point." She glanced up just as Katie and

Christopher came through the French doors. She read with accuracy the look of loving adoration on her niece's face and knew that she would have to do something quickly. Why, if Katie managed to catch him before she, herself, had a chance . . . "I'll do what I can, Andre."

"That's all I ask, ma cherie."

As the music ended, Suzanne became aware of Mark escorting Jacqueline La Zear off the floor, Irritation surged through her. How dare he show interest in someone else! Especially a babbling girl, barely out of the cradle.

"Lead me back to Mark for now. I'll have to think about what I'm to do."

"Of course. Would you like me to invite the nubile Miss La Zear to dance?"

"How did you know?"

"My darling," he spoke in hushed tones. "I know you as well as you know me. And Mark is your latest, isn't he?"

"You're very perceptive, too, Andre. I'm glad we understand each other."

"We did more than that once, Suzanne," he reminded her.

"Yes and we ended it by mutual consent."

"There are still nights when . . ."

"Spare me any leftovers, Andre. You're after Katie now and if I can help you to get her, I will."

They greeted Mark and Jacqui cordially as they joined them at the refreshment table.

Christopher and Katie had just come in the room when Robert Adams caught sight of them.

"Christopher!" he hailed loudly. "I've been looking for you."

"Robert," he acknowledged his friend. "I'd like you to meet Miss Katie Kingsford. Katie, this is my host,

140

Robert Adams."

"Ah, Isaac's niece. A pleasure, Miss Kingsford." He was taken by her stunning good-looks.

"Mr. Adams."

"Robert, why were you looking for me?" Christopher was concerned.

"I needed your opinion on some business matters. In fact, I still do if you can spare me a few minutes."

"Katie?" he looked at her questioningly.

"Please, go on. I can join Suzanne. If you'll excuse me, gentlemen?"

"Of course."

"I'll be back as soon as I can, Katie," he assured her, and was rewarded with a warm smile.

Katie moved gracefully across the room to join Suzanne.

"Are you having a nice time, my dear?" she asked sarcastically.

"Yes, I am," Katie answered innocently, not realizing that the other woman was criticizing her.

"Katie, we really must talk," Suzanne began condescendingly.

"Talk?" Katie was lost.

"Let's go into the library so we can speak privately." Suzanne led the way and Katie followed worriedly behind.

Once inside the darkly panelled room, Suzanne made a great display of closing the double hallway doors before turning to face her niece.

"I realize that this is all very new to you," she gestured about her. "But there are certain rules that one must follow in polite society."

"I'm afraid I don't follow you."

"My dear. A young, unmarried woman does *not* disappear out of doors for God knows how long with an eligible bachelor she'd only just met."

141

"You mean Christopher?"

"Of course I mean Christopher Fletcher. Have there been others?"

"No. But I didn't just meet him. He came down river with us."

"Still, Katie. Your reputation could be in shreds . . ."

"Is it?" She was curious.

"Not yet, but . . ."

"But, what?"

"I've heard some very unsavory things about him tonight. It might be best if you didn't spend so much of your time with him. There are many other young men who would love to be with you. Why, Andre Montard just told me . . ."

"Andre!" Katie knew now what was going on. "Has he been telling you lies about Christopher?"

"No, we didn't even discuss Mr. Fletcher," she lied. "He confided in me that he finds you very attractive and would like to call upon you."

Katie took a deep breath before facing Suzanne squarely. Only the knowledge of Christopher's love held her firm in what she had to say. "Suzanne, I appreciate your telling me all this, but believe me when I say that I have absolutely no interest in Mr. Montard."

"Katie." The older woman was taken aback by her abruptness. "Andre is very well received."

"He may be by you, but he isn't by me," she declared firmly. "I don't care to talk about it any further. And as far as Christopher is concerned, he is very dear to me."

"And just how well do you know this Yankee?"

"Well enough to know that he's more of a gentleman than Montard could ever hope to be." Katie refused to say more. "There's really no point in arguing about this."

"Katie, as a Kingsford you have to abide by certain standards," Suzanne spoke sharply.

"I realize that things are done differently here in the

142

South and I promise you that I will try," Katie offered in a conciliatory manner.

Suzanne only barely succeeded in controlling her temper. How dare this little bitch argue with her? Her expression was icy as she looked Katie up and down.

"See that you do," and with all her dignity intact, Suzanne strode gracefully from the room.

Katie lay upon her bed, wide awake. The ball had been so exciting . . . and Christopher . . . her lips curved in a soft smile and her hand touched her breast as she remembered their time alone together in the gazebo. He had been so wonderful and even though he hadn't told her he loved her, Katie felt that he cared for her.

A frown marred her perfect features as she thought of the rest of the night. Suzanne had been greatly upset, but Katie felt she'd handled her admirably. She vowed never to let Suzanne intimidate her again. Still, she couldn't help but wonder at the connection between Andre and Suzanne.

Curling up on her side, Katie hugged her pillow to her and closed her eyes. Christopher had promised to get in touch with her as soon as he'd settled in at Greenwood and Katie lived for that day. Sighing deeply, she hoped he was missing her as much as she was missing him.

Christopher lay, unable to sleep in his wide, comfortable bed at the Adams's plantation. Ever since they'd left the ball he'd been unable to put Katie from his thoughts. Her protestation of love had made him very uncomfortable.

True, they were attracted to each other, but love? It came to him then with crystal clarity . . . the reason she was constantly on his mind . . . the reason why he'd been so desperate to get her away from Andre. . . . He loved her.

The thought brought Christopher no joy. Why had he fallen in love now, when he was about to embark on a dangerous course of action that ultimately might cost him his life? And, if he truly loved Katie how could he involve her in a situation so fraught with risk?

Tossing restlessly, Christopher knew sleep would be hard to come by this night.

Six

The Danger

Having just fallen asleep, Christopher was irritated when the sound of hurried footfalls outside his bedroom door woke him. Tense, he lay still listening . . . waiting . . . but there was no further disturbance. Lighting a lamp, he got up and dressed. Leaving his bedroom, he heard the muffled sound of an argument from belowstairs. Stopping at the top of the staircase, he saw a dim light coming from the study and he hurried down, thinking that Robert might need his help. Angry voice muted by the half-closed door assaulted him and he hesitated before knocking.

"You should never have come here so openly! You have jeopardized our entire operation!" Robert was furious as he verbally lashed out, but he fell silent at the knock at the partially open door.

"Robert?"

"Thank God it's you, Christopher. Come in and close the door." Robert was openly relieved.

Christopher entered cautiously and was shocked by the scene that greeted him. Robert, clad only in night clothes, stood with an unidentified white man near the center of the room. Lying face down on the sofa was an unconscious black man, whose bloody back was wrapped in dirty bandages. The drapes had been drawn against prying eyes and the air was tense with desperate fear.

"What can I do?" Christopher offered.

"I don't know . . ." Robert nervously ran a hand through his sleep-tousled hair.

"Who is this, Adams?" the stranger demanded warily.

"It's all right, Dillon. This is the new man I was telling you about."

"You're Fletcher?" The man named Dillon eyed Christopher distrustfully.

"At your service, Mr. Dillon." Christopher noted his uneasiness.

"Dillon, just Dillon. No Mister." Turning back to Robert, he said, "What makes you think that we can trust him?" .

"He comes highly recommended."

"By whom?"

"Friends," Robert explained evasively.

"You the one who snookered ol' Montard outta his prize plantation?" Dillon's face lit up.

"Yes, but understand this . . ." Christopher resented his implication, "I don't cheat."

"I do admire an honest man," Dillon backed down. "And since we're being honest, Fletcher. This here Negra is one of your new slaves."

"Mine?"

"One of Greenwood's. Just got away tonight." He faced Robert. "He's too weak to travel. You're going to have to put him up a while."

"That's impossible. You know how difficult things are with the patrollers riding the main roads."

"If you turn him out, he'll be dead in a day," Dillon

146

stated the painful truth.

Christopher understood Robert's dilemma. If he forced them off his property the slave would be caught and returned to Montard. And in his present condition, it was a certain death warrant. If he stayed and was caught . . . the Southern aristocracy was ruthless when they found traitors in their midst. Many men before them had lost their lives in unfortunate "accidents" after having been discovered helping slaves to freedom.

"He's been whipped?" Christopher asked.

"Forty lashes," Dillon replied, grimacing.

"He'll have to stay, Robert. And if any problems arise, I'll take the responsibility. He is, after all, now my property," Christopher spoke the last words distastefully.

Robert's mood lightened at the thought, "By God, you're right. Let's get him out to the slave hospital, there are beds there."

"I'll help. I've had experience with this type of injury. Why don't you go get dressed?" Christopher offered.

"Good idea." Robert managed to smile briefly. "I'll meet you there."

"Bring Joel when you come," he requested as he and Dillon carried the tortured man out of the house.

By the time Robert and Joel joined Christopher and Dillon, they had already stripped the filthy wrappings from the abused man's back and had begun to wash away the dried gore from his wounds. The pain roused the man to semi-consciousness and he moved violently under their ministering hands.

"No, massa! Ah's sorry! Ah's sorry!" he moaned.

Joel recognized the voice as he came through the cabin door. "Hercules?"

The tossing man stilled at the sound of his name being called.

"Hercules. It's me, Joel." Joel knelt by the bed and gently touched his friend's shoulder.

147

The feverish, trapped-animal look left Hercules's eyes to be replaced by a watchful disbelief. "Joel?"

"I'm here," Joel reassured him. "These men are going to help you."

"Massa Dillon said he could get me out." Hercules spoke nervously as his hand gripped Joel's.

"He will, he will," Joel began.

"Why did Montard beat you?" Christopher interrupted, fury growing within him.

Hercules looked at Joel.

"He's a good man. Trust him," Joel confided.

Hercules looked over his shoulder at the tall white man and then back at Joel. The last time he'd seen Joel, he had been chained and beaten and was on his way to be sold downriver. Yet, here he was, a year later, clean and well-dressed, in the company of white gentlemen.

"How did you come to be here? You was sold downriver. Ah saw you leave . . ."

"Mr. Fletcher here, bought me. He took me up North and gave me my freedom."

Hercules was finding it all a little hard to believe, surely this was some cruel trick. "So why you come back, fool?"

"For Dee," Joel said simply and then the other man understood. "Now, tell Mr. Fletcher what he wants to know."

The slave shuddered visibly as Robert applied a healing salve to his lacerated back and then covered the cuts with clean, soft wrappings.

"Ah tried to run . . ." The whites of his eyes showed as he remembered the terror of that night, running in the dark with the dogs always close behind him. "Dey caught me and brung me back . . ."

"Why did you run in the first place?" Christopher wanted to know. "You saw what they did to Joel."

"Dey's saying that we gettin' a new massa, who's meaner than Massa Andre . . . Ah was scared."

"Who told you about the new owner?" Joel was curious.

"Massa Andre . . . He tell Dee . . ." Hercules gave Joel a sympathetic look. "He tell her to be ready to leave on Monday 'cause he doan want dis other man to have her. He tell her dis new massa is mean and Massa Andre says he doan want her hurt . . . So he is gonna sneak her out early like."

Joel stiffened at the news and looked up at Christopher. Christopher met his gaze coolly.

"We should have expected," he began. "Thank you, Hercules. You rest now. We'll talk more later."

Christopher stalked out of the small house closely followed by Joel.

Hercules watched them. "Massa Dillon, who was dat white man?"

"He's the new owner of Greenwood," Dillon explained.

Andre sat comfortably in the bed watching Dee move about the room straightening the clothes he had so hastily discarded upon his return from the ball.

"We'll be moving into New Orleans for a few weeks until the house is repaired at Fairwinds." He leered at her as she brought him a tumbler of bourbon. "Be sure you're ready to leave early on Monday. If you're not here, Fletcher can't claim you as part of the property. It will be awkward in the city, but I want to keep you as close to me as possible."

"Yes, suh."

"You want that too, do you?" He patted the bed beside him and she sat down obediently. He caressed her breasts idly as he drank his liquor.

Dee wondered at his fierce expression. She was surprised that he'd come to her tonight for she knew that there had been a big party at the Fontaine Plantation. But come to her he had, his mood remote; his actions mechanical. Dee knew that there was more on his mind than leaving Greenwood on Tuesday. But Andre was not one to share his thoughts. He merely came to her for the pleasures she provided and it was her job to see that she satisfied him to the fullest.

"I'm going to have that little bitch! And when I do . . ." Andre mumbled and squeezed Dee's breast painfully.

Dee wanted to pull away, realizing that he was going to take his fury with another woman out on her. But she also knew it would anger him further if she was reluctant. Gritting her teeth against the torment, she couldn't quite stifle the low moan that rose in her throat. The sound drew his attention and Andre looked at her questioningly.

Misinterpreting the reason for her groan, he assumed she was ready for him again. Having never been rejected by a woman in his entire life, Andre felt himself to be totally irresistible. And as such, he was confident that Dee loved him deeply, passionately and devotedly.

Setting his glass aside, he increased the pressure of his biting hold on her tender flesh. Pulling her across his lap, Andre kissed her wetly. What a shame that he couldn't keep Katie the way he kept Dee. He would love to lock her in a secluded cabin and tame the wildness from her at his leisure. The thought titillated him.

"Turn out the lamp," he dictated, and when she had he pulled her back to him.

Closing his eyes, Andre pretended that Dee was Katie.

Dee had no idea what to expect from him now, for he was not himself this night. Lying passively against him, she waited for him to tell her what he wanted.

Thinking of Katie, Andre kissed her brutally, raping her mouth with his tongue. But when he sensed no resistance on the part of the woman in his arms, his fantasy faded. Angry with Dee for not knowing what he

150

eeded, he grabbed her hair and forced her head back.

"Fight me, damn you! Don't make it so easy!" he demanded, his eyes blazing with a threatening fire that Dee didn't understand. "*She* would fight . . ."

Spurred to action by his fearful order, Dee struggled against his domination. What started as an act on her part became real as he tried to bring her under his control.

Andre, once again lost in his drunken fantasy of forcing Katie to love him, easily subdued her. Pinning her to the bed, he chuckled evilly.

Terrified by this unknown side of Andre, Dee began thrashing wildly about, trying to free herself. Surprised by her strength, he was unprepared when an accidental blow struck him in the groin. Reason fled.

"You no-good whore!" He slapped her viciously, rocking her head from side to side and splitting her lip.

"Doan hurt me, Massa Andre!" she pleaded, barely able to speak. "Doan hurt me no more!"

"Tell me you love me, Katie," he commanded.

Dee was nearly hysterical and his drunken ramblings made no sense to her. But when she didn't do his bidding instantly, he raised his hand to hit her again.

"Ah love you!" she managed and was relieved when she felt him relax a bit.

"That's better. Now, tell me you want me . . ." He moved against her.

"Ah want you," she mumbled through rapidly swelling lips. Anything, she thought, anything to hurry him . . . anything. Her mind was racing, trying to figure out what it was he wanted.

"More than Fletcher . . ."

"Ah love only you. Ah doan want no other man."

"Good."

Reaching down, he guided himself into her and when the full, hard length of him plunged deep within her without resistance, Andre drew back.

"Fletcher did have you!" he snarled. "Well, he may have had you first, but I'm going to be the one you remember."

As Dee accepted him into her once more, they moved together. Locking her legs about his waist, Dee rotated her hips hoping that it would hurry him on. Her breast was sore and her lips were throbbing from his brutality. Whoever this Katie was, Dee felt sorry for her. For if Andre ever did get her, she would suffer far more than she herself just had.

Christopher looked across the breakfast table at Joel. His friend had been noticeably silent since their talk with Hercules and Christopher knew why.

"Joel. Have a servant get our things ready. We're going to Greenwood today."

Joel looked up, a glimmer of hope shone in his eyes. "Thank you."

Christopher half-smiled. "Did you think that I would let her get away from us now?"

Joel was openly relieved, "No. But Andre is as slippery as a snake. Our only hope is to surprise him."

"Well, showing up two days early should catch them unaware. Robert has agreed to accompany us and has already put the flag up at the landing. We should be on our way sometime later this morning." And Christopher couldn't deny to himself that he was eager for the chance to see Katie once again.

It was Sunday afternoon when the steamer carrying Christopher, Joel and Robert docked at the Greenwood landing. Though not as imposing as Kingsford House, Greenwood had a charm all its own. It was white and two stories tall with galleries both front and back. Greenwood was spacious without being overpowering in size and Christopher openly admired it.

Standing at his side, Joel paid little attention to the

beauty of the place. He was tense . . . assailed by memories of all that had happened here.

"Don't worry." Christopher was confident. "The past is over."

"I know," Joel said, pushing the depressing thoughts from his mind. "I'm just afraid we won't be in time."

"As soon as we get up to the house, I'll leave instructions for you to be taken to the quarters so you can settle in. While you're there . . ."

"I'll find her," Joel spoke, determination evident on his stern features.

"Also, let Hercules's family know that he's safe," Robert instructed.

Joel nodded but didn't reply as the plank was lowered and they left the ship. Assuming the role of manservant to Christopher and Robert, he carried their bags and, keeping his eyes downcast, managed to look suitably humbled. A small open carriage was waiting for them and soon they were on their way up to the main house.

Emil Montard and his wife Marie were surprised and displeased by their unexpected arrival. Awaiting Christopher and Robert in the main parlor, their expressions were grim and their nerves were on edge.

"Emil, this is the most humiliating day of my life and it's all because of your reckless pursuits!"

"We have discussed this before, Marie, and I will hear no more on the subject."

"You will hear no more!" She was outraged. "Greenwood was mine. . . my dowry, my legacy from my family. And you have squandered it. . ."

Emil turned on her viciously. "Shut up. They will be here at any moment."

Marie quieted at the sound of horses on the drive. Giving her husband one last scathing look, she went out to greet the new owner.

"Robert, so good to see you." Her mask of civility in place, she met them on the porch. "Mr. Fletcher? I'm Marie Montard."

"A pleasure, ma'am," he bent over her hand.

Christopher's Northern accent grated on her, but she managed a strained imitation of a smile. "Come in. My husband is awaiting you in the study."

"If I may, I'd like to send my servant on to the quarters?"

"Of course." She dismissed the thought as trivial, not even looking at Joel. Speaking to the driver, she directed, "T.C., take care of the horses and then see to Mr. Fletcher's man."

"Yes, ma'am."

She conducted them into the cool dimness of the house. "The study is right through those doors."

"Thank you."

Marie nodded and walked stiffly from their presence.

Girding himself for what he was sure would be an unpleasant interview, Christopher exchanged looks with Robert and opened the study doors.

Emil glanced up from his seat at the desk as the two men entered. With an effort he maintained his cordiality and rose to greet them.

"Robert, good of you to come along. Fletcher." He was solemn in his appraisal of the other man as they shook hands. "I didn't expect you until Tuesday."

"I know. But I'd finished my business in New Orleans and could see no reason to further delay my arrival. I trust you won't find my presence burdensome?"

"No. Greenwood can easily accommodate you."

"Fine." Christopher walked around the room surveying with much interest the well stocked library. "Robert has agreed to witness the transfer of title. Is that acceptable to you?"

154

"Of course. He is a man of honor."

"Thank you, Emil," Robert acknowledged.

But Emil waved away his words. "The simple truth, my friend."

"Where is Andre?" Robert asked in seeming friendliness.

"Out riding." Emil's answer was curt and Christopher sensed some tension in his words.

"Well, I'm sure we will see him later," Robert said smoothly before turning to business. "Shall we tour the grounds now and then later this evening check your inventories?"

"Most certainly." Emil could think of little to say to them. "Would you like to see the house first?"

"By all means," Christopher assented.

"Come with me then," Emil told him and guided them out into the center hall.

As soon as the carriage had rounded the corner of the house and was protected from view, T.C. reined in the horses and turned to Joel.

"Ah cain't believe you is here!"

"Me either," Joel agreed, embracing his old friend.

"Where you been?" T.C. asked, remembering clearly the day when Joel was sent downriver to be sold.

"Up North mostly." Joel was deliberately vague. He knew how news travelled on a plantation. Within an hour everyone in a five mile radius would know of his return. "How is Dee? Is she still here?"

"Sho is. C'mon, let's take care of these horses and den find your wife," T.C. encouraged.

Joel breathed a sigh of relief and leaned back in the seat as the carriage started up again. Dee was here! And soon he would be with her.

Andre touched Dee's cheek gently. Usually he never regretted his actions, but today he felt a twinge of guilt over Dee's injured face and the marks he'd left on her

155

breasts and thighs.

"You'll be fine in a day or two," he said soothingly a he pulled her to him. "Damn, but I was hot for you las night!"

Dee didn't speak. She ached all over from the abus she'd suffered at his hands the night before and all sh wanted this day was to be left alone.

Andre paid little attention to her discomfort as h pressed intimately against her.

"Do you have everything you need to go?"

"Ah finished packin' this mornin'." Her speech wa slurred as she spoke though puffy, swollen lips.

"Good." Andre slid his hands down her back and pushed her hips to him so she could feel the desire h had for her. "We'll have one last night together here."

Dee nodded, too tired to do anything else. She wa worried. She knew that Andre had planned to take he to New Orleans with him, but he had made no mentio of Jebediah. As much as she hated to stir Andre's anger Dee knew that she had to ask. She couldn't leave h baby.

"Mastah Andre . . ."

"What?" he murmured, drawing back to look dow at her.

"Ah needs to know, suh . . . 'bout my baby."

"What about the child?" Andre's voice was cold as h waited for her response.

"Ah needs my chile wid me. Ah know you doan wan him but suh . . . if he could jes' stay wid de others i New Orleans?"

"No." His reply destroyed her hopes. "He stays. I' be lucky if I can get you out of here without any prob lems. I have no time for your black brat."

Dee's heart broke and she couldn't control the sob that escaped her.

"Mastah   Andre . . . Please . . . Ah'll   d anything . . ." She fell on her knees before him.

156

"You'll do anything, anyway."

His words cut into her, making her realize the hopelessness of her situation. There was no justice. There never would be as long as she belonged to him.

Andre looked down at her in disgust, rejecting all the tenderness he had been feeling for her. She was stupid! He was offering her everything and all she could think of was that baby. The desire he'd had for her drained from him. He would leave her alone for a night and see how she liked that!

Shoving her roughly aside, he stormed to the door.

"See that you are ready to go first thing in the morning," Andre ordered, his black eyes burned with anger as he looked at her sprawled brokenly on the cabin floor. Without a word he turned and walked out, leaving Dee behind, her world in a shambles.

Dee waited until he was out of sight and then spurred herself into action. No one was going to separate her from Jebediah! She had lost Joel and survived, but she doubted if she could live through the loss of her only child. She would rather die trying to escape with him, than suffer endless years of torment worrying about his fate. Changing into a darker colored nondescript dress, she went in search of her son.

Dee found him playing in the dirt and took him back to the cabin with her, ignoring the questioning stares of the other slaves as they noticed her injured face for the first time. Once she was safely inside she gathered the few necessities they would need and quietly slipped away.

No one paid much attention to her as she headed up the long track to the big house. And at first opportunity, she quickly moved off into the side brush, keeping low and making her way toward the creek. She knew she had a chance of eluding the patroller's dogs if only she could make it to the water.

* * *

157

T.C. finished watering the horses and then took Joel down the road that led from the stables to the quarters. They had seen Andre ride by earlier on his way back to the big house, so they were certain that Dee would be alone.

"Where does he keep her?" Joel knew there was no use denying Andre's use of his wife.

"He's had her in a cabin out back." T.C. led him to a shaded path that branched off from the main track. "Down there, 'bout half a mile."

"Thanks T. C." Joel was grateful for the help and hurried off to see his wife.

Joel had no problems locating the house and he entered excitedly, wanting to surprise her. But instead of the loving embrace he'd expected, there was only silence to greet him. The cabin was deserted. Running back outside, Joel was determined to find her. As he searched through the quarters for her, he was welcomed warmly by all who remembered him. But no one could offer any help about where she'd gone. They knew that Dee had been in the cabin with Andre a short while before but she hadn't been seen since. Frustrated and more than a little worried, Joel went back to her house once more to see if she'd returned.

Christopher was standing with Robert and Emil on the back gallery when Andre rode up. Keeping his expression carefully blank, Christopher greeted the other man.

"Montard," he nodded.

"Fletcher." Andre was thoroughly aggravated to see Christopher. What was he doing here? And how in the world could he get Dee away from Greenwood under Fletcher's watchful presence? "Robert."

"Good afternoon, Andre," Robert greeted.

"I've just been showing Mr. Fletcher around," Emil told Andre as he joined them on the gallery.

"What do you think of Greenwood, Fletcher?"

"It's quite a showplace," he said approvingly.

"Yes, it is." Andre's tone was bitter as he looked out over the land he loved. Then forcing politeness, he turned to them, "Well, if you'll excuse me. I'm going to get cleaned up. Gentlemen."

"If you would care to rest before dinner . . . ?" Emil offered after Andre had disappeared inside.

"Yes. Please," Robert and Christopher agreed.

Emil led them indoors and walked with them to their rooms, "We dine at 7:30. I'll see you then."

Andre stalked around his room as he waited for the servant to bring the water for his bath. Just when it looked like his plan was going to work, Fletcher had to show up and disrupt everything. Andre's only hope was that he wouldn't insist on a head count of slaves. If he did . . . Well, it was bad enough that Hercules had been gone for two days, but if Dee was listed as missing, too, there might be trouble . . . big trouble.

His thoughts were interrupted then by Lizzy, the servant, returning with the heated water. When the bath had been prepared and the slave turned to go, Andre stopped her.

"Lizzy, I want you to go out to Dee's cabin and tell her to be ready to leave tonight. Tell her I'll come at midnight. All right?"

"Yes, suh," she responded and hurried to do his bidding.

Determined to set his plan in motion a day early, Andre settled back in the tub and tried to sort out his thoughts. He couldn't take the chance of letting Fletcher find out what he was up to. He had to remain calm in the face of his hatred for the man. Andre knew that he would be hard pressed to control his temper. But control it he must, if he was to get Dee out. He knew that he had to concentrate only on Dee right now. He would worry about winning Katie later.

Feeling confident of success, he rose from the tub

159

and began drying himself. There was much he had to do before midnight.

Joel entered the big house through the kitchen just as he had in all the years before. The idea of playing the slave had not set well with him, but he knew it was the only way he could accompany Christopher on this trip.

"Lucille," he called the cook from her hot endeavors near the stove.

"Joel? Is dat you?" She dropped what she was doing and hurried to hug him. "What you doin' here?"

"I'm here with the new owner, Christopher Fletcher."

"You his slave?"

Joel nodded. "He bought me when Montard sold me last year."

"Well praise the Lord. You is back! Come, have a quick bite and talk wid me 'bout dis new mastah we got."

"I will later Lucille. Right now I'm trying to find Dee. Have you seen her?"

Lucille looked thoughtful for a minute. "Not today I ain't. Aint' she at de cabin?"

"No. I looked there first and then I searched the quarters. But no one's seen her."

"I heard dat Mastah Andre spent most of last night with her and he went back early this afternoon. But that's all I know."

Joel was frustrated. "I need to see Mastah Fletcher. Do you have anything I can take up to him?"

"Here," handing him a pitcher of fresh water and a stack of towels, Lucille laughed. "You sho doan look much like a maid!"

"Hush woman," he growled good-naturedly as he headed up the back steps. "Which room?"

"Front by the magnolia," she directed.

"Thanks," and he disappeared around the narrow turn of the staircase.

160

Surprised by the knock at his door, Christopher got up quickly to answer it.

"Somehow you aren't quite a chambermaid," he said wryly, taking the water and linens from Joel.

Joel came inside and closed the door behind him. "I know. Lucille, the cook, said the same thing."

Christopher smiled broadly at his friend. "Did you find Dee?"

Joel scowled. "No. And I can't find anyone who's seen her this afternoon."

"Would he have sent her away already?"

"If he had, someone would know," Joel replied heavily. "Christopher, I've got to find her."

"Check the quarters once more and if you don't locate her this time, I'll ask Montard about her."

Joel walked over to the window and stared with sightless eyes at the rapidly darkening countryside, "If I've lost her again . . ."

"You haven't. We'll find her." Christopher had no doubts.

Joel nodded and left the room to continue his quest, his heart heavy with concern for his wife.

"Mastah Andre!" The nervous call came at his bedroom door just as he was tying his cravat. Recognizing Lizzy's voice, Andre quickly answered the door.

"What is it?" He was concerned by the unexpected interruption.

"It's Dee, Mastah Andre. She ain't at the cabin and ain't nobody see her since this morning."

"What do you mean she's not there? I was with her just this afternoon."

"Ain't nobody at the cabin, suh. It's all dark and deserted. And Ah looked everywhere else . . . but she's gone."

A range of emotions shook him. Fury that she was gone . . . worry that she might be hurt . . . and finally

161

a cold, vicious loathing settled over him.

"What about the child?" he asked, remembering their last conversation. "Is her baby gone too?"

"Yes suh."

Andre smiled grimly. "You may go. I'll handle it from here."

After dismissing the servant, Andre pulled on his coat and went downstairs to see his father. Finding Emil alone in the study was a stroke of luck and Andre closed the doors quietly for privacy.

"I need the hounds," he said flatly.

"Why?" Emil looked alarmed.

"Dee's run away and taken that black brat of hers with her."

"When?"

"Sometime late this afternoon, so her trail should still be fresh . . . Since she was travelling with the baby, she couldn't have gotten too far."

"All right. But you realize that I'll have to explain all this to Fletcher, don't you?"

"Yes."

"Go ahead. Good luck. We'll have to let Fletcher decide the punishment."

"I may do a little of that on the way back."

"Why did she run?"

"I made the mistake of telling her that she couldn't take her child with her to New Orleans."

Emil nodded but didn't speak.

"This shouldn't take too long," Andre said as he headed out to the stables.

The sun had disappeared, leaving behind a purple-stained night sky. Only a few stars were out, but they were enough to help guide Dee. Knee deep in the middle of the muddy stream, she waded on. With the help of a sling made from part of her torn skirt, she was balancing Jebediah on her hip as she staggered ever forward.

To elude the dogs she had to stay in the water. It was her only hope if she wanted to avoid detection. She had been running for over four hours now and exhaustion was taking its toll. Somewhere during the first few miles, Dee had lost her shoes to the clinging, sucking mud and now her feet were cut and sore. But despite her misery, she kept moving . . . toward freedom.

Dee was proud of her son, for Jebediah had only stirred and fussed twice during the past harrowing hours. Luckily, she had managed to calm him both times with food . . . What she would do when the little she'd brought along ran out, she didn't know and she was determined not to worry about it now. She only had enough strength left to concentrate on putting one foot in front of the other . . . She had to get as far away as possible. Shifting Jebediah's sleeping body to a more comfortable position, she trudged downstream hoping somehow to escape the future Andre Montard had planned for her.

It was only after dinner had begun that Joel returned with the news. Christopher heard him arguing with the servant in the hallway and excused himself from the table quickly to see what was going on.

"She's gone . . . run away . . ." Joel told him as he joined him in the hall.

"We'll go look for her," Christopher said calmly.

"It's too late!"

"What do you mean?"

"Andre found out about it long before I did. According to T.C. he left with the hounds over an hour ago."

"Did he go alone?"

"No. He took three other slaves along. But the dogs . . ."

"I know," Christopher paused, deciding on the best course of action. "Wait here."

Christopher returned to the dining room.

"What was all the commotion about, Christopher?" Robert asked as he re-entered the room.

"My servant informs me that one of my slave women ran away this afternoon." Christopher stood near the table staring straight at Emil. "Why wasn't I informed? I am the owner of this plantation and everyone on it, am I not?" His voice boomed with an authority that he had not chosen to exert previously.

"We didn't want to bother you on your first night here," Marie said in falsely soothing tones. Her husband had told her the whole story and she had been thoroughly disgusted. Marie had had no use for her son's black wench and she secretly hoped that some terrible fate would befall her.

"My dear woman, these are *my* slaves now. I want . . . No, I demand to be 'bothered' when they take a notion to depart the premises," he cut at her.

"We've handled the situation, Fletcher. There's no need for such outrage," Emil defended his wife.

"And just how did you handle it? Have you dragged her back beaten and cowed or just sent the hounds to kill her on sight?"

"She hasn't been found yet, but she will be. Andre is seeing to it personally."

"That's what I was afraid of."

"Suh?" Emil came half out of his chair.

"Your son has a cruel streak in him and I don't want him damaging my property!"

Emil paled at Christopher's words.

"I want horses now," Christopher demanded of the servant standing at the door. "See to it!"

The slave didn't give Emil a second thought, but took off at a run for the stables.

"Robert, will you join me?"

"Of course. Emil, how long as Andre been gone?"

"Not more than an hour."

"Perhaps we can still catch up with him. I imagine

164

he's having a difficult time of it in the dark," Robert advised.

"For his sake, I hope so," Christopher threatened as he led the way from the room.

Dee scratched at the ground with her bare hands as she attempted to dig a shallow hole in the middle of a large clump of bushes. She needed rest. The gruelling pace she'd set for herself had worn her out. Drawing Jebediah's warm sleeping body to her, Dee curled up in the dugout and tried to relax. She lay still . . . listening for the baying of the hounds . . . waiting . . . She hadn't meant for it to happen, but as the minutes passed and all was quiet, her eyes grew heavy with fatigue. Almost of their own will, they closed and soon she was sound asleep.

Cursing the darkness, Andre headed back to the big house with the hounds yapping at the heels of his gelding. He had an idea where Dee was, but he couldn't find her in the blackness of the night. The search would have to wait until first light. There was no point in breaking his own neck or ruining a good horse chasing after her now. She wasn't worth it.

Christopher, Robert and Joel heard Andre long before they saw him.

"Andre!" Robert called, hoping to avoid a major confrontation between him and Christopher.

"Robert?" the answering call came.

"Yes," Robert replied, leading the way and carrying his lantern high.

"What are you doing out here?" Andre asked loudly over the barking of the dogs.

"The same thing you are. Trying to find the runaway. Did you catch up with her yet?"

"No. I have an idea where she is but I won't be able to find her while it's this dark. It'll have to wait until morning."

"Good idea," Robert encouraged. "Why don't we all head back to the house?"

"You go on," Christopher said, glancing at Joel. "We're going to have a look around."

"Suit yourself. But if my hounds can't find her, I doubt that you can." Andre didn't try to hide the sneer in his voice. Jerking hard at his reins, he rode off with Robert leaving Christopher and Joel alone in the woods.

"All right Joel, where is she?"

"By the stream," Joel rode confidently toward the water. "She's trying to hide her scent from the dogs . . ."

Making their way to the stream, they rode through the water, holding their lanterns high.

"How far do you think she's gone, Joel?"

"Not too much farther. Watch the banks . . . She's probably resting somewhere by now."

They scoured the embankments thoroughly on both sides but found no trace of Dee or Jebediah.

"You're sure this is the way she'd go?"

"Yes." Suddenly Joel's breath caught in his throat at the unmistakable cry of a small child. "Listen!"

They were both mesmerized and overjoyed at the noise and followed it to its source.

At the sound of the splashing horses, Dee gave up trying to placate Jebediah. She held him in her arms and crushed him to her chest. No longer mindful of the cutting barbs and snagging branches, she panicked and ran. Running in mindless terror, she vowed that she would never return to Andre! Never!

Racing headlong through the low hanging branches, Dee ignored Jebediah's squeals of pain as brambles tore at his tender flesh. Hoofbeats echoed through her soul as she glanced over her shoulder. A white horseman was bearing down on her and she screamed shrilly, praying for rescue but knowing none was possible.

Just as the white man's arm reached down to snare her, Dee tripped over a half-hidden log and fell heavily on the damp ground. The rider sharply reined the horse in, taking great care to keep the iron-clad hooves from striking her. Leaping down from his horse, Christopher approached slowly.

"Dee? I won't hurt you," he began as Joel dismounted and ran toward them.

At the sight of what she thought was another patroller, Dee lunged away from them, knowing death was preferable to the torture of life without her baby.

Joel put a restraining hand on Christopher's arm as he made to follow her.

"Dee! Stop running!" Joel called, trailing her easily, but not wanting to frighten her any worse than she was.

The voice Dee never thought to hear again came to her through the darkness and she paused in her flight. Could it be? Or was she losing her mind? Tears streamed down her face. It had to be her imagination . . . There could be no other reason . . .

"No!" she denied, struggling to keep going.

"Dee! Wait! Montard's gone. "Wait!" Joel picked up his pace and caught up with her.

Grabbing her by the arm, Joel turned her to him, but her eyes were glazed in terror. Dee was so hysterical that she didn't recognize him and she tried to fight Joel tooth and nail.

"Ah won't go back! Ah won't!" she cried as Joel subdued her, as gently as possible.

"Dee . . . Dee . . . Look at me, Dee."

His words slowly penetrated the fog of horror that surrounded her and she ceased her struggles.

"Joel . . ." her voice was faint as she stood unsteadily before him.

"Christopher . . ." Joel took the screaming Jebediah from her arms and handed him to Christopher.

Picking her up, Joel carried her back to his horse. She lay limply in his arms, too exhausted by her ordeal to offer any further resistance.

"I'm here, Dee. I'm here," Joel murmured, over and over as he tried to soothe and comfort her.

With Christopher's help, Joel mounted and held Dee across the saddle in front of him. Finally, when Christopher managed to get a tenuous grip on the wriggling tot, he too mounted and together they headed back to Greenwood and the waiting Montards.

Seven

The Lovers

Joel carried Dee carefully into the small shack he was sharing with T.C.

"Joel?" T.C. was surprised by his unexpected return.

"We just found Dee," he explained as he placed her gently down on the corn husk mattress that served as a bed.

"She hurt?"

"She tried to run with Jebediah," he told T.C. as Christopher entered the cabin with the child asleep in his arms.

"They all right?" T.C. worried. "Did the hounds get 'em?"

"No, no," Christopher assured him as he looked down at the peaceful babe. "They'll be fine. They're just tired."

"Let me take him, suh," T.C. offered. "Ah'll have one of the women keep him for the night."

"Thank you." Christopher handed Jebediah to T.C.

and then approached Joel. "She's asleep?"

Joel glanced up. "Yes, but I don't know for how long."

"Did she say anything on the way back?"

"Nothing that made much sense." He shrugged. "I wonder what made her run . . ."

"Look at her face," Christopher's voice was strangled with emotion. "She didn't get that way from running through the brush."

Joel stared at her cut, swollen mouth. "Andre." The name was a curse on his lips.

"Come on outside a minute," Christopher suggested.

They stood together in the moonless darkness, sharing a moment of tense silence.

"I've got to go back up to the big house," Christopher admitted reluctantly. "You stay here, out of sight."

"I know."

"Keep her here, too . . . until I can get rid of Andre."

Joel nodded. Christopher was about to leave when they heard Dee's frantic cry and they both rushed back inside. Dee was crouching on the bed, her eyes wild with fear.

"Joel!"

"I'm right here," he reassured her, kneeling beside her.

"Where's my chile? I want my baby!"

"Dee, Jebediah's fine. T.C. took him for the night."

"He's all right? You sure?" Dee calmed slowly.

"I'm sure," Joel bent to kiss her tenderly.

Despite the gentleness of his kiss, Dee winced as his mouth touched her injured lips. Joel drew back, his face reflecting all the concern and anguish of the past year.

"I'm sorry, Dee," he apologized from the heart. "I wish I had been here to help you."

Dee caressed his cheek lovingly, lost in the sweetness of having him near, "Joel, yore here now."

"Dee, this is Christopher Fletcher." Joel brought himself back to the present with an effort.

Dee nodded shyly to the big, handsome white man.

"He bought me last year when I was sold in New Orleans."

"Looks like he been takin' good care of you."

"He did. He gave me my freedom."

Dee's eyes widened in astonishment. "Den why you here?"

"I couldn't leave you or Jebediah. I had to come."

"Oh, Joel," she cried hugging him.

He held her a moment and then drew back, explaining, "Christopher's the new owner of Greenwood."

She looked at him speculatively and then smiled as best she could, "Good . . . there has been so much talk . . . Andre, he say . . ." the thought of her tormentor sent a shiver down her spine. Trembling with horror, she looked up at Joel, "Andre . . . is he still here?"

"He'll be gone soon," Christopher confirmed.

"But he's after me!" She gripped Joel's hand in panic.

"Not anymore, Dee."

"He's the devil, Joel! He's crazy!" Dee grew more frightened at the thought of him. "Last night . . . he hurt me . . . he hit me. And he kept callin' me Katie . . ." she sobbed as Joel took her in his arms.

"You're safe now."

Christopher stiffened at her mention of Katie. Why would Andre call Dee Katie? Did Andre want her so badly that he fantasized about her? The possibility troubled him more than he cared to admit. If Andre

171

was capable of such cruelty to Dee, his mistress, how would he treat Katie if she refused his advances . . . Worry gripped him . . . had Andre gone there now? He had to make sure Katie was all right.

"Joel, if you need anything . . ." he said, resting a hand on Joel's shoulder.

"We'll be fine now."

"I'll meet you in the morning then." Leaving the re-united couple alone, Christopher headed back to the main house, his concern for Katie clouding his thoughts.

As Christopher entered the main hall of Greenwood, he was relieved to hear Andre in the study talking with the others. Forcing himself to appear relaxed, he strode easily into the room to join them.

"Christopher!" Robert greeted him warmly. "We'd heard that you had returned with the woman."

"Yes, Joel and I found her. We just got back."

"How is she?" Andre asked quickly, eager to get his hands on the bitch.

"Do you really care?" Christopher responded sarcastically.

"Where is she?" When he got no response, Andre headed for the door. "I'll go find out for myself."

"You are not to go near any of my slaves. Do you understand?" His voice was deadly calm.

"You have no right . . ." Andre sputtered, stiffening as he was reminded of his new status at Greenwood.

"I have every right! In case you've forgotten, I now own Greenwood. It is my property, as is everything and everyone on it." Christopher's words were icy with disdain.

The fury and hatred that Andre had fought so hard to control were unleashed full force by Christopher's arrogance.

"You may think you've won it all, but you haven't!"

Christopher snorted in derision and made to turn away as Andre continued.

"You may have Greenwood right now," Andre faced him squarely. "But you'll never have Katie Kingsford!"

Andre stormed from the house in a rage and, mounting his horse, he raced off into the darkness.

After a long silence, Emil began, "Mr. Fletcher, I must apologize for my son's outburst. This has been a trying time for us . . ."

"Mr. Montard," Christopher turned to glare at the older man. "Your son is no longer a boy. He is a man. It is time he took full responsibility for his actions."

Emil was outraged, "You are . . ."

"Telling the truth, Montard. The slave woman I brought back had been physically and sexually abused. *By your son!*"

"She is my property . . ."

"No, she is mine! She has been since last week. Andre had no right to lay a hand on her!" Christopher was furious at the man's attitude.

"She is only a slave," Emil shrugged.

Christopher started toward Emil, his hands clenched, and only Robert's restraining hand on his arm prevented their coming to blows.

"Let's see to the books now, gentlemen," Robert suggested.

"Of course," Emil spoke smoothly. "I have everything right here."

Christopher was grateful for Robert's interference. This was neither the time nor the place for a confrontation.

"Robert, if you would be good enough to take care of this for me," he requested. "There is something urgent that I must see to."

"This is highly irregular," Emil spoke.

"But necessary. I trust Robert implicitly," Christopher said as he stalked from the room. "I'll speak with you later, Robert. Montard . . . if the books are in order, I'll expect you to vacate tomorrow. I see no need to delay your departure until Tuesday. Do you? Good evening."

And with that, he was gone.

Katie sat in her bedroom, pleased that she'd been left behind. The Kingsfords had been invited to a soiree this evening and though she had been included in the invitation, Katie had begged off, pleading a headache. Not that she didn't have one, she did . . . Suzanne. Katie found the prospect of spending another evening under her aunt's disapproving eyes quite debilitating. And if she heard another comment on the advantages of marrying Andre Montard she was going to scream.

She was musing happily on the thought of a quiet evening alone when the sound of hurried hoofbeats on the front drive drew her out onto the gallery. Leaning over the rail, she was thrilled to see Christopher dismounting below.

"Christopher!" she called excitedly and raced through her room and out into the hall.

He was just being admitted by a servant when she came running down the stairs to greet him.

"I'm so glad you're here! I've missed you so!"

"Katie." He was relieved to see her and overwhelmed by her greeting. "You're all right," he confirmed to himself, embracing her warmly.

Katie pulled back and looked up at him questioningly, "All right? Of course, I'm all right. Why

174

wouldn't I be?" she paused briefly, "Nothing's happened to Mark or Uncle Isaac, has it?"

"No, no. It's nothing like that." Christopher released her slowly, his handsome features marred with worry.

"Then what is it?" she demanded. "It must be important."

"Is there somewhere we can talk privately?"

"Outside?" she suggested.

"Fine." He followed her out onto the gallery and then down the steps to the lawn.

The night was dark but the lights of Kingsford House helped guide them to a small grove of trees midway to the landing.

"Here, sit down," Katie invited as she located the ornamental bench in the middle of the sheltering trees.

Christopher joined her, quite at a loss, now that he'd discovered that she was all right. The ride to Kingsford House had seemed interminable, as he'd raced to what he thought was her rescue, and he felt quite foolish. He'd acted like a lovesick knight, dashing off on his trusty steed to save the damsel yet another time. A self-deprecating half-smile quirked his lips and Katie wondered at it.

"Well?" she questioned eagerly. "What happened?"

He sighed heavily, "It was Andre . . ."

"Andre?" She was confused. "I think you'd better start at the beginning."

He nodded in the darkness, "I got word through a reliable source that he was going to sneak one of the Greenwood slaves off the plantation tomorrow. So, Joel and I decided to go to Greenwood a few days early."

"I'll bet he was upset!"

"Actually, he hid it quite well," Christopher smiled broadly, his white teeth gleaming in the darkness.

175

"Amazing," she put in.

"I know." Christopher leaned back wearily and stretched his long legs out before him.

"So what does all of that have to do with me?" Katie was openly curious.

"It was later, after Joel and I discovered that he'd been abusing one of the slave women that Andre lost his temper."

"He hit a woman?"

Christopher nodded curtly, "Yes."

"I think I always knew he was capable of it but . . ." She shivered nervously.

"Anyway," he wanted to interrupt her thoughts. "He told me that I might have Greenwood, but I would never have you." Reaching out, he took a small cold hand in his large, warm one, and marvelled at the softness of her skin. "He rode off in a fury and I was worried that he might have come here. That's why I came straight over."

"No, I haven't seen or heard from him since the ball. Although . . ."

"Although what?"

"Well, Suzanne can't stop singing his praises. She's of the opinion that I should marry him," Katie told him. "That's why I stayed home tonight. I didn't think I could stand much more of her 'motherly' concern."

"There's no one else at home?" It just occurred to him that they were truly alone.

"No. They've gone to a soiree at the — um — Chenaut Plantation. Suzanne said it would be a late night."

He sat quietly for a moment.

"We'd better head back up to the house," he encouraged cavalierly.

"Why?" Katie kept her tone innocent enough, but Christopher could read the invitation in her eyes.

"Katie . . ." he began, wanting to give her a good

176

reason why they should return.

"Oh, Christopher. I love you so much!" Katie had thought of nothing else all day except being with him, in his arms, kissing him. And tonight there was no chance that they would be interrupted. "Please . . ." she urged him.

With a groan, he took her in his arms and held her close. "You're so tempting, Katie. But . . ." he began, catching his breath as her arms slipped around his waist.

"Christopher," her voice was throaty. Her whole body was on fire with longing. "We have to . . ."

Before he could summon up a good argument for abstaining, the context of which escaped him at the moment, Katie kissed him.

Though not experienced in seduction, Katie was naturally sensual and knew instinctively what would please Christopher. Pressing against him, she drew his hand to her breast and arched herself to fill his palm. The heat of his touch burned through the material of her dress and a thrill of excitement stirred her.

"Katie . . ." he began, making one last valiant effort to stop, but she would not hear of it.

Moving a little away from him, she unbuttoned the bodice of her gown to give him free access to her aching breasts. Christopher watched hopelessly for a moment and then surrendered to the desire that flamed within him. He loved her. It was what they both wanted . . . why fight it any longer?

"I want to be with you, Christopher. I love you," she told him huskily, her face alight with her love and her passion.

Again her innocent, honest ways moved him and he stood, pulling her up to him.

"Katie . . ." Christopher murmured.

He gently pushed the dress from her shoulders to

expose the full, pink-tipped mounds of her breasts
Then, taking the time to admire her silken, ivory skin
he caressed her with a featherlight touch. Her nipples
hardened encouraging him further as his mouth
sought and found each peak. Enraptured, she held her
breath as the erotic movement of his mouth upon her
breast awoke her slumbering passions.

Releasing Katie, Christopher shed his coat and
spread it on the soft, fragrant grass. Coming back to
her, his eyes dark with passion, he smiled at her tenderly.

"I want to know all of you . . . to feel your softness
against me. Love me," he invited.

"Oh, I do," she came to him, trembling with the
force of her passion.

With Christopher's help, she soon stood unclothed
before him. Proud of her love for him and equally
proud of her body, Katie smiled sensuously.

Christopher was enraptured. Katie was perfection
No fantasized vision could ever hope to compare to
the reality of her sleek curves. With clumsy fingers, he
unbuttoned his shirt and stripped it off.

Without waiting for an invitation, Katie went to
him, wanting to touch the solid wall of his hair-roughened chest and to feel the heat of his body next to hers.
In a surge of blazing desire, they came together and
moved to lie upon their makeshift bed.

Katie was lost in the splendor of his embrace as
Christopher bent over her and kissed her softly. He caressed flawless flesh in long smooth strokes that traced
her from shoulder to thigh. Rolling to his side, he took
her with him, cupping her buttocks and pressing her
intimately to his strength.

Thrilled at finally being in his embrace, Katie
moaned in anticipation. It felt so right being with him.
Molding her hips to his, she wrapped a slender, bare

leg around his still clad thighs and moved eagerly against the hardness of his manhood.

Christopher shuddered as Katie's leg encircled him and he couldn't stop himself from moving sensuously against her offered softness. Clasping her to him, he pinned her lightly to the ground with the seductive weight of his lower body. Supporting himself on his elbows above her, he paused, wanting to make the moment last. The way things were going, if he didn't stop for a moment, their joining would be over almost as soon as it had begun.

"I want you, Katie."

"Christopher, please . . ." she entreated, wrapping both legs around his slim hips, the tight ache within her begging for the ultimate release.

Understanding her driving need for satisfaction, Christopher kissed her passionately and then slowly moved lower to explore the sweetness of her throat and bosom. Katie ground her hips into Christopher's, arching and driving against him in an innate effort to fill the emptiness within her. But he shifted away from her seductive twisting.

"I need . . ." she moaned breathlessly as his hand slipped between her parted thighs. "Oh!"

With tender, persistent strokes, Christopher teased her to the peak of passion as she writhed beneath his skillful hand.

Holding his head to her breast, Katie sobbed her pleasure to him as she experienced her orgasm.

Shaken by the power of her climax, she couldn't move as his kisses traced a lower path over her body. Wanting to discover her most sensitive spots, he lifted her hips to him and tasted of her. Katie bucked weakly at this unexpected, intimate invasion, but Christopher's hands stilled her. She lay languid and motionless as his lips and tongue forced her to arousal again.

When he moved away from her to shed the rest of his clothes, Katie cried out to him, her body aching for the heavy, sensuous weight of him upon her. He returned to her in moments, drawing her legs around his waist and positioning himself against her wet heat.

Excited by the contact, Katie reached down to explore this part of him. Holding him gently, she fondled him.

He groaned as her inexperienced fingers stroked him. Kissing her deeply, Katie tasted the essence of herself on his lips. Aroused, no longer able to refrain from having her, Christopher covered Katie's hand with his and, together, they guided him to her. He entered slowly. At Katie's urging, Christopher began to move, driving into her depths and branding her his own.

United, they soared together, giving and taking, until their world exploded about them in a cascade of fluid light and suspended motion. Clasped in each other's arms, they fell to earth, replete and content, enthralled with the love they had just discovered. In quiet, they rested, each reliving with great wonder the joy of their union.

"I love you, Katie Kingsford," Christopher's deep voice was rough with emotion as he lay beside her, cradling her next to him.

"I love you, Christopher Fletcher," she returned, smiling up at him.

She caressed his cheek with her hand and he turned to press a heated kiss on her palm.

"You've given me so much . . ." He bent to kiss her lips.

"I am yours, Christopher. All that I have . . . all that I am . . ." she pledged, trustingly.

"You can't imagine how much that means to me."

Katie looked at him questioningly. "I don't understand."

"I'm not what you think," he told her cryptically.

"You're not a gambler?"

"I won't deny that. I do know how to gamble and that I am good at it, but it's not my livelihood."

"Oh."

"I learned card playing when I went to the university he shrugged. "And usually I only play for sport."

"Well, if you only gamble for fun, how do you make a living?"

"I have business interests in Philadelphia . . ."

"You mean you're rich?" Katie was astounded. At his nod, she shook her head in wonder. "But why lie?"

"I didn't really lie. It was just easier in the beginning to let everyone think what they wanted. I don't like to talk about it. Most people are overly impressed by money and seem to treat you differently when they find out you're wealthy."

Katie grinned at him. "It doesn't matter to me one bit if you're a gambler or not. I love you anyway."

As Christopher bent to kiss her he thought of his future.

Was there room for this woman in his life? Should he keep her with him in spite of the danger he was facing? He had never been responsible for anyone but himself . . . Could he love her the way she needed to be loved?

Doubts assailed him. Logically, he knew he should run from such entanglements. He had his work to do and shouldn't let himself be distracted by a woman. But Katie wasn't just any woman. Confused, he kissed her once more and moved away to pull on his pants.

Sensing his withdrawal from her, Katie, too, began to dress. Christopher came to her and helped her with the multitude of petticoats and the voluminous skirts. Before rebuttoning the bodice, he cupped her breast and lifting it to his lips, sucked it gently. Then, quite reluctantly, he began to cover her.

Katie had stood spellbound as Christopher had toyed with her, working his magic upon her sensitive flesh. When he forced himself to stop, her frustration was great and she looked up at him questioningly.

"No, my love. We can't tempt fate . . ." he told her, pulling her to him.

"But it feels so good," she tried to explain.

"I know."

"Is it always this perfect?" she asked, resting her head on his chest.

"Between us, it will be." His voice was velvet. "Always."

When they had finished dressing, they began the walk back to Kingsford House, pausing at every concealing shadow to share a heated embrace.

A late rising moon shone down upon them as they finally drew near the gallery. Patsy observed their approach from her vantage point in Suzanne's room.

"I'll be in touch with you sometime this week," Christopher was saying as they stopped at his horse.

"I'll be waiting."

Mindful of the servants, he kissed her cheek tenderly. Katie closed her eyes as the touch of his lips brought serenity to her soul. How she wanted to spend the night locked in his arms, sharing love's most passionate embrace. When she opened her eyes again, he had already mounted his horse.

"Good night, Katie. I'll see you soon," he told her softly before riding off down the road.

Katie raised her hand in a mute farewell, feeling empty and very alone as she watched him disappear into the darkness of the tree-shrouded lane.

* * *

Andre stood with Suzanne drinking champagne in the main parlor of Windland, the Chenaut Plantation. The soiree had been pleasant enough but they were both decidedly bored.

"I can't believe you didn't force her to come," Andre mumbled under his breath.

"Frankly, I was glad to get away from her," Suzanne responded with a shrug. "Really, Andre, you must tell me what it is that you see in her."

"Blond hair, a beautiful body . . ."

"You can buy that in New Orleans, darling," she told him drolly.

"She's a challenge, Suzanne. The unattainable virgin." Andre voiced his deepest feelings. "And I intend to be the one to breech her defenses, so to speak." He smirked at the thought.

Suzanne looked at him, her expression one of great irritation, "I find it very hard to believe that someone of Katie's calibre has truly captured your heart."

"Jealous, love?"

"Hardly," Suzanne answered truthfully. "Just surprised."

"And well you should be. I've never felt this driving need for possession before."

"Not even with your black slave wench?" Suzanne asked sarcastically, knowing of his long-standing desire for Dee.

"That was different and it's over now, anyway. I love only Katie."

"Love? Andre, I don't think you're capable of that most tender of emotions," she chided.

"Maybe not the way you think of it, but I want her more than I've ever wanted any woman," he told her earnestly. Then realizing how that had sounded, he added, "No offense."

"None taken," Suzanne sipped her champagne in

ladylike elegance. "I'm doing my best to encourage her in your direction, but she seems to find you unappealing."

"I know. I made a mistake during our trip down-river . . . I pushed too hard." He remembered very clearly her parting words after his first attempt at seduction. "But now, I'm prepared to win her slowly."

"I wish you luck, Andre. She's quite enamored with Fletcher."

"I know that too." He paused deep in thought. "What do you think of him?"

"I found him quite handsome. Why?" She was noncommittal.

"Why don't you make a play for him? Surely he'd find a dalliance with a woman of your stature far more entertaining than the company of a young, unsophisticated girl."

"I had considered it."

"Don't consider it, woman. Do it!" Andre was losing his patience.

Setting her glass on the table beside them, she spoke over her shoulder as she walked away from him, "I'll see what I can do for you."

And, for the time being, he had to be satisfied with her answer.

Isaac, Mark and Suzanne sat in the quiet comfort of the carriage on their late trip back to Kingsford House.

"A lovely evening," Isaac spoke contentedly. "What a shame Katie didn't feel up to coming."

"I hope it's not anything serious," Suzanne added.

"I'm sure she'll be fine by morning." Mark was confident.

"Good," Isaac remarked. "I've been thinking. And I

184

believe it would be most suitable for us to have a party for Katie and Mark . . . say a week from next Saturday."

The idea nauseated Suzanne, but she smiled in agreement, "Of course, Isaac."

"That should give you plenty of time for your shopping trip and to prepare the house. What do you think, Mark?"

"It sounds fine," he agreed, hoping that the La Zear family would be included in the invitations. In spite of his attraction to Suzanne, he'd found himself watching for Jacqui all evening.

"I want the best of everything, Suzanne. Spare no expense. And if Katie wants one of those white ballgowns like Renee Fontaine was wearing, then get it for her."

"Naturally." She swallowed hard against the urge to scream.

"I have to go to New Orleans on Wednesday. If you wish you may travel with me that day."

"I would enjoy that." Suzanne's voice sounded hollow, even to herself.

So, he was going to her again! She wished there was some way to put an end to this other woman's hold on Isaac, but she knew from past experience that it was useless. Cherie Delabarre had been Isaac's mistress for over twenty years.

"Will you be returning to Greenwood with us?"

"No. I have affairs to take care of in town. I'll plan to be back the Thursday before the ball."

"Very well," she replied distantly, knowing with certainty what those affairs were.

Mark sensed a change in the mood of the conversation, but he didn't understand it. He only knew that Suzanne seemed greatly distressed by something Isaac had said. Wanting to distract her, Mark made an effort at pleasant conversation but her monosyllabic responses did not encourage him to continue. Puzzled, he sat back and tried to enjoy the rest of the ride home.

Suzanne excused herself and retired upstairs to her bedroom as soon as they reached Kingsford House. She was tired and most irritated. She didn't know why, but Isaac's infidelity still had the power to hurt her.

As she entered the room and slammed the door viciously behind her, she was surprised to find Patsy waiting up for her.

"Patsy? What are you doing here?"

"Ah knows how you like to know everything dat goes on 'round here . . ."

"Yes. So?"

"While you was gone, dere was a gentleman caller."

"For me?"

"No ma'am. He came ridin' up real quick like and asked to see Miz Katie. Said his name was Fletcher . . . Christopher Fletcher."

"And did she receive him?"

"Yes ma'am," Patsy offered eagerly. "Dey even went for a long walk outside—in de dark. And when she came back in . . ."

"Thank you, Patsy. I get the picture. You may go," Suzanne dismissed her curtly.

"You ain't mad, Miz Suzanne?"

"No. Not with you, Patsy. You did the right thing. Thank you."

"Yes ma'am," Patsy replied and withdrew from the room leaving Suzanne seething in silence.

Was there no controlling the girl? Had she and Fletcher planned the assignation the night before? It would seem so and Suzanne was furious at having been outwitted by a mere child. Never again would she leave Katie unchaperoned.

Readying herself for bed, she climbed beneath the covers dwelling on her plan for attracting Christopher Fletcher. Mark didn't even enter her thoughts as she plotted her next moves. And she would have laughed had she known that he lay sleepless in his room, waiting and hoping that she would come to him.

After leaving Katie, the ride back to Greenwood went swiftly for Christopher as he passed the time reliving in his mind their encounter this evening. Hard put not to return to her most willing arms, he stopped at the quarters to see Joel, hoping the visit would distract him from his sensuous thoughts of Katie.

Christopher found Joel and Dee alone in the cabin. Dee was asleep, so they went outside to talk.

"Where've you been?" Joel asked, curious. He had not expected to see him again until after the Montards had gone.

"I went for a ride," he replied, not wanting to reveal anything about his time with Katie.

"This late?" Joel was openly skeptical. "What happened?"

"Andre wants Katie . . . and he threatened . . ."

"I wouldn't doubt it. Dee's told me more about what's been going on with Andre. He's a very dangerous man."

"I've known that."

"He wants Katie in a very bad way."

"I know that, too. That's why I rode over to Kingsford House. I was afraid Andre had gone after her. But now I realize he has far more subtle ways . . . he would never confront her directly."

"So Katie's all right?"

"She was fine," Christopher said, his relief quite obvious. "But I warned her anyway."

"Do you love her?"

Joel's question jolted Christopher, "Am I that obvious?"

"Only to me. I've never known you to care so much about a woman before."

"I do care. Probably too much."

Joel chuckled, "She's sure special."

Christopher growled as a flashing thought of her naked body, writhing in his arms assailed him. Standing abruptly, he climbed on his horse.

"I'll send word as soon as the Montards are gone."

"I'll see you tomorrow."

Turning his mount down the path, he headed back toward the big house. Christopher had hoped to put Katie from his mind, but his conversation with Joel had only heightened his awareness of his need to have her with him always.

Marie Montard had already retired when Christopher entered Greenwood house and only Emil and Robert were there in the study to greet him.

"Andre's not back yet?" he asked taking the glass of bourbon Robert offered him.

"I'm sure he'll be late," Emil spoke casually. "He undoubtedly went to Chenaut's dinner party."

Christopher nodded, agreeing with Emil's inference.

He was surprised that he hadn't thought of it sooner. Andre would have gone there in search of Katie.

"Are all of the papers in order, Robert?" he asked, changing the subject.

"Everything is acceptable."

"Good." Looking at Emil with narrowed eyes, Christopher continued. "What time do you plan on leaving tomorrow?"

Emil turned his cold-eyed gaze to Christopher, "We will be gone before noon."

"That will be fine."

"If you'll excuse me?" Emil left, not trusting himself in the same room with Christopher.

Though Emil realized that the loss of Greenwood was his own fault, it didn't make it any easier to deal with the other man's high-handedness. Resentment flared within him. Someday . . . some way . . . he would even the score with this presumptuous Yankee.

Robert turned to face Christopher after Emil had quit the room. "You've just made an enemy, you know."

Christopher shrugged, refilling his glass. "He's not my first."

A sudden thought of Katie sent a tingle down his spine and he smiled in spite of everything.

"You seem quite pleased with yourself this evening," Robert noted casually.

"I am, Robert. Things have been going so well . . . The Montards will be, gone tomorrow . . . Joel's back with Dee . . . and I . . ." he stopped not wanting to say too much.

"And you?"

"I am very thankful that this has turned out better than we had anticipated."

"I know what you mean. We've been most fortunate." Robert let the subject drop. "I think I'll call it a night, too. Until tomorrow."

When he had gone, Christopher settled into a comfortable wing chair and drank his bourbon in silence. In the morning, things would seem clearer and he would be able to think more rationally and decide what to do. But for now, he was going to relax with his memories. Memories of a burning sweet surrender that had left him branded by its flaming joy.

189

* * *

Katie was relaxed and totally content when she awoke the next day. She smiled to herself as she dressed for her morning ride and wondered how she could possibly have slept so well after the excitement of being with Christopher last night. Humming merrily, she left her room and started down for breakfast.

Usually she ate the early meal alone, but this morning Mark was already at the table.

"Good morning," she greeted cheerfully as she poured herself a cup of hot coffee at the buffet and sat down across for him.

"You're certainly feeling better this morning," he observed.

Katie glanced up at him and was surprised to find that he looked exhausted. "I feel fine, but you look terrible. Didn't you get any sleep last night?"

"A little."

"Were you out that late? I'm afraid I was already asleep when you came in."

"No. I just had trouble falling asleep."

"There's nothing troubling you, is there? Will talking about it help?" Mark had always confided in Katie and she expected that it would be no different now.

"No. Nothing's wrong. It was probably just all the excitement."

"I missed something exciting?"

"On the ride home, Isaac decided that he and Suzanne would give a ball just for us, a week from next Saturday."

"A ball? For us?"

Mark nodded, "We're going into New Orleans with Suzanne on Wednesday to do all our shopping."

"That sounds very nice." Katie sounded unimpressed.

"Don't worry, we'll have a great time," he told her, assuming that she didn't want to go on a marathon shopping spree.

"I know but . . ." she began.

"But it won't be as interesting as staying home un-chaperoned. Will it, Katie?" Suzanne's autocratic voice cut into their conversation.

"Good morning, Suzanne." Mark stood as she approached the table.

"Mark," she acknowledged curtly, the full fury of her emotion directed to Katie. "Isn't that correct, Katie?"

"I don't know what you mean," Katie said honestly, caught totally unaware by her verbal assault.

"I mean this, young lady." Standing at the head of the table, her hands on her hips, Suzanne appeared quite formidable. "Last night, you pleaded illness and remained at home even though you were included in an invitation to a respectable party. Then, when you were sure you were alone, you had your lover sneak over here and you cavorted in the darkness with him until all hours, having no consideration for your own reputation or that of your family!" Suzanne charged heatedly.

Mark was outraged at Suzanne's disclosure. "Katie?"

"It's true that Christopher did stop by. But it was not planned. He was worried and . . ."

"Worried? Worried about what?" Suzanne pried.

Katie started to answer but thought better of it. "Nothing. If you'll excuse me. It's time for my morning ride."

Without giving Suzanne a chance to continue the argument, Katie quickly slipped out of the dining room.

Mark realized that Suzanne was still angry with his sister and he wanted to bridge the gap between them.

"Suzanne," he came to her, but did not touch her. "You mustn't let Katie upset you so. She's not accustomed to your ways yet. Give her time."

"Mark, if I give her any more time, her reputation will be a shambles," Suzanne hissed, covering up her real

191

feelings about the situation. "And I'll have been made the laughing-stock of the parish!"

"Hardly. Katie's actions are her own. They've nothing to do with you."

"I hope so . . ." She turned to Mark and rewarded him with a bewitching smile. "You've calmed me already."

"Sit down." He held her chair. "I'll bring you some coffee."

Suzanne sat quietly while he served her. She cared little about Mark now one way or the other for she'd set her sights on more challenging game. Christopher Fletcher. Somehow, someway, she was going to have him, but until her plans came to fruition, there was no harm in passing the time with Mark. Turning on her most charming manner, she set out to beguile him completely.

Eight

The Runaways

The roustabouts were busy loading the luggage on the steamer as Marie, Emil and Andre stood on the landing and took a long last look at their beloved home. Christopher had wisely chosen to stay away from them this morning and only Robert had come to see them off.

"I'm sure I'll be seeing you soon, Emil," Robert offered as they shook hands.

"We'll be staying in New Orleans for a few weeks until the house at Fairwinds is ready."

"Fairwinds is on Bayou Teche, isn't it?"

"Yes. It's not too far."

"Good. You'll still be close."

"Of course." Seeing that their final piece of baggage had been taken aboard, Emil knew it was time to depart. "Robert, take care. Come Marie, Andre. We must go."

With one final glance toward the white house, they boarded the boat and disappeared inside.

* * *

"To the new owner of Greenwood," Robert lifted his glass in toast to Christopher.

"Thank you."

"I'll bet you're relieved that they've finally gone."

"Relieved isn't the word for it." Christopher gave Robert a half-smile as he sighed deeply. "It didn't go as badly as I thought it would."

"You were just lucky to get here before Andre moved Dee out."

"I'm glad we made it for Joel's sake. He's been through a lot this past year."

Christopher was quiet as he thought of the changes that had occurred in his life during the last twelve months. He had embraced a cause that was altering the entire course of his existence. No longer was he the pleasure-seeking hedonist who travelled the world looking for new thrills. He had grown past that. He had witnessed unnecessary suffering and had decided to use all his energy and all of his considerable funds if necessary to aid the hopeless victims of slavery. He drained his drink and turned to Robert with renewed resolve.

"What's our first move?"

"We wait. There's nothing more for us to do," Robert confided. "You'll never know when they're coming."

Christopher nodded, "But once they arrive, I'm to secrete them away until it's safe to travel."

"Right. Move them out as quickly as you can. Use what ever means are available . . ."

"We've been over this so often, but still, the first time . . ."

"Is the worst," Robert grinned. "Unless, of course, you have Dillon show up on your doorstep with a beaten slave in the middle of the night when you have a house full of company."

Christopher chuckled, "Well, you can bring Hercules back as soon as he's able to travel. He has no reason to fear Greenwood's new master."

"Are you going to free all the slaves?"

"I don't know. There's nothing I'd like to do more than give them all their freedom, but I think it would be just a little too obvious."

"Everyone would be suspicious and no doubt you'd be ostracized from society."

"I'm not concerned about that," Christopher sneered. "I just don't want to stir up any interest in my business affairs."

"Take your time then. Probably, it would be best if you lost a few slaves to the Underground Railroad, too."

"You're right," Christopher agreed solemnly. Then reviewing their procedure one final time. "Once more—I send them from Greenwood to your place and you take over from there."

"Yes. You'll probably be dealing mostly with Dillon, but occasionally they come on their own," Robert instructed. "Well, I'd better get ready to head home. Can you have the flag put out for me?"

"Of course. Do you need any help packing?"

"No. I didn't bring that much with me." Robert headed upstairs. "I'll be back down in a few minutes."

Christopher settled in his chair at the desk. The morning had been hectic, giving him little time to think of Katie. Now, in the peace of his first real moment alone at Greenwood, memories of last night stirred his heart and body. How he wished she could be here with him to share this time. It amazed him that she had managed to become so important to him in such a short period of time, and he found the thought oddly warming.

* * *

Suzanne sealed the last invitation and set it apart from the others. She had spent long hours the night before preparing the guest list and, now that the necessary missives had been written, all that remained was to see them delivered as soon as possible.

Summoning Patsy, she gave her the invitations with explicit instructions as to what to do with them. Then, pocketing the one she'd put aside, Suzanne went up to her room to change clothes. Moments later, she came down, dressed in her riding habit, impatiently awaiting her mount.

"In case Isaac should ask, I'm going to ride over to Greenwood to deliver Mr. Fletcher's invitation personally," Suzanne informed Patsy. "I'll be back shortly."

"Yes ma'am," the servant acknowledged. Patsy couldn't help but wonder, though, why she had to hand deliver his invitation, but she held her tongue. That was none of her business, she had no right to question her mistress's comings or goings.

As Suzanne rode away from the house she was slightly nervous, but nervousness turned to exhilaration as she neared Greenwood. She loved a challenge. And that's what Fletcher was. Especially since he was attracted to Katie. Suzanne smirked. She'd see how long Katie could keep him once she turned her full attention to seducing him. The thought of winning him for herself made her smile. Unsophisticated Katie Kingsford was no match for her. Confident of her womanly abilities, Suzanne rode up Greenwood's main drive, eager to meet on a one to one basis with Christopher Fletcher.

After spending the entire morning riding the fields, Christopher and Joel were now closeted in the study reviewing every aspect of the planting schedule. They were deeply involved in trying to arrange a less arduous work day for the field hands when the announcement of Suzanne's arrival interrupted them.

"We can talk more about this later," Christopher suggested as he and Joel walked into the hall.

"Yes, massa," Joel played his role to the hilt and left the house by way of the kitchen.

Christopher was puzzled as he entered the front parlor where Suzanne awaited him. What reason did Suzanne Kingsford have for coming to call?

"Mrs. Kingsford, how good to see you," he welcomed her.

"I hope I'm not disturbing you, Mr. Fletcher?"

"Not at all. It's a pleasure."

"I've come for a most important reason," she confided.

"Is something wrong?" He immediately worried about Katie.

"No. Quite the opposite," she smiled at him seductively. "I've come to invite you to a ball we're giving a week from Saturday. I decided to bring the invitation personally so I could be sure you received it."

"Thank you for including me." He took the sealed note from her.

"Then you'll be coming?"

"I wouldn't miss it."

"Wonderful. We hardly had a chance to talk at the Fontaine ball," she pouted. "I think it's essential that we get to know each other better, don't you?"

"Of course, Mrs. Kingsford."

Christopher was stunned by her blatant suggestiveness. Had he not been in love with Katie he definitely would have taken Suzanne up on her offer. She was a very attractive woman.

"Please, call me Suzanne."

197

"And I'm Christopher, Suzanne," he gave her a knowing smile. "Would you care for some refreshment?"

"You're very kind, but perhaps another time?" she insinuated. "I must get back to Kingsford House. We're going in to New Orleans tomorrow and there is much that needs to be done."

Walking gracefully to him, Suzanne touched his arm and gave him a provocative, smoldering look.

"I'll see you a week from Saturday, Christopher?"

"Most assuredly. Thank you for coming by, Suzanne." He escorted her onto the gallery.

Christopher watched Suzanne until she was out of sight on the drive and then he turned to re-enter the house. He was only mildly surprised to find Joel waiting for him in the study.

"Watch that woman. I have a very bad feeling about her."

"You're not alone," Christopher concurred. "But I have to admit, what she had to offer was quite tempting. Suzanne Kingsford is a beautiful woman."

"On the outside, maybe . . ." Joel let the thought drop there.

"She's definitely not worth losing Katie over," Christopher grinned. "Somehow, I don't think Katie would stand still for my seeing her uncle's wife."

Joel gave an exaggerated shudder, "I hate to think what that little lady would do to you this time!"

"Once was enough. I'm sorry I even gave Suzanne a second thought." Christopher chuckled in vivid remembrance of his injured eye.

"You're learning, Christopher. You're learning."

"How's Dee today?" He changed the subject.

"She's much better."

"Did you mention to her about moving into some rooms here?"

"Not yet. I thought I'd let her get her full strength back before I tell her everything."

"Well, feel free whenever you're ready."

"I will." Joel rose to leave. "Let me know what Gasell says about our changes . . ."

"He wasn't too pleased at our questions today. I may have to fire him." Christopher was solemn on the subject of Greenwood's overseer. "And soon."

"That might be best. I could do his job or T.C. could take over."

"Let's see what happens tomorrow when we approach him with these changes. If he gives me any trouble, he's gone."

Joel nodded his agreement, "He's the nosy type and one thing we don't need is somebody snooping around here . . ."

"You're right. Things are going to be complicated enough without having to worry about Gasell finding out. I'll take care of him in the morning."

"I think I'll stay here and rest." Katie declined Suzanne's invitation to go on another shopping trip.

Suzanne was exasperated with the girl, but hid it behind a veneer of indifference, "Whatever you wish. We should be back before four."

Suzanne closed Katie's bedroom door as she left and, shaking her head in annoyance, joined Mark in the foyer of the Kingsford's home in New Orleans.

"She's decided to stay home this afternoon," she told him.

"Is she ill?" Mark was concerned.

"No, just tired."

"I suppose we'll just have to have a good time without her," Mark smiled warmly at Suzanne.

Suzanne read his meaning, but wanted to keep him

at bay.

"I'm sure we shall." She took his arm as they left the house.

"Suzanne, I need to talk with you privately. There are things I have to say . . ." Mark began earnestly after they'd entered the carriage.

"No!" She managed to sound shocked. "We must not speak of these things . . ." She turned her face away from him hoping to give the impression of being embarrassed.

"But Suzanne . . ." Mark grew more forceful.

The desire he felt for her was eating at him . . . tearing him apart. She had only come to him once, but she had haunted his every moment since. He took her hand and drew it to his lips.

"What happened between us was so special . . ." he wanted to explain.

Withdrawing from his touch, she felt a fleeting sense of panic. Suzanne was snared in a web of her own making. She had not expected this silly young pup to become so smitten with her . . . and after only one night. Grasping for a way out of her dilemma she forced tears and turned to face him.

"Oh, Mark!" she spoke in a guilt-strangled whisper. "I'm so ashamed!"

Hiding her face in her hands she gave a good imitation of great despair.

"I—I have broken my marriage vows . . . I feel so soiled!" she told him tearfully, gracefully dabbing at her eyes with her lace handkerchief.

Mark was shocked. He had been so enamored with the memory of her lovemaking that he had totally ignored the moral side of their night together. The weight of his guilt, which he had been successfully ignoring, fell heavily upon him. How could he have taken advantage of Suzanne and Isaac this way? His

200

mood was suddenly morose. Sitting back silently, he stared sightlessly out the window as the carriage rumbled along the city streets.

Suzanne cast a surreptitious glance at Mark and was pleased to find that she had distracted him from his amorous intent.

"Mark," she said in a breathless, shaky voice. "Don't feel guilty. It was all my fault . . . I was the one who couldn't resist you . . ."

Mark's heart swelled at her tremulous confession. What a warm, loving, honest woman Suzanne was. No wonder he cared so much for her.

"Suzanne," his troubled gaze probed hers. "You mean a lot to me . . . So does Isaac. I feel I have betrayed you both."

Suzanne smiled to herself. Her ploy had worked. She wouldn't have to worry about fighting Mark off any longer.

"We have both betrayed Isaac's trust," she told him, sharing the guilt. "But we can begin anew . . ."

"I still find you to be the most desirable woman I've ever met."

Suzanne had to control her urge to taunt him after he made the statement.

"I know it will be difficult, but for Isaac's sake—we must."

Mark smiled sadly at her and then turned his attention to the passing scenery as Suzanne once again thought of Christopher Fletcher and the joy she would find in his arms.

Christopher leaned back in the desk chair, stretching stiffly. The hours had flown as he had pored over Greenwood's accounts and he was surprised to find that it was past midnight. Shutting the ledger before

201

him, he rose from the desk, rubbing the back of his neck in a weary motion.

He had no complaints. Things at Greenwood were going smoothly enough. He had discharged the overseer Gasell yesterday and Joel had taken charge, much to the delight of the slaves. Money was not a problem, for Greenwood was debt-free, an unusual occurrence, Christopher was discovering, among Delta plantations. Rich though they might appear, most plantation owners were land and slave poor. All their cash was tied up in fields, crops, and laborers. It seemed they lived totally on credit and gentlemanly goodwill, both of which offended Christopher's Yankee sensibilities.

Leaving the study, he turned out the lamps and started upstairs. It was only as he reached the top step that he heard the faint but distinct noise at the back of the house. Without a light, he made his way to the kitchen and cautiously opened the door.

"Come in," he directed as he recognized Dillon.

After hurrying inside, Dillon and his small group stood silently in the dark room while Christopher closed the shutters. Then after lighting a candle, he turned to face them. Christopher was stunned by the condition of the three runaways.

The two women were starkly clad in only simple sackcloth shifts. Their bare feet and legs were scratched and bloodied, a testimony to their struggle for freedom. The young man with them had been whipped not long before for his back was a mass of slow-healing scars. He wore only a pair of loose trousers, tied at the waist with a length of rope. And though his legs were covered his feet had suffered the same abuse as the women's.

"They've been on the move all day and the patrollers are watchin'," Dillon told him.

"Sit down, rest," Christopher instructed the wary

group.

"Go on," Dillon spoke gruffly to them and they quickly moved to sit at the table.

"Did they see you?"

"No. We got past 'em all right. But it was damn close." He was obviously relieved.

"Do you want a drink?" Christopher offered, his expression worried.

"No. I've got to be leavin' now and I'll need all my wits about me. Maybe next time," Dillon paused and grinned. "The first time is the worst. Don't worry."

"It is enough to test a man's mettle," Christopher returned his smile.

He walked with Dillon to the back road and bid him Godspeed before hurrying back. He was glad to find Joel waiting for him in the shadows of the back gallery.

"Need help?"

"Definitely. Can you get them some food while I fix a place for them to sleep downstairs?"

"Sure." Joel followed Christopher inside.

The three runaways looked up nervously as they came back in the room. They still found it hard to believe that white men would help them and they watched Christopher's every move with an animal wariness.

"I'm going to prepare a place for you to sleep. And Joel, here, is going to fix you some food."

"When we leavin' here?" the man asked boldly.

"As soon as it's safe."

They nodded their fearful understanding and began to eat as Joel quickly set out some bread and cheese for them.

"When they've eaten their fill, bring them down," he told Joel before he went out to make the arrangements.

It was almost an hour later when Christopher and Joel had the fugitives safely hidden away. Breathing a sigh of relief, they sat in the study sharing a last drink before attempting once more to go to bed.

"Dillon said the patrollers were thick on the roads."

"We'll have to be extra careful, then. The patrollers aren't easy men to deal with," Joel advised.

"You heard or you experienced?"

"Both. Are you sure that Captain McCarthy is reliable?"

"He was recommended by some very powerful people when we were in St. Louis. Though he's very closed mouth about his views, he's an ardent abolitionist."

"How'd you manage to get him a captain's job on a Southern boat?"

Christopher looked quite pleased with himself. "I bought into the steamship line with Edward Courtois and James Williams over a year ago. Neither of them showed any interest in the management, so I dabbled in it a little." He shrugged. "They trust me. I've never given them any reason to doubt me. And Captain McCarthy is one of the best on the Mississippi."

"He knows the signal?"

Christopher nodded, "He stops, picks up our crates and then delivers them downriver to the Adams plantation."

"It sounds simple."

"With any luck it will be," he stated and then added. "I hope."

With the responsibility for the lives of the three people resting heavily upon him, Christopher fell silent. Their next move would be made cautiously and only when he was certain it was safe. Confident that they would succeed, they both retired eager to begin their plan the next day.

* * *

Mark sat with Isaac in the comfort of the Kingsford carriage. He had been surprised by Isaac's invitation to join him for a business meeting this evening. But eager to redeem himself in his own mind and anxious to prove his worth to his uncle, he had immediately accepted.

"There's someone I want you to meet," Isaac told him as they drew up in front of a small residence on Rampart Street.

"A business associate?" Mark asked innocently.

"So to speak." Isaac gave Mark an indulgent look tinged with good humor. "Come."

They climbed down from the vehicle and entered the house without knocking.

"Cherie? I'm home," Isaac called out.

A young fair-haired boy not much older than twelve seemed to come out of nowhere and jumped into Isaac's arms.

"Papa!" he exclaimed delightedly. "We've missed you so!"

Then seeing Mark, the youngster drew away from Isaac and with a grace admirable for one his age, turned to greet him.

"Monsieur. I am Denis Delabarre, at your service," he bowed formally to Mark.

Mark, dumbfounded by what he'd just discovered, could only stare in mute surprise at the youth who bore such a resemblance to Isaac. Turning questioning eyes to his uncle, he couldn't stop the question.

"Isaac? You have a son?"

Isaac chuckled at Mark's very apparent shock, but as he started to explain, Cherie Delabarre swept into the entry foyer.

"Ah, mon coeur! You have returned to me at last,"

the slender, petite woman of color embraced Isaac warmly, with the ease of long familiarity.

Isaac returned her enthusiasm and then, keeping an arm about her waist, turned her to Mark.

"Cherie," he introduced. "This is young Mark, whom I've told you so much about. Mark, this is Cherie Delabarre."

Mark had presence of mind enough to acknowledge her graciously, but an indignant anger flared to life deep within him. How could Isaac do this to Suzanne? Suzanne, who loved her husband devotedly, and was even now suffering untold anguish over her indiscretion with him.

"Mark, it's wonderful to finally meet you. Isaac has told us all about you and your sister, Katie. Come in and I'll arrange for some refreshments."

The visit seemed to drag on interminably for Mark who was studiously polite to Cherie, but refused to warm to her friendly overtures. He was too outraged by Isaac's behavior. Isaac considered himself a gentleman and yet, he was openly keeping a quadroon mistress and she had borne him a son!

Mark's heart ached for Suzanne and he prayed in his desire to protect her that she would never learn of her husband's unfaithfulness.

Later as they were leaving, Cherie drew Isaac aside for a few moments of privacy. Her usually sparkling eyes were clouded with worry.

"Isaac, I fear Mark has been offended," she confided.

"Really?" Isaac had been so enjoying his time with Denis that he'd paid scant attention to Mark's reaction.

Cherie nodded solemnly, "He seemed so distant. Is he so innocent in the ways of the world?"

Isaac pondered her question. "It's quite possible,

my love. Do not worry. I'll speak with him. I'm sure he will come to love you, too."

"I do not want *his* love," Cherie teased, a small smile curving her full, sensuous lips.

Isaac stared at Cherie, delighting in her gentle beauty. He had fallen in love with her at a Quadroon Ball when he was thirty-six. And as soon as the arrangements were completed, he had set her up in this house. They had been together for over twenty years now . . . Their relationship forged through the test of time, physical intimacy, and genuine friendship.

Isaac had often wished that a marriage between them would have been acceptable. But society dictated strict rules on the relationships between the races and Isaac and Cherie were caught in the maze of hate and prejudice.

Denis, Isaac was sure, would fare far better. The boy easily passed for white and Isaac planned to send him North for his schooling so he could break free from the restraining condemnation of the South.

"You're radiant," he remarked with great wonder. "And you are as lovely now as you were that first night I met you."

Cherie went into his arms and kissed him hungrily, "If only you could be with me always." Her voice broke as she spoke her most fervent wish.

"Easy," he held her gently. "Suzanne is returning to Kingsford House tomorrow."

"Only Suzanne?" her eyes brightened with hope.

"Only Suzanne," Isaac's mouth sought hers, sealing his promise. "I'll be with you for the next week."

"Oh, Isaac," she sighed contentedly. "Hurry back."

"I will," he told Cherie.

Walking back with her to rejoin Mark and Denis, his heart was already counting the hours until he could stay the night with her once more.

***

Joel met with the mud clerk on Greenwood's landing.

"You just got these three crates?"

"Yes, suh," Joel answered respectfully. "My master says that they're to go to the Adams Plantation."

"I know the place. We'll have them there late today."

"Thank you, suh."

Joel watched as two roustabouts loaded the heavy crates none-too-gently onto Captain McCarthy's steamer the *Magnolia Queen*. Then with a final whistle, the boat backed out to midstream and began the final leg of her journey to New Orleans. When she was out of sight, Joel walked back to the main house to report to Christopher.

Dee, who had taken over the housekeeping for Christopher, met him on the gallery.

"How did it go?"

"Very smoothly," he confided and, after giving her a jubilant hug, he hurried in to find Christopher.

Christopher quickly looked up from his paperwork as Joel entered.

"Well?" he asked nervously.

"Everything went very smoothly. Our freight should be with Adams later this afternoon."

Christopher grinned broadly and rose from the desk to clap Joel heartily on the back.

"Like Dillon said—The first time is the worst! I thought McCarthy was never going to get here!" he said with great relief.

"Well, we did it!" Joel was excited.

"We did it!" Christopher remarked solemnly.

Looking at Joel seriously, they embraced warmly as they both realized what they had accomplished. Their year of dealing and planning and studying up North had paid off. And from here on in, it could only get easier.

Katie sat in the middle of her bed at Kingsford House rereading Christopher's note yet another time. She had been so excited when they'd returned from the New Orleans trip and his letter had been waiting for her. Obviously not a man given to flowery verse, he had only sent word that he would be attending the ball and anxiously awaited being with her once more. He had signed it only "Christopher" and for that Katie was grateful for Suzanne had insisted upon reading the message.

Folding the letter and placing it beneath her pillow for safekeeping, Katie wondered how she could possibly last another five days without seeing him again. The weekend had passed quietly, for with Isaac out of town, there had been no social functions to attend. But the rest of the week loomed before her—long, boring days filled only with dress fittings and party preparations. Not that Suzanne would let her help. Suzanne had already made it quite clear that she intended to take care of all the arrangements herself. So, she was left to her own means to entertain herself.

Katie had tried to interest Mark in riding with her but he had been strangely preoccupied since their return from New Orleans. She had confronted him about his withdrawn mood, but he had dismissed her concern with a sharp word. Never one to pry into anyone's private affairs, Katie held her tongue, but she wasn't quite sure that she liked the changes that were taking place within her brother. Shrugging off the thought as one she could do nothing about, she left the room. Perhaps a ride would lift her spirits and she knew exactly where she wanted to go.

Katie didn't mind the heat of the early afternoon as she rode up to the front entrance of Greenwood. Dismounting with the help of a servant, Katie turned to find that an attractive black woman had come out on the porch.

"Good afternoon. Welcome to Greenwood."

"Good afternoon," Katie said cheerfully as she started up the gallery steps. "I've come to visit Mr. Fletcher. Is he in?"

"No ma'am. He left fo' New Orleans early dis mornin'," at Katie's crestfallen look, Dee continued. "I'm Dee, his housekeeper. Would you care to leave a message?"

"No . . . no," Katie retreated to her horse. "Just tell him Katie came over."

Dee's expression was suddenly shocked and Katie looked at her quizzically.

"Is there something wrong?"

"No ma'am," Dee turned quickly from the white woman to hide her feelings. "Ah'll tell him you was here when he gets back."

After thanking Dee, Katie rode off. She was confused by the servant's manner but paid it little mind. Right now, all of her thoughts were on Christopher. She was greatly disappointed that he hadn't been in. She missed him and longed to be in his arms. Why, just the memory of his hands upon her body thrilled her . . . and, at the remembering of his mouth upon her breasts, she felt the now familiar tightening deep within her. Sighing, Katie dragged her thoughts back to the present. The days until the party seemed to stretch out in an endless path before her and the prospect of seeing Christopher on Saturday was all she had to look forward to.

* * *

Mark lay listlessly on his bed. He was confused and angry and worst of all, he had no idea what to do about it. For days now, his temper had been short and though he wanted to get control of his life, he found it impossible.

Since the night he'd met Isaac's "other family," he'd been torn by viciously conflicting emotions. He loved his uncle. Isaac had been very good to him. But on the other hand, he hated Isaac, too, for abusing the trust Suzanne had in him. Mark knew that if he were married to Suzanne, he would never leave her for another woman.

Rising, he went to the washstand and splashed cold water on his face. He had to take some action. He couldn't stay in this limbo any longer.

Isaac had returned from his week in New Orleans with Cherie early that morning and was busily going over the accounts in the plantation office when Mark knocked at the door.

"Mark! Come in. I must say I've missed your company this past week," Isaac was jovial. He always felt better after spending time in undemanding solitude with Cherie and Denis.

"Isaac," Mark greeted him, his expression reflecting all of his conflicting emotions.

"Something's troubling you?" He noticed Mark's discomfort.

"Frankly, Isaac, there is and you're the only one I can talk to about it."

"Please, sit down."

Mark drew up a chair and glanced nervously about the room.

"Well?" Isaac prompted. "You don't have to be afraid to talk to me, Mark."

"Isaac," Mark stated bluntly. "I don't understand how you can betray Suzanne this way."

Isaac looked calmly at his nephew. Ever since Cherie's warning, he had been wanting to speak with Mark, but the opportunity had never arisen.

"In what way?"

"By keeping a mistress. Why, you even have a bas—"

"*Son!* I have a son," Isaac bellowed cutting Mark off.

Mark blanched at Isaac's shout.

"Denis is my son, Mark," he added more slowly. "I think I need to explain my relationship with Cherie to you."

"Please," Mark's voice was strangled.

"I have been with Cherie for over twenty years. I love her. She means everything to me, but being a woman of color, we cannot marry."

Mark nodded, "Do you love Suzanne, too?"

"Of course. She is a beautiful woman and she graces my life at Kingsford House splendidly."

"If you love Suzanne, as you say you do, how can you go to another woman? Surely, she is everything you could possibly want."

"Ah, you have fallen under Suzanne's spell. That is good. She is deserving of your affection, but your worries are not necessary. Suzanne is very aware of my life with Cherie and Denis."

"She is?" Mark was astounded.

"She's known for years. She even takes her own amusements on occasion and I see nothing wrong with that as long as she is discreet."

"Amusements?" he dreaded the explanation.

"She has taken lovers."

"And you don't object?"

"No. I realize that she has needs. But I prefer not to be the one to satisfy those needs. Cherie is all the woman I need."

"But why did you marry Suzanne?"

"She was the most attractive woman in the parish. I wanted her and she wanted what I could give her."

Mark was silent.

"I hope you don't find all this distasteful."

"No," he paused, still trying to reason out all he had heard. "Yours is a marriage of convenience, so to speak."

"Exactly." Isaac was satisfied with his explanation.

Mark's mind was spinning as he excused himself from his uncle's presence. He had much to think about. Returning to his room, he paced its confines nervously, his anger with Suzanne growing. What was her game? Did she think him a child she could play with and then ignore! All of her conniving had to be for some purpose. Or was she just a wanton creature who constantly searched for new and more thrilling ways to amuse herself? Certainly, seducing her husband's nephew would come under that category.

His heart grew cold as he remembered her tearful pleading in the carriage. What an accomplished actress! No longer would he feel any guilt about their one night together. She had wanted it . . . had planned it, probably . . . and he refused to believe that she regretted it.

Mark knew he still wanted her. But he had learned enough in the past few weeks to recognize his feelings for what they really were. He did not love Suzanne as he had begun to believe. He lusted after her. Smiling to himself grimly, he decided to start playing a few games of his own.

Christopher finally returned to Greenwood early Saturday morning. His meetings with his bankers in New Orleans had taken far longer than he had expected and he was glad to be back. Or so he thought, until Joel brought him the news that five runaways had shown up alone the night before. That in itself wasn't bad, but Captain McCarthy had just passed on his way north and he wouldn't be returning before Tuesday.

There were few safe options open to them. Christopher could forge passes for them or try to smuggle them out on a wagon bound for the city, but the prospect of hiding them in the canebrakes for a few days until the boat returned was far more appealing. It was a well-known fact that the negroes could easily elude the patrollers and their bloodhounds by hiding there. True, there were poisonous snakes in the canebrakes, but they posed less of a danger than the vicious patrollers who might catch them on the road.

"We'll have to wait 'til dark to run them out there," Joel was saying.

"I know." Christopher was aggravated. He had waited impatiently all week for tonight and now . . .

"What's wrong?"

"Tonight's Katie's party. I promised I'd be there."

"It shouldn't take long. It'll be dark by eight."

Christopher nodded and let the subject drop. He'd always known that there would come a time when his dedication to his work would conflict with his desire for Katie. And he knew that there was really no choice. It had been made a year ago. Katie would have to wait.

Nine

The Ball

The sounds of the lilting melody drifted softly from the festively lighted mansion. Drawn by the happy celebration, the slave children hid by the windows, enjoying the music and peeping in occasionally to watch the handsome gentlemen squire the beautiful ladies about the dance floor.

Isaac stood in the front hall with Suzanne, gracefully welcoming a group of late arrivals.

"Glad you could make it, Wade, Lavinia," Isaac greeted another neighbor warmly.

"The house looks lovely, Suzanne," Lavinia told her, admiring the fresh cut, beribboned rose boughs that framed the ballroom's archway off the main hall.

"Thank you."

"We're just dying to meet this niece and nephew of yours. Where are they?"

"Dancing, last time I saw them. Come on in and I'll introduce you." Isaac offered his arm to Lavinia and Wade followed them with Suzanne.

"I understand your niece was quite the belle of the

ball at the Fontaine's party."

"I hadn't heard that, but I don't doubt it," Isaac chuckled. "She's quite special, my Katie," he led Lavinia to where Katie appeared to be holding court.

Laughing merrily at some clever response from one of her ardent suitors, Katie glanced up to find Isaac approaching.

"Uncle Isaac!" she smiled coming to kiss his cheek.

"You're making new friends?" he inquired, a definite twinkle in his eye.

"A few," she replied.

"Katie, this is Lavinia Crawford and her husband Wade."

"Nice to meet you."

"Your gown is lovely." Lavinia admired the white flowing creation that set off the girl's attributes to the fullest.

"Thank you, Mrs. Crawford. Suzanne helped me pick it out," Katie told her.

"Your aunt does have the most marvelous taste in clothes," Lavinia complimented Suzanne.

"Thank you," Suzanne accepted the accolade. "But wherever did you find your gown? It's stunning."

Lavinia and Suzanne drifted away toward the refreshment table, followed by Wade and Isaac, leaving Katie once again surrounded by her admirers.

"Suzanne, are you and Isaac going to the island for the season?" Lavinia asked as she took the glass of champagne that Wade offered her.

"We're going the first of August," Wade told them. "We've already sent the servants ahead to prepare our cottage."

"It sounds heavenly," Suzanne sighed.

Isaac smiled indulgently at Suzanne's rapt expression. "I had planned to surprise you, but I may as well tell you now."

"What?" Suzanne questioned eagerly.

"I've made our reservations at the hotel . . ."

"You have?" Suzanne interrupted, clearly delighted. "Thank you, darling. You know how this deep summer heat affects me. How soon do we leave?"

"I've booked us for the entire month of August."

"That's wonderful."

"I'm sure Katie and Mark will enjoy it, too."

"No doubt," Suzanne added, thinking of them only as an afterthought.

Mark was standing near the hall doors watching Suzanne from afar. His emotions were still in a turmoil. He wanted her . . . the memory of her soft, naked body next to his was burned into his mind, giving him little rest.

But he now knew what kind of woman she truly was. Her lies had proven that to him. Mark intended to have her again, and when he did it wouldn't be like the last time. He would gird himself against the desire he felt for her and use her as unemotionally as she had used him . . .

"Monsieur Kingsford?" Jacqui La Zear touched his arm with her fan as she gazed up at him.

She had waited over an hour for Mark to notice her and finally had given up and decided to approach him herself.

"Miss La Zear." Mark was startled from his thoughts of Suzanne. "You look lovely tonight."

"Thank you," she smiled. "I was hoping you'd notice."

Jacqui shocked herself with her own brazenness, but she had decided after the Fontaine ball that she wanted to marry him and Jacqueline La Zear always got what she wanted.

Mark, used to Katie's open uninhibited ways, was unaffected by Jacqui's direct interest.

"Would you like to dance?" he invited.

"I'd love to." She moved easily into his arms, eager to be close to him.

Katie was dancing with another of the young men of the parish, trying to be charming and witty when all she wanted to do was cry. Where was Christopher? She had waited all week to hear something further from him but no word had come. Now the ball was almost half over and he still had not made an appearance. Katie was glad when the dance ended and her partner escorted her from the floor. She had no desire to be in another man's arms if and when Christopher finally did arrive.

"Katie." The hated voice greeted her.

"Andre. How nice that you could come," she responded politely.

"I wouldn't have missed a chance to be with you," he told her intimately. "Would you care for some punch?"

"Please," Katie knew there was no dismissing Andre in front of all these guests. Taking the cup from him when he returned, she thanked him.

"It seems you're most popular this evening," he complimented her.

"I have made a few new friends," she answered distractedly, her eyes still searching the crowd for Christopher.

"Your gown is most becoming. It suits your virginal beauty," Andre stated boldly and Katie blushed for more than one reason.

"Andre . . ." she began threateningly, glad that the décolletage on this gown was not was revealing as the

218

ne she'd worn to the Fontaine's.

This gown was white with puff sleeves and a full skirt that was draped in scallops over a pale yellow underskirt. Yellow ribbons and a sprig of fresh yellow rosebuds adorned her hair which Lottie had artfully arranged in a cascade of tawny curls.

"Will you dance with me this evening, Katie?"

His tone was so undemanding that Katie found herself agreeing. After all, there was no way she could avoid it without causing more hard feelings and she didn't want to cause Isaac and Suzanne any trouble tonight.

"Of course," she consented.

Andre could hardly believe his luck. Maybe Suzanne's prompting had helped after all. As if on cue, the musicians began a waltz and offering her his arm, Andre led Katie onto the dance floor.

Christopher hurried down the stairs at Greenwood, tying his cravat as he went.

"Joel!" he bellowed. "Did T.C. bring my horse up from the stables yet?"

Joel emerged from the back of the house.

"He's tied up out in front."

"Good. I'm leaving." He paused in front of the mirror in the hall to check his handiwork.

Dee joined them in the hall. "This is the first chance I've had to tell you . . ."

"Tell me what?" With the way the day had been going Christopher was sure that the news Dee had to impart was horrendous.

"Katie Kingsford came by earlier this week to see you."

"She did?" Christopher smiled at the thought.

"Christopher?" Dee began, having been encouraged

219

to use his first name. "Is she the Katie . . . ?"

"Yes," he answered flatly, his expression turning thunderous at the thought of Andre possibly holding Katie even now. "I've got to go. You know where I'll be if you need me."

And with that he hurried from the house, eager to be with Katie.

Isaac watched with enjoyment as Katie and Mark danced together for the first time that evening. How he wished that his brother George could be here to see them. But Isaac knew that George would balk at any suggested return to civilization.

Since the death of his wife all those years ago, George Kingsford had made only one trip to Louisiana. Isaac recalled how painful it had been for his brother to see the places where he had courted the beautiful Geraldine McKenna before he'd married her. And while George had sent his children back to Louisiana to learn something of the more cultivated life style, for himself he had chosen to continue on with the railroad, avoiding all contact with society.

Sighing, Isaac also wished that Cherie could share these moments with him. Her gentle, abiding love was the sunshine of his existence and he begrudged every minute that he had to spend away from her.

Isaac had taken care of one important need this past week which had set his mind to rest. He'd set up a liberal trust fund for Denis and had made certain that all the investments he'd made over the years for Cherie were safely in her own name. Not that he expected anything to happen, but one couldn't be too careful. Knowing Suzanne as he did . . . Isaac was glad that he'd had his will restructured. The changes he'd made were few, but they would have a lasting impact on the future of his holdings should he die any time soon.

Dismissing his practical, yet morbid, thoughts, Isaac turned to start out into the hall and found that Christopher was just arriving.

"Fletcher. So glad you could come."

"Mr. Kingsford. Sorry I'm so late, but I was delayed by plantation business. I'm sure you're familiar with the demands."

"Of course. And you're still learning." They shook hands. "Would you care for a drink?"

"A bourbon would go nicely. Thank you."

Isaac signalled one of the waiters and Christopher was quickly served his drink.

"Have you met everyone?"

"I believe so. I recognize most of your guests from the Fontaine Ball."

Isaac nodded. "Good. Ah, here's my wife now. Suzanne, darling, Mr. Fletcher has arrived."

"Mr. Fletcher," Suzanne extended her hand to him and thrilled at the touch of his lips on her skin.

"I'd be honored if you would call me Christopher," he invited Suzanne and Isaac.

"Christopher," Suzanne breathed his name, his eyes twinkling as they played out their charade. "I'm Suzanne."

"And I'm Isaac. Darling, I'm off to see Wade for a moment. Will you see to Christopher for me?"

"I'd love to," Suzanne smiled up at Christopher. "I'm so glad you've come. I've been watching for you all evening."

He couldn't believe the open invitation she was giving him. "I'm surprised you had time . . ."

"For you, I'd make time." As she spoke, she leaned closer, pressing her breasts against his arm in what looked to be a totally innocent gesture.

Christopher glanced quickly about the room, hoping to catch sight of Katie, but Suzanne was too fast for him.

"I'll take you up on that drink you offered the other day."

"What would you like?"

"Some brandy, I believe. There's some in the music room . . ." Taking his arm, she led him from the ball-room, down the hall to the back of the house.

Christopher's mind was racing. He felt ironically like a lamb being led to the slaughter. He had to put a stop to this before Suzanne compromised them both in her own house.

And where was Katie? He had come to see her, not Suzanne. But then, how did a gentleman tell his hostess that he wasn't interested in having an affair with her? Somehow, he instinctively knew that Suzanne Kingsford wouldn't handle rejection well. Christopher followed her into the deserted, candle-lit music room.

"The brandy is on the table." She indicated the small bar set up with crystal decanters, tumblers and snifters.

As Christopher went to pour her a drink, Suzanne shut the door behind them. At last, she was alone with him. She could hardly wait to be in his arms. Approaching slowly, her skirts swaying in a sensual rhythm, Suzanne was ready. And when Christopher turned to bring her her snifter, he was surprised to find her seated on the small loveseat awaiting him.

"Don't you think we should rejoin the others?" Christopher had been approached by other lovely, sophisticated women, but none had been as forward as Suzanne.

"In a moment. I'm in need of a little . . . rest." Her lips curved in a soft smile and she wet them seductively with the tip of her tongue.

Christopher handed her her drink but remained

standing.

"Sit down." She shifted her full skirts to one side to give him room to join her. When he didn't immediately sit beside her, she leaned toward him, thrusting her breasts out so they swelled dangerously over the top edge of the extremely low-cut bodice of her gown.

Christopher had to force back a grin as he expected her to pop out of the dress at any moment. "I prefer to stand."

Suzanne hid her annoyance. This was going to be more difficult than she had expected.

"You must tell me about yourself, Christopher," she continued. "Where are you from?"

"Philadelphia, originally. But I haven't lived there for quite a few years."

"Do you have family?"

"No."

"Pity." She sipped her brandy. "You must get lonesome."

"I keep myself busy," Christopher moved away from the tempting view she was offering of her bosom and went to stand near the hearth. "Family ties can be very restraining."

"I've found that on occasion," she agreed. Setting her glass aside with great care, she went to Christopher. "But I've also discovered that if one is discreet enough . . . one can do almost anything without attracting attention."

"True," he answered, thinking of his own situation.

"Would you . . ." Suzanne was about to make the most blatant overture of her life when the door flew open and Katie walked in.

"Christopher? Uncle Isaac said you were here . . ." She stopped in stunned surprise at the intimate scene before her. Suzanne and Christopher together, alone, in a candle-lit room! "You are really hard to believe,

Suzanne!" Katie shut the door behind her and advanced on her aunt menacingly. "You had the unmitigated gall to criticize me for spending too much time with Christopher at the Fontaine Ball. And you chastised me again for visiting with him unchaperoned last week! And yet here you are in your own husband's house hidden away in a dark corner with the very same man!"

"I am a married woman! I do not require a chaperone," Suzanne defended herself.

"It looks to me like you need a keeper!" Katie declared, her eyes glinting with fury. "You have a house full of company and you sneak off with a very eligible bachelor?" She threw Christopher a cursory look. "Did you want him for yourself? Is that why you condemned my friendship with him at every opportunity? And is that why you've done nothing but push the idea of matrimony to Andre Montard at me every waking minute?"

Suzanne didn't answer.

"Well, is it?" Katie stepped toward her threateningly.

"Your suggestions are disgusting. If you'll excuse me . . ."

"Oh, I'll excuse you all right, but you'd better stay away from me in the future, Suzanne."

"It will be my pleasure." Suzanne stormed from the room.

Katie folded her arms across her chest and laughed derisively at her aunt's hasty retreat. When she heard Christopher's chuckle, she turned her fury to him.

"What's so funny?" she demanded.

"You were wonderful. You defended my honor . . ." He was openly laughing now.

"Don't you dare laugh at me, you hyena!"

"You saved me, darling. I was wondering how to

gracefully extract myself from your aunt's 'overwhelming' presence when you walked in," Christopher opened his arms to her but Katie turned her back on him and stalked away.

"I'll bet. You expect me to believe that?"

His hand snaked out to take her arm, stopping her exit and she faced him again, even more angry.

"I've never lied to you, Katie," he began, but her fury ruled her.

"Let go of me, you —" she hissed at him.

Christopher wasn't about to let Suzanne's little games damage their relationship. Pulling her forcefully to him, he kissed her, his mouth devouring hers in a possession designed to punish her for doubting his faithfulness.

Squirming in his arms, Katie struggled against his domination. How dare he! But as his hand sought her breast her anger turned to passion. Vaguely, she wondered if his touch would always have this power over her . . . the ability to make her forget everything but him and the desire of the moment . . .

Aware of the change in Katie, Christopher didn't release her but pulled her down with him onto the loveseat. Wanting her submission to him to be complete, he sought to arouse her fully. Seeking out her most erogenous zones he explored them with bold caresses, teasing her to a fever of ecstasy. Katie, pliant to his will in her frenzy of need, welcomed his body upon hers as he pushed aside her skirts and entered her roughly. Her orgasm shook her at once as he moved excitedly within her. Clasping him tightly to her, she eagerly met his driving body, wanting to prolong the tempestuous thrill of her climax. Katie's provocative rhythm was so stimulating that Christopher could not hold back. With one final, frenzied thrust, he gained his release and collapsed, sated, on top of her.

Katie, the conquered and the conqueror, lay beneath him amazed by what had just transpired. Never had their passion seemed so sweet . . . so satisfying. He had subdued her with his love and she had enjoyed it. Smiling softly, she pressed a gentle kiss to his throat as he rested above her.

Christopher opened his eyes to stare down at her.

"Katie," he spoke, his voice hoarse with emotion. "I can't imagine being with anyone but you. I love you."

"And I love you, Christopher." Her eyes were filled with love as he moved slowly away from her.

"Never doubt me, love."

"I won't," she breathed, trusting him completely. "Never again."

Serenity restored, they embraced tenderly, cherishing what they'd just shared. Leaving the music room, they returned to the party hoping that they hadn't been missed.

Dee finished putting the kitchen in order and was wiping her hands on her apron as she turned to Joel.

"Who's this Katie? And what is she to Christopher?"

"She's Isaac Kingsford's niece. She's staying with them at Kingsford House."

"And?" Dee knew there was more to it than that.

"And Christopher loves her . . . more than he's willing to admit."

"But Andre wants her, too."

Joel nodded.

"Christopher best be careful. If Andre means to get her, he'll do anything."

"I know."

"How does she feel?"

"She hates Andre."

226

"That's good." Dee was thoughtfully quiet. "He's a mean man."

"He's out of your life now, Dee."

"Yes, Joel. Ah know." She went willingly into her husband's welcoming arms. "Ah'm fine now that you're wid me again."

They held each other close, savoring their nearness and the beauty of their new life together.

Suzanne drank deeply of her glass of champagne and smiled coquettishly at Mark.

"Are you enjoying the ball?"

"It's been a wonderful evening, Suzanne."

"Good. I'm glad you're happy."

Mark, aware that she was leading up to something, took the bait in order to lure her on. He had seen her hurried entrance into the ballroom and had sensed her eyes following him as he'd danced with Jacqui earlier.

"Would you care to dance?" he invited.

"Thank you," she accepted.

As the music began, she moved as close to him as she could.

"I was wrong, Mark," Suzanne said softly.

"About what?" he asked, squiring her around the dance floor.

"Everything . . . I can't go on this way. I've ignored the feelings I have for you enough . . . I want you, Mark."

Mark was mildly shocked by her sudden turnabout, but kept his expression carefully blank. He found it hard to believe that she was propositioning him in the middle of the ballroom, but he also found it very stimulating.

"And I still want you," he admitted aching to show her just how much.

Suzanne smiled at him seductively. "We'll have to do something about that."

She had been humiliated by her scene with Katie and was determined to prove herself irresistible this night. She had watched Mark as he courted the simpering Jacqueline La Zear and her rage grew. How dare he spend time with another woman! It didn't matter that she had thrown him over. Mark had professed a great desire for her and she intended to take advantage of that weakness tonight.

Stealing him away from the girl had been no problem, being his aunt gave her that privilege. The difficulty now was in finding a private place in this house crowded with friends and neighbors.

The drugged throbbing in her loins urged her on and Suzanne felt much like a lioness at hunt as she gazed up at him from beneath heavy-lidded eyes.

"I don't want to wait, Mark. I need to have you now . . . to feel you inside me . . ."

Her words were a seduction in themselves and Mark tensed in anticipation.

"I'll meet you upstairs . . . the sewing room?" he suggested the little used room.

"Five minutes?" she panted.

"Five minutes," he agreed, releasing her as the music ended.

Suzanne swept away from him and went directly upstairs. She attracted little attention as she disappeared into the small room, for the ladies lounge had been set up in the connecting chamber and there had been ladies going in and out all night. As she awaited his coming, she lit one small candle and placed it on the table next to the sofa. Her wait was not long as Mark slipped quietly in, closing the hall door behind him.

Her gaze swept over him as he stood silently in the deep, half-shadows. He looked older to her now . . .

more mature and Suzanne wondered at the cynical glint in his eyes. She didn't speak, but went to him, pulling his head down for a fiery kiss. Her hands took liberty with his body, exploring all of him without hesitation. She needed a man . . . now. The fact that she could so easily arouse him thrilled her and she gave a throaty laugh as her hand caressed his hardness through his clothes.

"Can Jacqueline La Zear arouse you the way I do?" he taunted, thinking her power over him was absolute.

But she was soon terrified as Mark thrust her painfully away from him.

"Don't ever compare yourself to Jacqui," he growled.

"What? . . ." she was speechless.

"Just shut up and lie down," he ordered.

"Mark!" she was totally shocked as he pushed her down none too gently on the sofa.

He stood above her for a moment, a massive, strongly built man. And Suzanne suddenly realized that she was not the one in control. Afraid, yet somehow oddly inflamed by his masterful manner, she did as she was told.

Knowing that he was in command, he dropped to his knees beside her. Dipping within her bodice, he lifted her breasts from their restraint and pressed heated kisses to the lush mounds. Brushing her skirts aside his hand slid up her leg to explore the nest at the juncture of her thighs. He found it most amusing that she wore no underwear and he wondered if she had planned all of this. Positioning her legs, Mark rose above her and freeing himself from his pants, he plunged into her wet, willing heat.

* * *

Jacqui entered the room quietly. She was flushed from dancing a polka with her father and had come upstairs to the room set aside for the ladies to rest for moment. Fanning herself, she sat at the mirrored van ity to catch her breath.

What an exciting evening! Her dreams were coming true! Mark Kingsford had been at her side most of the night. She sighed happily. It had been worth taking the chance to approach him. Not only had he been recep tive but he'd given her every indication that he would be calling on her very soon.

Staring into the mirror, Jacqui smoothed her hair back into place. Then, sure that she looked present able, she rose to leave.

A muffled sound drew her attention and she glanced about the empty room searching for the source. The noise came again, indistinct and blurred from beyond the partially open connecting door. Hes titantly, Jacqui crossed the room and was about to push the door open when she caught sight of the re flection in a free standing mirror in the next room.

She stood frozen, unable to move or speak as the mirrored images shattered all her hopes. It was Mark . . . and he was lying on the sofa with Suzanne Suzanne's breasts were uncovered and Mark appeared to be kissing them, although, in all her innocence, she couldn't imagine why he would want to. She watched their figures in the mirror for only a few moments, bu the vision of Mark moving restlessly against his aunt' partially nude body left her both shocked and sick ened. Suzanne Kingsford was old and married. Why would Mark want to do those things with her?

Shuddering, Jacqui backed away from the door wishing that she'd never gone to investigate the strange sounds she'd heard. Pale and shaken, she hurried out onto the upstairs gallery, trying to regain her compo sure before rejoining the party.

Suzanne lay limply on the sofa, too exhausted to move.

"Mark, darling." She held out a hand to him as he stood above her buttoning his pants. "You were wonderful."

Mark looked down at Suzanne and realized that the hold she had on him was still very potent. She was a very sensual creature and her surrender to him just now had increased the physical desire he had for her all the more.

Suzanne watched Mark as he moved away from her, both physically and mentally. If she wanted to keep him enamored with her, she would have to convince him that she couldn't resist him.

"Do you need help with your gown?" he asked casually.

"No. But Mark . . . kiss me once more," she invited.

"No, Suzanne. We've been away too long as it is," he dismissed her brusquely. "If you don't need my help, I'll be going."

As she lay stunned by his indifference, Mark left the room to return to the ball. When he had gone, she sat up slowly, trying to understand what had just occurred. She felt used . . . like a dockside trollop. Mark had whispered no endearments, had made no declarations . . . nothing. He had only used her and then left her and Suzanne definitely did not like the feeling.

Mark shared a drink with his uncle in the men's gamingroom before returning to the ball to search for

Jacqui. He was becoming more enchanted with her all the time and he was anxious to be with her again, hoping that her sweet freshness would erase the memory of Suzanne's heavy passion from his mind.

"Katie, have you seen Jacqui La Zear?" he asked his sister when he found her on the gallery with Christopher.

"I just saw her going down the front steps . . . She was alone. I guess she was going for a walk."

"Thanks." He hurried off leaving Katie and Christopher smiling after him.

Mark searched the lawns for Jacqui and finally caught sight of her in the garden at the rear of the house.

"Jacqui? I've been looking all over for you," he told her as he came to her.

"You have?" she asked dully, wondering how he could face her so calmly after having just been with Suzanne.

"What's wrong?" He was worried. Jacqui's face was pinched and pale and her eyes looked up at him with little emotion.

"There's nothing wrong, Mark. Please, leave me alone." She turned away.

"But why?"

Jacqui took a deep breath as she tried to decide what to do. Her experience with men was limited. She knew by rumor that men were not virgins when they married, but until tonight that had meant nothing to her. Now, it did. Jacqui had seen the man she loved with another woman and she didn't know how to handle it. Honesty? Jacqui knew she wouldn't be able to enjoy his company ever again. And Suzanne Kingsford? Well, the woman obviously was a slut.

"Jacqui?" Mark took her by the shoulders and turned her to him.

"Don't touch me, Mark Kingsford!" she hissed. "I saw you!"

"Saw me?"

"Just a little while ago . . ." she said brokenly.

"You saw me?" Mark swallowed nervously.

"Upstairs . . . with your *own aunt*! She was naked and you were . . . Mark! How could you?" Jacqui was sobbing hysterically. "I loved you . . ."

"I love you, Jacqui!"

An anguished cry tore from her. "Please . . . leave me alone. Just go away."

"Darling," he tried to take her in his arms but she pulled away and slapped him.

"Leave me alone!" her voice was chilling.

Mark backed away, stunned by the consequences of his actions. How would he ever convince her that Suzanne meant nothing to him?

Suzanne took the champagne Andre brought her and sipped it slowly.

"How did you fare with Katie?"

"Better, although once Fletcher arrived I couldn't get near her." Andre paused to take a drink. "I thought you were going to do something about him."

"I tried, but Katie interrupted me just as I was getting started," Suzanne said flatly.

"Then where were you? I was looking for you for over an hour."

"If it's any of your business, I was with Mark."

"Second choice, was he?" he asked smugly.

"In the dark . . ." she began, not wanting to let Andre know what really had happened.

"I know . . ." Andre laughed. "Isn't he courting the La Zear girl?"

"He was . . ."

"You should let him. That way no one would ever suspect that you two were lovers."

"No one suspects now. And besides, I don't like sharing the men I sleep with."

"You're sharing Isaac," Andre pointed out cruelly.

"And I'm not sleeping with Isaac either!" she returned hotly.

Andre shrugged, "Suzanne there's no need to get angry. I was just trying to help."

"Why don't you worry about your own problems . . . like Katie."

"Katie's not a problem," he stated arrogantly. "We've already danced tonight."

"Well, when Katie caught me with Fletcher she accused me of pushing you on her just so I could have him."

"So, she's clever enough to figure out the truth . . ." Andre was thoughtful. "I'm surprised. She struck me as being too naive . . ."

"Obviously, she's learning very quickly." Suzanne's response was tart with dislike.

"I suppose our only real hope is to discredit Fletcher in some way. I'll have to start checking . . ."

"Has Suzanne told you about the trip we've planned?" Isaac asked as Katie and Christopher joined Mark and himself.

"No."

"I'm sure you'll enjoy this, Katie. I've made reservations for us for the month of August at the hotel on Last Island."

"Last Island?"

"It's an island resort in the Gulf. Suzanne and I have gone every summer for the past three years. It's wonderful. There's riding and hunting and dancing . . . a

234

little something for everyone."

"When are we leaving?"

"The first of August," Isaac informed them. Then including Christopher, he added, "Look into it, Christopher. August is no time to stay in the country. The yellow fever . . ."

"I will sir," Christopher replied.

"Good. A few years ago it was very primitive, but now it's quite the place to be. A number of families have built their own summerhouses there. The hotel is relatively new, too. If you have any trouble getting reservations just let me know."

Christopher found the prospect of a few weeks on the Gulf relieving, for the heat was already oppressive and he knew August would be even worse.

The knock at Katie's bedroom door startled her and she sat up quickly in her bed.

"Who is it?"

"It's me, Katie. May I come in?" Mark's voice was muffled through the door.

Getting up, she pulled on a robe and unlocked the door to let her brother in.

"What time is it?" she asked lighting the lamp by her bed.

"Almost four," he told her. "I couldn't sleep."

"Obviously," she responded drily. "Sit down."

Katie climbed back into bed while Mark pulled up a chair.

"What's wrong, Mark? Something's been bothering you for quite a while now, hasn't it?"

Mark nodded, his mood despondent. "I thought I could handle it . . . But I think I've ruined everything."

"Ruined what?"

"My relationship with Jacqui La Zear."

"Relationship?"

"I love her, Katie."

"Mark, I am so glad! She's very nice and . . ."

"But she doesn't want to see me any more, Katie."

"Why?"

"You're not going to like this . . ."

"How will I know if you never tell me?" She was getting irritated.

"This is the hardest thing I've ever had to tell you, but I've — uh — I've been having an affair with Suzanne," he blurted out the painful truth.

"Suzanne?" Katie was incredulous.

"Suzanne," Mark confirmed.

Thinking that Katie was about to lose her temper with him, Mark hastened to explain.

"Right after we got here . . . she came into my room in the middle of the night . . ."

But Katie wasn't listening to Mark's embarrassing confession. "The woman is a damn vulture."

Mark looked at her in surprise. "I know that . . . now . . ."

Katie glanced at Mark as if for the first time, "She was after Christopher all this time, too. I caught her with him tonight in the music room."

"What time was that?" Mark was stunned.

"About ten, I guess . . . Why?"

"It was right after that that she came after me . . ."

"And you . . . ?"

Mark nodded.

"Where, for God's sake?"

"In the sewing room."

"But that's right next to the room the ladies were using to freshen up in."

"I know," Mark sounded defeated. "Jacqui saw us."

"Not while you were . . ."

236

"Yes, in the act."

"No wonder she's finished with you. Why the girl is hardly more than a child and to watch you . . . with Suzanne . . ." Katie shook her head in disgust. "Poor Jacqui . . ."

"What can I do, Katie?" Mark was upset. "I didn't realize until it was too late that I really cared for Jacqui."

Katie thought for a long moment, "Why did you really go with Suzanne?"

"I was angry."

"About what?"

"Suzanne had told me that she was feeling guilty about our lovemaking and that she didn't want to continue . . ."

"I wouldn't have expected . . ."

"She was lying. I found out from Isaac that she's had numerous lovers in the past."

"And he doesn't care?" Katie was indignant.

"No. In fact, he's glad."

"How can he be happy about his own wife committing adultery?"

"Because he's got a mistress."

"Uncle Isaac?"

Mark nodded. "He keeps her on Rampart Street. They've even got a son."

"Mark . . . this is . . ." Katie stammered, trying to understand everything he'd just revealed to her.

"I know. That's why I got mad. Suzanne had been using me. She only fed me that line about feeling guilty to make me feel guilty. That's why when she offered tonight, I took her up on it . . . just to give her a taste of what it felt like to be used."

"But she's turned the tables on you again . . . I mean if she went after Christopher first and then approached you . . ."

237

Mark sighed. "I still don't know what to do about Jacqui."

"Right now, nothing. She's probably shocked, disgusted and very disillusioned," Katie told him honestly. "How much did she see, anyway?"

"Enough." his voice was emotionless.

"Time is your best bet. Maybe she'll forgive you . . ."

"Do you really think so?" Mark cheered considerably at the thought and he sounded like a small hopeful boy.

"The truth?"

"Yes."

"I doubt it. These Southern girls are different, Mark."

He looked disheartened. "I think you're right."

Jacqui paced her bedroom torn between anger and despair. It seemed that all of her dreams had been shattered that night. Images of Mark taunted her — their dances, the strength of his arms, the comfort of his embrace . . . How she loved him. Unbidden, came the remembrance of Suzanne and Mark sharing a lover's embrace. It hurt to think of them so . . .

The knock at her bedroom door caused her to jump nervously.

"Yes?"

"Miz Jacqui? What you doin' up?" Mattie, her mammy, scolded as she came into her room.

"I can't sleep."

"Has somethin' upset my baby?"

"Oh, Mattie!" Jacqui sobbed and flung herself into the other woman's arms. "I don't know what to do!"

"Tell me, child. What's wrong?"

"Everything . . ." she cried.

"You sit down and tell ol' Mattie all 'bout it, now," Mattie guided her young charge to the canopy bed. "Now what happened?"

"Tonight," she sniffed. "At the Kingsfords."

"Yes. You like dat young Mr. Mark, don't you?"

"Oh, Mattie. I love him! But . . ."

"But what, honey?"

"He loves someone else."

"How could he love any girl but my lamb?" Mattie hugged her. "Did he tell you that?"

"No." Jacqui struggled to tell her what she'd witnessed. "He didn't have to tell me. I saw him."

"Saw him do what?"

"I saw him with the other woman!"

"Lotsa men be with other women at a party but it don't mean nothin'," she tried to dismiss Jacqui's fears.

"But Mattie . . . he was making love to her!"

Mattie drew a sharp breath, "What did you see, chile?"

"Mark was lying on top of her . . . Her dress was down and he was kissing her breasts." She blushed as she remembered the intimacy of Mark and Suzanne's embrace.

"Lawsy, lawsy," Mattie groaned, hugging Jacqui. "Who was de woman?"

"It was his aunt," Jacqui whispered.

Mattie was shocked but not surprised . . . she had heard things about Suzanne Kingsford before.

"What am I going to do, Mattie? I still love him!"

Mattie thought long and hard. Miz Jacqui had never learned the realities of life. She had always been cosseted and protected. But Mattie supposed now was as good a time as any to tell her.

"You love him, truly?"

"I want him, Mattie. Or at least, I did until I saw him with her . . ." Jacqui made a face. "How could he make love to his own aunt?"

"She's his uncle's wife. There's a difference."

"I suppose. But Suzanne Kingsford is so old!"

Mattie chuckled, "She ain't that old that she don't appreciate a good man, Jacqui."

Jacqui blushed again.

"Honey. Do you know anything 'bout what a man does with a woman?"

"No," she admitted hesitantly.

"Well, when a man wants a woman, he can't stop till he gets her . . ."

"What do you mean?"

"Has Mark Kingsford kissed you yet?"

"No. Do you suppose he finds me unattractive?" Jacqui worried.

"No. He respects you. That's good . . ."

"Sometimes, I think I'd rather not be quite so respected!" Jacqui pouted. "I want him. I would have let him kiss me if he'd tried."

"Jacqui. Menfolk need more than a kiss. They got a power within 'em that don't give 'em no rest till it's eased."

"What kind of power?"

"When they find a woman who stirs 'em, they get all hot and hard . . ." Mattie was finding this conversation to be very awkward.

"You mean like Papa's stallion?"

"Right," she agreed happily. "And a man, well, when a woman gets him that way, then he has to have that woman."

"You mean Mark is attracted to Suzanne that way, but not to me?"

"Not necessarily. Miz Suzanne, well, she a woman. She knows what she wants and she gets it."

240

"Suzanne Kingsford wanted Mark?"

Mattie nodded.

"But she's married."

"Don't make no never mind to some folks. Some white folks no matter how rich they is, is still white trash."

"I understand, Mattie."

"Good."

"I have to make Mark want me," Jacqui murmured to herself. Then to Mattie, she said, "What does it feel like? What does a man do? Suzanne sure looked like she was enjoying it . . ."

Mattie smiled, "Ah'm sure that she was."

"It's nice?"

Nodding, she responded, "Don't you go gettin' any ideas now."

"I want to know! Tell me, or I'll find out on my own!" Jacqui threatened.

Mattie looked at Jacqui and realized that she meant what she said, "They like to touch you and when they get ready, they put themselves inside of you."

"Like the horses?"

"Yes."

"Mattie, does it really feel good?"

"Yes, darlin'."

"I want Mark Kingsford and I intend to get him."

"Den be a lady," Mattie ordered as she left the room, closing the door soundly behind her.

Jacqui curled up on the bed, recalling again Mark's body thrusting on Suzanne's. Oh, how she wished it had been her and not Suzanne. She had been a lady this long and it had gotten her nowhere. If that was what Mark wanted in a woman, then that was what she was going to give him. She wondered how it would feel to have him touch her so intimately. Touching her breast, a thrill of forbidden pleasure shot through her.

She was going to have Mark Kingsford and after she did, she would make sure that he never wanted another woman again!

Though the single lamp did little to pierce the darkness of the study, Christopher made no effort to light another. Alone in the peaceful quiet of the house, he sat staring into the shadows of the now-familiar room. No longer could he deny the truth of his need for Katie. The time he'd spent with her at Kingsford House tonight had only served to emphasize to him how empty his life was without her. Christopher was no longer satisfied with just a few hours of Katie's company. He wanted her with him, always.

The decision to propose was not a hard one. He loved her and marriage was the perfect solution. The difficulty came from trying to decide whether or not to tell her about his involvement with the Underground Railroad. He knew it would be virtually impossible to keep the secret from her once they had married and she was living with him. But how would she react to the news? Somehow, he knew he had to find out, but he wasn't quite sure how to go about it without giving away their entire operation. Extinguishing the light, Christopher made his way up to his solitary bed, determined to find a way to have Katie with him as soon as possible.

Ten

The Plot Thickens

It was with great frustration two days later that Christopher read the letter from his business advisor up North informing him of some major problems they were having and requesting that he return to Philadelphia to handle things personally. There was no doubt in his mind that he had to go; what worried him was leaving Joel alone to deal with the fugitives.

"Dee said that you wanted to see me." Joel drew Christopher's attention as he entered the room.

Tossing the letter across the desk to his friend, he said, "Bad news."

Joel read it quickly and looked up expectantly. "You're going?"

"I have to. But I'm worried about things here. Can you take care of everything by yourself?"

"With T.C.'s help, I should be able to handle it."

Christopher still looked worried. "Maybe I should contact Robert . . ."

"No." Joel was emphatic. "We'll do it. You know what might happen if we don't."

"All right, but I could be gone as long as a month . . ."

"I'll be fine. And if worse comes to worse, I know these swamps and canebrakes better than anyone else." Joel smiled trying to relieve his fears.

"That's all I need . . . to come back and find the place overrun with patrollers and you and Dee hiding out with the snakes in the swamps!"

"It'll never happen. Go and take care of your business."

"I have to," he replied heavily.

Joel nodded. "Will you get back in time for your trip to the Gulf?"

"I hope so." Christopher smiled. "If I don't I know a female who is going to be very angry with me," he paused thoughtfully. "Speaking of whom, I'd better let her know that I'm leaving. Have somebody start packing for me, I'm going to ride over to see Katie."

"Watch out for her aunt," Joel teased.

"Don't worry, I will!"

Katie was delighted when Lottie came to tell her that she had a visitor. Anxious to see who had come to call, Katie hurried downstairs.

"Christopher!" she cried happily as she saw him at the foot of the stairs.

"Good afternoon, Katie," he greeted as she flew into his arms and kissed him.

"I am so glad you've come. I was missing you already," her eyes sparkled as she looked up at him. "Let's go in the parlor and talk for a while."

"Is it safe?" he whispered melodramatically.

Katie laughed, "Very. Suzanne's gone over to the Crawford's for the day."

"Good. Where's Mark?"

244

"I'm not sure. I haven't seen him since breakfast, but he's probably out riding the fields with Uncle Isaac."

"Katie," he began after she'd led him into the parlor. "There's something I have to tell you that . . ."

"Oh, oh. This sounds ominous."

"No, it's not that bad." He grinned, sitting down next to her on the sofa.

"Thank heaven," she sighed exaggeratedly. "Well, you might as well tell me and get it over with. What's wrong?"

"My business agent in Philadelphia has requested that I return home. They've got problems that they need my help with . . ."

"You're going?"

"I leave tomorrow."

"How soon will you be back?"

"Hopefully in time for the trip to Last Island."

"Good. I'm looking forward to that."

"I am too, Katie." He lifted her hand to his lips. "We don't get to spend enough time together."

"I know," her breath caught as he pulled her closer.

"We'll have to see what we can do about that when I return," he said softly just before his lips found hers.

His kiss was devastating and when Christopher released her, she moved away.

"Katie?" He had no idea where she was going.

Katie walked straight to the door and closed and locked it, giving him a smile with just a hint of wickedness.

"I'm going to miss you," she said coming back to him.

Her eyes were alight with anticipation as she stopped before Christopher and slowly began to unbutton her blouse.

"I haven't gone yet," he smiled, standing to help her

245

with the buttons.

"I know," she smiled invitingly.

Kissing her passionately, he parted the soft material and explored the softness of her breast.

Held tightly to him, Katie could feel his arousal and she boldly caressed the strength of him. Christopher started at her unexpected touch and a low moan escaped him.

Clinging together feverishly, aware that at any moment they could be discovered, Katie and Christopher moved back to the sofa. Pressing full length against each other, their need to be one overwhelmed them. Slipping her riding skirt down, Christopher lowered himself over her as Katie unbuttoned his pants and guided him to the heat of her.

Their joining was rapturous as they moved together as one, sharing and saving all their love so that their memories would help to keep their time apart from seeming so desolate.

Climaxing simultaneously, they lay on the sofa spent and yet elated by the joy of their union.

"Do you have to go?" she murmured wanting to hold him a prisoner of her love.

With a protesting groan, Christopher rose and buttoned his clothes.

"You know I don't want to, but the sooner I do, the sooner I'll get back," he told her as he helped her to dress. "Miss me, Katie?"

"I will, Christopher. You know I will."

And watching him ride away, she felt a wave of loneliness wash over her. How was she going to last through the whole month of July without him?

"Frankly, William, you've been doing an excellent job."

"Thank you, Christopher. I can't say it's been easy, but I do try my best."

"I'll see that you're well rewarded," he assured his agent.

"I did worry about asking you to come . . ."

"You did the right thing, so don't let that bother you. Besides, I had other business that I needed to take care of while I was here."

"Well, thanks for your support. And if I can be of any further service while you're in town . . ."

"I'll be sure to call on you." He rose and shook hands with William. "Goodbye."

"Goodbye, Christopher."

Christopher left the business offices feeling relaxed and confident. His trip had been more than successful. Not only had he taken care of his family's business affairs, but he'd made important contacts with a group of abolitionists who had direct dealings with William Still, head of the Philadelphia anti-slavery office. Christopher's numerous meetings with them over the last few weeks had given him added insight into the problems that he dealt with at Greenwood. It was with a renewed determination to succeed that he now prepared to return to Louisiana.

The Bird of Paradise Gaming-house was doing a brisk business on this hot evening in mid-July. Andre Montard had been winning steadily at the tables since late afternoon and was more than a little disappointed when the game broke up. As he headed for the bar, he caught sight of Edward Courtois and James Williams and went to join them.

"Good evening, Edward . . . James," he greeted them as he ordered a drink.

"How'd you do in the game?" James asked.

247

"Very well," Andre smiled confidently. "It seems that my luck is finally changing."

"Your luck was always good." Edward replied, grinning. "I still remember last summer when Monique picked you over me!"

"Ah, Edward, my friend. You're not still holding a grudge over the sweet Monique, are you?" Andre chuckled as he recalled the incident. Confidingly, he added, "She was not worth your concern."

"How are things with you? We had heard the news of Greenwood."

"Yes, well, we are living in town right now, while repairs are being completed at Fairwinds."

"Fairwinds is a beautiful plantation."

"Yes, it is," Andre's reply was short and James and Edward knew that the wound from losing his home had not yet healed.

"Well, what are your plans for the rest of the summer? James and I are leaving for Newport next week."

"And that's not a minute too soon as far as I'm concerned," James said. "The heat this year has been horrible."

"I'd like to get away, but we're tied up with this move."

Michel Bardeleau, the owner of a plantation north of Greenwood stopped to speak with them.

"Andre! I was hoping to run into you."

"Good to see you, Michel. Join us for a drink."

"I have something serious to discuss with you. Do you mind if we take a table?"

"Not at all."

James and Edward exchanged questioning glances and followed the two other men to the secluded table in the corner.

"Is there something wrong?" Andre asked as soon as they were seated.

"Yes, there is definitely something wrong. I've been losing slaves."

"The fever?"

"No." Michel's answer was tinged with disgust. "Runaways. They disappear in the night . . ."

"What about the patrollers?"

"They've seen nothing on the roads. Although . . . and this is why I wanted to speak with you . . . I've heard rumors that there was a lot of activity in the back canebrakes at Greenwood."

"Greenwood?" Andre was puzzled. "We lost two ourselves in early June, but . . ."

"No, no," Michael continued. "This has been just recently . . . the last three weeks or so."

"I'm afraid I can't help you there. You see, we no longer own Greenwood."

"What?" Michel was shocked by the news.

"It has changed hands. A Christopher Fletcher of Philadelphia now owns it. In fact," Andre insinuated. "He took control a little over a month ago."

Edward and James bristled at the inference. "Suh. We are both well acquainted with Christopher Fletcher and resent your implying that he would be involved in such a dastardly plot!"

"He is a Yankee," Andre shrugged.

"But he is also a slave-owner," James defended. "Besides, he's intelligent enough to know how foolhardy it would be to try to run slaves out of the South."

Andre looked at James and Edward, his expression clearly doubtful. "Maybe. I only mentioned it for what it's worth, Michel."

"Of course. Well, I'm sorry to have bothered you with this."

"Not at all. If you ever find out anything, please let me know."

"I will. Gentlemen." Michel left them at the table.

Andre's eyes were gleaming as he, too, excused himself and left. He was anxious to get home so he could speak with his father. Perhaps he had just discovered the key to Christopher Fletcher's downfall.

"You say Bardeleau thinks there's some connection between the increasing number of runaways and Greenwood?"

"He only mentioned that there appeared to be activity in the marshes around Greenwood . . . and that the patrollers were having little success on the roads."

Emil was pensive. "Perhaps this is what we've been waiting for. Where did you say Fletcher was from originally?"

"Philadelphia. I believe."

"We'll start there," Emil told him, determined to find out all that he could about Christopher Fletcher's activities. If what they suspected was true, the Montards would have their revenge at last!

Eleven

The Island

The only thing that had gotten Katie through the rigors of the July social season had been the promise of a sojourn by the sea with Christopher in August. She supposed that the continuing round of parties and barbeques wouldn't have been so boring if Christopher had been there. But with him away all month in Philadelphia, the days had dragged by on leaden feet. She knew that she loved him, but she hadn't realized how much until he had gone. Any doubt that she might have had about her feelings for him had been laid to rest. She wished now that she hadn't told him of her aversion to getting married, for there was nothing she'd rather do than spend the rest of her life with him.

Standing with Mark at the rail of the island-bound steamer, she watched excitedly as Last Island came into view.

"Oh, Mark!" she exclaimed as she saw its primitive subtropical beauty for the first time. "Isn't it gorgeous?"

Last Island—or Derniere Island as it was known to

the Creoles — had derived its name from its location in the Gulf. The westernmost of a chain of barrier islands that rimmed the Louisiana coast, it was situated ten miles out from the mainland and was only accessible by water. Blessed by nature and as yet unspoiled by man, it was a virtual paradise. Endless miles of smooth, white beaches framed its lush greenery and entranced all who came to visit. Walkers and riders alike eagerly explored the shores while those more prone to sport took to the gentle, shallow waters of Caillou Bay to either swim or fish. Unsurpassed in natural beauty, Last Island won the hearts of all who enjoyed vacationing by the sea.

"It sure is," Mark answered. "Our hotel is on the Gulf side, isn't it?"

"Right on the beach," she replied without looking away from the scenic view before her. "Promise me, you'll walk with me on the beach as soon as we get settled."

"I promise," he laughed at her enthusiasm.

"Promise to do what?" Suzanne interrupted their conversation as she joined them on deck.

Mark stiffened perceptively. He had avoided Suzanne as much as possible during the past month, but she still had the power to make him extremely nervous whenever she was near.

"Mark's promised to take me for a walk on the beach," Katie explained cordially.

She, too, had steered clear of Suzanne since their confrontation at the ball, and amazingly enough, Suzanne seemed to like it that way.

"Oh." Suzanne showed little interest.

She greatly begrudged the fact that she was being forced to spend her vacation with Katie and Mark. It was bad enough that Isaac was going to be late arriving, but to leave her alone with these two was almost more than she could bear.

Ever since the night of the party, Mark had been acting very strangely. Suzanne had tried to maintain a comfortable relationship with him but his stilted, withdrawn manner had forced her to give up. Taking his youth into consideration, she dismissed him as not worth the effort. As far as she was concerned, if Jacqui La Zear wanted him, then she was welcome to him.

The pilot guided the steamer expertly up to the landing at the entrance to the Village Bayou. Once it had been tied up, they left the boat and were taken directly to the hotel at the far end of the island where they were shown to plain yet comfortable rooms.

"I will be resting this afternoon," Suzanne told them as she entered her suite. "So I won't be seeing you until dinner."

"If you should need us, we'll be outside," Katie offered.

"Fine." The older woman dismissed them and shut her door.

Katie looked at Mark and shrugged happily, "I'll meet you downstairs in ten minutes."

"Right."

It was over an hour later when Katie and Mark finally slowed their pace. They had explored the sand and rolling surf with the delight of children and now, slightly damp but no worse for the wear, they headed back toward the hotel.

"That must be the Adams's cottage." Mark indicated a small house that was still closed up.

"It is," Katie stated with certainty.

"How can you be so sure?"

"I asked Lottie before we left."

"You're sure that Christopher is coming?"

"I'm positive. I'm just not sure when he's going to arrive."

"You've missed him, haven't you?"

"Very much."

"Do you love him?"

"Yes," she confirmed. "And I didn't realize how much until he was gone."

"You're almost as bad as I was with Jacqui. But, at least Christopher's coming back to you."

"You're not doing well with her?"

"I'm not doing as well as I'd like to, but . . ."

"But what?"

"She let me kiss her last weekend."

"That's wonderful!"

Mark reddened. "Yes, it was."

"All is not lost. Believe me, Mark. If Jacqui didn't care about you any more, she wouldn't even be speaking to you."

Mark smiled. "I can hardly wait for this trip to be over. How am I ever going to stay away from her for a whole month?"

Katie laughed. "If I can manage without Christopher for a month, you can stay away from Jacqui that long. And who knows? She might start to miss you."

"There's only one thing that worries me, Katie."

"What's that?"

"Being alone with Suzanne."

"I thought it was over between you?"

"It is, but damn, every time she's around me, I get nervous. She's so beautiful and to know what it's like to have her . . ."

"Mark Kingsford!" Katie glared at him. "The only thing you need to know is how you felt after the last time you were with her . . ."

Mark paled as he remembered how disgusted he had been with himself.

"Right, Mark?"

"Right, Katie."

"Besides, Uncle Isaac will be here soon."

"I hope so."

"Why do you say that? He only had a few meetings, didn't he?"

"Actually . . ."

"What?"

"Actually, he didn't have any meetings at all. He's spending this time with his mistress."

"His mistress?" Katie fell silent for a moment. Then questioned, "Mark?"

"What Katie?"

"What is she like?"

"Cherie?"

"Yes."

"Well, I tell you. When I first met her I was determined to hate her."

"Why?"

"Because of Suzanne. All I could think of was that Isaac was hurting her. But now that I understand the situation better, I see Cherie in a different light."

"What do you mean? She's still a kept woman."

"But, Katie, she's very nice. Cherie went out of her way to be kind to me that day and I was totally unresponsive to her."

"You were just surprised."

"And angry. But Isaac explained it all and I feel kind of sorry for Cherie now."

"Why?"

"Isaac would have married her years ago, except that she's a quadroon. You know how impossible it would be for a white man to marry a free woman of color . . ."

"They probably would have been killed for daring to cross color lines, wouldn't they?"

"That's right."

Katie stopped walking, her body tense with useless anger. "The whole situation is ridiculous! I mean, it's perfectly all right for a white man to sleep with a black woman as long as he doesn't marry her."

"It is ridiculous, Katie, but there's nothing we can do about it."

"I wish there were, Mark," she declared.

"Katie," Mark dragged her back to reality. "We're here on holiday. Let's have fun."

"I'm sorry, Mark." Katie temporarily gave up her plans to change the world.

Grinning at each other, they continued their walk on the beach, taking the time now to admire all the delights that nature had created on Last Island.

The next week passed in a panorama of seaside activities. Katie and Mark were busy exploring the island during the day and attending various parties at the private summer cottages in the evenings.

Suzanne attended the soirees and cotillions, too, enjoying the chance to visit with her friends. But as the week wore on and Isaac still hadn't joined them, her mood had grown more tense. Where was he? Was he spending all this time with his mistress? It still pained her to realize that Isaac preferred the company of his mistress and their bastard son to her. But she had given up fighting that arrangement years ago.

Suzanne supposed that she wouldn't have been so concerned about Isaac if Christopher Fletcher had been on the island. But he, too, was late in arriving. She was looking forward to spending some time alone with him again, for after all, he hadn't rebuffed her the first time. They had only been rudely interrupted at a very inopportune moment and had not had a chance since then to continue their very interesting conversation. She was going to do everything in her power to get Christopher alone and when she did . . . well, the thought made her smile.

Isaac looked worriedly at Cherie, "I think we'd best call in a physician."

"What's wrong?" Cherie asked tearfully.

"I'm afraid it's the fever," he told her solemnly.

"No!" the word came from her in a gasp. "Not Denis!"

Rushing past Isaac, she entered her son's bedroom and knelt by his bed.

"But he was fine last night . . ." she touched Denis's cheek tentatively. "Isaac, he's burning up!"

Isaac left the room to find the maid. After sending her for the doctor, he returned to Denis's bedside with a bowl of cool water and clean cloths.

"I'll bathe him. It should help bring his fever down."

But the gentle strokes of the cooling cloth did nothing to lessen the heat emanating from the child's fever-wracked body.

"Papa," he mumbled in feverish confusion. "I'm so hot. I hurt so bad . . ."

"I know, son. We've sent for the doctor. He'll be here soon . . ." Isaac held his son's small hand tightly, wishing that he could bear the pain for him.

When the knock came at the front door, Cherie rushed to answer it.

"Dr. Lucien! Thank God you've come. It's Denis!" Cherie led him quickly to the sick room. "He was fine last night and now he's burning with fever . . ."

"Mr. Kingsford," Dr. Lucien greeted Isaac. "If you

will take Miss Delabarre from the room, I'll examine the boy."

"Of course," after taking a last look at Denis, who was only semi-conscious, Isaac took Cherie out into the hall. "Let's wait downstairs, my love."

"But Denis may need me . . ."

"Dr. Lucien will call us, I'm sure."

The minutes dragged by, stretching their nerves taut, as they waited in silence for the doctor to finish his examination. Cherie could not sit down, and pacing the parlor in helpless anguish, she fought against remembering the horrors of the last yellow fever epidemic in 1853. Nearly one in every ten had died that summer from the ravaging disease that could kill within three days.

At the sound of Denis's door opening, Cherie and Isaac rushed into the hall to confront the doctor as he came downstairs.

"Dr. Lucien?" Isaac asked, keeping a supporting arm about Cherie's waist.

"It is the fever," he confirmed.

Cherie sagged against Isaac. "Oh, no. Denis is all I've got . . ."

"What can we do?"

"Very little. Keep him as cool as possible . . . perhaps some broth . . . Once it strikes, the outcome is in the hands of the Lord."

Cherie groaned. "Is there nothing more? Surely we can do something?"

"I'm sorry." he wished he did know the cure. "I'll check back with you later . . ."

He let himself out as Isaac and Cherie returned to their son's bedside to begin their vigil.

The candle had burned to a stub and the melted wax had puddled and hardened in the holder on the table-top, but no one took notice. Hours had passed. Day

258

had turned to night and night to early morning with no change in Denis's condition. His fever raged uncontrolled in spite of frequent sponge baths and constant fanning. Denis had been unconscious most of the time, rousing only occasionally to call for Isaac and his mother. He could keep no liquid down and grew continually weaker as the new day dawned.

Isaac watched as Cherie worked tirelessly over the inert body of their child.

"Cherie, you must rest or you, too, will take ill."

"No. I will not. I must save him." She looked at Isaac levelly, her earlier emotions now frozen by her grim determination to succeed.

Isaac came to her and embraced her. "Then let me help you. Sit down and I will take over."

"Isaac, I have to save him . . . He is all that I have in this world," she said desperately.

"You have me," Isaac tried to comfort her.

"Do I? Really?" moving from his embrace, she returned to Denis. "I have you only when it is convenient for you. I am alone in this."

Turning her back on him, she once again began bathing her son.

Isaac, stunned and hurt, left the room quickly. Going into the study, he poured himself a double shot of bourbon and downed the fiery liquid without thought. Refilling the glass, he strode to the window and pushing the drape aside, stared out at the first light of morning.

He had had no idea that Cherie had been discontented with their life. She had always been glad to see him and had never made any demands on his time. Until now, she had given him no indication that she had needed more from him. He had thought their relationship was as near to perfect as possible . . . and it grieved him to find that he had somehow been lacking.

His thoughts were interrupted by the knock at the door and he went to answer it almost mechanically.

"Dr. Lucien?" Isaac was surprised.

"I thought I should check back with you as soon as possible." The doctor looked haggard. "There have been more cases reported . . . I've been out all night."

"Come in. Would you like some coffee? Or perhaps something a little stronger?" Isaac ushered him inside.

"Coffee would be wonderful, thank you."

"I'll get it right away."

"I'll go on up."

"Fine. Cherie is with him," he told him as he went to get the coffee.

Cherie was fanning Denis as the physician walked in.

"Miss Delabarre —"

"Oh, Doctor. I'm glad you're back. I've been sponging him down all night, but I don't know if it's helped or not."

"Has he awakened?"

"A few times."

"Does he know you?"

"Yes, he did . . ."

"That's good. Why don't you rest for a few moments while I see what I can do?" Cherie looked worried, but he walked her to the door. "Go on."

So dismissed, she left the room and started downstairs to find Isaac. Isaac was on his way back when he met her in the main floor hall. She looked so stricken that for a moment he thought the worst.

"Denis?" he asked, his voice choked with emotion.

"He's the same," she responded, nervously glancing upstairs. "Dr. Lucien sent me out of the room."

"Cherie —" Isaac breathed a small prayer of thankfulness that his son was still alive. "Cherie, he will be ll right."

"How can you be so sure?"

"Denis is a healthy boy. I'm sure he'll make it."

"Oh, Isaac," her veneer of calm finally shattered. "What if he doesn't? What if he doesn't?"

For Christopher, the trip from New Orleans to Last Island had seemed to take longer than travelling from Philadelphia to Greenwood. It had been late afternoon before he finally arrived at the resort and by the time he settled in, it was dusk. Anxious to find Katie, he'd headed for the hotel after learning of the cotillion being held there tonight.

The hotel was ablaze with lights and the melodic strains of a waltz drifted out across the sandy beaches and shell-lined drives as Christopher rode up to the entrance. Eager to reclaim Katie, he left his horse with a stableboy and hurried inside to find her.

Katie had almost decided not to attend the dance this evening, but Mark had encouraged her to go. Now, as she stood listening politely to Lavinia Crawford and Suzanne exchanging small talk, she wished she'd not let Mark talk her into it. Excusing herself, she left them to walk out on the hotel's side gallery alone.

The moon was bright that night, etching the island in stark relief of black and white. The murmuring of the surf as it lapped hungrily at the shore had a hypnotic effect on Katie as she leaned on the balustrade, sighing deeply. The night could be magical if only Christopher were here. A cooling breeze from the north chilled her and Katie was turning to go back inside when she saw him coming through the ballroom doorway.

"Christopher," she whispered her heart's desire.

261

Without speaking, she went into his arms. Restraining himself with great effort, Christopher didn't kiss her.

"I finally got here," he grinned, looking almost boyish in the dim moonlight.

"I was beginning to think you weren't going to make it," Katie couldn't take her eyes off his lean, tanned features.

"You never have to worry about that. I'll always . . ."

"Here you are, Christopher," Suzanne interrupted them as she came outside with Lavinia. "I thought I saw you come in."

Christopher quickly released Katie and turned to greet the other ladies. "Good evening Suzanne."

"Christopher, this is Lavinia Crawford. She and her husband Wade own Millbrook."

"Mrs. Crawford," he acknowledged the introduction.

"Mr. Fletcher, I've heard so many nice things about you from Suzanne," Lavinia babbled, impressed by this handsome newcomer. She had seen him at the ball at Kingsford House but had not managed an introduction that night. "I understand that you own Greenwood now."

"Yes ma'am."

"Such a lovely place."

Katie was about to scream. Her first moment alone with Christopher in over a month and Suzanne had to ruin it. And while she was tense with frustration, he seemed quite relaxed as he stood by her side.

"Why don't we rejoin the party?" Suzanne maneuvered cleverly. "Perhaps you'd like some refreshments?"

"Of course," Christopher agreed, understanding her plotting. "Katie?"

He ushered them back inside and summoned a waiter to bring him a bourbon. It was going to be a long night.

The hours passed in miserable slow-motion for Katie as she was forced to endure Suzanne's constant company. Her only relief came when Christopher danced with her and then there was little that they could say to one another. As the musicians began another waltz, he swept her quickly into his arms and out onto the dance floor before Suzanne found some way to prevent it.

"I'm sorry, Katie. I didn't want our first night back together to be like this."

"Neither did I," her eyes filled with tears.

Christopher groaned when he saw her misery. "Ah, Katie. I missed you so . . . and to be stuck here . . ."

"Will you meet me later? On the beach?" The idea gave Katie some hope. "I need to be with you so badly."

His hands tightened on her as he thought of the possibility. "Will you be able to get away?"

"I think so," she determined.

"All right. I'll be waiting for you on the beach below the hotel. Say, about an hour after the dance ends?"

Katie smiled, "I'll be there."

Katie's mood had definitely improved as the dance ended and they walked slowly back to the others. Christopher, unable to put it off any longer, asked Suzanne for the next dance, which much to his aggravation was another waltz. He had hoped for a polka or a schottische so he wouldn't have to hold her too intimately.

Suzanne was obviously delighted by the invitation and moved gracefully about the dance floor in his arms as Katie watched from the side.

"You know, Christopher. It's really a shame that we

didn't get to finish the conversation we were having the night of the ball at Kingsford House," she purred.

"Oh?" Christopher tried to remain aloof. Attractive though Suzanne was, he understood the type of woman she was and he wanted no part of her.

"There was so much I had to say to you . . ."

He knew what was coming and decided to go ahead and get it over with. "Such as?"

Suzanne was puzzled by Christopher's manner. She couldn't tell if he was interested or just being polite. Throwing caution to the wind, she pushed onward, for Isaac would be arriving soon and her free time was limited.

"Such as, I find you very attractive."

"Thank you," he responded and let it drop, forcing her to continue.

Suzanne wasn't quite sure what Christopher's ploy was. Probably, she reasoned, since she was a married woman, he didn't want to make the first move.

"Christopher," her voice was sultry. "Would you like to meet me later so we can do more than talk?"

Christopher remained impassive as he looked down at her coldly, wanting to discourage her once and for all.

"Suzanne, I am very flattered by your offer, but I must refuse," he told her flatly. "You are a lovely woman, but I make it a point never to get involved with married women. I'm sorry."

She stiffened at his refusal and then wanted to laugh out loud. A married woman! Ha! She hardly felt like a married woman. How unfair!

"If you will please escort me back," she requested as the music ended, keeping all emotion from her voice. "Thank you for the dance, but I fear I'm quite winded," she said as they joined the others.

"My pleasure," he responded and after giving Katie

a quick reassuring look, he excused himself and left the ball.

When Christopher had gone, Suzanne too made her excuses and retired for the night, leaving Katie alone to search out Mark. She found him in the lobby visiting with a group of planters from upriver.

"Katie," he greeted and introduced her to his new acquaintances.

"I was wondering if we could talk for a moment?"

"Of course. Gentlemen, if you will excuse me?"

Walking with Katie outside onto the gallery, he smiled down at her. "Well, I saw you with Christopher. How is he?"

"I didn't get much of a chance to find out."

"What do you mean?"

"We weren't together two minutes before Suzanne found us."

"She's a regular bloodhound, Katie," Mark teased. "How did Christopher handle it?"

"I don't know. They danced once and then he left for the evening."

"Don't worry. I'm sure he had a good reason."

"I know," she sighed unhappily.

"You'll see him tomorrow, I'm sure," Mark consoled her.

Katie hesitated, debating whether to tell Mark about her rendezvous with Christopher.

"Mark, I'll need your help."

"With what?"

"I'm meeting him later on the beach and I need you to cover for me just in case Suzanne should come looking for me."

Mark's eyes widened at what Katie had just revealed. "You're meeting him tonight?"

"I have to. I've missed him so badly . . ."

"I understand," he told her, knowing that he'd go to

meet Jacqui if the opportunity ever arose.

"Then you'll help me?"

"Just tell me what you want me to do."

It was very late when Katie, dressed in her comfortable clothes, slipped undetected from the hotel. Barefoot, with her hair unbound, she raced across the sandy expanse searching for Christopher.

"Katie!" his hushed call drew her directly to him and they came together in a heated embrace.

Needing to be as close to him as possible, she kissed him passionately.

"You feel so good in my arms," he told her between breathtaking kisses.

"I don't ever want to be anywhere else," she hugged him.

"Let's walk." He took her hand and led her off down the long, deserted beach.

They walked for a distance in silence, relishing the moon and the surf and each other. They stopped in front of the Adams's cottage, where Christopher had spread a blanket in anticipation of their being alone.

"Sit down," he invited as he sat and pulled her down next to him. "I've wanted to be with you for so long . . ." he told her, drawing her into the warm circle of his arms.

"It's all I've thought about, too," she confided, as his lips found hers in the darkness.

Their kisses were wild with hunger as they strained against each other.

"Make love to me, Christopher," Katie pleaded and he pulled away from her slightly.

"First," his voice was husky with emotion. "We have to talk."

"Talk?" conversation was the farthest thing from

Katie's mind.

"Talk," he confirmed, smiling tenderly at her confusion. He gave her a quick kiss and sat apart from her, clearing his throat. "Katie Kingsford, would you do me the honor of becoming my wife?"

Katie blinked in surprise at his proposal. "Will I what?"

"Marry me, Katie. I love you."

"Oh, Christopher! Yes. Yes, I will."

He hugged her tightly before kissing her deeply. Lowering Katie to the blanket, Christopher stretched full-length beside her savoring the feel of her hips pressed eagerly to his. Their hands knew not a still moment as they quickly undressed each other, wanting to be free of their clothing's inhibiting restraints. Finally, naked in the shimmering moonlight, they joined in a piercingly sweet union that explored to the fullest love's most treasured blending.

Christopher felt as if he had come home as his body melded with Katie's. Giving and taking, they came together, not daring to speak lest they spoil the magic of the moment. Moving in the age-old rhythm of love, they explored with renewed wonder the glory of their love for one another.

The shattering bliss of their union left them panting and breathless and they lay in each other's arms, lost in the splendor of what had just occurred between them.

Andre arrived at the Montard's New Orleans home late that night. He was tired, but excited as he roused his father from a deep sleep. Emil was glad that his son had finally returned and hurriedly dressed so he could join him in the parlor.

"How did it go?" Emil inquired eagerly.

"Very well, although the first days I had my doubts about finding out anything useful."

"So what did you learn?"

"While Fletcher was there this past month, he made direct contact with the abolitionists working out of William Still's Anti-Slavery Office."

"Did he, indeed?" Emil's eyes lit up at the thought. "What else?"

"I also got the names of a few people who might help us find out more, but they're in St. Louis. I thought I'd come back here first."

"That's fine. In fact, take a week or so and enjoy yourself. I can send someone else to St. Louis . . ."

"Where's Fletcher now? I know he left Philadelphia before I did."

"From what I understand, he's gone out to Last Island for the rest of the month."

Andre tensed at the thought of Katie and Fletcher together at the resort. "If you have no objection, I think I'll go out to the island for a week or so."

"Of course not," Emil agreed, quite pleased with the information his son had turned up. "There's a lot of checking I can do from this end now that we have an idea of what to go after."

"Right. I'll go ahead and leave tomorrow then, so I can be there for the weekend. I'll plan on being back by the twenty-first. How's that?"

"That should give me time to find out more. You go and have fun."

Isaac sat in the study of Cherie's home, his expression somber, his shoulders slumped as if the weight of the world was upon him. He knew that he should be rejoicing, but the decision he had just made was a serious one.

For the past few days, as Denis had lain at death's door, Isaac had had time to take a good look at his life. With painful forthrightness, he'd admitted to himself that he had made many mistakes, but none so grievous as marrying Suzanne. He had married her for all the wrong reasons. He had married her because she was beautiful, charming, with the appearance of a perfect lady, not because he loved her. He was fond of her, true, but the only love he really felt was for Cherie and Denis. The thought of living without them was abhorrent.

Heading upstairs to the master bedroom, Isaac summoned the maid. He was instructing her as to what clothes to pack for his trip to Last Island when Cherie found him.

"You're leaving?" She was weak with fatigue. The unending hours of worry had left her drained of all feeling.

"We need to talk." He dismissed the servant and drew Cherie into the bedroom and closed the door.

Cherie couldn't keep the question from her eyes as Isaac sat on the bed and pulled her down next to him.

"You know I was due at the island last Tuesday . . ." He patted her hand gently. "I didn't even think of it until late last night . . . I'm sure they're concerned . . ."

"Is there a boat out tomorrow?"

"Yes, I've already booked passage. I must leave very early."

Cherie didn't respond. He was going, just as he always did. She was glad that she was too tired to argue — to tell him how she needed him — how Denis, now that he was recovering, needed him. No, she wouldn't use that ploy. Isaac had to come to her because he desired no other, not because he had been forced to.

"What I want to say, Cherie, is this . . ." he said sincerely. "When I do return to you, it will be to stay. Permanently."

She looked at him blankly, not quite grasping his meaning. "Of course."

"Cherie, I know I haven't told you this often enough but I love you. Only you. These long hours I've spent alone here worrying about Denis helped me to see . . . I can't live without you. I don't want to even try. You two mean everything to me."

"And I wouldn't want to live without you," she said softly.

He smiled and kissed her softly. "When I get to the resort, I'm going to tell Suzanne of my decision."

"Decision?"

"I'm leaving her. I should never have married her. I realized now the pain I caused you by taking her as my wife. She can divorce me . . . I don't care. All I want . . . all I need is to be with you and our son. I cannot go on any other way."

Cherie's eyes brimmed with tears. "You can't leave her."

"I can and I will. I want to be here. Watching Denis grow to manhood."

Her prayers had been answered and her tears fell unbidden. "Isaac, I love you so."

He held her tenderly. "I'll be back as soon as I can make all the arrangements. We may have to make some changes, but we'll worry about that later. If things get too bad, we can always move North."

Cherie nodded. "Will you tell Denis? It would cheer him so."

"Let's both tell him."

Together they went to Denis's bedroom to tell him of Isaac's decision to live with them permanently.

* * *

"Christopher?" Katie spoke softly, stirring in his arms.

"Um," he responded contentedly, not wanting to move from their blissful rest.

"There's something I want to do with you that I've never done before."

He opened one eye and looked at her skeptically. "There is?"

Katie laughed at his nervousness. "Don't look so worried. I don't think it's painful . . . at least I hope not!"

"Well, don't keep me in suspense any longer," he said sitting up, his curiosity aroused.

"I want to go swimming."

"Now?" he asked incredulously.

"Of course, now. C'mon." Jumping lithely to her feet, she ran gracefully to the water's edge.

Mesmerized, Christopher watched her frolic in the surf, alternately chasing the waves and running from them.

"Christopher! C'mon. The water is warm." Her inviting call stirred him to action.

Running out to Katie, he picked her up and waded farther out into the foaming swells. Laughing delightedly, Katie looped her arms around his neck. "Isn't this a wonderful idea?"

"Absolutely. But I don't know how much swimming is going to get done," he agreed as he stopped in waist-high water to let Katie slide down his arms, pressed full against him.

"Don't you want to swim?" she asked archly as she came in contact with his arousal.

"Not yet, my little water nymph . . . maybe later." His kiss was devouring as he braced himself against the incoming waves.

"Oh, Christopher," Katie surrendered to his touch,

enjoying the novelty of their position.

Katie was virtually weightless in the water and Christopher grasped her hips, lifting her legs to encircle his waist.

The moonlight . . . the white-crested waves . . . the sand still warm from the day's blazing sun all combined to make Katie more aware of sensuality than she'd been before. Rubbing her breasts against him, she delighted in the wet slickness of his chest. With slow deliberation, she licked at the salty droplets of seawater on his neck and shoulders.

Christopher bit back a groan of pure animal pleasure and Katie moved restlessly, brushing in seeming innocence against his throbbing erection. His body was demanding that he take her quickly but the night was too perfect. He wanted to go slowly . . . to treasure each moment of this Elysian night.

Katie, aroused and ready for Christopher's possession, didn't understand his slow pace. Feeling decidedly wicked, she reached down to encircle his manhood. His breathing was harsh in her ear as she fondled his male essence, stroking him knowingly. Finally, when he could stand no more, he covered her hand with his and guided himself to her softness, entering gently.

Katie arched away from him, her head thrown back in ecstasy as she rode him. Glorying in the joy of having her for his own, Christopher pressed passionate kisses on her throat and bosom as they rocked together.

His lovemaking drove her on to a fever pitch and Katie collapsed against him as the sweet tight pain in her exploded in ecstasy, pulsing through her in waves of wildfire. As he felt Katie's tumultous climax, his own body sought and found that same ultimate release and he joined her in the mindless, quiet peace of love's aftermath.

Twelve

The Storm

A stiff, northern breeze roughened the usually calm waters of Caillou Bay as the steamer churned her way toward Last Island.

Isaac had been surprised to find that Andre, too, was travelling out to the island. And, though Andre was not one of his favorite people . . . being too loud and conceited in Isaac's opinion, he was glad for the company for it distracted him from thoughts of his upcoming confrontation with Suzanne. Sharing a drink in the saloon together, they passed the hours in friendly companionship.

"So, you've just been up North?" Isaac inquired, as Andre made mention of his recent trip.

"As a matter of fact, I did just return from Philadelphia. I was taking care of some business matters for Father." Andre hedged on relating the true purpose of his visit there.

"Your father is lucky to have you. I've been trying to convince Mark to come into the business with me and I think he will, once he finishes school."

"That will be fortunate for you," Andre said courteously. "Isaac, there is something else I've been wanting to speak with you about."

"Yes?" Isaac was curious.

"Katie . . . I plan to ask her to marry me and I wanted your consent," Andre told him smoothly.

When Isaac chuckled, Andre looked irritated. "Are you making sport of me, sir?"

"Hardly, Andre," Isaac tried to appear contrite. "You have my permission to court her, but I can't say that my approval will carry any weight with her. Katie is a strong-willed young woman."

"I know. But her beauty makes up for some of her less admirable traits." Andre thought of her altercation with Fletcher.

His smug remark angered Isaac, but the older man held his tongue. He knew how Katie felt about Andre and realized that his chance for success was minimal.

"Have you spoken to Katie about your intentions?"

"Not yet."

"I see," Isaac said knowingly. "Well, I wish you luck."

"Thank you, sir."

When the boat docked a short time later, Isaac and Andre were taken by carriage to the hotel. The bumpy ride over the shell-covered road seemed far too short for Isaac as he wrestled with the problem of how to break the news to Suzanne. Andre, however, thought they would never get to the hotel. He was anxiously anticipating proposing to Katie and thoroughly expected to win her hand today. As the conveyance drew to a halt at the front entrance of the large rambling building, they climbed down and went inside to register.

It was late afternoon and Katie was waiting on the beach for Christopher to return with their horses.

Having met him after breakfast, they'd spent the day together exploring the island and enjoying each other's company. Katie had felt exhilarated all day . . . in love with life after her night in Christopher's arms and she could hardly wait for their engagement to be officially announced. The sooner she became Mrs. Christopher Fletcher, the happier she would be.

"Katie!" the sound of Andre's voice shook her painfully from her reverie.

"Andre? I didn't know that you were coming out to the island. I thought you were away on business."

"I was, but I got back early," he explained. "And New Orleans was very lonely without you, Katie."

Katie blushed at his statement. "I'm flattered, Andre, but . . ."

Before she could explain anything to him, he continued, "I needed to see you. I've been thinking about you a lot, Katie."

"You have?"

Andre nodded. "Walk with me, Katie." He needed more privacy in order to propose.

Glancing around, she saw no sign of Christopher and realized that there was no way to avoid it.

"For a moment, but I'm meeting someone here anytime now."

"This will only take a minute." Andre took her arm and led her off down the beach.

Preoccupied with trying to figure out how to propose, Andre walked in silence until Katie broke in.

"The surf wasn't nearly this rough yesterday." She indicated the tumbling, almost violent, waves.

"There must be a storm out at sea," he commented, distractedly. Then his thoughts finally in order, he began. "Katie, there is something important I must ask you."

"What?" Katie had no idea what he was leading up to.

"Katie," Andre was suddenly solemn as he took her hand. "I want you to be my wife." At her stunned expression, he hurried on, "I know this may seem precipitate to you, but I've thought of nothing else since the first time we met."

"Andre," Katie stammered, trying to find a way to refuse tactfully. "This is so unexpected . . . I'm honored by your proposal but . . ."

"I know. You want to think about it," he finished her sentence for her, arrogantly certain that she was overcome by his offer. "There's no rush. I just wanted to let you know that my intentions are strictly honorable."

"Sorry I'm late," Christopher gladly interrupted the intimate little scene and wondered why Andre was holding Katie's hand.

"Fletcher," Andre's tone reflected his total dislike.

"Hello, Christopher," Katie smiled, relieved that he'd rescued her again.

"Our horses are ready, if you are," he told her.

"Andre," Katie turned to him. "I'll let you know."

Nodding curtly, he responded, "Fine. I'll speak with you later."

As Andre stalked away, Christopher looked down at Katie, his expression questioning. "Are you all right?"

"I'm fine."

"When I saw him holding your hand, I wanted to kill him."

Katie took his arm and hugged it to her, "You have nothing to worry about."

"What did he want?"

Looking up at him, she grinned. "I just received my second marriage proposal in two days."

"Andre proposed?"

"Yes, he did."

"What did you tell him?" Christopher was mildly amused.

"I didn't get a chance to tell him anything. You showed up."

"Well, good. He'll find out you're mine soon enough anyway," he sounded inordinately pleased with himself.

"You're a conceited lout," she teased.

"You're mine, Katie, make no mistake," Christopher was suddenly fierce.

"There is no one else I care to be with, Christopher," she told him. "But you realize there'll be no getting away from Andre on this little island, don't you?"

"And there I had hopes of spending some time with you . . . alone."

Katie laughed, seeing the humor, "With Suzanne and Andre around, we don't stand a chance."

"Maybe we should plan on a very short engagement."

"I agree!"

Isaac arrived at the hotel to find that Suzanne had gone out for the evening. Not in the least disappointed, for he was dreading the upcoming confrontation, he passed the evening quietly dining with Mark, Christopher and Katie in the hotel dining room.

"Well, Christopher, how are things going at Greenwood?" Isaac asked cordially, wanting to learn more about this young man who was so important to Katie.

"Just fine," he answered.

"Katie told me you went to Philadelphia last month?"

"Yes. There were a few problems that my business

277

agents couldn't sort out, so I had to go."

"You have ties in Philadelphia?"

"Not any more." He looked at Katie intimately. "Greenwood is my home now."

Andre, who was approaching their table, was hard put not to hit Christopher when he heard his last statement.

"Isaac," Andre greeted. "Mind if I join you?"

"Of course not." Isaac motioned for Andre to take a chair.

An air of tense silence hovered momentarily as Andre eyed his adversary dangerously. Then, shaking himself mentally, Andre knew that this was not the time to deal with Christopher Fletcher. He would wait until later . . . when he had all the necessary proof.

"Andre has just returned from the North, too," Isaac remarked innocently.

"Oh? Where were you?"

"Philadelphia."

"Really? On business?" Christopher sensed Andre's hostility.

"Partially," Andre replied evasively. When Christopher showed no reaction, he dropped the subject. And turning to Katie, he commented, "You look lovely this evening."

"Thank you."

"Have you been enjoying the island?" His question was meant for Katie, but Mark answered.

"It's beautiful. We've been having great fun on the riding trails and we even went hunting," Mark looked fondly at his sister. "Katie outshot everyone."

Andre fought to keep the distaste he felt from showing. My God! The woman not only fought like a man . . . She was a marksman, too.

Isaac chuckled, "George taught you well, didn't he?"

"He taught me everything he taught Mark," she answered simply.

"My brother is a very wise man."

Andre was totally frustrated as he listened half-heartedly to their exchange. Tonight he had wanted to court Katie, but, instead, he was forced to endure Christopher Fletcher's hated presence. Andre was almost relieved when Katie announced that she was retiring for the evening.

Christopher, too, was frustrated for with Andre in attendance, he had had no chance to ask Isaac for Katie's hand. And now that she and Isaac were both calling it a night, he knew there wouldn't be another opportunity until tomorrow. Taking Mark up on his challenge to a game of billiards, Christopher decided to bide his time in relative good humor while Andre disappeared into the bar, sulking.

The following morning dawned dark and threatening. Katie and Mark were fascinated by the Gulf's wild beauty and spent the better part of the day watching the waves crash upon the shore and the sky grow ever more menacing.

Suzanne, however, had witnessed Gulf storms before and she urged Isaac to make plans for them to return to the mainland. Isaac agreed that bad weather was imminent, but there were no boats available for the trip back to the coast. The water was so rough now that even the arrival of the steamer *Star*, which was due in that evening, was in doubt.

Determined to have a good time in spite of the weather, the cotillion went on as planned. The partygoers, their gaiety forced, danced and drank, as they kept a nervous lookout for some sign of the *Star*'s arrival.

Christopher squired Katie about the room to the smooth, soothing strains of a waltz. What he had hoped would be a relaxing enjoyable evening together had become for him an exercise in self-control for Andre had been pursuing Katie relentlessly all evening. Christopher had tried to meet with Isaac alone all day to make his engagement to Katie official, but his efforts had come to no avail. So, now, he was forced to endure with pretended unconcern, Andre's obnoxious advances on Katie. Jealousy was a new emotion for Christopher and it was a struggle for him to force himself to maintain his air of indifference. Finally, drawing upon his experience as a gambler to disguise his turbulent feelings, he brought himself under control, but it still rankled him that the same man who had beaten and abused Dee could freely court Katie.

For her part, Katie was doing an admirable job of staving off Andre's amorous attentions. Being polite but firm, she danced with him but gave him no other encouragement. Katie longed to discourage him by telling him of her betrothal to Christopher but she knew that they would have to speak with Uncle Isaac first.

"The storm seems to be getting worse," Christopher remarked as the howling of the wind could be heard over the music.

"I know," Katie sounded a little nervous. "Isaac said earlier that we were going home tomorrow if it doesn't look any better."

"I thought there was no way back."

"There will be when the *Star* gets here."

"She was due at nine."

"I know," she stated. "And it's after eleven already."

Christopher chuckled, hoping to ease her mind, "I always wanted to be stranded on a desert island with a beautiful woman."

"I don't think you had a few hundred other people in mind, did you?" she quipped.

"It does cut down on intimacy," Christopher commented good-naturedly and Katie laughed.

Andre, who was standing at the hall doors watching Katie, was having a wonderful time. He had sensed Fletcher's irritation with him and was taking every opportunity to flaunt his courtship of Katie in front of his hostile rival.

"You look like you're enjoying yourself," Suzanne noted the smug look of satisfaction on Andre's face.

"I am," he told her. "Where is Isaac?"

"With Wade Crawford, I believe. Why?"

"Just curious . . . By the way, what is happening with you and Fletcher? You haven't been giving me much help . . ."

Suzanne pierced Andre with a deadly gaze. "I'm afraid I'm out of the picture where Christopher is concerned."

"What happened?" Andre had been counting on her help to distract Fletcher from Katie.

"He informed me quite bluntly that he makes it a practice to never get involved with a married woman."

Andre snorted in disbelief. "As gorgeous as you are, I find that hard to believe."

Suzanne was surprised by his declaration. "Well, it's true. But thank you for the compliment." Changing the topic to something less embarrassing, she continued. "You seem to be making some progress with Katie."

Andre smiled. "I am. In fact, I proposed . . ."

Suzanne was incredulous. "You proposed?"

"Yesterday. She has yet to give me her answer."

"Are you sure that's what you want?" Andre's obsession for Katie still mystified Suzanne.

"Since I can't get her any other way, I'll have to

marry her," he answered simply.

"A marriage lasts a very long time, Andre," she reminded him, a touch of regret in her voice.

He glanced at her sharply.

"What will you do when the thrill of conquering her is gone and you're left with a nagging shrew of a wife?"

"I mean to have her any way I can."

"But Andre . . ." Suzanne wanted him to see what a mistake he was making.

"Suzanne, I've heard enough from you on this matter," Andre silenced her effectively.

"It's your bed . . ."

"I know," he smiled at her wickedly. "And I intend to be in it with Katie very soon."

Lifting her glass, she toasted him mockingly, "If she says yes, you have my condolences . . ."

Andre knew that Suzanne was trying to protect him in her own way, but her remarks still irritated him. Their friendship was a strong one, though, and would endure. It had already lasted through her marriage to Isaac and their own brief, tempestuous affair the year before. Passionate and innovative, Suzanne had been quite his match in bed and there were still times even now when he regretted the break-up of their relationship. But Suzanne had been the one to end it after she'd learned that he was keeping Dee for his pleasure at Greenwood. Andre supposed, now that he thought about it, that she had been jealous, but at the time he had been too involved with Dee to realize the choice he was making. He smiled at the thought of Suzanne being jealous and she gave him a curious look.

"Something's funny?"

"I was just thinking about us. You know in my own way, I still care about you."

"Spare me, Andre," she said sarcastically.

"All right, don't believe me," he came back. "But you are a very special woman."

Suzanne gave him a long-suffering look, "Why don't you go dance with Katie now that you have practiced your lines on me?"

Shrugging off her ascerbic remarks, he moved away. "If you insist. But remember what I told you . . ."

Mark's night had been slow in passing. With great effort, he had eluded Suzanne all night and had spent his time drinking and dreaming of Jacqui. Christopher and Katie both had urged him to ask one of the other eligible young ladies to dance, but he was too smitten with Jacqui to even consider it. Miserably unhappy, he sat at the hotel bar nursing his drink.

With only a glance from the bar room door, Katie could tell that he was drunk. She was anxiously considering how to get him upstairs when Christopher joined her.

"What's wrong?" he questioned as he came to her side.

"It's Mark," she spoke confidentially. "I have to get him upstairs to bed."

Christopher took one look at Mark and chuckled softly. "I'll help, as long as he doesn't take a swing at me."

Katie laughed, "He won't tonight. All he can talk about is Jacqui La Zear."

"Love strikes again, does it?" his tone was intimate and Katie blushed.

"Help me get him upstairs," she directed.

Engaging Mark in light banter, Christopher encouraged him out into the hall and with Katie's help and a friendly arm around the shoulders directed him up to his room.

Thirteen

The Fury

Sunday . . . The day of the Lord . . . A day of rest . . . A day of peace and contentment . . . For those who were stranded on Last Island, about to face the fury of nature unleashed, there was no peace.

There had been a small ray of hope earlier in the day when the *Star* had hove into sight. But all hope of rescue from their precarious situation was dashed when the buffeting winds drove the old steamer aground.

Faced now with no possible avenue of escape, everyone waited, watching in petrified horror as the waters of the Gulf and bay rose ever higher and threatened to inundate the island.

Christopher slept well that night. Secure in his relationship with Katie, he was looking forward to meeting with Isaac the next day. He realized, of course, that the wedding would have to wait until her father could be with them, but that didn't matter. What was important to him was publicly claiming Katie as his own, so Andre would back off.

When Christopher woke up late Sunday morning,

the storm had worsened. At the advice of the servants, he decided to close the cottage and take refuge in the more sturdy hotel. It was afternoon before the packing was completed and they began the now treacherous trek up the beach.

The wind was savage and it whipped the sand viciously about, blinding all who dared to try to look up. Shielding their faces as best they could, they stumbled on toward the island's most protective haven. Rain lashed them in torrents and the salt spray from the now-monstrous waves stung painfully. Helping the drenched, frightened servants onto the hotel porch, Christopher fought to open the door to the lobby as the full force of the gale battered him.

When a helping hand from inside threw the offending portal wide, he ushered his weary companions into the welcome dryness.

"Mark!" Christopher was surprised to find that Mark was holding the door. "Thanks."

Putting his shoulder against it, Mark pushed the door shut and turned to Christopher.

"Are you all right?"

"I think so," he responded, after sending the servants off to seek comfort.

"Good." Mark was relieved. "We've been hearing reports that cottages have been blown down . . ."

"I wouldn't doubt it. This is more than a storm, I'm afraid."

"I know. The talk here is hurricane."

"Did the *Star* manage to get in?" he asked, shedding his slicker.

"Yes, for all the good it did."

"What happened?"

"The wind drove it aground."

"Damn!" Christopher was furious, for he knew now that there would be no escape from the fate that

285

awaited them.

"Well, I'm just glad you're here. Katie's been worrying about you."

"I've been concerned about her, too. Has anything been done?" His tone was critical.

"Nothing that I know of . . ." Mark admitted.

"Why not?" he demanded as the rising crescendo of the wind rattled the windows and shook the entire structure. "Where the hell is Katie?"

"In the dining room," Mark began.

Breaking into a run, Christopher went to find her, his instincts dictating that he move and move fast.

"I'm sure we'll be safe here in the hotel," Isaac was saying. "It's been through storms before and survived."

"I agree," Andre supported. He, too, was completely confident of their safety.

Relaxing at the table with the Kingsfords, Andre had been enjoying the time in Katie's company without Fletcher. It was with total disgust that he looked up to see his nemesis barging across the room in their direction.

Christopher was angry. Why weren't these people doing something? Surely there were precautions that could be taken . . . This was no ordinary storm . . .

Outside, bolt after bolt of jagged lightning illuminated the green-black sky. The wind furiously battered the rising water ever higher until in one last cataclysmic surge the waves met and clashed, devouring each other in a foaming frenzy that inundated the entire island.

Katie would remember forever the look of desperate fury on Christopher's face as he was crossing the crowded dining room to join her. She smiled serenely at him, overjoyed to find him safe, and was rising to meet him when it happened.

Christopher had not expected it so soon. He had thought that there was time to reach Katie and formulate some plan for their safety . . . but the savage killer-storm struck first. He was caught in mid-stride as the windows were blown out and the walls were ripped apart.

"Katie!" he yelled lunging forward in a grim final effort to reach her. Christopher would have made it to her side had not a storm-tossed timber struck him a glancing blow. Falling heavily, he lay unconscious on the flooding floor.

"Christopher!" Katie's scream was lost in the screeching tumult of the hurricane and she was knocked down by the force of the winds. Struggling to right herself, she tried to get to Christopher, but Andre restrained her.

"Don't be a fool, Katie. He's probably dead. Forget him and come with me," Andre tried to pull her along with him as he searched for better shelter, but she broke free.

Dragging herself to Christopher's side, she tried to rouse him as water swirled through what had been the dining room. Trying to keep his head above the violent current, Katie held tightly onto him as the water washed them away into the lightning studded sky.

The destruction was over in a matter of minutes as the combined strength of the wind and waves ripped every structure on the island apart and feasted on them, gaining strength from the sustenance. The terrified screams of the victims soon gave way to the groaning power of the tempest as it stripped the island of all life.

Though the winds had died off, the rains continued all night, beating down mercilessly upon all who had managed to survive. The *Star*, thought to be useless before the hurricane because of her beached state, became ironically the savior of all. The captain had cut away her superstructure during the storm to keep the boat afloat and had worked tirelessly with his crew pulling aboard all who floated by borne on by the rushing waves. Dawn's first light found the steamer aground far inland, her deck crowded with survivors.

Bruised and exhausted, Suzanne clung numbly to Andre.

"Do you have to leave me?" she cried, the horror of what she'd just witnessed still terrifying her.

"The captain needs me to help search the island, Suzanne. But I'll be back." He set her from him gently and moved away.

Suzanne looked wildly about for a familiar face but there was no one she knew. Trembling from both weakness and shock, she sat back down on the boat's deck and tried to recall the events of the day before. They had been eating in the dining room when the building had seemed to disintegrate. She had seen Isaac fall and had watched helplessly as he had been swept away by the rising tide. Andre had grabbed her and they had stayed together in the rushing waters until the crew of the *Star* had plucked them from the raging sea. There had been no sign of the Crawfords or of Katie and Mark all night. And it was with sudden heartbreaking sorrow that she remembered Christopher being felled by the falling timber. Sobs shook her as she realized that they were probably all dead.

Carrying Isaac as best he could, Mark stumbled and fell to his knees as he slowly made his way up the ruins of Last Island's Gulf beach. The rampaging waters had left wreckage strewn everywhere. Shattered

288

boards and remnants of personal possessions littered the once beautiful landscape, but Mark had no time to dwell on what had happened. He had to get help for Isaac.

Quite by accident, they had found themselves together after the initial blast. Locating a board, they had drifted aimlessly in the current until shortly before dawn when it drove them back ashore. Unknown to Mark, his uncle had been seriously injured by the flying debris during the first hours, but Isaac had not complained. Instead, he had steadfastly maintained his determination that they would be rescued. It was only after they were safely on the beach that Mark had discovered the extent of Isaac's injuries. Refusing to leave him behind, Mark had begun the long walk back in the direction of the hotel, carrying Isaac who had fainted from the pain.

"Mark!" The call penetrated his stupor and he looked up to see Andre coming toward him.

"Andre! Hurry!" Mark yelled as he carefully lowered Isaac down on the beach.

With Andre's help, they made the trek back to the boat. When Suzanne saw them coming, she ran out to meet them.

"How is he?"

"He's alive, but I don't know for how long," they told her as they brought him to the shelter of the *Star.*

After Isaac had been made as comfortable as possible, Suzanne went to speak with Mark.

"Mark, are you all right?"

"I'm fine, but how is Isaac? Is he going to make it?" Mark inquired anxiously, his concern very real.

"I don't know . . ." she began. "Have you seen Christopher or Katie?"

"No. Not since the storm began."

"I could have saved her," Andre said bitterly.

"Saved who?" Suzanne questioned.

"Katie."

"What happened?"

"I told her to come with me . . . but she went after Fletcher. He was already dead. I saw the timber hit him full-force. But Katie wouldn't listen. The stupid little bitch . . ."

At Andre's last remark, Mark lost the tight control he had over himself. Without a word of warning, he threw himself at Andre, taking him by surprise and knocking him to the ground. Mark pummeled Andre with punishing blows until three other men dragged him off.

"Katie loved him, you fool! She would rather have died with Christopher than lived without him!"

Glaring at Mark accusingly, Suzanne ran to Andre's side.

Mark, disgusted by the whole scene, shook off the restraining hands of the men who had pulled them apart and stalked off across the sand. He needed time . . . time to come to grips with himself. He knew he would be of little help to anyone else until he had his own emotions under control.

Katie blinked and tried to focus. She had not expected to survive the onslaught of the turbulent waters, yet here she was alive and, seemingly, in one piece. Christopher! His name screamed through her mind. Where was he? She couldn't remember anything after the first terrifying moments when the waters rushed over them. Had she been dreaming or had he really been roused by the water? Regardless, they'd somehow ended up drifting together on the remains of a cottage wall.

Sitting up painfully, Katie felt battered and sore.

Her throat was raw from swallowing sea water and her movements brought about wracking spasms of nausea as her body rid itself of the briny poison. Coughing and gasping, she managed to get to her feet and aching and wet, she staggered forward to search for Christopher.

It was with great relief that she finally found him a few minutes later lying face up on the swampy shore. Katie hurried to him as fast as her weakened legs would carry her.

"Christopher!" Her voice was a croak as she knelt by his side.

Putting her ear to his chest, she was reassured to hear the steady thudding of his heart. Gripping him as best she could, she jockeyed him up to drier ground. It seemed an eternity to her before he finally stirred and opened his eyes. When he looked at her with recognition, she took his hand and kissed his knuckles.

"Thank God you're alive!"

"Where are we?" he asked, his voice as hoarse as hers.

"I can tell you where we aren't . . . but I have no idea where we are," she told him, smiling slightly.

He tried to sit up, but waves of dizziness and nausea struck him and he lay still, waiting for the discomfort to pass.

"I'll be all right in a minute, Katie," he tried to convince her and himself.

Holding her hand tightly, he closed his eyes, but disturbing visions of their storm-tossed night assailed him.

"What's wrong?" She noticed his stricken expression.

"I can't believe we're both alive . . . last night I didn't think we were going to make it."

"I know . . . I know." Crying tears of happiness,

Katie broke down and clung to him for reassurance.

Holding her against him, he pushed her wet hair away from her face and kissed her tenderly.

"The worst is over, love. The worst is over . . ."

Mark headed back toward the wreck of the *Star* after having spent long hours staring out at the still restless sea. He knew that help would be coming for them as soon as word reached the mainland, but he hoped something could be done for Isaac before that. His uncle's condition was serious and Mark didn't want to take any chances while they awaited rescue. It was hard enough dealing with the loss of Katie, but if Isaac dies, too . . .

As he rejoined the group on the *Star*, Mark was surprised to find Suzanne sitting away from the others.

"Suzanne, Isaac isn't —"

"No . . . no. He is the same. But Mark . . ." she sobbed. "They found Lavinia and Wade . . . They're dead!"

Mark stood awkwardly for a moment watching her cry and then, throwing chance to the wind, took her in his arms to comfort her.

"I'm sorry, Suzanne," he spoke softly. "I know how close you were."

Suzanne held tightly to Mark. In the space of a few short hours she had witnessed such carnage and destruction that she doubted she'd ever be the same again.

"I'll take care of her," Andre spoke from behind Mark. "Isaac's been asking for you."

Suzanne went willingly into Andre's waiting arms as Mark walked away without speaking.

Isaac lay with the rest of the injured in a place partially protected from the elements by the hull of the oat.

"Isaac?" Mark spoke. "Andre said that you wanted o see me."

With an effort, the older man's eyes flickered open.

"I'm glad you came," he said painfully. "There's nuch I have to tell you."

"You should rest," Mark tried to quiet him.

"I can't rest until I tell you . . ." His cough was trangled.

"Tell me what?"

"My will . . . I changed my will . . . Suzanne oesn't know. No one does," he gasped for a breath. "I vanted Denis protected. So I made you exec- tor . . . Take care of Denis and Cherie for me. They eed someone and I love them so."

"You'll be taking care of them yourself just as soon s we can get you back to New Orleans."

"Mark." Isaac was suddenly grave. "Mark, I'm ying. I know it. Promise me that you'll do as I ask."

Mark looked away to hide the emotion reflected in is eyes.

"Mark!" Isaac's voice was stronger, demanding an nswer.

"I'll take care of them for you," he promised sol- mnly.

"Good. Good." The tenseness drained out of Isaac t Mark's answer. "I can rest easy now."

The lonely cries of the swamp creatures echoed erily through the blackness of the night as Chris- opher and Katie lay close together, seeking rest. The ong day had been made all the worse by the swarms of ungry, blood-sucking insects which wanted them for heir dinner. In desperation at sundown, Christopher ad fashioned a protective tent of sorts out of Katie's once frilly petticoats.

"Christopher?" Katie spoke.

"What?" he turned to her, pulling her closer.

"Do you really think we should wait here for someone to rescue us or should we try to walk out?"

He admired Katie's courage and stamina, but he also remembered vividly everything Joel had told him about the bayous and canebrakes.

"We have to stay put, Katie," he told her, knowing it wasn't the answer she had wanted to hear.

"But why? No one even knows we're here!"

"They'll come. And when they do, we'll be waiting for them."

For the first time since she was a child, Katie was afraid. She found it hard to believe that anyone would be able to locate them in this Godforsaken place. "We have to get out of here!"

Christopher cradled her near, calming her. "Sweetheart, Joel's told me about travelling in the bayous and it would be suicidal for us to try. We don't even know for sure where we are. So how could we possibly find our way back?"

"I know you're right," she confessed. "But it's hard for me to wait here and do nothing."

Christopher smiled in the darkness, his teeth showing in a flash of white.

"Katie, do you realize that we are alone. I mean really alone for the first time ever?"

Katie managed a smile at the thought. "I hadn't looked at the good side of being stranded with you . . ."

"Don't you think it's time you did?" he asked, bending over to kiss her.

"Absolutely," she agreed, returning his kiss with abandon.

Moving between her legs, he fit himself intimately

to her, rubbing suggestively against her. Her body responded to his urgings without thought as her hips surged upward craving contact with his hardness.

Excited, needing to be one with Katie, Christopher broke off the embrace long enough for them to undress. Finally, she lay nude beneath him and he plunged within her. Lost in the wonder of their embrace, Christopher and Katie surrendered to the fire of their emotions and were swept away in a rush of heated desire. They reached completion together in a crescendo of ecstasy and lay marveling at the wonder of their love.

Katie awoke first the next morning just as the first rays of the sun streaked the eastern horizon with rainbow shades of pink and gold. Slipping carefully from Christopher, she freed herself from their protective shelter and stretched her stiffened, cramped limbs. Never again would she look askance at the canopy bed in her room at Kingsford House. There was a lot to be said for the comforts of civilization.

Thoughts of Kingsford House brought back her worries full force. She had not seen anything of Mark, Uncle Isaac or Suzanne as the storm hit and concern about their safety weighed heavily on her. Thankful that she had Christopher with her, she glanced back over her shoulder to where he lay sleeping. Then leaving him to his rest, she started down toward the water's edge.

The hand that snaked out and grabbed Katie startled her so badly that she couldn't make a sound as she was pulled tightly back against her attacker.

"What have I got here?" The man's sour breath assaulted her as she tried in vain to twist away. "Not a sound, dearie or I'll slit you open without a thought."

He brandished a knife menacingly.

"That's a good girl." He released her arm and spun her about to face him. "You're a pretty one, you are."

He leered at her tattered clothing, his eyes dwelling on her barely covered bosom.

Katie wanted to run away screaming but she realized that she would probably only get herself killed. Deciding to brazen it out, she turn to face him squarely.

"I've been stranded here since the storm on Sunday. I was vacationing at Last Island."

"And you was washed up all the way back here?"

"Yes and . . ."

Holding up a bulging bag, the man laughed wickedly, "You see this sack of jewelry?" At Katie's nod, he continued, "This all came from your island. Now what do you have for me?"

"Nothing, sir," she answered honestly. "But if you take me back to New Orleans safely, I'm sure there would be a substantial reward."

"I think I'll take my reward now." He lunged at Katie and grabbed her.

Katie screamed in terror as his hands tore at her already ragged gown.

Startled to wakefulness by Katie's horrified cry, Christopher sat up. Then, tearing his way out of the small makeshift tent, he ran toward the sound of her desperate call.

At the sight of the stranger attacking Katie, Christopher lost control. Without thought, he attacked, pulling the man from atop her and beating him viciously. Blood streamed from the scavenger's nose as Christopher landed blow after bone-crunching blow. When the man finally sank to the ground, he rushed to Katie's side.

"Are you hurt? If he's touched you, I'll kill

him . . ." Christopher vowed.

Katie was shaking from the shock of it all and trying to hold the bodice of her gown together, she smiled tremulously.

"Hold me . . . Please hold me."

He surrounded her with his warm, powerful arms and pulled her protectively to him. Pressing her to his heart, he rocked her soothingly.

"What will we do with him?" Katie turned to look at the man but in the short moment of their quiet embrace, he had slipped away in his skiff and was now far from the shore, paddling hastily.

"Good riddance," Christopher swore.

"But he might come back . . ."

"If he does, I'll be ready for him," Christopher stated coldly, showing her the knife he'd wrestled away from the looter during the fight.

Katie nodded, but didn't respond. The swamps were more dangerous than she'd imagined . . . and the most vicious beast there was man . . .

Jacqueline La Zear had paid scant attention to the bad storm over the weekend. There had been no social functions to speak of, so she'd spent the time at home, thinking of Mark. Her plans to win him seemed to be going well, but now that he'd gone to Last Island with his family for a month-long vacation, she was worried. If Suzanne Kingsford and Mark still wanted each other, there would be nothing to keep them apart. He had only been gone two weeks, but to Jacqui it seemed an eternity.

She looked up from her needlepoint as Mattie came into the parlor.

"What is it, Mattie?"

"There's somethin' here in the newspaper you'd better see."

"In the paper?" She took it from her and glanced at it curiously.

It took a minute for the headline to sink in . . .

"Mattie? This can't be true! It can't!" she cried coming to her feet in panic as she read the first accounts of the tragedy. All feared lost . . . No survivors . . .

Jacqui was frightened that it might be true, but she felt that if something had really happened to Mark, she would have known. Taking the paper with her, she rushed into her father's study.

"Papa." She handed him the newspaper. "Is this true?"

"I don't know for sure . . ." he began.

"I have to go to Mark. You have to help me get out to the island!"

"According to the report, Jacqui, the island was devastated. There's nothing left."

"But the Kingsfords were there . . . Mark was there . . . He can't be dead! He can't!" she cried and her father came to hold her.

"You go on upstairs and rest while I send someone down to the newspaper office to look into this. As soon as we find out anything new, I'll let you know," he soothed.

"No! I'm not going to sit here for hours waiting. I'm going down to the office myself," she declared.

"But Jacqui . . . it's no place for a lady," he protested.

"Papa, right now I don't feel much like a lady!" she looked at him seriously. "Would you be able to sit back quietly and wait if you thought something had happened to me or mother?"

"That's different. You're family."

"It's not different, Papa. I love Mark Kingsford and I intend to marry him as soon as he proposes!"

And without another word, she turned and left the room.

Joel listened to Robert in stunned disbelief.

"It's not true," he declared, Christopher couldn't be dead!

"I double-checked my sources. I knew you would want me to be certain . . ."

"But how?"

"You know how bad the weather was here Sunday . . . Well, in the Gulf, it was a hurricane."

"And it wiped out the whole island?"

Robert nodded in affirmation.

"Were there any survivors?"

"There was a partial list . . ."

"But he wasn't on it," Joel concluded. "Where are they taking the people who were rescued?"

"There's a boat due in New Orleans in the next day or two . . ."

"I've got to meet it."

"I'll go with you."

Cherie reread the newspaper again to make sure and then went to speak with Denis. She hated lying to him, in fact, she had never had to before, but he was still so weak from the fever . . . Denis's only joy these last few days had been the prospect of Isaac returning to live with them permanently. She found out about the disaster long days ago but had deliberately sheltered Denis from all news of it; the child had suffered enough. And she refused to think the worst, even if Isaac's name wasn't on the list of those who'd been rescued.

"Denis, darling," she greeted him with a kiss. "I

must go out for a while. Will you be all right?"

"Of course, maman."

"Good. I shouldn't be long . . ."

"Don't worry about me," he stated bravely and Cherie smiled.

"I keep forgetting that you are almost a man. I'll see you when I get back."

After kissing him goodbye, Cherie left her home and hastened to the riverfront. The steamer carrying the survivors was due in at any time.

Mark was overjoyed as the port of New Orleans hove into view. Since their evacuation from the island, Isaac's condition had steadily worsened. He had been incoherent most of the time and to Suzanne's mortification, had called repeatedly for Cherie and Denis. Finally, in a frustrated fury, she had stalked away so humiliated that she vowed never to return. Since then, Mark had stayed by his side, witnessing his decline and he knew it was imperative to get him to a surgeon as quickly as possible.

Hurrying back to check on Isaac, he met a steward and asked, "Have any plans been formulated for transporting the injured to the hospital?"

"Yes sir, Mr. Kingsford. We sent word ahead. There should be vehicles waiting at the dock to transport them."

"Good."

Jacqui, with a protesting Mattie in tow, shoved her way through the crowd. For the better part of the week, she had been a waiting word of the survivors' arrival and now, at last, they were here. Her eyes scanned the decks of the steamer as it slipped smoothly into its berth. She knew the possibility of Mark's being on board was small for his name had not appeared on the lists of those still alive. But she still had to come . . . just in case. What had happened between them before didn't matter anymore. If he returned to her safely, she would never let him go again.

Joel and Robert stood back, tense and silent, as the boat docked. There had been no further word on any of the survivors and it was with heavy hearts that they watched the passengers come down the gangplank.

"Mattie! Look! There's Andre Montard and Suzanne Kingsford!" Pushing forward Jacqui ran to them, leaving her servant to follow in her wake. "Suzanne! Thank God you're all right. Andre!"

She hugged them both, but before she could ask about Mark, Suzanne pulled forcefully away from her to glare at the small quadroon woman standing nearby.

"How dare you!" Suzanne hissed loudly. "How dare you show your face in the presence of gentle folk! Slut! Whore!"

Jacqui watched in surprise as Suzanne broke down and Andre had to carry her away to a waiting carriage. The woman Suzanne had made the scene over was not deterred by her attack and pressed on trying to get a glimpse of those leaving the boat.

"Mattie," Jacqui whispered. "What was that all about?"

"I'll tell you later. Ain't nothin' for discussin' in public."

"Mark!" she cried as she waved excitedly to get his attention.

Mark heard her call and broke into a run, "Jacqui!"

Catching her to him, he kissed her eagerly, giving no thought to appearance.

"Mark, thank God you're alive . . . You weren't on

301

the lists . . . I tried for days to find out if . . ."

"Shut up and kiss me, Jacqui. And then tell me you'll marry me."

She threw her arms about his neck and kissed him exuberantly.

"Yes, Mark. I'll marry you. Right now, if you want!"

"I want!" His gaze warmed as he looked at her, but then reality intruded and he frowned.

"What is it?"

"It's Isaac. I have to stay with him . . . he's been injured."

"I'll go with you," she offered.

"No. The hospital is no place for you." Mark caught sight of the stretcher bearing his uncle leaving the steamer and he turned to go. "Go on home and as soon as I know he's going to be all right, I'll come for you."

"All right," she agreed. "I'll be waiting. If you need anything . . ."

"I'll send word." He kissed her softly and then walked to Isaac's side as Jacqui and Mattie happily headed for home.

Cherie had been startled by Suzanne's outburst. The only reason she could think of for her to lose her temper was that Isaac had told her of his plan to leave her. Embarrassed, but not discouraged, Cherie kept a sharp lookout for Isaac, anxious to know that he had made it safely home. It was Mark's conversation with Jacqui that she'd overheard in small bits and pieces that alerted her to Isaac's condition. And when Mark had rushed back to aid the stewards with the stretcher, she had known it was him.

"It's Isaac?"

"Cherie! I'm glad you're here. He's been asking for you."

"He has? With Suzanne aboard?" Cherie was in-

302

credulous.

"Yes. Come with me. We're going straight to the hospital." Mark led her to a carriage and gave the driver instructions.

As he was climbing in, Robert Adams and Christopher's man Joel hailed him.

"Mark! You made it!" Robert shook his hand.

"Robert, it's good to see you. Joel," he acknowledged.

"I saw Isaac as they took him away. Is he going to be all right?"

"I don't know, Robert. I'm on my way to the hospital now . . ."

"We won't keep you . . . We were just wondering if there was any word on Christopher."

Mark looked stricken. "I'm sorry . . . I saw him go down . . . A timber caught him and then . . ." Mark paused. "Where are you staying? Can I meet you later?"

"At my townhouse. Please come any time. And if you need anything—please let us know."

"I'll try to stop by tonight, but it will all depend on my uncle's condition."

"Of course. We'll be waiting to hear from you."

With a nod, Mark climbed inside the carriage where Cherie awaited him and they drove off toward the hospital.

It was night and Suzanne was glad. Dressed in a flowing negligee, she sat before the mirror at her vanity brushing her hair in angry strokes. It had been bad enough that her husband called for his mistress while he was delirious, but to come face to face with her first thing off the boat . . . well, the incident had totally shattered her sense of well-being.

Suzanne was through playing games with Isaac. If he wanted a divorce, as shameful as it was, she would give it to him. No longer would she suffer the humiliation of being second . . . no third . . . in his life. It was over.

Suzanne was grateful that Andre had been there to help her. He had seen her home and helped to calm her considerably before going home himself.

The maid's knock at her bedroom door surprised her and she called to her to come in.

"Miz Suzanne."

"Yes, Lucy?" Suzanne regretted Patsy's death on the island and she wondered how long it would take her to find another servant as good and as trustworthy as she had been.

"Mr. Montard is here to see you."

"Andre?"

"Yes, ma'am."

"Tell him I'll be right down." Suzanne felt happy for the first time in weeks. "Then you may go for the night."

Lucy's eyes widened perceptibly, but she answered a humble, "Yes, ma'am."

Suzanne waited long enough for Lucy to reach her quarters before going to see Andre. Leaving her hair down she perfumed herself and donned a silky wrapper before descending to greet him.

"Andre," her tone was warm with welcome, and more, as she moved gracefully across the parlor to him.

Andre's gaze devoured her scantily clad beauty and he realized, not for the first time, that he had been fool to ever have let her go.

"Suzanne. I'm glad to see you're feeling better," he smiled.

"It's all because of you, Andre," she told him. "You

made me feel wanted at the most desperate moment of my life and I love you for that."

"You are wanted, Suzanne. A man would be a fool not to want you . . ." he complimented, thinking of Fletcher's rejection of her.

"Don't be a fool, then, Andre," she spoke seductively, going into his arms. "Love me."

Andre had only a fleeting sense of regret that she wasn't Katie before he succumbed to his natural desires. Suzanne, whose only motive was to forget her humiliating scene with Isaac's slut, had no thoughts at all. Fletcher was dead . . . as well as her marriage . . . Andre was the answer to her prayers. He would make her feel attractive again and tonight that was just what she needed.

"I'm going to leave for a few hours, Cherie. But I'll be back as soon as I can," Mark informed her.

"I'll be here," she said. "I've already sent word home that I wouldn't be back until very late, so there is no need for you to hurry."

"Well, if you need me, I'll be at Robert Adams's residence."

"Fine."

Mark and Cherie had been at Isaac's bedside since their arrival that afternoon and during that time they had become friends. No longer was Mark ashamed or intimidated by her. He found Cherie to be a very warm, intelligent woman and now he completely understood Isaac's predicament.

As he left the hospital, Mark knew he would have to hurry back, if for no other reason than to relieve Cherie. She had been with Isaac all day and Mark was truly impressed by her devotion.

As his carriage arrived at Robert's house, Mark was

welcomed by Joel and Robert.

"Come in. Sit down." Robert gestured him into the manly comfort of the study.

"Thank you, Robert."

"Would you care for a drink?"

"No thanks, but coffee would go well."

After they'd settled in, Robert broached the subject he'd dreaded.

"I know this will be painful for you, but we must know . . . Did you see what happened to Christopher?"

Mark understood. "I was in the hotel lobby and he was trying to reach Katie in the dining room when all hell broke loose . . . The windows blew out and then the walls went . . . I saw a board or something knock him down and he didn't get back up."

"What about Katie?" Robert asked as Joel stood silently in the background.

"Andre said she was with Christopher when the water . . ."

"They were together?"

"From what I can find out."

"And their bodies weren't recovered?" Joel pressed.

"No."

Robert looked at Joel, their expressions equally determined.

"Where have the search parties been looking? Have they gone back in along the coast?"

"They've just started there. Evidently the scavengers have been hiding out in the bayous . . ."

"Scavengers?"

"There were looters everywhere and we had nothing to fight them off with . . . They were like vultures, preying on the dead . . ."

"We have to look, Robert," Joel stated firmly.

"I agree, Joel. And the sooner we get out there, the

better."

"You're going out?" Mark interrupted.

"At daybreak."

"Then I'll come, too."

"What about Isaac?"

"There's nothing more I can do to help him. Cherie is with him now."

"Meet us at the Adams's Warehouse landing at sunup, then."

"I'll be there," Mark assured them, glad that they were going to take some action.

He had felt so frustrated and defeated. At least now he would know that he had done all he could to save them.

Fourteen

The Aftermath

Joel stood on the steamer's promenade deck and watched in grave disappointment as Last Island faded from view. They had searched the beaches thoroughly but had found no trace of Katie or Christopher—alive or dead.

Joel and Robert had both been stunned by the total devastation wreaked by the hurricane. The once subtropical paradise was no longer a thriving resort community. Stripped bare by the storm, the island lay unprotected against the elements. The useless, hulking remains of the *Star* so deeply imbedded in the sands only added to the air of death and decay.

Shaking his head in a forlorn gesture, Joel contemplated the possibility of a future without Christopher. There would be no way that he alone could continue their work at Greenwood and Dee still had not been freed.

"What's wrong, Joel?" Mark asked as he joined him on deck.

"I'm worried, Mark. I had really expected to find

Christopher today."

"I think we all were," Mark agreed.

"Where are we bound now? Robert isn't heading back to New Orleans already, is he?"

"No. We're going to check the coastal areas, just on the chance that they might have been washed up on shore."

"Good. Somehow I feel we're so close . . ."

"I know," Mark paused. "I hope it's not just our imaginations working overtime."

"What is?" Robert broke in as he came out on deck.

"Joel and I both feel that Christopher and Katie are alive . . ."

"I feel the same way, too," Robert confided. "Why else would we be searching these isolated back-washes for them?"

"I'm glad we're not going to give up yet," Mark said gratefully. "I wouldn't be able to live with myself if I thought I hadn't done everything possible to find them. Especially after having made it through myself." He smiled crookedly at Robert and Joel. "There's a lot of guilt connected with being a survivor . . ."

Robert and Joel didn't respond. They were familiar with the trauma of watching friends and family in dire trouble and being unable to go to their aid.

"We're going to do our best to find them . . . we'll just have to pray that our best is good enough."

It was late afternoon and the August heat was oppressive. In their makeshift shelter, Katie napped fitfully.

A short distance away Christopher sat unmoving. His shoulders slumped in defeat; his expression was one of sad acceptance. No longer could he pretend that help was on its way. He had finally been forced to face the ugly truth. If they were to survive they would have to save themselves.

Guilt plagued him, as he shook his head in self-condemnation. Had he killed the scavenger who'd attacked Katie, they would be in possession of his boat. But his concern for her that day had overridden his common sense. Without a skiff, their trek back to civilization would be long and treacherous, especially since they'd both lost their shoes during the storm. Barefoot or not, though, Christopher knew that they had to try walking out.

Glancing over at Katie, his gaze softened, easing the grave lines of worry that were newly carved into his features. Somehow, some way he would see her to safety.

Getting slowly to his feet, he went back to her and kissed her awake.

"Katie, darling," he whispered against her lips.

Katie opened her eyes to look up at him with undisguised adoration. "Hello," she murmured sleepily. "Have I been sleeping long?"

"About an hour or so, I guess."

"I'm sorry."

"No need to be. You were tired."

Katie reached up to caress his cheek gently. "You look really worried, is there something else?"

"We can't wait here any longer Katie. If help was coming it would have been here by now," he explained seriously.

"I knew we'd have to do something soon, but I wasn't sure what . . ."

"We'll have to walk out, it's the only way."

"Are we going to follow the bay?"

"That's the safest. I don't think we'd last long if we tried to go inland."

"I know what you mean. I heard the tales about the alligators in the swamps." Katie shuddered at the thought of the big, hungry, log-like creatures.

"According to Joel, those are not tales, they're true stories."

"Then let's be sure to stay out of their territory, all right?" she smiled.

"Good idea. We'll plan on heading east first thing tomorrow morning," Christopher felt a little more hopeful as he kissed her again.

The enforced intimacy of these past days together had made him realize more than ever just how precious she was to him.

Katie lay still, enjoying the sensuous play of Christopher's lips upon hers. During this time they'd spent together, she had come to know him better and the more she learned about him, the more she had loved him.

"I love you, Christopher," Katie told him honestly.

Christopher pulled away and stared down at her. He treasured their closeness, but he was also aware for the first time of what a great responsibility loving someone could be. The days of only taking care of himself were over. He loved Katie and wanted to protect her from all harm.

"Oh, Katie," he sighed. "How did we end up here?"

"I thought you liked being alone with me!" she complained in false indignation. "You mean you're not having a good time?"

Christopher couldn't hold back his smile and Katie was relieved to know that she had lightened his mood.

"Of course I'm having a good time," he insisted. "I'm alone with you in a remote," Christopher cleared his throat. "Very private resort, of sorts. The accommodations are rustic and leave a bit to be desired . . . but on the whole it's been memorable."

Katie laughed happily. "You forgot to mention how much you've been enjoying the wild life."

"Oh, yes," he kissed her quickly. "Our friends the mosquitos, who are almost big enough to ride and all the other assorted wonderful creatures of the night. Remind me to take you somewhere a little less exciting on our next vacation. All right?"

"All right. But frankly, there's one part of this I wouldn't have traded for the world."

"What?" he couldn't find anything to be optimistic about.

"Making love with you any time I want to," she smiled invitingly as she pulled him down to her. "Like right now."

And Christopher didn't protest as Katie took the lead in their mating.

With no thought to modesty, she shed her clothes and unbuttoning his pants, stroked him to hardness with expert caresses.

"No," she denied him as he reached out to touch her. "I want you to relax and enjoy."

Smiling at Katie quizzically, he folded his arms behind his head and lay back as she undid his shirt and pushed it aside to expose his chest. Trailing her fingers over the powerful muscles of his shoulders she paused to tease his flat male nipples before slipping lower to trace a path of tempting fire over his lean, trim stomach.

Christopher tensed as she moved up over him to touch her lips to his, trapping his hardness between them. The satin of her belly created an exquisite friction as she rubbed against him. When he could bear it no longer, he clasped her to him and in one easy movement, rolled, bringing her beneath him.

"You're right, Katie," he murmured as he slipped within her hungry body. "There are definitely benefits to coming to these out-of-the-way resorts."

Smiling softly at him, she drew him down to her, meeting him in a poignant kiss that stirred his heart.

Fused in love's embrace, he sought release from the reality of their situation, if only for a little while. Thrusting desperately into her welcoming warmth, he climaxed quickly with Katie and, then he lay together with her enjoying the peace of the moment.

Mark and Joel were frustrated and angry. Robert had just informed them that they would have to give up the search and head back to New Orleans the following day.

"Damn! I knew it was coming, but I had no idea it would be this soon," Mark declared heatedly.

"I know. But Robert's got a point. We've been checking the coast for the better part of four days and there's been no sign of them. Maybe they've already been picked up and taken to New Orleans," Joel said optimistically.

"Do you really believe that?" Mark was skeptical.

"No, but until I have proof I refuse to accept that they're really dead." Turning away from Mark, Joel stared out at the coastal shore again hoping against hope for some sign of Christopher.

Travel had been slow the past few days, but Christopher and Katie both felt that they were making steady progress. Carrying the remnants of Katie's petticoats with them to provide their nightly mosquito netting, they had trudged barefoot ever eastward along the marshy shoreline.

Katie, whose long ragged skirts had proven to be quite a hindrance, had torn the offending material off at knee's length so she could keep up more easily with Christopher's long strides. But now, as they stopped to rest, Christopher found the sight of her slim, well-shaped calves most distracting.

Katie, however, was giving little thought to anything but her sore feet. Rubbing them tenderly she glanced up to see his eyes upon her.

"I don't know how the slaves do it," she remarked.

"Do what?"

"Go without shoes."

"I suppose they get used to it after a while. Just like we're going to," he grinned at her as he lifted her legs across his lap to massage them for her.

"That feels wonderful. Thank you," she groaned, gratefully. "You know when I was little I used to run barefoot all the time. I thought it was fun, then. But in those days, I always knew what I was stepping on. Now, when I wade through that muck . . ." she shivered in exaggerated disgust.

"Unnerving, isn't it?" he agreed. "It's hard to believe that Dee did this alone carrying her baby."

"Dee? Your housekeeper?"

Christopher nodded darkly, "Yes. She was running away from Andre because . . ."

"Why?" Katie looked at him questioningly.

Katie wondered what fate in life could be so horrible that a woman would brave the unknown of the wilderness with a small child rather than face it head on. She found running away from trouble hard to understand. No problem was ever solved by hiding from it.

"She was the slave I told you about . . . the one he'd abused."

"It must have been horrible for her . . . I mean if she chose the swamps over slavery . . ." Deep in thought Katie fell silent.

"It was. Slavery is a horrible institution," he spoke

314

his true feelings without thought.

"But you own slaves!" Katie accused, confused by his statement.

"That's true. Since I won Greenwood I am a slaveowner."

"But what about Joel? He came downriver with you."

"Pretending to be my servant," Christopher concluded for her.

Katie was really puzzled now. "He's a free man?"

"It's a long story, Katie, and I'm not sure you'll want to hear it."

"Why?"

"Because . . . things are not always what they seem to be." His answer was evasive.

"What do you mean?" Katie pressed.

"You are right. I don't own Joel. I gave him his freedom right after I bought him and took him up North."

"Good."

"Good?" Christopher was surprised by her reaction.

Since Katie was the niece of Isaac Kingsford, one of the biggest slaveowners in Louisiana, he had expected her to support the Southern institution without question, just as Edward Courtois and James Williams had.

"Mark and I were just talking about all this . . ."

"You were?"

Katie shook her head, "Uncle Isaac has a quadroon mistress named Cherie. He's been in love with her for years, but he can't marry her because she's black. So he keeps her in a house on Rampart Street and supposedly she's happy. But I wonder . . ."

"It's even worse when the woman is a slave, Katie. For then she has no choice or option. The man can do as he pleases with her and no one cares," Christopher

315

said bitterly.

"Is that what Andre did to Dee?"

"Yes. For over a year, until Joel and I managed to get Greenwood away from the Montards. Joel and Dee are married."

"So you came back here to save Dee?" Katie understood.

"And anyone else we could help."

"How?"

"We're working with the Underground Railroad."

"You are!"

Christopher nodded.

"I am so proud of you!" Katie hugged him.

Christopher was relieved by Katie's acceptance and admitted to her, "I was worried."

"About what?"

"About telling you the truth. I wasn't sure how you would react."

"Well, there was no need to worry. My father taught us that it was wrong to buy and sell human beings. That was one of his main reasons for leaving the South so many years ago."

"Your father was right. Too bad he didn't stay to fight against it."

"I'll help you, Christopher." Katie waited expectantly for his answer.

The last thing he wanted to do was to expose her to danger, but, regardless, as his wife she would be involved.

"I could use your help." He reached out to touch her cheek gently. "We'll be good together."

"We already are," she told him confidently as they started off once more in search of civilization.

It was long hours later when they rounded a point in the bay and began searching for a dry, relatively safe place to spend the night. Tired and nearly famished,

Katie paused by the water's edge to gaze out across the quiet blue expanse while Christopher explored farther back into the wilds.

The cry erupted from her without conscious thought, "Christopher!"

Thinking that Katie was in danger, he ran quickly in her direction, knife in hand. When he broke free of the trees, he caught sight of Katie and the boat at the same time. Snatching up the bundle of her petticoats, he untied it and waved the yards of white cloth in the air, desperately trying to attract their attention.

"Look!" Joel shouted as he spotted what looked to be a white flag on a small point of land.

"Someone's out there!" Mark took off at a run for the pilot house. "Get Robert!"

It seemed to take forever for the ship to draw near and Katie collapsed happily into Christopher's arms as she finally recognized Mark on deck.

"Mark's alive! And he didn't give up!" she cried.

"Neither did Joel or Robert. Look!" They broke apart waving excitedly at the steamer.

"It's them!" Mark shouted as he recognized his sister in the distance.

A skiff was lowered and two deck hands rowed directly toward them, their powerful strokes sending the craft skimming lightly across the water.

"Thank you! Thank you!" Katie hugged each of her rescuers.

Christopher was more restrained but just as happy as they climbed into the boat and headed back toward the steamer.

Katie was hauled unceremoniously out of the boat and into Mark's arms as the deck hands quickly secured their craft.

"I can't believe it!" Mark was overcome with joyful emotion and kissed her repeatedly. "Do you realize

317

that we were about to give you up for dead?"

"Oh, Mark!" was all Katie could say as she hugged him fiercely. "I am so glad you didn't."

Christopher climbed up on deck and embraced both Joel and Robert.

"Thank you." His voice was hoarse with emotion. "I don't know how much longer we could have gone on . . ."

"Don't even think about it," Robert smiled, greatly relieved to find his friend alive and well.

"You would have made it," Joel put in drily. "Katie wouldn't have let you quit."

Katie heard him and came to kiss his cheek. "You're right, Joel."

Smiling she greeted Robert as Christopher shook hands with Mark.

"Are you hungry?" Mark finally asked as the steamer backed away from the shore and headed for New Orleans.

Katie laughed loudly. "Hungry isn't the word for it! Do you have any idea what it's like to live on raw fish and rain water?"

"No and I don't want to find out. Come on. I'm sure there's plenty to eat in the galley."

Ready for a hot meal, they eagerly followed Mark inside.

Katie knew that in all her life she'd never tasted anything so delicious as the stew the cook served her. Devouring every bite with undisguised gusto, she finally sat back contentedly and looked up to find the men watching her proudly.

"It was good," she smiled and they laughed, appreciating her honesty.

"Tell me," Christopher spoke up as he finished his meal, too. "How were you rescued, Mark?"

"I was with Isaac . . ."

318

"Uncle Isaac? Is he all right?" Katie worried.

"He was injured, Katie. When I left New Orleans, he was in the hospital and Cherie was with him."

"Cherie?" Katie was confused.

"It's not a pleasant story."

"Was Suzanne killed?"

"Far from it."

"Then why . . . ?"

"Isaac and I hung onto a board together the whole night of the storm until right before sunup, the current pushed us back ashore."

"Thank heaven."

"I know. But once we were on land, I found out how badly Isaac had been injured."

"What did you do?"

"I started walking back in what I thought was the direction of the hotel, carrying him."

"Did many survive?" Christopher asked.

"Quite a few, thanks to the captain of the *Star*."

"You mean the *Star* made it through the storm?"

"It was the only thing that did. Captain Smith and his crew spent the entire night dragging people out of the water."

Katie shuddered in remembrance. "So what happened to Uncle Isaac?"

"Andre found me and helped me get back."

"Andre made it?" Christopher asked, not exactly pleased by the news.

"Andre and Suzanne both," Mark informed him. "But when I got Isaac back to the boat, he was delirious and kept calling for Cherie."

"Oh, no!"

"Who's Cherie?"

"His mistress," Mark explained. "Anyway, Suzanne was with him at the time and was completely and totally embarrassed. She stormed away from him and never came back."

Katie groaned. "Did Uncle Isaac realize what had happened?"

"No. He's been incoherent since we were rescued."

"What about Cherie?"

"She was waiting on the dock in New Orleans when we tied up and she's been with him ever since."

"She truly loves him, doesn't she?"

"Yes, she does, Katie."

"So, Suzanne has left Uncle Isaac?"

"It looks that way. She was furious."

"Have you spoken to her?"

"No. And I don't intend to, anytime soon, either. The La Zears have offered me a place to stay and when we get back I'm taking them up on it."

"Who am I supposed to stay with?" Katie asked, not wanting to move back in with Suzanne.

"You'll be getting married right away, won't you?" Mark smiled at Christopher. "Now that you've been compromised, so to speak, there's no choice but to have a hasty wedding."

"I hadn't thought of that," she brightened.

"It sounds good to me," Christopher agreed. "We'll make all the arrangements just as soon as we get back."

"I still want to know what happened to you two during the storm."

"I was unconscious for quite a while after the board hit me." Christopher touched the bruise that remained from his injury.

"Andre wouldn't let me go to him," Katie related. "So I had to fight him off. By that time the waves were coming in and it was all I could do to keep Christopher's head above water. I don't remember too much after that. We ended up floating on some kind of timber and then the next thing I knew we were washed up back in the bayou."

"I know I came around for a while. I think just long enough to get us up on those boards, but then I must have passed out."

"How long were you stuck in the bayou?" Joel asked.

"Since the Monday after the storm."

The three rescuers shook their heads in sympathy.

"I'm sorry we didn't get to you sooner," Robert apologized.

"Robert, we are grateful that you showed up at all." Katie and Christopher looked at each other seriously before turning back to their friends. "Thank you."

It was late morning when they had arrived back in the city and they had gone straight to Robert's house to freshen up. Christopher and Katie had both needed new clothes, so a servant had been quickly dispatched on that errand while another had been sent ahead to the hospital to check on Isaac's condition.

Katie took the time alone to indulge in a long, soothing bath. Bathing was one feminine luxury that she'd never fully appreciated until she had been deprived of it for so long. Now, as she lingered in the perfumed water, she relished the silken feel of it upon her sunburned limbs. A small, impish smile lifted her lips as she thought of what Suzanne's reaction would be to her reddened face and arms. It was only the servant's knock that finally drew her from the warm comfort of the bath.

Dressed, and once again looking the proper young miss, she descended to the study to join the men.

Christopher grinned as he noted Katie's sunburned nose. Setting his drink aside, he went to her and kissed her cheek.

"I must say, Katie, you look stunning," he admired her trim figure in the cool-looking muslin day-gown she wore. Then in a stage whisper, he added, "But I like the other dress better. Did you save it?"

If Katie blushed, no one could tell.

"As a matter of fact, I did. I thought I might start a new fashion trend. It was certainly a lot less constricting than this," she teased. Then turning to Mark, "What have you heard from the hospital?"

"The news is not good, Katie," he informed her. "They don't expect him to hold on much longer."

Sadness clouded her usually animated features. "We'd better go, then."

"I'm coming, too," Christopher told her and they left the house together.

The Adams's carriage pulled to a stop in front of the hospital. Mark and Christopher climbed down first and then Christopher turned to help Katie out. She smiled at him gratefully, for she was having trouble re-learning how to maneuver in her ponderous hoop-skirts. Once she was safely on the ground, he offered her his arm and they followed Mark into the building.

They found Isaac's room easily and as usual Cherie was at his side. Katie was horrified by the change in her uncle's appearance. Gone was the robust man who loved to tease her. Now, there remained only a shell of the former man. His coloring was gray and lifeless and his features seemed somehow shrunken. Katie hesitated in the doorway, but Mark went on in. Christopher stood supportively behind her, his hands resting protectively on her shoulders.

Cherie rose to greet Mark. "I'm so glad you're returned. The messenger you sent said you'd found her . . ."

"Katie," Mark called softly, motioning her into the room.

"Cherie, this is Katie, my sister. Katie this is Cherie Delabarre."

Katie was all set to say the polite, correct thing to Cherie, but when the small woman hugged her tenderly, all thoughts fled.

"He has been worrying about you since the beginning . . . refusing to give up hope. Perhaps now he will rest easy. Come . . ."

Cherie took Katie to Isaac's bedside and touching his arm gently, she tried to rouse him.

"Isaac, Katie's returned." When there was little response, Cherie turned to Katie. "Speak to him . . . Maybe the sound of your voice . . ."

"Uncle Isaac," she began nervously. "Mark has rescued me again."

The teasing note she tried to keep in her tone was almost strangled by her concern for him.

"Katie . . ." When he spoke, his words were muffled and strained.

"I'm right here. Mark found me." She took his hand as he tried to focus on her.

"Are you all right?"

"I am, now that I'm back."

"Good." He sighed heavily and then drew a shuddering breath. "Your young man . . . ?"

"He's here too." She called over her shoulder. "Christopher."

He came to stand at her side.

"Do you intend to marry her?" His voice was suddenly more fierce as he defended his niece's honor.

"I do, sir. As soon as possible."

Isaac nodded tiredly in response. "See that you do. She loves you."

"And I love her," he told Isaac seriously.

"Mark," Isaac called him to his bedside. "Write to your father . . . and see that they are married right away."

"Yes, sir." Mark smiled at the thought of his ordering Christopher and Katie to do anything they didn't want to do.

Isaac's breathing was labored as he lay back against the pillows and closed his eyes.

"We'd better go," Katie whispered to Mark and Christopher.

Cherie followed them outside. "I am so glad that you are safe."

"Thank you." Katie already liked her and she wondered briefly why Isaac had ever married Suzanne.

"Have you heard anything from Suzanne?" Mark asked.

"No, nothing. And at this point, it's best that she stay away," Cherie said fiercely. "I don't want to upset him."

Katie and Mark both nodded in understanding.

"We'll be back again tomorrow. Do you need anything?"

"No," she responded. "No, I'm holding up all right."

"Should you need us for anything, we'll be at Robert Adams's house tonight."

"Thank you, Mark." Her expression was earnest and Mark kissed her cheek before following Katie and Christopher from the hospital.

"What do you think, Mark? Do I look good enough?" Katie worried, glancing again at her reflection in the cheval glass.

"You look beautiful, Katie," he said earnestly. "You couldn't have found a more perfect wedding dress."

Katie wore an ivory satin gown of simple yet striking design that they had chosen that morning on a very hurried shopping spree.

"You really think so?"

"I know so." He pulled a jewelry box from his coat pocket. "Here, I have a surprise for you."

"A present? For me?"

"I'd be honored if you'd wear it tonight."

Katie opened the velvet box to reveal a single strand of creamy, iridescent pearls.

"Oh, Mark! They're lovely. Help me put them on." She handed him the necklace.

"I wish Father could be here to give you away, Katie," he remarked as he fastened the delicate clasp.

"You did write to him?"

"Yesterday, as soon as we got back from the hospital."

"Good. It's a shame that Uncle Isaac can't be here either."

Mark nodded in agreement as he turned her to face him.

"Are you sure that you're doing the right thing?"

She smiled at his brotherly concern. "I'm positive. I love him, Mark. I don't want to ever be without him."

Mark returned her smile, then, reassured by her certainty. While he knew that the Southern code of conduct demanded that Christopher marry her, he would not let any stupid moralistic rule ruin his sister's life. If she didn't want to marry him, she didn't have to.

"Good. Let's go on down. Christopher was already downstairs waiting for you when I came up."

"He was?"

"I think he's as eager for this marriage as you are," Mark teased, guiding her from the room.

Christopher had indeed been waiting in the study with Robert and Joel. Thanks to Robert's influence with church officials, the wedding had been arranged on only one day's notice and for that he was grateful.

There was nothing he wanted more than to join his life with Katie's. He felt somehow incomplete whenever they were apart and fully intended that they never be separated again.

At the sound of Mark and Katie on the stairs, he hurried to the door to watch her descend. In her full-skirted ivory gown, she seemed an ethereal vision to him. Her hair was pinned up in a sophisticated style of soft looping curls and around her neck she wore an elegant pearl necklace.

"The reverend is ready," Robert said from behind Christopher, breaking into his thoughts.

"Of course." Tearing his gaze away from Katie, he accompanied Robert and Joel into the main parlor where Jacqui and the minister awaited them.

Katie had caught a glimpse of Christopher in the hall by the study door before he'd disappeared into the parlor.

"Are you ready?" Mark asked, his question steadying her excitement.

"Oh, yes," she told him anxiously.

And Mark led her into the parlor and presented her to Christopher where he stood before the minister.

"And you give this woman in matrimony to this man?"

"I do," Mark answered solemnly.

"Then let us begin . . ."

As his voice droned on, bonding their lives together, Katie found herself remembering all the times she'd been with Christopher. Their first explosive meeting—his concern for her—the first time they'd made love . . . Yes, she loved this man. Of that she had no doubt.

Staring up at him during the final recital of their vows, Katie studied his lean good looks, memorizing every nuance so that years from now she would be able to recall every detail of their wedding. Christopher felt Katie's gaze upon him and turned to look at her as he pledged his life to her.

"I, Christopher, take thee Kathleen . . ."

Katie thrilled as he spoke the words that would bind them together for all time. She repeated her vows with the same intensity and watched, enthralled, as Christopher slipped the plain gold band on her ring finger.

"I now pronounce you man and wife. What God has joined together let no man put asunder."

At the culminating words, he swept her into a possessive embrace and kissed her deeply.

"I'm sorry we didn't have time for more," he apologized, worrying that she might have wanted a big wedding.

"It doesn't matter. What's important is that we're together. Now and forever." She reached up to kiss him quickly before turning to receive the best wishes of the others.

After feasting on the special dinner Robert had arranged for them, they were whisked off by carriage to the St. Charles Hotel where Mark had reserved the bridal suite in their name.

"Mr. and Mrs. Fletcher. Welcome to the St. Charles," the desk clerk greeted them. "Lyle will see you to your suite."

"Thank you," Christopher replied, smiling at the thought of having finally made Katie his own.

They were quiet and reserved as they followed the bellboy to the most elegant suite of rooms in the hotel.

Andre downed his drink at the bar of the St. Charles. He had just met with one of the investigators, who had been checking on Fletcher's background, to tell him that there was no need to continue the investigation. With Fletcher dead and no relations to speak of, it would be a simple matter for the Montards to purchase Greenwood from his estate.

Andre was pleased that at least something had worked out well. Not that he was unhappy with the way things were. He and Suzanne had resumed their passionate affair and had spent most every night together since their return.

Andre's only concern was the gossip that might ensue from Suzanne's refusal to visit Isaac. He had tried to convince her that for appearance's sake she should go to the hospital, but she steadfastly refused. Knowing better than to press Suzanne, he had let it drop.

Andre thought of Katie as he finished off his drink. There had never been another woman who had affected him as deeply as Katie had and he regretted that they hadn't gotten closer before her death. He had wanted Katie badly and he supposed the disappointment would haunt him the rest of his days. But Andre was a realist to a certain extent, too. He knew that life went on and that there was no use dwelling on "what-might-have beens."

He refused to believe that she loved Fletcher enough to die with him, as Mark had seemed to believe. More than likely, she had never seen anyone injured before and the shock had caused her to behave irrationally.

Paying the bartender, he left the saloon and headed across the main lobby.

"Mr. and Mrs. Fletcher. Welcome to the St. Charles . . ."

The desk clerk's words stopped Andre in mid-stride and he glanced quickly toward the desk. Andre blinked in confused surprise as he saw Christopher escort Katie up the magnificent central staircase. Mr. and Mrs. Fletcher? How could that be? They were supposed to be dead!

328

When they were out of sight, he approached the desk clerk.

"Was that Christopher Fletcher?"

"Yes, sir. It was."

"I didn't know he was married."

"They're on their honeymoon. I believe he and Miss Kingsford were just married this afternoon."

Andre nodded, stunned. "Thank you."

Andre walked away, confused. How had they been rescued? And from where? He shook his head in dismay.

Instead of being happy that Katie had survived, he was furious that she had married Fletcher. Why? After all, he himself had proposed to her! The only answers that made any sense to him at all were that she thought him killed during the storm . . . or that circumstances had forced her to marry. Determined to find out the truth, he would meet with Katie alone, as soon as possible.

In the meantime, Andre went in search of the man he'd just met with; since Fletcher was still alive, the investigation had to be continued at all costs.

Katie smiled invitingly as Christopher shed the last of his clothes and joined her on the wide, comfortable bed. Lying down next to her, he took her in his arms and held her close. Their eyes met, speaking volumes without uttering a single word, and his mouth sought hers in a fiery kiss that left her breathless with its intensity.

Murmuring her name in a litany of desire, Christopher molded her to him. Katie, aroused by his nearness, moved restlessly beneath the erotic weight of his body.

"Do you realize," he whispered softly, stroking the

329

long fine strands of her golden hair back away from her face. "That this is the first time we've ever made love in a bed?"

"Um," she nodded, seeking his lips for a short, quick kiss. "And it's not a moment too soon as far as I'm concerned."

Aggressively pulling him closer, Katie took the initiative. Pressing kisses on his throat and chest, they rolled to their sides, legs intertwined, straining together. The feel of his manhood, hard and proud, against her thigh encouraged her and she no longer wanted to wait. Reaching down with eager fingers, she guided him to her.

Christopher groaned at her sensuous invitation and slipped within the hot-velvet sheath of her body. Once imbedded tenderly in her moist, silken depths, he paused to savor the deep sense of oneness that this most intimate joining with her gave him.

Katie looked up at him as he supported himself above her. His eyes were dark with carefully controlled passion as he dipped his head to kiss her gently.

"You feel so good to me, Katie."

And without answering she wrapped her legs around his hips pulling him even more deeply inside her body. Christopher shuddered with the rush of sexual pleasure that her movements brought and gave up the thought of prolonging this moment as she arched temptingly beneath him. Meeting her twisting hips with excited thrusts, he slipped his hands beneath her and, cupping her buttocks, held her tightly to him.

As a sudden explosion of delight rocked her, Katie clung to him, his hard, driving body sending her spinning off into passion's paradise. Sensing her ecstasy, Christopher could hold back no longer as love's deepest pleasure drove him on, over the brink of total fulfillment.

When at last he could speak, long moments later, the words were hoarse with emotion.

"Mrs. Fletcher, you are wonderful."

Katie smiled dreamily, curling on her side against him.

"Thank you," she murmured softly, running her hand over the mat of hair on his broad chest.

They lay quietly together amidst the rumpled bedclothes, replete and content, yet eagerly ready to begin their new life together.

Suzanne welcomed Andre with a passionate kiss. Now that they were lovers again, she wondered how she'd ever managed to let him go in the first place. But when he returned her embrace with less than his usual ardor, she drew back, frowning.

"What's wrong?" she asked, accurately reading his mood.

"Quite a lot, actually. I just left the St. Charles Hotel and guess who was in the lobby?"

Suzanne was completely stumped. Who could have upset Andre so thoroughly?

"Don't play games," she said irritably. "Just tell me."

"You'd better sit down, then," he said sarcastically. "Because it was your precious niece and her new husband."

"Niece? Husband?"

"Katie is alive and according to what I was able to find out, married Christopher Fletcher late this afternoon."

"How can she be alive? She's been missing for almost two weeks . . ." Suzanne was angry and confused. "And Christopher . . . Surely when that timber hit him . . ."

"They are both alive and well, Suzanne. Make no mistake, for I saw them myself." Andre's tone was bitter.

Suzanne nodded and took his earlier advice, sinking down on the loveseat. "I wonder where they've been staying . . . all of them."

"With Robert Adams."

She looked up. "I had wondered where Mark had gone."

"Surely with Isaac in the hospital you hadn't expected him to come back here?"

She shrugged, "It doesn't matter now. I'm done with them . . . all of them."

"Well, I'm not!" Andre was still seething over Katie's marriage. "There was no reason for her to marry so quickly . . . especially to Fletcher."

"You're not going to pursue this any further?" she condemned.

Andre slanted her a dangerous look. "You needn't concern yourself with what I intend to do, my dear."

Suzanne fought down the urge to feel insulted. "Of course not, but surely if she's gone ahead and married Christopher, that's some indication of her feelings."

"Not necessarily. Circumstances . . ."

"You're a fool if you believe that!" she drilled the words at him with emphasis. "Need I remind you that during the storm she fought you off so she could get to his side?"

"Shut up, Suzanne."

"Leave, Andre!" she shouted. "I refuse to be your substitute for Katie. If and when you decide that you want *me*, I'll be here. Until then, don't waste my time."

Morning came far too soon for Katie's wishes. Having made love for the better part of the night, she wanted to spend the entire day in bed, but Christopher roused her early. After sharing a light breakfast in their rooms, they left for Robert's house. Katie met Mark so that together they could go to the hospital to visit Isaac and Christopher went with Joel to meet with their factor and to take care of some other business arrangements.

Cherie, worn and exhausted from a night of waiting for the end, looked up dully as Katie and Mark entered the room.

"Cherie?" Mark worried.

"Thank heaven you've come." She stood wearily and hugged Mark. "They say he could go at any time now . . . I've been here with him all night."

"Do you want to rest? Katie and I will stay."

"No . . . I can't leave him now." Her voice was pitiful as she glanced at Isaac's inert body.

Mark walked her back to her chair and held her hand supportively.

"Has he been conscious at all?"

"Off and on. He always asks for Denis . . ." Cherie began to cry softly. "I'm sorry . . . I just hate to see him suffering so."

"We feel the same way, Cherie." Katie came to stand by the bed.

Isaac's eyes flickered open and he stared at them unknowing for a moment before sanity appeared in his gaze.

"Cherie?" he whispered, his breathing shallow and labored.

"Yes, darling. I'm here . . ."

"Good." He sighed as she quickly moved closer to him and took his hand.

"Katie and Mark are here too," she told him, trying to sound cheerful.

"Katie?"

333

"Yes, Uncle Isaac?"

"Did he do the right thing by you?" The question drained him.

"We were married yesterday," Katie answered honestly.

Isaac nodded. "I need to talk to Mark . . . alone "

Cherie looked at Mark questioningly but he motioned for her to go on outside with Katie.

"Mark . . ."

"Yes Isaac."

"You'll take care of Cherie . . . and Denis?" his voice faded.

"I will," Mark choked.

"Thank you," Isaac wheezed, paling. "I'm so tired . . . so tired . . ."

Isaac closed his eyes and Mark quickly called Cherie and then ran for a doctor. But it was too late. Isaac had left them . . . his tortured look of pain erased by death's peaceful release.

Fifteen

The Murder

Andre stood with his parents near the ballroom doorway watching the festivities going on around him. He had not wanted to come, but his father had insisted. It didn't matter that his last encounter with Mark had destroyed all friendship between them. What was important was that the Montards were lifelong friends of the La Zears and it would be a snub if Andre did not attend their daughter's engagement party . . . even if he did hate the man she was to marry.

He had been waiting for over an hour now for Christopher and Katie to arrive. Somehow, tonight, he was going to discover the truth behind their marriage. Andre had even enlisted his mother's help in finding out the latest gossip about their sudden wedding. He had been patient for a month now but he could wait no longer, he had to know.

As Andre watched Mark greeting the guests with Jacqui on his arm, Suzanne suddenly crossed his mind. He hadn't visited her since the night they'd exchanged heated words over Katie and Christopher. He had seen

335

her at Isaac's funeral and after observing her success, playing the grieving widow, he had privately complimented her on her performance.

Suzanne hadn't been able to reply to his observations, but instead had flashed him a triumphant smile. Then, as others had approached, she had quickly masked her pleasure at being single again and had resumed the role of mourning wife.

Andre had heard later that Isaac had altered his will and that the changes had so upset Suzanne that she had retired to Kingsford House in a fury. He'd never found out the whole truth, but he was curious and hoped he could learn more about it tonight.

Christopher put Katie from him reluctantly as the carriage slowed.

"We're almost there," he explained as she looked at him questioningly.

"But I was enjoying myself," she pouted happily, loving the fact that her kisses always had the power to arouse him, even after an entire month of being together constantly.

"So was I, too much. We have a party to go to."

"Do we have to?" she flirted.

"He's your brother." Christopher's eyes glinted with good humor at the thought of forgetting the party and going back to their suite to make love.

He had been delighted to discover that their relationship had only improved with time. Many couples he'd known had grown bored with each other. But not them. Katie was constantly surprising him. She was like a blossom unfolding and each day he discovered a new facet of her love.

"You're tempting, but we're very late already," she smiled and then paused in thought. "We don't have to stay late, though, you know."

"I know," he said with emphasis and regretfully they left the carriage to attend Mark and Jacqui's engagement party.

The evening passed in a pleasant blur for Katie. It was her first social outing since Isaac's death and she enjoyed renewing her acquaintances.

Christopher was always near, his presence protective and much appreciated for they had both caught sight of Andre earlier in the evening.

It was during Christopher's dance with Jacqui that Andre made his move, cornering Katie in the main floor hall.

"Katie." His tone was sincere as he greeted her. "I was overjoyed when I heard that you'd been rescued."

"Thank you Andre." She tried to end the conversation, but he persisted.

"I need to talk to you, Katie. Somewhere where we won't be interrupted."

"Andre, I'm a married woman now."

"That's precisely what I want to talk with you about."

Katie looked at him questioningly. "Why?"

"Come with me for just a moment." And when she hesitated, he added, "Please."

"All right. For a moment," she finally agreed and went with him into the deserted study.

To Katie's dismay, he shut the door behind them.

"Andre, I hardly think anything we have to say to each other is that important," she bristled.

He was irritated by her attitude but tried not to let it show.

"What I have to say is," he insisted. "And I don't want the whole world knowing my business."

Eyeing her in the soft lamplight, it took all of his willpower not to ravish her then and there. She was beautiful . . . her golden hair . . . her breasts swelling

337

daringly above the d5ecolletage of her evening gown. God, how he wanted her. Fighting down his baser instincts, he faced her squarely.

"I love you, Katie. You must have known that when I proposed to you on the island."

Katie tried to stop him . . . to keep him from embarrassing himself but Andre continued, waving aside her attempts to speak.

"If you were forced into this marriage by circumstances beyond your control, all is not lost. We can still be together . . . You can get an annulment."

"Andre! I . . ." she began, wanting to set him straight on the matter, when the door flew open and Mark and Jacqui entered laughing gaily.

"Oh!" Jacqui was startled to find them there.

"Katie?" Mark asked, surprised to find her alone with Andre.

"I was just leaving. You're welcome to the study." With a swish of her skirts, she was gone.

"Mark, Jacqui," Andre nodded, his eyes following Katie's retreating back. "If you'll excuse me . . ."

Mark watched Andre leave, noting the tenseness in his manner and the glare in his eyes.

"Where were you?" Christopher asked as Katie joined him.

"With Andre."

"What did he want?" Christopher stiffened.

"I'll tell you later. Can we leave now?"

He noticed how pale she was. "Of course. Let's get out of here."

They made their excuses to Mark and Jacqui and quickly left.

Seated in the carriage, Katie leaned heavily against Christopher. Putting his arm around her, he held her

338

protectively to him.

"What happened?"

"The man is a fool!" She was angry at having let him upset her so. "He wanted me to get an annulment, so I could be with him!"

"He what?"

"Andre thinks I only married you because I was forced to. He wants me to leave you and marry him."

"That's ridiculous!"

"I know. I tried to tell him, but he wouldn't listen. And then Mark and Jacqui walked in . . ."

"Walked in?"

"Andre said that we had to talk in private . . ."

"Don't ever go anywhere with him alone again! Do you understand me?"

"Yes, Christopher."

"The man is dangerous and when he finds out the truth, I don't know how he'll react."

Katie nodded. "I wanted to tell him but he wouldn't let me get a word in."

Christopher tilted her chin up and kissed her softly. "I'm glad Mark and Jacqui interrupted. It probably saved you from a very awkward situation."

"I know."

Mark smiled down at Jacqui as the last of their guests departed.

"What a night. It was wonderful!"

"It was," she agreed. Then admiring the diamond and sapphire ring he'd given her, she said, "Thank you for my ring. It's lovely."

"You're welcome. It was my mother's. I'm glad that you like it." Mark wanted to kiss her, but her parents were just in the other room.

"I'm sorry your uncle couldn't be here tonight."

"I miss him," Mark said simply. "He was very good to me."

"He was a good man," Jacqui paused. "Have you heard any more from Suzanne?"

"Not a word since the reading of the will."

"It really upset her, didn't it?"

"That's putting it mildly."

"Why do you suppose he made you the executor?"

"Because he knew I'd take care of Cherie and Denis. I promised him that I would."

"But to give you and Katie the townhouse and put you in charge of all his business dealings . . ."

Mark shrugged. "He trusted me. He knew I'd do a good job."

"Have you thought much about school?"

"There won't be time now. I've got too much work to do."

"You won't be dealing with Suzanne much, will you?"

Mark smiled at Jacqui's jealousy and kissed her in spite of her parents' nearness. "Hardly at all."

"Good," came her reply. "I don't trust her."

"Well, we agree on that at least," Mark chuckled. "Now, how soon do you want to get married?"

"Tomorrow?" she responded hopefully.

"Tonight," he murmured teasingly, kissing her again.

Andre listened attentively as his mother related everything she had found out talking with the other women at the party.

"And Suzanne didn't visit him once the whole time Isaac was in the hospital," Marie Montard confided scandalously.

Andre knew all that, but didn't let on.

"Why?" He tried to sound genuinely confused by her behavior.

"Well, it seems that Isaac had a mistress and he wanted her with him, not Suzanne."

Andre nodded.

"Of course, when he died, there was no way around it. Suzanne had to go and she put on a pretty convincing act, too. Why, even I was fooled," Marie sounded smug. "It must be miserable for her now, having to mourn him for almost a year when obviously she didn't love him and he didn't love her."

"What of Katie's sudden marriage?"

"Oh, the niece?"

"Yes."

"Well, she was stranded alone with Christopher Fletcher for over a week . . . What else was there to do, but insist on a wedding. I mean, her reputation was in shreds."

"Oh."

Marie looked at her son shrewdly. "Why did you want to know?"

"I had been courting her and I wondered why she up and married Fletcher. Of course, now that I know she was compromised . . ."

Marie nodded. "I understand . . . who'd want her after she'd spent all those nights alone with him . . ."

Her comments infuriated him and he got up and stalked from the room. Were Katie and Christopher lovers? The thought enraged him but he knew that he had to face up to the possibility.

His only chance was to find the opportunity to speak with her alone where they wouldn't be interrupted. Maybe then they could straighten everything out between them.

Mark drank his coffee and smiled warmly at Cherie. "Is Denis doing better?"

"Much. The first few weeks were terrible for him, but now he's finally accepted Isaac's death."

"Good. Acceptance is the hardest part," Mark paused. "And you? Are you well?"

"I'm fine." Cherie gave him a sad half-smile. "We have some adjustments to make yet, but Isaac seems to have taken care of everything . . ."

"He did do that. Why Denis's inheritance is a fortune. He'll be a very rich young man when he reaches his majority."

"Money is not everything . . ."

"No, it isn't. But it can help both of you to find some peace in your lives."

"You're right." Cherie felt guilty about her bitterness. "I'm sorry."

"There is no need to apologize, Cherie. I understand. I only wish I could find some way to ease your pain . . ."

"You have done so much already."

"But if you ever need me—for anything—please, don't hesitate to call upon me."

"I won't Mark," she told him as he rose to leave. "And thank you for everything."

Joel waited impatiently on Greenwood's Landing for the steamer to tie up. He had returned to Greenwood right after Christopher and Katie's wedding and had been anticipating their arrival for quite some time now. He was glad to see that they had finally made it home.

"Joel," Christopher greeted him with restraint, maintaining an air of master and servant. "Please see to Mrs. Fletcher's bags."

"Yes, suh," Joel answered obediently, aware of the watchful eyes upon them from on board the boat.

Christopher helped Katie into the small, open carriage as Joel loaded the luggage. When they were all seated,

342

Joel took the reins for the short trip to the house.

"How are things going?" Christopher asked as they moved off up the drive.

Joel looked at him uncertainly.

"Katie knows everything. You've no need to worry. We can trust her."

"All right," Joel confided. "The patrollers seem to have let up. And traffic's been so light that there's been no need to hide anyone in the canebrakes since I returned."

"Good. When was McCarthy through here last?"

"Three days ago."

"Did we have any freight?"

"Not that trip."

"Have you seen or heard from Dillon?"

"He was here about ten days ago, but he hasn't been back since."

They fell silent as they arrived at the house.

While Katie went to settle into her new home, Christopher met with Joel in the study to review all the plantation business of the past weeks. When he found that the books were in order, he shared a drink with Joel and then retired upstairs to spend some time with Katie.

The drapes were drawn in the master bedroom, blocking out most of the bright sunlight. But even in the deep shadowed stillness of the room, Christopher could make out Katie's sleeping form on the massive four-poster bed. Standing at the foot, leaning against one of the posts, he took the time to study the young beauty who was his wife.

Who would have thought, all those months ago when she'd attacked him on the steamboat, that she would have become the most important person in his life? Certainly not he, and yet, she was.

Turning away from her scantily clad body for a moment, Christopher stripped off all but his pants and then

343

joined her on the bed. He had left strict orders that they were not to be disturbed until dinner, so he knew that they would have at least a few hours of privacy.

Even though the bed dipped under his weight, Katie didn't stir. Stretching out beside her, he toyed with a sun-streaked curl, marvelling at its softness and the sweet fragrance of it. Then unable to resist the offering of her barely concealed breasts, he moved lower to kiss their tempting pink peaks through the sheer material of her shift.

Katie awoke at the touch of his hot, wet mouth upon her bosom. Sensuously writhing against him, she murmured his name in a sultry welcome.

Christopher rose above her and kissed her more fully awake as his hands slipped the barrier of her shift from her slender body.

"No matter how many times I take you, your beauty still stirs me," he told her, touching her breasts in awe. "You are so perfect . . ."

Katie's desire for him deepened at his words and she pulled his head down to her aching bosom. Her breasts swelled as his mouth explored them and she moaned her pleasure when his questing hand sought the softness between her legs. Yearning for completion, Katie moved restlessly beneath his practiced caresses, seeking the ultimate union with his big, hard body.

But Christopher was in no hurry as time and again he teased her to her limits, leaving her panting and on fire with her need for him. It was only when Katie begged him for release from his exquisite torture that he shed his pants and joined his body with hers.

The feel of his masculinity possessing her so deeply drove Katie into of frenzy of longing. Clinging to Christopher, bucking eagerly against him, she bit back a cry of passion as the pulsing joy of her excitement rocked through her.

Christopher, too, was carried away by the power of her love. Meeting her in a peak of rapture, they achieved love's ultimate gift and drifted peacefully together through the enchantment of their hearts' haven.

During the week after the engagement party, Andre had anxiously tried to come up with a way to catch Katie alone, but to no avail. Before he could arrange anything, Katie and Christopher had left New Orleans for Greenwood. Frustrated but not defeated, Andre immediately planned a visit with Suzanne at Kingsford House. He was confident he could convince her that he was there to see her, not to pursue Katie.

Early on the day of Andre's departure, Emil summoned him to his study. Sitting at his desk, looking most pleased with himself, he motioned Andre into the room.

"And close the door!" he directed excitedly. "I have something here I think you'll be interested in."

"Oh, really?" Andre was openly curious.

"It just arrived by special messenger. It's from St. Louis."

"St. Louis! Did they finally find out what we needed to know?"

"See for yourself." Emil handed him a small leather portfolio which Andre opened eagerly.

He read the missives once quickly and then reread them again more slowly.

"It's unbelievable!" he muttered in astonishment, unable to understand how Christopher could have fooled everyone so completely.

Folding the letters carefully, Andre returned them to their place of safety.

"They've already picked up that Dillon person and from what I understand, he was very uncooperative. It took the most extraordinary measures to get the rest of the information out of him."

"But we've got the facts, now!" He was almost jubilant. "When do we go to the authorities?"

"Not so fast, son," Emil looked pensive. "I think we can do a lot better for ourselves if we don't rush into anything . . ."

Andre looked at his father quizzically. "What do you mean?"

"What I mean is we'll wait until the time is right . . . We'll let Fletcher sweat a little . . . Then we can get what we want just by asking. Later, when there's nothing more to be gained, we'll tell the sheriff."

Andre smiled at his father's cunning. He would enjoy watching Fletcher squirm as they tightened the noose on him and his operation.

Suzanne had been surprised when Andre had arrived at Kingsford House. She had thought their last confrontation had been the final word on their relationship . . . and yet, here he was.

"Andre," she greeted him warily. "This is, as you can well imagine, an unexpected pleasure."

Andre, understanding Suzanne only too well, smiled at her veiled sarcasm. "I thought you might be lonely living out here in the country, all alone."

"I am. But I'm not sure you're the one I want to help liven up my life." Suzanne started back indoors. "Come in."

Andre followed her without speaking, trying to figure out a way to keep in Suzanne's good graces while he arranged a private meeting with Katie. When they were seated in the parlor and Suzanne had ordered refreshments, he spoke.

"Have you given up mourning already?" he noted her fashionable gown.

"Why should I mourn something that died years ago?" she flashed at him. "We both know how Isaac really felt about me. I'm just sorry that I didn't find out before I married him."

"Ah, but then you wouldn't own Kingsford House."

Suzanne shrugged. "The money is nice, but I wonder if it was really worth it. All those years of my life . . ."

"You're still young."

"Thank you for that much," she glared at him. "Now, enough small talk. Why did you come?"

"To see you," Andre replied truthfully.

"Oh," she watched him cagily. "Why?"

"I missed you."

"Really," she said tartly. "Somehow I find that hard to believe."

"Isaac's treatment of you has made you bitter, Suzanne," Andre observed.

"Isaac was not the only man I've been involved with who needed more than what I could give him," she said pointedly.

"Touché. But now that he's dead, things will be different."

Suzanne didn't deign to reply to his optimistic observation.

"Did you miss me?" Andre asked.

"Occasionally," she admitted.

"Well, that's a start. We'll begin anew," he lied, knowing that he had to win her trust once again.

After trying to figure out his ulterior motives for wanting to resume their relationship, she agreed. "I'd like that."

"Good."

"I take it you're planning on staying?"

"If you have no objections."

"Very well. You might as well make yourself at home."

"Thank you." He was relieved that Suzanne believed him.

Now it was just a matter of catching Katie alone next door at Greenwood. And, from those reports on Fletcher's comings and goings, that didn't look to prove too difficult.

"Father received some information yesterday that was quite exciting," Andre told her, setting his coffee cup aside.

Andre found the possibility of trapping Fletcher enormously entertaining and he wanted to share it all with Suzanne. Andre had no doubt that she would be glad to see him suffer, for after all, he had rejected her.

"Really?" she answered drily.

"Really," he asserted. "After we lost Greenwood, we decided to do some checking into Fletcher's background."

Suzanne did not appear interested. "So? What's to know? He's rich and handsome and married to Katie."

"Ah, but there's more," he told her cryptically. "He's also an abolitionist and has been working with the Underground Railroad, moving slaves out of state."

Suzanne arched an eyebrow at Andre's disclosure. "Christopher?"

"Yes. We just found out yesterday," he related growing more excited as he thought of finally seeing Fletcher get what was coming to him.

"Have you gone to the sheriff?"

"Not yet."

"What are you waiting for?" Suzanne thought him stupid for not turning the information over to the authorities right away.

"I want revenge, Suzanne," Andre suddenly seethed.

"Revenge? For what?"

"He's taken everything I ever wanted."

"Are you still thinking about Katie?" she demanded.

"I'm talking about Greenwood," Andre replied, hoping he sounded convincing. "I want it back."

"And just how do you propose to go about it?"

"Blackmail, of course," he grinned evilly.

"I wish you luck," she sighed, seeming bored. "Frankly if I was handling this, I'd let the law take care of it."

"Well, you're not handling it, I am. And I intend to see him sweat a bit before I'm finished."

"I'm sure," she dismissed him and his plotting. "But leave me out of it. I want nothing more to do with any of them."

"All right. I will. But at least now you'll know where I am if I ride off the plantation occasionally." Andre felt triumphant as he found the opening he'd been looking for.

"Andre," she looked at him levelly as she stood up. "You do not have to check in and out with me. Now, if you'll excuse me, I believe I'll go up to my room for a while."

Suzanne left the room quickly, aggravated with Andre. She had had her fill of dealing with the Kingsfords. If she never heard their names again, she would be happy. Yet here was Andre, determined to dig up the past. Revenge was stupid, she thought to herself. Better to let the authorities have him, than to play games and take the chance that he might escape . . .

Christopher and Joel were pacing the study worriedly. It was near dawn and four fugitives had just arrived bearing the news of Dillon's death.

"Why would anybody kill him?" Joel wondered aloud.

"They're sure it was murder?" Christopher asked.

Joel nodded. "They said he'd been tied up and

dumped in the river."

"We'll have to assume that he talked before he died," Christopher concluded.

"Then we'd better do something and fast."

"When's McCarthy due?"

"Not 'til next week."

"Without Dillon or McCarthy, we'll have to take them out."

"I'll go this afternoon," Joel offered, but Christopher refused.

"No. I've got some business to take care of in New Orleans so I'll go this time."

"Are you sure of the way?"

Christopher grinned with false bravado. "Of course, we've gone over it often enough, haven't we?"

"Talking and doing are two different things," Joel worried. "What if they know about you?"

"If they knew about me, they would have been here by now," Christopher reassured him.

"I suppose you're right, but . . ."

"No buts. I'll be careful. You've taught me well. We'll disguise the slaves . . . nobody will suspect."

Joel reluctantly agreed with Christopher and together they began to plan the trip.

"I'm going for my ride now. Do you want to come?" Katie asked, peeking into the study where Christopher was meeting with Joel.

"I'll be right with you, darling," he responded. "Have the stableboy bring my horse around, too."

"Oh, good. I'll meet you out front." Katie went to see to the horses.

Christopher glanced up at Joel. "I'll tell her about the trip this morning."

"Are you going to tell her about Dillon?"

"No!" he answered sharply. "The less she knows, the less she has to worry about."

"All right."

"I'll be back in an hour or so." Christopher glanced at his pocketwatch. "Have the runaways ready to go by two."

Secluded in a grove of trees, Andre watched in disgust as Katie and Christopher rode past. He had had his hopes set on speaking with her today, but it was not to be. Since he'd found out about her early morning rides four days ago, Andre had been coming here each morning to watch and wait for her. Now, again, his quest was to end in frustration.

Turning his horse, Andre headed toward Kingsford House, disappointed but not ready to give up.

Katie jumped lightly to the ground and led her horse to drink at the small pond.

"Are you going to rest a while?" she called back over her shoulder to Christopher who had just ridden up.

"Yes, now that I've finally caught up with you. You've led me a merry chase this morning."

"You needed the exercise! All you ever do any more is sit in the study and do paperwork!"

"I seem to recall taking part in some vigorous physical activity last night," he teased, coming to her side.

"That's different," Katie blushed.

"Indeed?"

But Katie ignored his attempts to goad her.

"I do have something to discuss with you."

"Oh? What?"

"I have to leave this afternoon."

"Why?"

351

"I've got to get this latest group to New Orleans right away."

"What about Captain McCarthy?"

"He won't be back for another week."

"Won't you be in danger?"

"No," he told her confidently. "We haven't seen much of the patrollers lately. It should be an easy trip."

Katie frowned her worry but didn't speak of it. "How long will you be gone?"

"Four days at the longest."

"I'll be waiting."

Christopher sensed her upset and swept her into a protective embrace.

"Don't worry darling," he kissed her. "You know I'll always come back to you."

"I know," she sighed.

His mouth possessed hers in a heart-branding kiss that left them both panting when they finally broke apart.

"How private is this pond?" Katie asked suggestively.

"Not very, I'm afraid," he told her in mock frustration.

"That's a shame." She gave him a sultry look as she moved a small distance from him. "But I guess it will give you something to think about while you're gone."

"And to hurry home to!" he chuckled and in a lightning move, pulled her to him once more, kissing her deeply.

Christopher began the trip to Robert's house optimistically. The four runaways were travelling incognito . . . one man was the driver . . . two of the men were disguised as women . . . and the woman was dressed as a boy. Christopher had forged identification papers for them and had made out counterfeit passes just in case they were somehow separated.

352

Traffic was light all afternoon as they headed due south on the River Road. It was only as dusk came upon them that the sound of pounding hooves struck a chill of terror into their souls. Pulling the carriage to the side of the road, they waited. The foam-speckled horses, galloping at full speed, veered to the side and were viciously reined to a halt.

To the four disguised runaways the patrollers looked like demons from hell. Their eyes bright with blood-lust, their hands itching to use their guns, they stared at Christopher and his group with open interest.

"Well, well, what have we here?" the leader of the pack of human bloodhounds asked sarcastically.

"I, sir, am Christopher Fletcher, owner of Greenwood Plantation. These four blacks are my property."

"Mr. Christopher Fletcher, where are you bound with these niggers?" the patroller spat a wad of tobacco juice casually from the side of his mouth.

Christopher looked at the man arrogantly. "If it's any of your business, we are heading for New Orleans."

"New Orleans, eh?"

Aware that these men might just be looking for him, he now doubted the wisdom of so freely offering his own name.

"Do you have reason to doubt the validity of my travel plans?" Christopher disliked being questioned by these lowlifes.

" 'Course not, Mr. Fletcher. We just heard tell of some bucks runnin' from up-country and thought we'd better stop and question everyone we see."

"Well, Mr. . . . ?" Christopher began. "I don't believe I got your name."

"Jones. Leo Jones."

"Well, Mr. Jones, I appreciate your vigilance, as I'm sure all my neighbors do," he told him more cordially. "But as you can see, Lulabelle, Becky, David and Martin are hardly the slaves you're looking for. Why Martin there is just barely old enough to do a good day's work." When Jones nodded in agreement, Christopher continued. "That's one of the reasons why I'm taking him to town to try to hire him out. He's eating more than he's worth!"

Jones laughed, showing broken, decayed teeth. "That's the trouble with them niggers. They just ain't worth what you pay for 'em."

Christopher gritted his teeth and smiled as best he could. "You're so right, Mr. Jones," he answered, knowing their value as human beings far surpassed any dollar amount.

Tipping his battered hat, Jones called to his men and they were off at top speed, setting out again in search of the missing four.

When the patrollers were out of sight down the road, Christopher was so relieved that he almost collapsed back in his carriage seat.

"We made it," he spoke in low tones. "Let's get out of here!"

Picking up their pace, they headed on until darkness overtook them and they were forced to camp for the night.

Katie was without her usual joie de vivre as she came down the stairs the following morning. Though she wouldn't admit to it, she was concerned about Christopher's safety. The Underground Railroad was serious business and Christopher was deeply involved. The chance that he could be caught was very real . . . and Katie knew what the slaveowners did to runaways and the people who aided them.

Pushing such thoughts from her mind, she greeted Dee in the breakfast room with a big smile.

354

"Good morning."

"Good mornin', Katie." Dee's expression was solemn this morning and Katie was puzzled.

"Is something wrong?"

Dee looked uncomfortable for a moment and then answered her. "Yes. There's something wrong. Andre Montard is staying at Kingsford House."

"Andre? But why?"

"I don't know for sure, but I think he's taken up with Suzanne again."

"Again?"

"They were lovers . . . about a year ago."

"Andre and Suzanne?" Katie was surprised to finally find out the truth.

Dee nodded.

"She must not have mourned Uncle Isaac at all," Katie shook her head sadly. "You don't think that's the only reason Andre's around, do you?"

"No ma'am."

"Dee, if you're concerned about your own safety, you can go in to New Orleans and stay with my brother there."

"Katie," Dee was serious. "It's not me I'm worried about. It's you."

"Me?"

"Andre's been wanting you for months. And when he wants something or someone, he doesn't stop until he gets it."

"But he knows I'm married now."

"Katie, if you think that's gonna discourage him, you'd better think again."

"He may want me, but I don't want him," Katie was irritated by the truth of her words.

"That hasn't stopped him before . . . Just be careful."

"I will be."

355

Katie took to the trails this hot, sultry morning with less than her usual enthusiasm. Dee's warning had taken the joy from her day. Riding at a loping pace, she paid little attention to her surroundings. Her thoughts were clouded with worry over Christopher's trip and Dee's advice about Andre. It angered Katie that he could still be entertaining thoughts of winning her. She was done with the man and it was time he realized it.

When she reached the pond, she dismounted and led her horse to drink. Memories of her ride yesterday with Christopher made her smile and lost in thought she waited patiently as her mount cooled.

Andre had heard from the Kingsford servants' gossip that Christopher had left for New Orleans and he had watched Katie's approach with unmitigated joy. It was true. She was alone! At last! As soon as she had passed him, he was in the saddle ready to ride. Today was the day! Andre waited until she had dismounted by the pond before riding after her. And even then, he kept his pace under control.

"Katie!"

Katie heard her name being called and couldn't imagine who would be out looking for her so soon. When she turned to see Andre riding toward her, she could have groaned aloud.

What was he doing here on Greenwood property? Dee's warning chilled her and she fought not to panic.

"Good morning, Katie," he spoke cordially, his gaze swept over her in warm appreciation.

"Andre," she returned coolly. "I'm surprised to see you."

"I thought you liked surprises," he countered.

"Sometimes. What are you doing here?"

"I needed to speak with you alone . . . to finish our conversation."

Katie couldn't believe that he could be so persistent

after the way she'd dismissed him at Mark's party.

"I thought we *had* finished our conversation."

Andre's expression darkened at her curt reply.

"Hardly, my love. If you'll just . . ." He climbed down from his horse and made to approach her.

Katie's stance became defensive as she grew angry with his bold assumptions.

"I am not your love, Andre," she told him straight out, her hands on her hips for emphasis.

"Ah, but you will be . . . Katie, there is so much that I can give you . . ."

"Andre, I don't want anything from you." Katie began to realize that arguing with him was useless.

"You will," he laughed and in one quick move he took her in his arms and pulled her forcibly against his chest. "I love you, Katie."

His mouth covered hers in a wet possession that disgusted as well as alarmed her. His hands were a painful vise on the soft flesh of her upper arms and she twisted and squirmed trying to escape from his grasp. When he released one arm so he could fondle her breast, Katie doubled up her fist and hit him with all her might.

The blow glanced off his cheek and surprised him more than it hurt him. Shocked by her reaction to his protestations of love, Andre shoved her away from him.

"Katie? What . . . ?"

"I don't love you, Andre. I never have."

"But I can give you the world!"

"I don't want the world! I have everything I could ever want or need right now."

"Kate, I love you. I know you only married him because you had to. But we can work things out," Andre told her, not paying any attention to her protests.

Katie was angry. The man was so obsessed that he wouldn't listen to reason.

"Andre! I don't love you. The only man I've ever

cared for is Christopher. We are very happy together."

Andre stopped as her words penetrated his self-induced over-confidence. A red haze of fiery hate clouded his thoughts as he finally realized that she truly didn't care for him.

"Why you stuped little bitch!" With one vicious swing he back-handed her, splitting her lip.

Andre glared at her for a moment, enjoying her pain and then visibly relaxed. He still planned to have her, only now it would be on his terms.

"Well, darling, since you won't come of your own free will . . . I've a little news you might find inspiring . . ." he grinned malevolently. "I am very much aware of Christopher's activities."

At Katie's gasp, Andre continued, "So, you're not such a sweet innocent after all . . ."

"I don't know what you mean . . ." Katie tried to bluff her way out of the situation, but it was too late.

"You're a terrible liar, Katie. But there's no need for you to panic. I'm more than willing to keep quiet about everything I know . . . for a price."

Katie wasn't sure what to do. For her own safety, she wanted to run . . . to flee his disgusting presence, but what about Christopher? If Andre did know the truth, he could have him murdered before she could warn him.

"So, what is it that you think you know?" she finally asked, trying to keep her tone light.

Andre sensed her uncertainty and he loved the feeling of power it gave him.

"Be a little nicer to me and I just might tell you." He grabbed her and pulled her slowly to him, heightening her awareness of what he wanted to do to her.

"Tell me and I just might be nice to you," she countered brashly.

Andre smiled and ran a hand intimately over her breasts.

"Katie, I do admire your spirit. Even in the face of defeat. I know Christopher has left Greenwood. I know you're all alone here . . ."

She stiffened in repugnance as his fingers teased her nipples through the light material of her shirt.

"Enjoy that, do you?" Andre attributed her tensing to pleasure, not revulsion. "I have wanted to see you naked for so long . . ."

Katie remained standing still as he unbuttoned her blouse, but as he was about to slip it from her, reason returned.

"No!" she screamed.

The suddenness of her protest startled him and caught him off-guard. Shoving him with all her might, she broke free long enough to spring into the saddle and kick her mount to action.

Andre regained his balance and mounting his horse, rode after her at top-speed. Defy him, would she? He intended to slake his desire for her *now*! He was done with going easy with her. When he caught up with her this time . . .

Katie rode like the wind, heading straight for the house. Joel would be there . . . he would help her get rid of Andre.

Dee was sweeping the gallery when she saw Katie coming at breakneck speed up the drive.

"Joel!" she called him nervously. "Something's wrong with Katie. Come quick!"

Joel, who'd been working in the study, came out on the porch.

"Katie? What's wrong?" He bounded down the steps to grab her reins and steady her horse. Noting her clothing in disarray, he pressed, "What happened?"

"It's Andre!" she cried, breathlessly, looking over her shoulder to see him racing up the road after her. "He knows about Christopher! He wanted to . . ."

359

Joel reached up to help Katie down and was setting her on the ground when Andre reined to a halt nearby, his horse dancing in excitement.

"Get your hands off her, nigger!" Andre ordered, sliding his mount nearer to Katie.

Joel let her go and turned to reach for Andre's reins to calm the prancing steed.

"Did you think you could get away from me?" he seethed.

Katie, who was nervously holding her blouse together, glared up at Andre.

"Get off Greenwood! You're trespassing!"

"Why—" New fury rocked him. She dared to order him from what should be rightfully his! Andre reached down to grab Katie, but Joel stepped between them.

"You better do what the lady says, Montard," Joel ordered, blocking his way. He knew the evil Andre Montard was capable of and he wanted him away from Katie and off Greenwood.

Andre was in a frenzy of frustration . . . Katie had escaped him and now Joel had the audacity to challenge him! Without conscious thought, Andre drew his revolver and shot Joel point blank. At close range the bullet blasted through his chest, killing him instantly and knocking him forcefully to the ground at Katie's feet. Frozen in place, Katie could only watch in horror as Andre dismounted and swaggered toward her.

"Stupid nigger! He should have known better than to talk back to me." Andre grinned at Katie's undisguised fear. "Now, Katie . . ." He reached out and grabbed her wrist and pulling her to him, forcing her to step over Joel's prone body. "Why don't we go inside and make ourselves more comfortable?"

Dragging her up the steps, he pushed the door open and walked in ahead of her with familiar ease.

At the sight of Andre riding up, Dee had taken refuge

inside, wanting to hide from him. Aftering witnessing, in total helpless agony, the murder of her beloved husband, Dee went for Christopher's gun. As the door opened, Andre entered the hall, pulling Katie in behind him. When he came face to face with Dee, he stopped.

"Well, well . . . Now I have both of you, don't I?" dropping Katie's arm, he walked leisurely toward Dee. "Have you missed me, darling? You can join Katie and me upstairs . . . Would you like that? You always knew I'd be back, didn't you?"

"Yes, Andre. I've been waiting . . ." her voice was toneless as she remembered all of his evil deeds.

Andre smiled in cocky assurance as he stopped in front of her. "Good."

Dee lifted the gun she'd concealed in her skirts and fired repeatedly at him, emptying the gun into him.

Andre's look of stunned disbelief turned to one of pain, then fright as he collapsed on the floor.

"Katie . . ." his voice gurgled as blood rushed from his mouth and his head lolled to the side as death took him.

Sixteen

The Fugitives

Seated in the parlor of Robert's house, Christopher relaxed for the first time since he'd begun the trip.

"I take it your trek downriver was a bit 'exciting'?" Robert asked, giving him a sympathetic smile.

"It was downright nerve-wracking," Christopher grinned. "Thank God I learned early in life how to bluff my way out of tight situations. I thought the patrollers had us for sure."

Robert handed him a glass of bourbon and then sat down across from him.

"You say Dillon didn't bring this group?"

"No, in fact—" He took a deep, steadying drink— "They said that he's dead."

"Dillon? But how?" Robert was upset.

"Murdered . . . That's why I was extra cautious on this trip."

"Do you think it was the patrollers?"

"I don't know who it was . . . The runaways told me that his body had been found in the river and that he'd been bound and gagged."

"It had to be . . ."

"That's what Joel and I thought."

"They must have gotten some information from him or they never would have killed him."

Christopher nodded his agreement. "But I figured that if they were after me, they would have had me already."

"Possibly . . ." Robert looked at him pensively. "What do you think about getting out of town for a while?"

"Do you really think it's necessary?"

"I do. It's better to quit while we're ahead than to take unnecessary chances."

"I understand. What do you suggest?"

"How about a delayed honeymoon for you and Katie?"

"That sounds good. I can leave Joel in charge. That way it won't look too suspicious."

"We're agreed, then?"

"I'll finish up my business in town and then head north with Katie."

"Good."

"What about you?"

"No one would ever suspect me. I was born and raised here. I'll be safe."

"You're sure?"

"Positive. Where will I be able to reach you to let you know when it's safe to come back?"

"I don't know yet, I'll send you word after I discuss it with Katie."

"All right. You'll be leaving here tomorrow, then?"

"Yes. I've got a few business matters to clear up in the city and then I'll return to Greenwood."

"Fine. If I hear anything in the next day or so, I'll get word to you right away."

"Thank you, Robert. Thank you for everything."

"You're more than welcome, Christopher. We work well together. I just hope this isn't the end . . . there are so many others we could help . . ."

"The time is coming for a major change in this country . . . and I hope we'll be a part of it. Things can't go on as they are. This bartering of human souls has to be stopped."

"The question, my friend, is how to stop it? The plantation owners have most of their money tied up in their slaves. If they are forced to free them without compensation . . ."

"It's a problem for which I fear there is no easy solution." Christopher understood the economics of the situation.

They both fell silent wishing that there was more that they could do to help their cause.

Emil Montard arrived at Kingsford House, his features haggard with worry. A carriage was waiting for him at the landing and it took him quickly up to the mansion where Suzanne anxiously awaited his arrival.

"Emil —" she welcomed him solemnly.

"Where is my son?" he demanded, his eyes aglow with fiery hate.

"In here," she led him indoors to the back parlor where Andre's body lay, already prepared for burial.

A sob tore through him as he saw that it was no misunderstanding. Andre was dead.

Suzanne backed out of the room, leaving him to his grief. Later, there would be time for talk and explanations.

She was in the front parlor when he found her almost an hour later.

"I want to know who did this to my son," he spoke flatly, his gaze glittering with the desire for vengeance.

"Sit down, Emil. I'll get you a drink and tell you everything I know."

His movements were jerky and tense as he crossed the room to sit on the settee. After accepting the liquor from her which he downed in one gulp, Emil turned to face her.

"Well?"

"I was contacted by the sheriff yesterday afternoon. From what he told me, evidently Andre had gone to Greenwood and killed one of their slaves . . . Fletcher's man Joel, I believe."

"So?" Emil hardly thought the life of one black was worth that of his son's.

"That wasn't all. He apparently tried to attack Katie."

"Attack Katie? Why for God's sake?"

"He's wanted her for as long as I can remember," Suzanne told him bitterly. "In fact, he swore to me that he was done with her. That was the only reason that I let him stay. He told me that he would be going out to check on Greenwood, but supposedly it was just to spy on Fletcher."

"So, did Fletcher kill my boy?"

"No, he isn't even there. He's out of town on some business trip. It seems that Dee shot him when he was molesting Katie."

"Dee shot him?"

"Yes."

"It's all lies! It must be. Andre would have no reason to attack Katie. Why, all women loved my son."

Suzanne gave Emil a look of disbelief. "I'm afraid you're mistaken there. When it came to Katie, Andre was making a damned fool out of himself!"

"What do you mean?" Emil resented hearing anything disparaging about Andre.

"I mean, Andre wanted her and he was stupid enough to try anything to get her . . . including rape or blackmail . . ."

Emil came to his feet in defense of Andre. "I'm sure you're wrong. He would hardly have been interested in a woman who didn't want him. I'm sure she must have encouraged him in some way."

Suzanne couldn't believe that Emil would not face the truth.

"May I borrow a horse?"

"Of course, but . . ."

"I won't be gone long," he strode from the room, his heart on fire with the need for revenge.

Katie and Dee were walking slowly back up to the big house. The ceremony for Joel had been short yet poignant and both women felt drained of all emotion.

The ordeal of the day before was over, but not forgotten. The sheriff's probing questions—the confrontation with Suzanne when she'd come to claim Andre's body . . . They were numb from the shock and yet deep within them dwelled a fear that at any moment, the truth about Christopher would be known.

The sound of galloping horse drew their attention. Looking down the front drive, they were terrified to see Emil Montard riding toward them at top speed. Reining in roughly, he was pleased to see the fear in their faces.

"Just buried your nigger, did you?" he asked hatefully.

"What do you want, Montard?" Katie was brusque, her stance defensive and protective of Dee.

Emil surveyed her coolly and Katie could almost feel his glacial gaze touching her.

"I'll tell you exactly what I want . . . I want the deed to Greenwood signed over to me along with all the slaves including her!" he pointed at Dee.

"No deal. Now get off my property."

"I think you're reacting a little hastily, Katie," he spoke

366

in silky smooth tones.

"And I don't. Leave, Montard," she ordered.

"Oh, I'll leave all right after you hear what I've got to say."

"I'm not interested."

"In saving your husband's life? Pity . . ." he started to ride away when Katie stopped him.

"What do you mean?"

"I mean that unless you sign Greenwood over to me, along with all the slaves—no exceptions—I'll be forced to turn your husband in to the authorities."

Katie looked stricken.

"Let's face it, unless I have the deed in my hand in twenty-four hours . . . Christopher Fletcher is a dead man."

Without another glance, he rode off, leaving Katie and Dee staring after him in stunned terror.

"Dee?" Katie was pulling herself together with an effort.

"What?" Dee was confused. She couldn't let Christopher die because of her . . .

"Get Jebediah. We're leaving."

"Where can we go where he won't find us? And what about Christopher?"

"We'll go to my father. He'll take care of us," Katie was certain that her father's strength would be their haven in the storm. "I'll send another note to Mark so he can warn Christopher."

"But Montard said he'd be killed . . . I can't let that happen."

"What do you want to do? Stay here and let yourself be killed?" Katie appreciated Dee's selflessness, but she would have no defense against the evil of Montard if she remained here. "Christopher's a grown man and he can handle himself quite well. Don't worry about him. He'll be all right."

"Shall I have T.C. put out the flag?"

"Yes. We'll leave on the next boat north. That will give us a good day's head start on Montard just in case he decides to come looking for us."

T.C. helped load the few bags that Katie and Dee had packed onto the steamer and then turned back to the women.

"You be careful."

"We will, T.C. And thank you," Katie told him earnestly. "If for some reason, Christopher should not get my message and come here, please send him to St. Louis."

"Yes ma'am. I'll tell you've gone to be with your father there."

"Right." Katie cast a melancholy glance back at the main house. "Thank you for everything."

T.C. shuffled uncomfortably under her heartfelt praise. "You're welcome ma'am. I hope you do fine."

"Dee? We'd better hurry."

Dee hugged T.C. quickly and, holding Jebediah tightly in her arms, she followed Katie up the gangplank. As the steamboat backed out to midstream, Katie and Dee settled into their cabin. They were exhausted from the tension of the past two days and were looking forward to some uninterrupted peace.

"Katie?" Dee asked after putting Jebediah to bed in one of the bunks.

"Yes, Dee?" Katie was sitting on her bed, remembering the first time she'd travelled on the Mississippi.

"What do you think Mr. Emil will do to us if he catches us?"

Katie answered confidently, "He won't, so don't think about it."

"Are you sure?" Dee was scared.

"Positive," Katie reassured her. "And my father will take care of us once we're there, so we'll be safe."

"What about Christopher?"

"With any luck, he'll get our message and head for St. Louis right away."

Dee evidently believed her for she dropped the subject, but Katie couldn't help but worry . . . what if he didn't get the message in time . . .

Emil rode up the drive at Greenwood, feeling triumphant . . . as if he'd fought and won a great battle. Without a doubt, he was positive that by the end of this day he would once again own Greenwood.

He thought little of it that no one met him in front of the big house. Easily dismounting, he tied up his own horse and climbed the front steps. Pausing for only a second as he tried to decide whether to knock or not, Emil finally threw open the door and walked in.

Expecting a nervous skittering of servants, he was almost unnerved by the quiet stillness that greeted him. It made his entrance seem an invasion and left him most uncomfortable.

"Katie?" he called imperiously. "I'm here for your answer."

But there was no response. Striding purposefully down the hall he checked each room but found no sign of her or Dee. Charging up the staircase he stomped into the master bedroom and went straight to search the armoire. He was livid with frustrated fury. How dare she defy him! He would find her and when he did . . .

Hurrying from the room, he went downstairs and back outside where he found T.C. working in the stable.

"Where is Mrs. Fletcher?"

"I don't know, suh," T.C. replied.

"What do you mean you don't know? When did she leave? And who did she take with her?"

"I don't know, suh," T.C. watched fearfully as Emil reached for a horsewhip.

"Shall we see if I can refresh your memory?" Emil slowly unwound the leather and cracked it, testing it. "Where is Mrs. Fletcher?"

T.C.'s eyes were wide with fright but he shook his head.

Emil didn't make idle threats and he brought the whip down in a lightning strike that raised a bloody welt on the slave's shoulders.

"Shall I ask again? Or will you tell me now? Where is Katie Fletcher?" When he didn't respond, Emil struck even harder, this blow driving him to his knees. "Now?"

T.C. felt the hot stickiness of his own blood running down his back as the whip cut him for the third time.

"They left . . ." His cry was strangled as he was whipped again and again.

"When did they leave?"

"Yesterday!" he admitted trying to roll away from the punishing blows.

"Where did they go?" Emil stopped.

T.C. was sobbing in painful surrender, "St. Louis, they went to St. Louis . . ."

Emil with aristocratic disdain threw the whip in the dust beside the fallen slave and walked casually away from the stable. He had no doubts about what he had to do. First, he would turn in Fletcher and then he would go after Katie and Dee.

Returning to Kingsford House, he quickly packed and made ready for his trip to New Orleans with Andre's body. He would leave for St. Louis right after the funeral. That black bitch wasn't going to get away with killing his son!

"So you're going on a honeymoon, are you?" Edward asked Christopher as they settled in at a table at the saloon during his second night in town.

"As soon as I take care of my business. I've got one more meeting with our factor in the morning and then I head home."

"Have you made any plans?" James asked.

"Not yet. I'll have to check with Katie first. Maybe we'll go back east to Philadelphia . . . I'll leave the final choice up to her."

"Well, enjoy yourself. You deserve it."

"Thanks," he smiled at his friends. "I intend to."

It had been a long time since he'd had the chance to spend an evening with his friends and the hours in their company passed quickly. Finally, in deference to his early appointment the next day, he called it a night and went back to his hotel. He had been having such a good time with his friends that he hadn't noticed the small, darkly-clothed man watching him all night.

Checking in at the desk to get his key, the clerk stopped him.

"Mr. Fletcher, sir. We have a message for you . . . Here it is." He handed him a small envelope.

"Thank you." He tipped the man and went on upstairs to his room to read the letter.

Locking the door behind him, he tore it open.

Christopher —   7 pm
   Must see you at once.
                              Mark

Christopher was confused. Why would Mark need to see him? It couldn't have anything to do with the railroad for Mark knew nothing of his true activities. Heading out once again, he rushed off to Mark's townhouse.

The streets were dark and a heavy mist was rolling in off the river as he climbed down from the hired carriage in front of the Kingsford home. After paying the driver, he started up the stairs to the door. There was still a light on in the sitting room and the warmth of its yellow glow seemed to take some of the chill from the night air. Before he could knock twice, Mark opened the door for him.

"Christopher! You got my message! Come in," he ushered him inside.

"Has something happened to Katie?" he worried, following his brother-in-law into the sitting room.

"I don't think so . . . here, read her note . . ." He handed him Katie's first letter.

Mark —

There has been serious trouble here and I need Christopher to come back as soon as possible. He should be staying at the St. Charles. Please find him and send him home.

Katie

"What kind of trouble?" Christopher frowned.

"I don't know!"

"I'll leave tonight."

"It's too late now. I checked the steamer schedules and there won't be another one out until seven in the morning."

"Thanks, Mark."

"Sure," Mark replied. "Listen, why don't you spend the night here? Then I can take you down to the river front first thing."

"I will," he paused. "Let me go pack and I'll be right back."

"I'll wait up for you."

Christopher had only been gone a few minutes when there was loud knocking at both his front and back doors. Roused from sleep, the servants were frightened by the loud, boisterous attack on their home.

"Mark Kingsford! Are you in there?" a voice bellowed.

"Who's out there?"

"This is Special Deputy Fritch . . . we're lookin' for one Christopher Fletcher. Is he in there?"

"No."

"We have a warrant to search the premises. Will you open up?"

Mark fumbled nervously with the lock and finally opened the door to admit four seedy-looking official deputies.

"What's this all about, Deputy Fritch?"

Fritch was busy directing his men to search each room and it was a few minutes before he answered Mark's question.

"Christopher Fletcher is a wanted man. He's part of the Underground Railroad."

"Christopher?" Mark was totally shocked.

"Either you're a very good actor or you weren't aware of his involvement."

"I had no idea . . . You say he's been helping run slaves out of the South?"

"That's right . . . and if you help him in any way now that you know about his activities, then you're just as guilty as he is."

Mark was worried . . . Christopher was due to return at any time. He hoped that these men completed their search before Christopher made his appearance.

"Did you find anything?" Fritch asked his men as they regrouped in the parlor.

"Nothing, sir. He hasn't been here . . . yet."

"Mr. Kingsford, if Fletcher shows up here you would do well to turn him over to the authorities. He is a wanted man."

"Yes, sir," Mark answered, grateful that Christopher hadn't returned as yet.

When they had gone, Mark reassured his servants that all was well and sent them on to bed before indulging himself in a stiff drink. It was going to be a long night waiting up for Christopher.

Christopher took Mark's carriage on his return trip to the hotel and checked out in record time. He was so intent on getting back to Mark's that he didn't notice the rider following him. Worried thoughts of Katie in trouble assailed him. She needed him and there was no way he could get to her before tomorrow. He was stranded in New Orleans.

As he turned down Mark's private, darkly-shadowed street the shot rang out. The fiery projectile exploded through his shoulder, knocking him sideways in the driver's seat.

Christopher lay stunned by the force of the blow. His breathing was labored as he tried to figure out where the shot had come from. Blood poured freely from the raw wound and he tried in vain to staunch the flow. He could hear footsteps running toward him and he knew that he had to get away. Struggling awkwardly to right himself, he grabbed the reins and urged the horse forward. When he'd gained a lead on his assailant, he slowed the carriage long enough so that he could climb out and then slapped the horse into action once more.

With slow uncoordinated movements, he stumbled into a dark alley. Dizzy and in great pain, he fell. As the blackness of unconsciousness flooded through him, he thought of Katie and wished sadly that they could have had more time to build a life together.

Mark was pacing the parlor when the sound of the single gunshot sent him running to the window. When he couldn't see anything, he threw open the front door and rushed outside.

The fog was thick and visibility was severely limited. Moving quietly through the shadows, he paused only momentarily as the night breeze parted the mist and revealed his own carriage, driverless, standing idly some distance down the street.

Breaking into a run, he grabbed the horse's rein and led it back to the front of the townhouse. It was then as he walked back to check the seat that he discovered blood on the floor of the vehicle.

Mark ran back inside and woke John, one of his servants.

"What's happened, Mastah Mark?" John asked.

"I don't know, John. It looks like Christopher has been shot, but I don't know where he is . . ." Mark looked around worriedly. "We'll have to look for him. I'm sure he's hurt, but first let's get rid of this carriage before the patrollers come back."

"Yes, suh," John said as he took charge of the horse and vehicle.

"I'll wait for you inside. Then we can go together."

In a few short minutes, John was back, after having cleaned the carriage of traces of blood.

They began their search at the end of the street, checking all the dark corners and any place where a wounded man might crawl to hide himself. It was almost an hour later before they found him, unconscious in the narrow alley. Mark sent John back to get the enclosed carriage and when he returned they carefully laid him inside on the floor and drove off toward Rampart Street.

Cherie's house was the only place Mark could think of where Christopher would be safe. No patrollers would ever think of looking there for him.

Cherie looked frightened when she answered her door a short time later.

"Who is it?"

"It's me, Mark," he spoke softly. "I'm in trouble and I need your help."

"Come in." She opened the door for him and gasped when she saw who they were carrying.

"What's happened?"

"From what I've been told, Christopher is part of the Underground Railroad and the patrollers have just found out. They're after him and from the looks of things they almost got him."

"Take him upstairs. I'll send for the doctor right away."

"Do you think that's wise?"

"Of course. Dr. Lucien has helped his share of runaways before. We can trust him."

"Thank you, Cherie."

"You're welcome, Mark. Now, let's see what we can do for Christopher."

When they got him upstairs and into bed, Mark stripped off his jacket and shirt to reveal the raw, bloody wound in his shoulder.

"It looks bad. He's lost so much blood," Mark told her.

"There's not much more we can do without the doctor. We'll just have to hope that he hurries."

It was almost an hour before John returned with Dr. Lucien in tow.

"Miss Delabarre, Mr. Kingsford. John, here, tells me someone's been shot?"

"My sister's husband. He was ambushed."

"Where is he?"

"Upstairs . . . Follow me," Cherie said.

Cherie and Mark led the way up to the bedroom and ushered the doctor inside. If anything, Christopher looked worse. His coloring was pale — almost deathly — and his features seemed sharpened by his pain.

He didn't stir as the doctor cut away the makeshift bandage Mark had applied. His examination took long minutes and Mark and Cherie waited at the foot of the bed, anxious and worried.

Mark knew he would have to send word to Katie as soon as he knew something positive. He didn't know exactly what problems she was having at Greenwood, but it couldn't possibly be more important than Christopher's being shot.

"I'm afraid the bullet didn't pass through. It seems to be lodged against the bone and I'm going to have to probe for it."

"Can I help?" Mark offered.

"I may need you to help hold him down . . . It may take you and John both."

"I'll get him."

Mark went in search of his servants while Cherie went to wait in the parlor. The physician was preparing for surgery when they returned. Dr. Lucien had his shirt sleeves rolled up and was washing his hands.

"He may not feel this at all, but I can't be sure. I'll need one of you on each side," he explained as he readied his instruments. "And when I tell you don't let him move — I mean it!"

"Yes, doctor," they replied taking their places and waiting for orders of what to do.

With skillful precision, Dr. Lucien explored the wound drawing moans of protest from Christopher as he twisted violently against the restraining hands, trying to avoid the pain. On his third attempt to extract the bullet, Dr. Lucien succeeded and he quickly pressed a cloth to the ragged injury to stop the flow of fresh, bright blood.

"It's out," he confirmed, as he removed the cloth and sterilized the raw flesh.

Mark dismissed John and returned to Christopher's side as the doctor finished wrapping his shoulder.

"Will he be all right?" Mark asked anxiously.

"If there's no infection, he should be fine in a few weeks. But he's going to be very weak for a while . . . he's lost a lot of blood."

"I know."

"Just keep him quiet."

"Will he regain consciousness soon?"

"Any time now. I'll leave some laudanum with you just in case he needs a pain killer. And I'll check back with you tomorrow."

"Thank you, doctor."

Mark showed him out and then, before returning to Christopher's side, he wrote a note to Katie telling her that there was an emergency and that she should come to New Orleans at once.

The sun was rising as he finished the short letter and Cherie sent one of her servants on the trip to deliver the missive to Greenwood and bring Katie back.

After Cherie retired to her room to get a few hours' rest, Mark went back to Christopher's side. Entering the master bedroom quietly, he pulled a chair near the bed and sat down, waiting patiently for him to stir.

"Katie . . ." Christopher's voice was dry and hoarse and shook Mark from his half-sleep.

"Christopher!" Mark came quickly awake.

"Where's Katie? I've got to get her away . . ." He tried to sit up but was forced to fall back against the pillows.

"Christopher, it's me, Mark. You're safe. You're here with me. Relax . . ." he tried to console him.

"Mark?" Christopher tried to focus on him. "Don't

you see — they know. I've got to get to Katie . . . She's not safe. We've got to hide . . ."

"Christopher . . ." Mark's voice was stern, trying to calm him. "You're safe, please, take it easy . . ."

He eyed Mark warily. "Where am I?"

"At Cherie's house. It was the safest place I could think of."

He managed a small nod. "You know?"

"Yes. Right after you left, the patrollers showed up looking for you . . ."

Christopher closed his eyes wearily, "Someone's got to warn Katie . . . they'll be looking for me everywhere."

"I know; that's why I can't stay here. They may come back to my place again looking for you and I want to be there."

Christopher looked at him again. "Will you send word to Katie?"

"I already have. Now you just rest. I'll be back as soon as I can get away."

"Thanks, Mark."

Mark gave him a reassuring smile before heading back home.

It was much later that morning when Dr. Lucien returned, "How's he doing?"

"He started bleeding again, but I think it's under control now," Cherie told him.

"I'd better check."

The doctor followed her to the bedroom and found Christopher awake.

"Mr. Fletcher, I'm Dr. Lucien."

Christopher studied him seriously before speaking, "Doctor, thank you for all you've done for me."

"You're welcome. And, by the way, Mark and Cherie have told me everything and you have nothing to fear from me. I have often helped Robert Adams when the fugitives are injured coming downriver."

Some of the tenseness seemed to drain from him as he closed his eyes.

"I've got to rebandage your wound. It may hurt but it's necessary to prevent further bleeding."

"All right," he agreed, his voice a strained whisper. "I'll hold steady for you."

And he held perfectly still while the physician cleaned and dressed his shoulder.

"How bad is it?"

"You're weak from the blood loss, but I think two weeks of bedrest should have you back on your feet."

"I don't have two weeks!" Christopher argued.

"If you try to move before then, I can almost guarantee that you'll end up in a hospital. This is a deep, serious bullet wound, Mr. Fletcher," Dr. Lucien confronted him with the truth.

Christopher gave up the fight. What the doctor said was true. He would be little use to anyone in his present weakened state . . . why, he couldn't even get out of bed on his own . . . He would have to rest and hope that Katie would soon be here with him, so he'd know that she was safe.

It was mid-afternoon when Mark received Katie's second note explaining her reasons for leaving for Missouri right away with Dee and Jebediah. It all became clear to Mark then . . . Emil Montard was behind it all. He had discovered the truth about Christopher and after failing in his blackmail attempts, had informed the authorities.

As he was about to leave to tell Christopher the whole story, the patrollers returned, pounding loudly on his doors once again.

"Open up, Kingsford. We know you're in there,"

Fritch demanded.

Mark opened the door in a casual motion. "Deputy Fritch, what can I do for you?"

"We know that Christopher Fletcher was seen in the neighborhood last night and he might have been wounded. We need to search your house again."

"He's not here and hasn't been here all night."

"Well, we need to see for ourselves. If you don't mind." Fritch looked at Mark suspiciously.

But when Mark shrugged indifferently and stepped aside to let him in, they were surprised.

"Not at all, gentlemen. Please make yourselves at home."

Mark stood back quietly as they once again checked each room and returned empty-handed. He listened to their conversations, hoping to learn more, but nothing important was said.

"I guess you're not hiding anything, Kingsford, but just remember what I told you last night."

"I haven't forgotten, Deputy."

"Good. We'll be in touch. And you let us know if you hear anything."

"I'll do that."

When they had gone, Mark cancelled his trip to Cherie's for fear that they might be following him. Sending a note indirectly through a servant, he let them know that he would come the next day when the searches weren't so intense.

Seventeen

The Escape

The only sound in the dining room was the faint clink of the china as Marie and Emil Montard ate breakfast the following morning. They had not spoken to each other yet and the tension was almost tangible.

Marie was beside herself with grief. She was furious that this could have happened to her . . . her only son — dead. She choked back a sob and looked down the table at her husband. Emil seemed so cool and unemotional that she felt herself fill with hate for him. Frustrated at every turn, she directed all of her rage at him . . . wanting to see him break — if only for a moment.

"How can you just sit there so calmly?" she belittled him. "You just buried your only child yesterday and today you act as though you haven't a care in the world."

Emil gave her a withering look. "What would you have me do, madam? Air my emotions openly for all to see and leave myself vulnerable to attack? No. I will not."

He turned his attention back to his food, ignoring her baleful stare.

"Emil, I'll never forgive you. You have ruined my life . . ." she cried, undone by his cold words. "Oh that I had taken to the veil. Then I wouldn't have had to face such losses as I've had to endure these past few months."

Emil continued to eat, paying no attention to her diatribe. When she finally paused in her verbal attack, he managed to get a word in.

"I will be leaving for St. Louis this afternoon."

"St. Louis? But, why? How can you leave me at a time like this?"

"I leave you because I have to. If Dee is to be brought to justice, then I must do it."

"If you hadn't been stupid enough to let her get away in the first place . . ."

"Marie, your cutting remarks are wearing on me. I've explained to you what happened . . . I did not expect them to run . . ."

"More the fool you, then," she sneered.

Emil stood up abruptly. "I must pack."

"Don't bother to come back unless you take care of this matter . . ."

Emil left the room wishing that he could depart on an earlier boat.

Christopher awoke early the next morning and felt as if he were surrounded by an air of unreality. How could so much have happened in such a short period of time? Thank God for Mark and his quick thinking. He had saved him from a certain death.

Now, if he could only make sure that Katie was safe . . .

Cherie peeked in and was glad to see that he was awake and looking much better.

"How do you feel this morning?"

"Better, I think . . ." He gave her a smile that seemed closer to a grimace.

After helping him to a sitting position, she plumped his pillows to give him extra support.

"Do you want something to eat?"

"No. Not right now," he dismissed the thought of food as unimportant. "Have you heard anything from Mark or Katie?"

"No. Mark hasn't been back, but he sent a note yesterday afternoon. It seems the patrollers were watching him, so he deliberately stayed away. I'm sure he'll be by sometime today and maybe he'll have some information then," she assured him, trying to calm his fears.

"I hope so. This not knowing is hard to deal with."

"I know. I went through the same thing when you were all reported lost on the island." Her expression saddened as she remembered her long hours at Isaac's side. Then, wanting to put the past behind her, she forced a smile. "Now, how about some broth? I'm sure you'll be able to tolerate that."

Christopher shrugged, "Whatever you say."

"Well, if you want to get out of that bed as quickly as possible, then you'd better start eating. It'll help you get your strength back."

"Yes ma'am," he grinned sheepishly.

Cherie smiled at him fondly and patted his arm before leaving the room. "Don't you worry. Katie's just fine. I'm sure she'll be here as soon as she can."

Cherie made her way to the kitchen, her thoughts dwelling on Christopher. She felt good knowing that Katie's marriage was a happy one. Christopher obviously loved her very much and she was sure that Isaac would have been pleased.

A short time later, while Christopher was forcing down the hot chicken broth Cherie had served him, Mark arrived.

"Good morning, Christopher. You look a lot better today."

"Thanks, but I think anything besides a corpse would have been an improvement over yesterday," he answered wryly, as he awkwardly set the lap tray aside with his good hand.

"That's for sure." Mark dragged a chair back over by the bed.

"What's this about the patrollers coming back?"

"Yes, yesterday. They searched the whole house again."

"What did they have to say?"

"Not much. They know you've been shot but that's all they know. I don't think they suspect me, but I didn't want to take any chances . . ."

"I appreciate that. I have no desire to be strung up in public . . ." He shifted uncomfortably and paled slightly as he accidentally moved his injured shoulder.

"Bad? The doctor left some medicine . . ."

"No. I'll make it. I don't like to take anything if I can possibly avoid it."

Mark nodded.

"Have you had any news from Katie?" he asked and when Mark hesitated, he pressed, "Mark?"

"It's a very long story . . ."

"What is? Katie's all right isn't she? She hasn't been hurt, has she?"

"To the best of my limited knowledge, she's fine."

Christopher didn't like the way he left the sentence hang. "I think you'd better start talking and fast."

Mark cleared his throat. "From what I found out . . . the day after you left Greenwood, Katie went

385

for her usual ride and was accosted by Andre. When she refused his advances, he turned ugly and threatened her with blackmail."

"Blackmail?"

"The Montards are the ones who found out about your connection with the Underground Railroad and they were going to use the information to blackmail you."

"The Montards?" Christopher was caught by surprise. "I never would have thought . . . You mean Andre was that obsessed with having Katie?"

"Emil wanted Greenwood back and he was planning to use the threat against you to that end, but then Andre ruined Emil's plan by threatening Katie."

"How is she? He didn't hurt her, did he?" Rage welled up inside of him.

"No, she got away. She did manage to get back to the house, but he followed her."

"All the way to the house?" Christopher was incredulous at the brazen act.

"He must have known that you were gone," Mark explained. "Anyway, when Joel tried to send him on his way, Andre shot Joel."

"Joel?" He was instantly alert. "How bad is he?"

"I'm afraid he's dead."

Christopher's jaw tightened as he fought down the painful emotions that twisted deep within him.

"I'll kill the bastard. I swear I will." He looked away from Mark until he had himself more under control. Shaking with anger and furious at his own helplessness, he finally turned back. "And Katie? What happened to her?"

Mark read his bleak expression and hastened to reassure him.

"He didn't hurt her. Dee got your gun from the desk and killed him as he was forcing Katie to go inside."

386

"Dee killed Andre?"

Mark nodded. "She's a very brave woman."

"Well, thank God they're all right." He stopped to think about it. "Where are they now?"

"I got this note from her yesterday. Evidently, when Emil found out what had happened, he went to Greenwood and threatened them again. He told Katie to sign over the plantation along with Dee or he would turn you in. He gave her a day to make her decision."

"What did she do?"

"She and Dee didn't wait to give him an answer, they took the next boat North. According to her letter, they're going to St. Louis to be with our father. Katie figured that they'd be safe there. And she also sent a warning for you to be careful, for she didn't know what Montard would do when he found out that they had gone."

"I'm glad that she didn't give in to him." Christopher was proud of her actions and he was glad to know that she'd gotten safely away.

"The way I figure it, once he realized that they had run away, he turned all his information about you over to the patrollers. That must have been when they started hounding me . . ."

"I don't doubt it. He's a vicious man. I always knew that he was capable of anything . . . He and Andre were just alike."

"Yes, but when the news gets out, the people around here will think he's a hero . . ."

Christopher shrugged. "I'll just make sure that they don't see me as I leave. I've made it this far and I don't want to get caught now. Mark could you do me one favor?"

"Anything."

" Check on Emil Montard and find out what he's up to. I won't rest easy until I know Katie and Dee are safely out of his reach."

"I'll see what I can find out."

Emil stood at the railing of the steamboat's promenade deck, a look of determination on his face. He was glad to be away from Marie's spiteful presence. But in spite of their bitter words, he knew she was right. He had blundered when he'd given Katie a day to make up her mind. He should have forced the issue then and there.

But, no matter. That was over and done with. He was going after them and he when caught up with Dee, she would pay for shooting his son.

He dreaded the long days it would take him to reach St. Louis. But Emil knew that the trip would give him time enough to plan what he was going to do once he found them.

Christopher took no notice of the bright cheerfulness of his room. He was lost in thought . . . tortuous thought. Joel was dead . . . Joel who had struggled so valiantly to improve himself . . . Joel who had died fighting his fight. Christopher slammed his fist into the mattress. If he hadn't insisted on making the trip himself . . . if he'd let Joel take the slaves to Robert's, he'd still be alive . . .

It was almost a relief for him when Mark came in, dragging him away from his guilt-ridden feelings.

Mark noticed Christopher's dark scowl and wondered how to broach the next subject. He wasn't going to like what he had to tell him.

"Christopher," he smiled, sitting down next to him. "Any better?" Mark indicated his shoulder.

"As long as I don't try to move . . ." he said conversationally. "Have you found out anything?"

"I started checking yesterday, but I didn't get the final word until this morning."

"Well?" Christopher was suddenly impatient.

"Emil Montard left town shortly after Andre's funeral."

"Left? Without his wife?"

"Yes."

"Where did he go?"

"He took a boat North . . . presumably to St. Louis."

"Oh, no . . ." Christopher's thoughts were of Katie. "How much of a head start did they have?"

"Day and a half to two days . . ."

"What kind of connections does your father have in St. Louis?"

"Not much, really. We were out in the camps, mostly."

"You mean Katie could get there and there would be no one to help her?"

Mark looked away from Christopher's piercing glare, "It's a possibility."

"We've got to go. We can't leave her alone to defend herself against the likes of Emil Montard." He threw off the bedclothes and swung his legs over the side of the bed. "Hand me my pants!" he barked at Mark.

"Christopher, wait! You can't get up . . . not yet!"

"The hell I can't!" pushing off the wall he stood, swaying dizzily. "If you think for one minute I'm going to lie here while my wife is in danger, then you're crazy! Give me my clothes!" he bellowed loudly.

Cherie, who heard the commotion, rushed into the room, "Christopher! What are you trying to do?"

"I'm trying to help Katie . . ." His legs started to buckle and Mark quickly helped him back into bed.

Cherie came to him, her hands on her hips. "And

you think you'll be helping her by killing yourself? Hardly."

"Cherie, she's in very real danger. I've got to help her."

"Mark, what is he talking about?" she demanded.

"Emil Montard followed Katie and Dee upriver . . ."

Cherie was not surprised by the disclosure. "Something must be done . . . but what?"

Christopher closed his eyes, trying to gather strength as Cherie paced the room trying to come up with a solution.

"All right. This is what we'll do . . ."

Katie entered the cabin to find Dee playing on the floor with Jebediah.

"We should reach town tonight," she informed her happily.

"Then what do we do? Is your father in town?"

"I don't know for sure . . . probably not. But we'll check into a good hotel and then I'll go by the Pacific Railroad office tomorrow morning. They'll be able to tell me where he is and then we'll make our plans from there."

Dee was still worried about Emil, "Katie, you don't think Mastah Emil will follow us, do you?"

Katie sat down on the edge of the bunk and looked at Dee seriously. "The truth is, Dee, I have no idea what Emil is likely to do . . . If he is as crazy as his son, he might, but we've still got a good head start on him. I honestly don't think he'll find us even if he does come looking for us."

Dee's fears were not relieved by Katie's words.

"Maybe Ah shouldn't have shot Andre . . ." Dee agonized.

"He killed Joel and he was about to hurt us . . . You know what he would have done to us, don't you?"

"Ah, know," she replied, her dark expressive eyes filling with tears. "Ah know."

"Then you also know that you did the only thing possible under the circumstances. Believe me, Dee, if I had had a gun, I would have shot him myself! You were very brave." Katie put her arms around the other woman and hugged her.

"Do you really think so?"

"You saved my life and for that I will always be in your debt."

"But I feel so alone without Joel," she said.

"I wish there was some way that I could take away your pain, Dee," Katie told her, her feelings for her running deep. "You know how important you and Jebediah are to Christopher and me."

Dee nodded as she tried to bring her shattered emotions under control. Jebediah, who had been playing quietly nearby toddled to his mother and hugged her tightly, babbling in baby talk. Dee looked up at Katie and smiled tremulously.

"As long as I have my baby, I know I'll be all right."

Katie looked with tenderness at the sight of mother and child and wished wistfully that she had Christopher's babe to coddle and love.

When the steamer finally tied up at the St. Louis riverfront, it was almost dark. The mountains of merchandise and the bustle of the levee activity intimidated Dee, but to Katie it was as good as home. Delighted to at last be on familiar ground, she easily took charge, hiring a carriage and supervising the loading of their few bags.

"Where to ma'am?" the driver asked after he'd

helped Katie in and retaken his own seat.

"To the Planter's House, please," she directed as she sat back to enjoy the sights.

St. Louis was a thriving river city and Katie always found her visits to the growing metropolis exciting. They reached the hotel in short order and were quickly registered and shown to a large, comfortable room on the second floor.

Jebediah was tired from all the excitement and fell asleep as soon as they put him down, leaving Katie and Dee with the entire evening to relax and figure out what they were going to do. They ordered dinner in their room and discussed their plans for the next day as they ate.

"I'll get up early and go to the office. They should be able to tell me where my father is. Then as soon as we know. I'll make arrangements for our transportation."

"Is it gonna be hard gettin' out to the camp?" Dee worried about a cross-country ride with the child.

"No, it shouldn't be. We can probably ride the train the better part of the way."

Dee was relieved to hear that. "Your father won't mind you bringin' us along, will he?"

"No. He'll be glad to meet you, I'm sure."

"Good. Ah didn't want to be in the way."

"Nonsense, Dee. We've gone through this whole thing together. We're not going to separate now. Don't worry. You'll like my father and I'm positive that he'll like you."

That resolved, they passed a quiet evening and retired early, exhausted from the pressure of the trip.

"Are you sure this will work?" Mark asked Cherie doubtfully.

"It should. The patrollers aren't looking for an old man in a wheelchair." She smiled at Mark. "Don't look so worried. All we have to do is get him up the gangplank and into the cabin. It'll be dark and no one will even notice."

"Lord, I hope so." Mark was clearly nervous as he looked at Christopher in disguise. "I guess you do look like an old man," he finally admitted.

"See? I told you so." Cherie bustled about the room getting Christopher's few things packed and ready to go. "How soon does the boat leave?"

"Ten o'clock." Christopher spoke up from beneath the camouflage of blankets and a shawl.

"It's half past eight now. We'd better get going. Mark, are you all packed?"

"Yes. I'll leave now and go on aboard ahead of you. I've got the cabin right next to yours so we should be in good shape."

"The hardest part will be getting you on board. Once you're safe in your stateroom, you don't come out until St. Louis. You stay in bed the entire trip. Agreed?" Cherie threatened.

"Agreed," Christopher answered.

Cherie had agreed to help him go upriver only if he promised to spend the five days of the journey in bed in his cabin. He'd been reluctant to go along with her but he realized that there was no other way. He knew he would never be able to make it on his own. So travelling incognito, with Mark close by in case he needed help, Christopher was at last on his way to find Katie.

Cherie and her servant helped Christopher into her carriage and they rode to the riverfront quietly, in great fear of being discovered.

"Mark said that the patrollers haven't been around since yesterday." Cherie tried to cheer him up.

"Good," Christopher grinned, feeling as old as he

looked.

Cherie had first powdered his hair and used some lamp black to create the illusion of the wrinkles and the sunken cheeks of old age. Then she had handed him a mirror and he'd been hard pressed to believe that the old man reflected there was him. Truly grateful for her ingenuity, he thanked her for her help as they pulled up at the landing.

"Shush, I'll hear no more of it. We're family, in a way, and a family always takes care of its own."

Christopher groaned convincingly as he was settled into his wheelchair and Cherie pushed him up the gangplank with the help of her servant. There was only a short, tense moment as they waited to receive directions to the cabin and then they were safely inside the little stateroom.

They all breathed a deep sigh of relief and then quickly got Christopher out of the chair and into the bunk.

"By the time I get to St. Louis, I hope I won't have to use that damned contraption!" he complained as he rested back on the bed with a low, protesting moan.

"Just don't take any chances, Christopher," Cherie told him. "Take care of yourself."

She came to hold his hand and he lifted hers to his lips.

"I will. Thanks to you."

His voice was soft and sincere, reminding her of Isaac many years before and she blinked back sudden stinging tears.

"Keep in touch," she kissed his cheek, being careful not to get any of his disguise on her. Bidding him goodbye, she left the cabin, stopping only long enough to give the key to Mark before going ashore.

Christopher had only been alone a few minutes when Mark knocked at his cabin door.

"It's Mark," he identified himself in low tones as he entered. "How are you feeling?"

"I must be as bad as the doctor said. I feel horrible from just taking that short ride."

"Well, don't worry. You've got a good five days of bedrest ahead of you. By the time we get to the city you should be doing much better."

"I hope so. I won't be able to help Katie if I can't get out of bed for more than twenty minutes." He was disgusted with his own weakness.

"That's why I'm here," Mark championed himself.

"If we get into a fight, just make sure that you're sober!" he teased, and Mark had the decency to look a bit shamefaced.

"Don't worry, I've sworn off heavy drink."

"Good," Christopher smiled, relaxing a bit. "Did you let Jacqui know that you were leaving?"

"I sent her a note," Mark told him. "I figured that if I tried to explain it to her face to face, I'd probably give it all away. So, I just told her that I had to go back to see my father and that I'd only be gone a few weeks."

"Then everything's taken care of."

"I think so. Now, all we have to do is catch up with Katie."

Katie left the hotel right after breakfast and went straight to the Pacific Railroad office. Bidding the hired driver to wait for her, she hurried inside and approached the clerk at the front desk.

"Can I help you?" he asked.

"Yes, I was wondering if you could tell me if George Kingsford is still working out on the line or . . ."

"George Kingsford. Why no, he's not," the man replied abruptly.

"Oh," Katie paused, hoping he'd continue and tell her where her father was. "Well, then, could you tell me where he is working?"

"Are you a relation?" the clerk looked her over carefully.

"Yes, as a matter of fact, I am!" Katie was losing her patience. "I'm his daughter."

"Oh, well, in that case, Mr. Kingsford is here . . ."

"He's in St. Louis?" she was thrilled. "Where can I find him?"

"Right now, he's in the back office. Go on in."

"Thank you." With all the eagerness of a child Katie wrestled her skirts through the narrow, low gate that separated the waiting area from the desks.

Pushing the door open wide, she flew into the room.

"Father!" she cried joyfully.

"Katie?" George Kingsford looked up from his work and then stood up quickly to hug his daughter. "Katie, what are you doing here? I thought you'd just gotten married."

"I did Papa, see." She held up her hand to show him her wedding ring.

"Oh, Katie. I'm so glad that you're here. I've really missed you, little one."

"And I've missed you. But what are you doing in town? I thought I was going to have to chase you down out in the wilds."

"As a matter of fact, I just came into the office to arrange a leave of absence."

"What for?"

"To go to Louisiana to see you and meet Christopher. Where is he?"

"He'll be along soon," she hedged and her father knew it.

"Katie Kingsford, you're not telling me the whole

story," he accused.

Katie sighed, suddenly feeling that it was time to share all of her worries.

"Can we go somewhere to talk? I have so much to tell you."

"Of course. Have you eaten?"

"Yes, I have."

"Let's go back to the hotel then, so we can have some privacy."

"Fine. Where are you staying?"

"I'm at the Planter's."

"We are, too."

"We?" George was curious.

"I have a friend with me, but I'll explain all that to you later."

Dismissing her hired carriage, they took George's own and rode back to the hotel speaking only of pleasant things. George, ever sensitive to his daughter's moods, recognized her agitation even after a long separation, but he was wise enough not to make mention of her tenseness. Finally, in George's luxurious suite of rooms, Katie felt safe enough to tell him of the horrors she'd just been through.

"Can you talk about it, Katie?" he asked gently after the silence between them had grown heavy.

"Yes, with you I think I can . . ." she told him as he sat next to her on the small sofa.

"I know about the hurricane and your marriage. And Mark wrote again when Isaac died."

"It was so sad . . . Cherie loved him so," Katie confided, close to tears.

"Cherie? You mean he was still with her?"

"Yes. Do you know her?"

"Isaac had just begun their liaison when I left Louisiana with your mother."

"Oh."

"Where was his wife — Suzanne?"

"Well, when Uncle Isaac was really sick he kept calling for Cherie, not Suzanne, and she got mad and left. Do you know, she never came back." Katie was still mystified by her behavior.

George shook his head, "Cherie took care of him then?"

"She never left his side . . ."

"Cherie Delabarre is one very special woman."

Katie nodded, "Anyway . . . the reason I'm here . . ."

"Yes?"

"Do you know the Montards?"

"Of course," George smiled broadly. "Emil and I grew up together. Why?"

Katie looked at him skeptically. "Andre Montard was the cause of our problems."

"Andre?"

"He said he wanted me, even though I told him time and time again that I didn't care for him."

"You can't blame him for trying," George commented good-naturedly.

"But he didn't give up. Not even after I married Christopher."

George frowned, "What do you mean?"

"Last week, he found me alone and tried to . . . Well, when I wouldn't, he threatened to hurt Christopher."

"Hurt Christopher? How?" George was growing angry.

"He was going to turn him over to the authorities."

"For what?"

Katie looked her father straight in the eye. "Christopher works for the Underground Railroad. He's been helping slaves get out of the South."

George was stunned by her revelation and then

smiled. "I always knew when you picked a husband he would be someone special."

"Then you're not upset?"

"No. You've always known how I felt about slavery."

Katie was relieved.

"But you're telling me that Andre was blackmailing you to sleep with him by threatening to report Christopher?" George asked, his emotions under tight control.

"Yes, Papa," she answered. "But I didn't!"

"Good girl! That boy must be the lowest . . ."

"That's not all . . ."

"Oh?" he looked at her questioningly.

"I got away from him and he chased me back to the house. When we tried to make him leave he killed Joel, Christopher's partner. And then he was going to rape me, but Dee shot him."

"Dee?"

"Joel's wife."

"Thank God. She must be a very strong woman."

"She is. She's the friend I brought with me."

"I'd like to meet her, to thank her for saving you." George smiled at his daughter fondly. "But where was Christopher all this time?"

"He had taken a group of runaways into New Orleans. Evidently, Andre knew that he was gone, and that's probably why he took so many chances."

"Is Andre dead?"

"Yes," Katie stated. "And I can't say I'm sorry. He was a cruel and vicious man."

"So you're here for a visit?"

"No. I—we—needed to get away. Emil came to Greenwood and told me to sign over the plantation plus Dee or he would expose Christopher."

"Emil?"

"Emil," Katie confirmed. "That's why Dee and I ran away. I didn't know where Christopher was, so I sent word to Mark in town that we were heading North and then we took the first packet out of there."

"I understand and I'll take care of you, darling," he assured her. "Do you think Emil would really turn Christopher in?"

"I think so . . ."

"Well, don't worry any more. I'll do some checking on my own and we'll see what we can find out."

"Thanks."

"Now, let's go meet Dee."

Eighteen

Confrontation

It was mid-afternoon. The sun was hot for September and it almost seemed like a summer's day. Business on the levee was brisk and newly arriving packets were having trouble finding a place to dock.

Emil, withdrawn and aloof, waited in his cabin as the boat tied up. He had not socialized during the entire trip. Instead, he had remained in the seclusion of his stateroom, trying to figure out the best plan of action. Now his decisions made, he knew exactly what he had to do.

Leaving the boat, he checked into the Planter's Hotel and decided that after a short rest, he would begin his search.

Stretching out on the plush bed in his elegant room, Emil relaxed and closed his eyes. As he tried to sleep, the events of the past few months haunted him . . . losing Greenwood . . . Andre's death. Though he mourned his son, Emil was beginning to see that Andre had behaved very foolishly. Had he not lost his head over Katie Kingsford, Greenwood would have been theirs by now.

As it was, Emil had been forced to play his trump card and, though Fletcher might well be dead, he had gained nothing from it. Instead, he had probably lost the plantation forever.

Anger at his own inability to right a most complicated situation drove him from his attempted rest and he left the room after freshening up, intent on his search for Katie and Dee.

Seated in the hotel dining room with her father, Katie laughed lightly at something he said and smiled warmly at him.

"I am so glad I came here," she told him, wanting him to understand how comforting his presence was to her.

"I am, too, honey," he patted her hand. "And don't worry too much about Christopher. I'm sure we'll hear something soon."

Her eyes clouded for a moment, "I know. I'm sure Mark will write as soon as he knows anything."

Changing the topic, George asked, "How's Jebediah feeling?"

"He's much better tonight. It was just an upset stomach I think."

"It's a shame Dee couldn't join us."

"She wanted to keep him quiet until tomorrow."

"I can certainly understand that. When you and Mark were little and took sick you gave your mother and me fits. You were very demanding children," he teased.

"But we turned out so well," she countered.

"That you did. Now, tell me all about Mark's fiancee . . . Jacqueline?"

"Yes, Jacqui La Zear."

"Good family . . . I knew of them when I lived there."

"Yes, they're very nice people and Jacqui is very pretty. She's perfect for Mark and I know he really loves her."

"And he's decided to take over some of Isaac's business affairs?"

"Before he died, Uncle Isaac asked Mark to help out. And Mark does like it."

"So he won't be coming back here?"

"I really don't think so, Papa. With Jacqui's family there, I imagine he'll stay in Louisiana."

For a moment, George looked sad. "Well, whatever makes him happy . . . Has he made plans for the wedding yet?"

"No. I think they're going to wait a while."

George was glad, for that meant that he would be able to attend. He had missed Katie's wedding and he didn't want to miss Mark's.

Across the crowded dining room, Emil Montard was shown to a table for one. He ordered a drink to be served right away and sat back to enjoy the potent liquor.

Pondering his success, Emil was quite pleased with himself. He had located them and with a minimum of effort. He had hardly believed his luck, when checking the registry at this very hotel, he found the names of Katie Fletcher and travelling companion. Now, all he had to do was find Dee and . . .

Emil had been idly surveying the room when he was suddenly jolted by the sight of Katie having dinner with her father. He had not seen George Kingsford in years and the sight of his old friend surprised him. What was he doing here? George's presence complicated things. Emil didn't relish the idea of a confrontation with him. George Kingsford was a very influential, powerful man. Trying to figure out a way to avoid such a scene, the thought suddenly struck him . . . this would be the perfect opportunity to find Dee while she was alone. Then he could be gone from here with her before anyone ever knew.

Rising casually, he cancelled his dinner order and strode easily from the room trying not to attract any attention. Out of the Kingsfords' line of sight, he hurried upstairs and located Katie's room with relative ease. Taking a deep breath, he steadied himself. Cautiously trying the doorknob, Emil found to his relief, that it was unlocked and in one quick, smooth move, he entered and closed the door behind him.

Dee, who had been resting with Jebediah, looked up sleepily from her bed. "Katie?"

Her eyes widened as she saw Emil Montard blocking the door, looking like the devil incarnate.

"Hello, Dee," he said in a soft, dangerous voice. "Weren't you expecting me?"

Dee was paralyzed with fear and couldn't make a sound. She wanted to scream . . . to run, but terror held her captive.

"You can make this easy or difficult. The choice is yours, but the outcome will be the same. You are going back to Louisiana and you're going with me!" he told her as he approached her menacingly. "Now, let's go."

"No—Ah—"

"Now!" he snarled ferociously.

Grabbing Dee's arm he dragged her forcefully from the bed, waking Jebediah, who began to cry.

"My baby—" Dee managed.

She tried to reach for him but Emil pulled her toward the door. Jerking her around to face him he ordered.

"Do you want him to stay alive?"

Dee could only nod.

"Then walk out this door with me and make it look good. If you give me any resistance . . ."

"Ah understand . . ." she quaked.

"Then let's go." Opening the door, he pushed her ahead of him out into the hall. He shut the door solidly behind them, muffling Jebediah's frightened cries.

"Don't look so damned scared!" he muttered threateningly.

"Yes suh," she mumbled, stumbling as she walked.

Without pause, they moved off down the hall to the staircase and then climbed the steps to the third floor and entered Emil's room. Locking the door behind them, he quickly began to pack. When he'd finished, he gathered his things together and they headed down to the lobby. Emil stopped at the desk to turn in his key and then they exited the hotel.

Katie and George were almost back to her room when they heard the baby's screams. Katie gave her father a worried look before breaking into a run. She was surprised to find that the door was unlocked and she rushed inside.

Katie was terrified to find only Jebediah in the room. There was no sign of Dee.

"Where do you suppose she went?" Katie asked her father as she tried to calm the distraught child.

"Did she go or was she taken?" he questioned. "Surely she wouldn't have willingly gone off and left him alone."

"Oh God! Montard!"

"Let's check at the desk downstairs. Maybe someone saw them."

George took the baby and they l urried down to the lobby.

"Did a black woman leave the hotel recently?" he demanded of the startled desk clerk.

"Let me see . . . Mr. Montard checked out a few minutes ago and he had his black wench with him . . ." the man spoke sneeringly. "Damned attractive for a . . ."

"Thank you." George cut him off, not wanting to hear another slur. "He's got her all right and my guess is he's heading for the riverfront. Come on, Katie! Let's go!"

A hired carriage was parked in front and George called up to the driver, "Did you see the white man leave with his slave woman?"

"Yes, sir."

"Did you see which way they went?"

"Better than that," the driver replied. "I heard."

"There's an extra $10 gold piece for you if you can catch up with them."

"Yes, sir!"

After Katie, Jebediah and George were in and seated, he slapped his horses into action, sending them rampaging down the street in the direction of the levee.

"We'll catch them." George was confident as their conveyance tore along at breakneck speed.

"But will we be alive when we do?" Katie gasped clasping Jebediah to her.

Trying to lighten their mood, he gave her an encouraging smile, "Why, Katie, I've never known you to be afraid of a little rough riding!"

For a moment Katie saw the humor of their riotous chase. "I'm not afraid as long as I'm the one doing the driving!"

"I see your point," George agreed grasping the side of the vehicle to keep from losing his seat as they rounded a corner without slowing. And Katie couldn't quell the smile that came as she watched her father trying to regain his balance.

"We're almost to the river. I hope this driver knows what he's about."

The carriage rolled to a stop near the vehicle that had transported Emil, just as he stepped down dragging Dee with him.

George was out of the carriage and heading for Emil before he spoke.

"I believe you have something that belongs to me," he called out loudly, hoping to attract attention.

Emil froze and then, cursing under his breath, he turned to face George.

"I have no fight with you," he responded tightening his grip on Dee. "I've got what I came after and now I'm leaving."

He made to turn away but George's next words stopping him.

"She's Katie's property and if you take another step, I'll have you arrested for slave-stealing." His words were spoken conversationally but the threat was not to be taken lightly.

"George," Emil protested. "She shot and killed my son!"

"While he was trying to ravish my daughter!" he ground out.

He paled as he realized that there was no getting away.

"Emil, let's not air our differences publicly. Come, let's go back to the hotel and talk . . ." He offered him a way to save face before the small crowd that had gathered.

After hesitating a moment, he released Dee and spoke, "I'll come with you, George."

George turned to Katie, "You take Dee and the baby in the other carriage. I'll meet you later."

"Yes, Father." She ran to Dee, handing her her son and hugging them both.

Emil looked like an old man as he walked toward George, his steps dragged in defeat. They didn't speak, but looked at each other long and hard before climbing into the waiting conveyance and driving away.

"Mark, if I don't get out of this bed soon, I may never be able to!" Christopher grouched as he half-sat, half-lay on the small confining bunk.

"Sorry, Cherie's orders!" Mark grinned at his discomfort.

"Did anybody ever die from bedsores?" He rubbed his backside wearily and tried to shift to his other hip without jarring his slowly healing shoulder.

"I don't think so, but you could always be the first!" he joked and received a glare for his trouble.

"I am going to sit on the side of the bunk for a while," he declared.

"Christopher!" Mark began, but realizing that he was not to be deterred, he quickly moved to help him.

Christopher's face whitened as he held himself erect and his jaw clenched tightly as he fought against the dizziness and the shooting pain that almost forced him back down. But, as he waited, the agony passed and he turned smiling to Mark.

"See, I told you I could do it." He sounded just like a little boy bragging about some great feat.

"If only Katie could see you now," Mark smiled back.

"I wish she could." His good humor dimmed momentarily.

"We'll be there in only two and a half more days, and you'll see . . . She'll be fine. Katie's just like a cat

408

sometimes, she always lands on her feet . . ."

"I hope so," he answered.

"I tell you what . . . just to take your mind off your troubles, I'll let you beat me at poker. What do you say?"

Christopher grinned fleetingly. "How much money do you have?"

Mark laughed as he pulled a small table over and brought out a deck of cards. "Not enough to play with you. How about penny-ante?"

"You're on."

The bar of the Planter's Hotel was crowded and noisy as George and Emil made their way, drinks in hand, to a secluded table at the rear. Emil sat down stiffly, his back to the room, leaving George the seat against the wall. Swiftly downing his drink, he signalled the barkeep for a refill.

"Here you are, sir." The bartender came with a fifth of his best bourbon.

"Leave the bottle."

"Yes, sir," he replied, surprised for it was a very potent, very expensive brand.

When he'd gone, Emil poured himself another portion of the amber liquid and looked up at George for the first time.

"Why did you go against me to protect that damned wench?" he asked disgustedly.

George looked at his old friend with pity in his eyes. "I know what happened at Greenwood and Dee did the only thing she could to save Katie and herself. Andre had already killed the overseer, for God's sake!"

"It was only that no-good black buck, Joel, he shot," he dismissed George's contention.

"He was a free man, on his own property and Andre

shot him down in cold blood."

Emil glared at George, but didn't respond.

"If he'd been smart, he would have left then . . . he wouldn't have pushed his luck. But Emil, he was going to attack Katie."

Emil snorted derisively. "Women loved Andre. She probably encouraged him!"

George slammed his glass down on the table and came half-way out of his seat. "You, sir, are talking about *my daughter*! Your offspring, if you care to refer to him as yours, treated my daughter in such an unchivalrous manner that were he still alive, I, myself, would call him out!" He stormed on, "Andre acted the rogue and the scoundrel and met a suitable end for his dastardly deeds!"

Emil blanched before George's righteous anger. All along he had thought only in terms of Dee shooting Andre. Katie's involvement, as far as he had been concerned, had been academic. The slave had killed his son . . . Now he was beginning to understand and he didn't like the picture that was being painted of Andre. Had his son been so intent on pursuing his own pleasures that he'd thrown his honor to the wind? If George Kingsford's word was to be believed, it would seem so. Emil felt sick.

George realizing that Emil was finally accepting the truth, sat back down, drained his drink and waited.

"It is very hard for me to accept the fact that the boy I raised to manhood, could have done such an appalling thing," Emil managed.

"You have been too consumed by your grief and your desire for revenge to realize," George sympathized. "And I can understand that."

"You have my deepest apologies. I hope Katie suffered no harm at Andre's hands."

"No. She was just frightened."

410

Emil was relieved.

"Katie told me that you had threatened her the day after the shootings . . ."

"I am not proud of what happened, but it was not without provocation. When I discovered that Fletcher was involved with the Underground Railroad and that he was using Greenwood as his base . . . I was livid. I wanted revenge on both Dee and Fletcher."

"So, did you follow through on your threat? Did you turn him in?" George asked coldly.

Emil looked him straight in the eye. "I told one of the Special Deputies with whom I had had dealings in the past, that I suspected him. Yes."

George bit back a furious reply, "Had they caught him when you left?"

"No."

"Thank God for that."

"Then you are not going to deny his involvement?"

"No," he answered. "As a matter of fact, Emil, I am damned proud of it. You know how I feel about slavery."

"Yes, George. I know and I've never understood how how you could turn your back on your heritage and just walk away."

George shrugged, not caring to justify his motive to anyone and then turned his thoughts to his new son-in-law. There was no doubt about the fact that he admired Christopher for his brave stand on a very controversial issue and he wondered what could be done to rescue him from such a dangerous situation. Hopefully, he hadn't been captured yet and was just hiding out until he could make good his escape.

With narrowed eyes, George studied Emil and debated approaching him with a compromising offer.

"Emil," his tone was considerably lighter as he sought to come to an agreement that would settle everything.

"Yes?"

"I know you want Greenwood back."

"Of course, that goes without saying," he admitted, trying to understand this new twist in the conversation.

"What would you say to striking a bargain?"

"Bargain?" he was instantly cautious. "What kind of bargain?"

"Would you be willing to drop the charges you made against Christopher?"

"And why should I?" he countered tersely. "Christopher Fletcher is a criminal under the Southern code and deserves whatever he gets!"

"Ah, but right now, you have nothing. No Dee and no Greenwood. Suppose—just suppose now—that I could get Katie and Christopher to agree to sell Greenwood to you for a reasonable price in return for you dropping your testimony against Christopher." George continued, "Everyone would benefit from it, too. Christopher would be cleared of all wrongdoing. You would have Greenwood and Mark could marry Jacqui and stay in Louisiana without the fear of being connected with all of this."

Emil was impressed by the offer. Right now, he had only the satisfaction of knowing that he'd gotten the law onto Fletcher. But if he were to get Greenwood back—that might help to placate Marie.

"Your proposal is worth considering . . ."

"I'm glad you feel that way." George sat back in his chair. "You realize that I'm not in a position to make you a firm commitment until I know that Christopher is safe and alive and I have both his and Katie's approval."

"Of course." Emil secretly prayed that Fletcher had escaped the certain death that awaited him in

Louisiana.

Emil smiled, lifting his glass. "Then let us hope that Christopher Fletcher is safe."

"I'll drink to that."

Katie opened the door eagerly when George finally came to her. It had been long hours since the confrontation on the levee and she had waited impatiently with Dee in their hotel room for him to let them know the outcome.

"Well?" she asked eagerly as he entered the room.

"I think I've hit upon a solution . . . but I have to talk with you about it first."

"About what?"

George sat on one bed while Katie and Dee sat with Jebediah on the other.

"First, Dee, you're no longer in danger from Emil."

"Thank God," they muttered. "How did you manage to dissuade him?"

"Just a few, not so idle threats . . ." he grinned. "On certain occasions they work wonders."

"Thank you, Mr. Kingsford," Dee said tearfully.

"George, please, my dear. And you're most welcome."

"But what about this 'solution' of yours?"

"Let me ask you this, Katie," George said. "Do you want to return to Greenwood?"

"*No!*" the answer erupted from her. "I don't care if I never see that place again."

George chuckled, "I had a feeling that that would be your answer."

"So . . . ?"

"So, what I proposed to Emil is this . . . that he goes back to Louisiana without Dee and as soon as he gets there, retracts the charges he made against

413

Christopher."

"He agreed to that?" Katie looked at her father in wide-eyed disbelief. "And just what does he get in return for this sudden change of heart?"

Katie sounded cynical and George couldn't blame her.

"If Christopher is reunited with us, alive and well. Then we will sell Greenwood back to Emil for a nominal amount, provided that Christopher's name has been cleared."

"I only have one objection."

"What's that?"

"I refuse to sell him our slaves. I want all of the plantation's slaves to be given their manumission papers. He can have the land, but he'll not get another chance to abuse the servants." Katie drove a hard bargain.

"I'll tell him."

"Do you think it will affect his decision?"

"I don't know. We'll just have to find out." George rose to leave. "Well, I'm going to call it a night. Why don't you do the same?"

"When will you see Emil again?"

"I'll speak with him in the morning. And as soon as I do, I'll let you know what he says."

"Thank you." She kissed his cheek.

Emil had decided to breakfast in his room and was about to begin when George knocked at the door.

"Good morning, Emil. May I come in?"

"George," he acknowledged and opened the door wider to give him entrance. "What can I do for you?"

"I wanted to let you know that I did speak with Katie last night."

"Yes. And?"

"She has one change to make in our tentative 'arrangement'."

"What's that?"

"She wants the slaves." He noticed Emil's shock and hurried on. "Katie is most willing to sell you the house and the grounds but she is determined to keep the servants with her."

"I should have known. She is, after all, your daughter," Emil meant his remarks disparagingly.

"I'll take that as a compliment," George grinned at him maddeningly. "Well, what do you say? Are you still interested?"

"Of course, I'm still interested," he snapped. "Would she take a separate offer for the blacks?"

"No," his tone was final. "They are not for sale."

"And what if I refuse to clear Fletcher's name?" Emil tried to get better dealing power.

"I am sure," he informed him coldly. "That a very good case could be made against you for your blackmail attempt against Katie and your kidnapping of Dee just last night. You're in Missouri now, Emil."

Stalemated, they mentally circled each other, searching for a weakness.

George took the hard line, knowing that the worst that could happen would be that Christopher's name would not be cleared. He waited for Emil to accept his terms.

Emil felt as if Katie was deliberately trying to humiliate him with her request and it angered him to know that he had no effective way to counter her demand. Recognizing his position, he grudgingly agreed to her terms.

"Very well."

"Now. How soon are you leaving for New Orleans?"

"There's a steamer out tonight. I plan to be on it."

"Good. As soon as I'm assured of my son-in-law's safety, we will conclude our arrangement. Is that satisfactory to you?"

"Yes. And I will send word to you at once when I find out something."

"We'll be waiting. But be warned. If Fletcher's dead, you won't have seen the last of us."

Katie tossed restlessly in her bed in the darkened hotel room, as sleep eluded her. There should have been some word from Mark by now and the continued silence was undermining her determination not to think the worst.

She missed Christopher. Her entire being longed for him . . . his touch, his nearness, the gentle sound of his laughter. It seemed an eternity since he'd last held her and loved her. And yet, even now, she could recall his every caress and warm memories of his demanding desire stirred her.

"Oh Christopher," she moaned to herself. "Where are you? Please, please come to me."

So much had happened since he'd left on his trip. Joel's murder — Andre's death — her escape to her father's protection. She wondered if he knew about it at all or if he was still in hiding unaware of the great changes that had taken place.

Tears stung her eyes and, in the shadowed darkness of the room, she let them fall unheeded. Christopher was her whole world. Why, if something happened to him . . . No, she decided. He was safe. Katie wouldn't let herself even consider the alternative. Christopher was coming to her. Of that much, she was sure.

Nineteen

The Reunion

They would arrive in St. Louis the following morning and Christopher was torn between apprehension and excitement. Was Katie safe? He had fought thinking about it for the whole trip but no longer could he deny the possibility that Emil might have found her . . .

Swearing under his breath, Christopher sat up on the edge of the bunk. In the beginning, when he had been denying his attraction to Katie, he had known that something like this could happen. But his common sense had lost out in the war of his emotions. Love had conquered all, even his hard logic.

He couldn't help but smile . . . it was one battle that he would never regret losing. Katie was his world . . . his life. In just their short time together, she had shown him how wonderful real love could be. Christopher knew now that he would do everything in his power to protect Katie and to keep their life together free of fear.

Having made the final decision to give up his abolitionist work, he wasn't distressed. In fact, if anything, he was relieved. For if he found Katie alive and well, he was going to spend the rest of his life being thankful for their second chance at love.

Standing up with considerably less effort than it had taken him the day before, Christopher took several halting steps across the small cabin. He was pleased to find that the dizziness had passed. He couldn't say he felt wonderful but at least he was ambulatory and that was major progress.

"You're up!" Mark was surprised as he entered the stateroom unannounced. "Are you sure you're strong enough?"

Christopher grinned. "Probably not, but I'm doing it anyway. I have no intention of leaving this steamer the same way I got on it."

"Yes, sir," Mark chuckled at his good-natured vehemence. But as Christopher's smile became more of a grimace, he invited, "Sit back down for a while. Don't wear yourself out today. Save all that energy for tomorrow."

A grunt of pain escaped him as he sat down heavily. "So, how are you this morning?"

"I'm fine. I just spoke with the captain and he says we'll be tying up in St. Louis right at dawn."

"Good. Now, where did you say you stayed whenever you came to town with your father?"

"We didn't make the trip that often, but when we did, we stayed at the Planter's House."

"All right. That'll be our first stop."

"If she's not there, we can check at the railroad office. I'm sure she'll have left a message for you there."

Christopher nodded, anxious for this last day to be over. "Damn! I feel like we're never going to get there."

"I know. But we will."

Mark sounded calmer than he felt. With each passing day, his confidence in Katie's ability to protect herself had waned as all the "what-if's" played havoc with his peace of mind. But tomorrow, their journey would be over and hopefully, they would find Katie safe and happy, awaiting their arrival.

"Bring the table over," Christopher directed as Mark tried to get his thoughts together.

"Not again," he groaned in humorous frustration.

"Can you think of any other way to idle away the hours? It's going to be one very long day."

Without another word, Mark pulled the table over and brought out the now dogeared, deck of cards.

"We'll be waiting to hear from you, Emil. But if I haven't received any assurances about Christopher's safety in two weeks' time, then Katie and I will be coming South."

"I'll be in touch before then, George," Emil stated firmly as he watched the roustabouts take his baggage on board.

"I'm counting on it. And the news had better be good," he added one final threat.

"Goodbye, George."

"Emil."

George watched as Emil mounted the gangplank and strode down the main deck to the companionway. Then, turning away, he headed back to the hotel to dine with Katie and Dee. They had ordered dinner to be served in his suite and he was looking forward to their small celebration. Emil was gone and Katie and Dee were safe at last.

Christopher finished off his meal mechanically. He

had had no appetite, but knew that he had to eat to build his strength. Nervous and edgy, he got up to pace the room.

When Mark had left him alone to rest earlier, Christopher had forsaken sleep. Instead he had practiced walking and had almost attained his normal stride again.

He knew he had to give the appearance of vitality even if it was an illusion. He couldn't take a chance on facing Montard from a position of weakness.

"Finish eating, yet?" Mark joined him.

"I just got done."

"How about a drink?" He held up a bottle of bourbon and two glasses. "What do you say?"

"I say, you're a mind-reader."

"Not really. I'm just as nervous as you are," he admitted, pouring out two stiff drinks. "And I thought this might help to get us through the night."

Christopher picked up his tumbler and took a deep drink, sighing afterward. "That's the best medicine I've had yet."

Mark sat down on the single chair in the cabin as Christopher stretched out, once again, on his bunk.

"Make sure not to get in any fights tonight," he chided Mark.

"I have no intention of leaving this room," he countered. "And I definitely have no intention of picking a fight with you."

"Good, although right now, I've no doubt that you could lay me low with one punch."

Mark laughed and refilled both their glasses. "But it wouldn't be much of an accomplishment to beat up a man who has spent the past week flat on his back in bed recovering from a gunshot wound."

"Guess not," he agreed. "Although there was a time when I think you would have taken great pleasure in it."

"That's for sure. That first night — during the cardgame . . . you were so cool about the whole thing . . . so professional."

"I had a reason to be. I wanted to get Dee back for Joel and since Andre had refused to sell her . . . winning Greenwood was the only quick way."

"But you acted like you didn't want to gamble for the plantation."

"If I'd seemed too eager, Emil might have backed down."

"It was all a ruse?"

Christopher shrugged eloquently. "I didn't plan it that way. I just took advantage of the opportunity offered me."

Mark shook his head in admiration as he downed his whiskey. "You know, I'll admit I didn't like you in the beginning, but now I'm damned glad Katie married you."

"I'm damned glad she married me, too," he grinned and took another drink. "Katie's unlike any woman I've ever known."

"She is something. Until we came South, we had never realized how open and unrestricted our lives had been. We both had trouble getting used to all these 'do's and don't's'. Katie more than me, because she didn't want to be here."

"I know. Katie told me all about your father forcing her to come with you."

"Father never really forced her. It was more like gentle coercion."

"Well, no matter, I'm just glad he did it."

Mark smiled lopsidedly as the whiskey began to affect him. "Me, too."

* * *

"I told Emil that if we hadn't heard anything from him in two weeks' time that we would be coming South ourselves."

Katie nodded her assent. "Frankly, I'm ready to go to New Orleans right now to look for him. I don't know if I can last two more weeks."

"It's better that we stay put, for the odds are that Christopher is on his way here. Emil said that they hadn't caught him yet when he left to follow you North. And in my experience, the first twenty-four hours of being hunted are the most dangerous. Once Christopher found out that they were after him, I'm sure he took every precaution."

"I hope you're right."

"Your father is right, Katie. Mark was watching for him and I'm sure he took care of everything."

Katie smiled softly at their attempts to cheer her. "Thanks," she patted Dee's hand. "I know that you're just trying to cheer me up."

"Not really," George explained further. "If we left now, we might very well pass him on the river and never know it."

"I hadn't thought of that."

"I'm sure we'll be hearing from Mark real soon, Katie," he reassured her.

The first light of day found a bleary-eyed Mark helping Christopher to dress.

"I think we've got it," he said as he pulled the shirt up over Christopher's injured shoulder and then aided him with his sling.

"Thanks. In another week, I'll be able to do it myself. How close are we?"

"They're just looking for a place to dock," Mark answered. "Then it's just a matter of a few minutes. Why don't you lie back down until we're tied up? I'll come and get you when it's time to leave the boat."

"Fine." Christopher needed the extra rest for his head was aching as badly as his shoulder. "How's your head?" he finally asked wryly.

"I don't want to talk about it," came his answer as he headed for the door. "I'll be back."

"Shut it softly," he called.

And Mark laughed as he went out on deck.

The Mississippi River looked black and smooth in the early morning light and Mark watched it flow past, fascinated by its deceptive appearance. It looked tame . . . this wide waterway . . . as if one could float forever undisturbed, but Mark knew in its dark, swirling heart, it was a treacherous beast. Beneath the river's calm surface, lurked immeasurable dangers that were waiting—just waiting—for the right time to catch the unprepared unaware.

As their steamer glided up to the riverbank, hard muscled roustabouts grabbed the thick hemp ropes that were thrown and hauled the boat in, tying the massive stern-wheeler to the metal rings buried deep in the levee.

When the plank had been lowered, Mark went ashore and hired a carriage for them. Then, after directing the driver to get as close as possible to the steamer, he went back for Christopher.

"Ready?" he asked entering the stateroom.

"I've been ready for a week now. Let's go."

Slowly, with precise movements aimed at minimizing pain, Christopher stood up and left the cabin. The trip down the gangplank seemed the longest of his life and by the time they had crossed the uneven cobblestones of the levee to reach the carriage, his knees were weakening. Climbing in with an effort, he sat back heavily.

Mark noticed that Christopher had paled with pain and he wished there was something he could do to help him.

"Christopher?"

"I'll be fine in a minute," he said, his voice strained. "Let's get to the hotel."

Mark nodded. "The Planter's House, please. We'll register, so we can leave our luggage and you can rest for a while, too. I have no idea how long it will take us to find them, but we'll make our hotel room our base of operations."

"All right," he agreed.

The city was slowly coming to life as their carriage rumbled forth heading in the direction of the hotel. Pulling to a stop at the entrance, Mark and Christopher got out while the driver got their bags.

The lobby was deserted as they crossed the highly polished floor and the sounds of their footsteps echoed loudly through the high-ceilinged room.

"Good morning, gentlemen," the desk clerk greeted them. "Can I help you with anything?"

"We'd like rooms, please. Preferably a suite if one is available."

"Of course. If you'll just sign here." He pushed the registry to Mark.

Mark signed and offered the pen to Christopher, but he waved it away. Shifting positions, he leaned against the counter, disguising his discomfort by his casual stance.

As the clerk turned the book to check his signature, he frowned.

"Kingsford? Are you any relation to George Kingsford?"

"I am," Mark looked up attentively. "I'm his son."

"Then you'll be delighted to know that he's here."

"Here?"

"Upstairs in the suite next to yours." The clerk handed them their key. "Suite 202."

Christopher and Mark exchanged incredulous looks before heading for the main staircase. Christopher took the steps easily, his thoughts totally on finding Katie. There was no time for weakness of pain. She was close . . . he knew it.

The second floor hall loomed before them—wide and dimly lighted.

"202 . . ." Mark repeated to himself in frustration as he checked room numbers up and down the hall. "Damn! Where is . . . Here it is!" He half-called and pounded loudly on the door.

Christopher, who'd been checking the other side of the hall hurried to join him.

George had spent a restless night worrying about Katie. He knew that she was upset and discouraged, but right now, there was very little that they could do—one way or the other.

When the sun had first begun its ascent, bluing the purple and red stained sky, he had given up his useless attempt to sleep. Rising, George had pulled on his pants and had gone to sit by the window in his small parlor to watch the dawn.

The pounding on his door startled him and his immediate thought was that it had to be bad news . . . He dreaded opening the door and he girded himself against the upcoming scene.

"What is it?" he growled, throwing the door open wide, expecting the worst.

"Father!" Mark was excited. "I am so glad that you are here!"

"Mark?" George looked at him questioningly. "Mark!"

When he realized that his son wasn't an apparition, he embraced him warmly. Then with a quick look at Christopher, he ushered them inside.

"Come on in! We've been so worried! Come in!"

As he started to close the door footsteps sounded in the hall and Katie called.

"Father? Did you hear all that commotion? What was it all about?"

Entering the room, she gasped, her eyes widening, at the sight of her husband standing before her, his arm in a sling.

"Christopher!" She flew to him and was enveloped in his warm, one-armed embrace. "Oh, Christopher! Are you all right? What happened to you?" she asked tearfully.

"Katie," he groaned her name, holding her as best he could and bending down to capture her lips in a sweet, long-awaited kiss of reunion.

Katie melted against him, thrilling to his touch . . . his nearness. They broke off the kiss only as they became aware of the others' eyes upon them.

"I take it you two know each other?" George spoke in gruff good humor.

"Papa, this is Christopher," Katie told him proudly, holding his uninjured arm possessively.

"I had hoped as much," he laughed, clapping him on the back. "I'm glad I finally got to meet you. I've certainly heard enough about you these past few days." George's eyes were twinkling.

"It's good to meet you, too, sir."

"George, please."

"George." Christopher felt an immediate liking for this man who was his wife's father.

"Sit down. We've much to talk about," George directed sizing up Katie's young man and deciding instantly that he liked him.

426

Mark and George sat in wing chairs facing Katie and Christopher on the sofa.

"Where were you? When you didn't follow us right away . . . we were frantic!" Katie told him.

"I was waylaid . . . so to speak," Christopher explained. "I had been on my way to Mark's when I was ambushed. I managed to get away, but if it hadn't been for your brother . . ."

"The patrollers had come by the townhouse looking for him earlier," Mark went on. "They even did a room by room search. I knew he was coming back but I couldn't get a message to him without setting the patrollers on to him. Then when I heard the shot outside . . . Well, I went out and managed to find the carriage easily enough, but Christopher wasn't with it. It was covered with blood and he was missing."

"Where were the patrollers?"

"I didn't see them, I guess Christopher managed to decoy them away. Anyway, with the help of a servant, we scoured the whole neighborhood."

"Where was he?"

"We finally found him in an alley. I knew that it would be foolhardy to try to sneak him back into the townhouse so we took him to Cherie's."

"And you've been there all this time?"

"Yes, Cherie was wonderful," Christopher told her.

"You should have seen Christopher, though, once we'd found out that Emil had followed you North. He wouldn't rest until finally Cherie figured out a way to smuggle him out of New Orleans."

"Cherie did it all."

"She smuggled you out?"

"In a manner of speaking," he grinned now thinking of his very effective disguise. "She knew that I shouldn't get out of bed, so she made me up to look like an old man and then got this wheelchair . . ."

"Katie, you would not have recognized your own husband! He had gray hair and wrinkles and he was all wrapped up in this big old shawl . . ."

"It worked, though, right?"

"It worked beautifully. They got me on board and into the cabin with no trouble at all."

"Remind me to thank her," Katie said earnestly.

"I will . . . but what about you? Mark and I were out of our minds worrying about you and Dee up here, unprotected . . ."

"It would have been dangerous except for Papa."

"What happened?" Mark asked George. "And what were you doing here in town?"

"I had come into the office to arrange a leave of absence."

"A leave? But why?"

"I was going to come South for a visit."

"Well, it was a very lucky thing he was here," Katie spoke up. "Because the same day that I ran into him accidentally in the railroad office, Emil showed up."

"How did you find out that he was here?"

"We didn't until it was almost too late. Papa and I were having dinner in the hotel dining room and Emil went up to my room and kidnapped Dee."

"She's all right, isn't she?" Christopher worried.

"She's fine, thanks to Papa. When we found out that Emil had left the hotel with her, we chased them down to the levee."

"I'll bet that was a scene," Mark smiled as he imagined his father and Emil Montard squaring off.

"Actually," George said. "It wasn't too bad. A few well chosen threats . . ."

"Thank God you got her away from him." Christopher was relieved to find out that Dee was safe. "She's suffered enough already." His tone was bitter as he thought of Joel.

"But where's Emil now?" Mark asked. "How did you get rid of him?"

"He's gone back to New Orleans. And supposedly, he's withdrawing his charges against Christopher."

"He's what?" Christopher was astounded. "How did you manage that?"

"That's something we still have to discuss. With Katie's tentative approval, I made a deal of sorts."

"What kind of deal?"

"We agreed to sell him Greenwood—minus the slaves—in return for his clearing your name and leaving Dee alone."

"He wants Greenwood that badly?"

"Definitely," George stated. "But our whole arrangement depended entirely on your being safely returned to us. And now that you are here . . ."

"I've had a lot of time to think this past week and one thing I know for sure is that I don't want to go back," he admitted. "I don't want Katie put in any danger, ever again."

He looked at her, his gaze tracing her features lovingly.

"We'll sell."

"Good. Mark can take care of all that when he goes back."

"What should I do about Greenwood's slaves?"

"I want them all freed," Christopher stated without hesitation. "Find out the easiest way to handle it, Mark, and then let me know."

"I'll check as soon as I get back."

"Thanks."

"How about breakfast?" George suggested.

"Sounds great," Mark was hungry.

But Katie noticed that Christopher was looking tired and after meeting his gaze in understanding, she refused the invitation.

"I think we'll wait . . ."

"Christopher, why don't you and Katie take over our rooms? I can stay here with Father," Mark offered.

"That sounds fine."

"Dee will have her own room, too, then."

"We'll meet you back here this afternoon," Christopher stood slowly, drawing Katie up with him.

"And I'll make arrangements for a doctor to check your shoulder later today."

"Thank you, sir."

"George, please."

Christopher nodded.

Katie kissed her father and brother and then hugged Mark. "Thanks, little brother."

"You're welcome," Mark smiled fondly at her as she left the suite with her husband.

"Well, shall we go eat?"

"Yes."

"I want to hear all about New Orleans and what it is you're doing now. Katie tells me that you've taken over some of Isaac's business interests."

"Yes, I . . ." their voices faded out as they headed down the hall toward the staircase to the lobby.

Katie closed the door behind them.

"Do you want to see Dee now?"

"No. I'll speak with her later . . ." He knew his reunion with her would be painful for them both.

Katie smiled at him and moved to kiss him softly.

"What do you want to do?"

"Right now, the only thing on my mind is you. I want you, Katie."

His words sent a thrill of desire coursing through her.

"Love you," she whispered as they walked slowly to the bedroom.

Christopher sat on the bed as Katie undressed. His eyes followed her every move, admiring her trim figure as she shed the last of her petticoats and her shift and stood before him naked. Reaching up behind her, in a motion that thrust her breasts up and out invitingly, Katie pulled the ivory pins from her hair, releasing the silken mane and letting it fall caressingly about her. With cat-like grace, she approached the bed, burning with the need to be one with him.

Christopher watched, mesmerized, as she moved to stand before him. The sight of her slender, bare limbs enthralling him, he reached out and pulled her between his thighs, making her his willing captive.

"I'd like to keep you this way . . . always." His voice was hoarse with his need. "You are so beautiful."

Leaning forward, Katie kissed him, full and flaming on the mouth. She had waited an eternity it seemed and, at last, he was here. With impatient fingers, she freed the buttons of his shirt and ran her hands gently over his partially bandaged chest.

"Help me, darling," he asked as he broke off the kiss.

Katie slipped the sling from his arm and then stripped his shirt from him. She gasped as she saw the size of the bandage.

"Will I hurt you?" she asked, fearful of injuring him further.

"I'll only suffer if I don't have you Katie," he grinned, bending to kiss her quickly.

Then with Katie's help he finished undressing and lay back on the bed pulling her down with him.

Curling up against his good side, she rose up on an elbow to stare at him.

"I knew you'd come to me," she told him

confidently.

"Oh, you did, did you?" He smiled tenderly and smoothed a long, golden strand of hair away from her face. "What made you so certain?"

"Didn't you remember our last ride, down by the pond?"

"I remembered all right," he groaned. "That and every delectable inch of you, as a matter of fact."

"Good," Katie purred, throwing her leg over his and running her hand across his flat stomach teasingly.

His reaction to her was immediate as his body throbbed to life. And Katie, pleased with her power to excite him, trailed hot kisses down his neck and uninjured shoulder while her hands worked their magic on his lower body, coming near but never quite touching him.

"Oh, Katie," he spoke huskily as her lips followed the path her hands had taken.

"I want to please you, Christopher," she told him.

Rising up, she kissed him and then moved lower, surrendering herself to his pleasure.

Christopher's breath caught in his throat as she explored him with her lips and tongue, bringing him to the edge of ecstasy. As his climax neared, his body tautened and in one agile move, Katie mounted him, taking his pulsing manhood deep within her.

Balancing herself with her arms to keep her weight off his torso, she offered him her breasts. He nuzzled hungrily at her nipples, sucking one then the other as her hips ground steadily against his.

The ever-tightening coil of her excitement built to a frenzied peak. Calling his name, she strained closer to the hardness of his loins as the throbbing splendor of her desire took her to completion and beyond.

Christopher felt her climax and gave in to the power of her love, emptying himself within her sweet depths.

"I love you, Katie," he murmured as she rolled to lie at his side. "I love you so much." Levering himself up on his strong arm, he leaned over and kissed her.

Then, with her nestling at his side, they slept.

Mark looked at his father across the table. "Isaac trained me in several aspects of his business before we went out to Last Island."

"And you like that type of work?"

"Yes. I find it very challenging."

Mark was aware of what his father wanted to know, but he couldn't bring himself to say the words. For years, Mark had known that George wanted him to join him working on the railroads . . . and he realized, now, that his decision to remain in Louisiana was going to destroy those dreams.

"So," George said with evident finality. "You have decided to stay down South."

"Yes, sir."

"If it's what you really want and if it will make you happy, then I'm all for it."

Mark was surprised. "I was worried about telling you . . . I knew how you felt about my working with you . . ."

"That was my dream, Mark. Not yours."

They stared at each other for a long moment, Mark recognizing that his father had accepted him as an adult and George realizing that his son had become his own man.

"Thank you for making it easy for me."

George smiled, "Life is difficult enough without those we love adding to the problems." Then, changing the subject, he asked, "When's the wedding? Katie's told me about Jacqui."

"We haven't set a date yet."

"Well, just make sure I get plenty of notice. I may have missed Katie's, but I have no intention of missing yours."

"Yes, sir."

Christopher stirred and came awake as his shoulder began to throb. Glancing down, he studied Katie's gentle beauty and for a moment, completely forgot his pain.

She had been so giving . . . so tender . . . so open in her desire to please him. Her every touch had been designed to arouse his passion with little thought given to her own.

Christopher marvelled at her selflessness and wanted to love her as she had loved him. Shifting himself to a more comfortable position, he stroked the velvet flesh of her breasts.

"Christopher?" Katie's voice was soft and slurred as she looked up at him with sleep-drugged eyes. "Hello."

"Hush, now," he told her quietly. "Let me love you this time."

Katie sighed with delight and stretched sinuously, arching her back.

Christopher was in no hurry and continued his exploring caresses from breast to thigh, pausing only briefly with each stroke to brush over her sensitive aching peaks.

"Please, Christopher," she whispered as the fire he was building within her burned ever hotter.

"No, love. Not yet."

He lowered his head to suckle her breast as his hand slipped between her legs seeking the moist secrets of her womanhood.

Katie moaned her passion as her hands slid down

his chest to his erection, but Christopher shifted his hips away, not yet ready to complete their union.

"Easy darling."

"I want you."

"And I want you. But we're going slow, this time."

Pressing a hot, wet kiss to each breast he slid lower over her body, his mouth tracing patterns of fire over her silken stomach.

Katie knew what Christopher wanted from her this time and she lifted her hips for him, offering him all of herself. The joy of his most intimate caress left her shaking, as he delved warmly into her love nest. Abandoning herself to his skillful lovemaking, she moved against his mouth. And, as he reached up to pinch gently at her nipples, her orgasm rocked explosively through her. Holding his head tightly to her pulsing body, she arched convulsively in ecstasy and then lay spent.

Christopher lowered her hips and kissed the inner sweetness of each thigh before covering her sated body with his. He slid easily within her depths and waited until Katie began to move.

Murmuring her love to him, over and over, she wrapped her legs around his slim hips and let him have his way with her, glorying in his driving possession.

It was long minutes later, as they lay in each other's arms that she remembered his injury.

"Your shoulder!"

"I didn't feel a thing," he grinned and she returned his smile.

"You may not have, but I sure did."

"You're a wanton, Katie Fletcher."

"If I am, it's because you made me into one!" she teased.

"Yes. And I'm loving every minute of it." He kissed her deeply.

Dee heard the knock and, busy with dressing her son, just called out, "Come on in."

She was expecting it to be George or possibly Katie, although Katie would have no reason to knock. Hurrying to fasten Jebediah's clothes before he squirmed away, Dee cast a hasty glance over her shoulder to see who it was.

Christopher paused for a moment in the doorway until Dee looked his way.

"I'm back Dee." His tone was solemn.

Dee stopped what she was doing and turned to face him, allowing Jebediah to escape her restraining clutches.

"Christopher . . ." She was so happy to see him but so forcefully reminded of Joel that her pain and her pleasure mixed and she started to cry.

"Dee, I'm so sorry." He came to her and held her tenderly, his own eyes burning with the long suppressed grief he felt over Joel's death.

Their embrace went on for long minutes as they sought solace from each other. While many had known Joel, only Christopher and Dee had been truly close to him. They had suffered with him and rejoiced with him and they had loved him. Finally, Dee composed herself and drew back to look at him.

"Where's Katie? Have you seen her yet?"

"She's with her father. I wanted to see you alone."

"Thank you," Dee understood. "Did Katie tell you about that day?"

"Just what was in her letter . . ."

"It was terrible. He came chasin' after her up the front drive, and Joel, he didn't even have a gun . . ." Dee trembled as she related the horrors of that fatal morning.

"You don't have to talk about it," Christopher hugged her again.

"I need to," Dee explained. "It helps me remember what a good man Joel was."

"He was that." He could still recall Joel's reaction to the injustices of the slave pens that first time he'd seen him. It seemed so long ago. "He was a very good man. I miss him, Dee."

"I know. I do, too." Putting aside her sorrow, she worried at his arm. "What happened?"

"The patrollers caught up with me in New Orleans, but Mark and Cherie got me out." He minimized his brush with death.

"I'm so glad. Katie's been almost sick worryin' 'bout you this past week. We didn't know where you were or ever if you were safe."

"I had to hide. But it's all over now."

Dee's eyes darkened with concern as she moved to pick up Jebediah who was fussing on the bed. "You ain't plannin' on goin' back, are you?"

"No. We're not going back," he answered firmly and Dee smiled tremulously.

"Good."

"I haven't talked it over with Katie yet, so I'm not sure where we're going. But wherever it is, Dee, you are going with us."

"Thank you," she murmured, her words heartfelt.

"I've got to get back to George's suite. He's arranged for a doctor to take a look at my shoulder, so I'd better be there when he shows up. I'll see you later this afternoon."

As Dee watched him leave, she felt a sense of peace and contentment wash over her, soothing her pain and lightening the burden of her grief.

* * *

437

The doctor carefully cut the bandage away from Christopher's shoulder and tossed them aside before examining the ugly-looking wound.

"How long ago were you shot, Mr. Fletcher?"

"It's been a little over a week."

"You're healing nicely," he told him. "If you take it relatively easy for another week, you should be fine."

"Good."

Christopher sounded excited and the physician quickly slowed him down.

"If you try to do too much, you're liable to break this bullet wound open again . . . and it takes longer to heal the second time around."

Christopher frowned, accepting that he still had some healing to do.

"However, if it doesn't hurt, you can leave your arm out of the sling, now."

Brightening at the chance to at least look normal, Christopher flexed his bad arm. While there was a tinge of pain, the discomfort was not unbearable.

"I think it'll be fine."

"Well, you're done then," he told him as he finished rewrapping the wound. "I believe you'll find this small bandage a little easier to live with, too."

"It feels better already," Christopher responded as he managed to pull on his own shirt for the first time since the shooting.

"Good. I'll check back on you toward the end of the week."

When the doctor had gone, Christopher finished dressing and walked out into the little sitting room to find George there alone.

"Where did Katie go?" he was curious.

"I sent her out with Mark to get you a change of clothes. From the looks of things, I take it you didn't get a chance to pack when you made your exit."

"You're right," Christopher grinned.

"How about a drink?"

"Bourbon will do fine, thanks," he replied as George poured the liquor into two glasses.

Handing Christopher his glass, George waved him to a chair and they both relaxed, savoring the smooth taste of the expensive whiskey.

"I'm glad you're not going back," he said seriously. "For although Emil will, no doubt, be able to clear your name, I would still be concerned that the seeds of distrust had been planted. You might never really be safe there again."

"I know. And I have other friends in the area whom I want to protect. If I returned, someone might decide to do a little more investigating and end up causing all kinds of trouble."

George nodded. "How did you get involved in the Underground in the first place? I've always been fascinated by it, but I've never had the opportunity before to meet someone who was actually active in the movement."

"You probably have met them, all right, it's just that nobody talks about it. The risks are too great."

"But what encouraged you?"

"I went to my first, and I hope my last, slave auction," Christopher would never forget the terror and heartbreak of that day under the blistering summer sun. "I bought Joel that day . . . he had been beaten and abused."

"Who was his owner?"

"Montard. In fact, I found out later that the reason he was being sold was because Andre wanted Dee."

George was beginning to understand everything much more clearly. "So Andre got rid of Joel to have free access to his wife?"

"Yes. Plus, Joel and Dee had tried to run . . . Dee

couldn't tolerate the things Andre was doing to her and she wanted to get away from him."

"No wonder they were so furious when you won Greenwood."

Andre tried to send Dee away before we took possession, but luckily we got there in time."

"Which only served to make Andre even more furious."

"Right. And then there was Katie."

"Katie?"

"Andre was trying his best to win her, but she didn't want anything to do with him. From the way things turned out it seems he was almost obsessed with having her. And, if it hadn't been for Dee, he would have. I hate to think of what might have happened to them if Dee hadn't had sense enough to go for the gun." Christopher suppressed a shudder.

"I'm glad things worked out as well as they did, although, I am sorry about Joel. Were you involved with the abolitionists before you bought him?"

"No. We went North later so I could free him more easily and I got him a tutor so he could learn to read and write. But he didn't care much about all that, all he wanted to do was go back and free Dee and Jebediah," Christopher paused. "I made the necessary contacts. It took quite a while, because everyone was so suspicious, but eventually, we knew what we had to do and we headed back South."

"Were you planning on using Greenwood as your base?

"No. It was just luck that I won it in that poker game. Joel and I had originally planned to get Dee and Jebediah out on the Underground."

"So, what will you do now?" George asked as the conversation lulled for a moment. "Have you made any plans at all for the future?"

"No. I haven't thought much beyond today."

"Do you need to work? I can get you a job with the Pacific, if you're interested."

"Where are you building?"

"We're heading west. The going is slow, but it's where the future is for this country."

"I know. I don't think that the North and South can go on much longer without coming to violence. It's such a tense situation . . ." Christopher was torn between resuming his structured life in Philadelphia or heading west into the unexplored wilds of the Rockies.

"You don't have to make any decisions right now. Take your time. But, remember, you'll always have a job with me if you need one."

"Thank you."

"Your father's offered me a job on the railroad," Christopher told her as they dressed for dinner that evening.

Katie smiled at the thought. "What did you tell him?"

"Nothing, really, just that we hadn't made up our minds about the future yet." When she didn't respond, he went on. "What would you like to do, Katie? Do you want to go to England? Or maybe the Continent? You name it. You know that money's not a problem."

She looked at him affectionately. "I'm happy here. You don't need to take me to Europe."

"All right, then, pick a city. I still own the family home in Philadelphia, so we could move back there if you like. Or . . ."

"Christopher?" she interrupted him.

"What?"

"Are you sure that you're finished with your abolitionist work?"

441

"Yes."

"Is there any place that you particularly want to go?"

"No."

"Then I want to go west."

"West?"

"I had my fill of putting up with the dictates of society. I want to go where people accept you for what you are, not for what your family owns or doesn't own."

"Do you want to stay with the railroad? I have no objections to doing some honest labor for a while." He smiled as he pictured himself toting the huge railroad ties and driving the spikes deep with sledgehammers.

"We could try it just to see if you like it . . ."

"All right. We'll do it."

Katie hugged him excitedly. "Do you know, when we lived at Greenwood, I was so afraid that I'd never get back here . . ."

He kissed her gently and pulled her close. Katie was wearing only her chemise and she wriggled her hips invitingly against him, stirring his blood.

"I like the feel of both your arms around me," she said in a sexy voice, kissing his neck.

"Katie!" he pushed her firmly away. "We're due to meet your father and Mark in ten minutes. You'd better get dressed."

But Katie enjoyed playing the temptress and she embraced him from behind, rubbing her hard-tipped breasts against his back and slipping her hands inside the waist of his pants.

"We could be a few minutes late, don't you think?" Katie sat down on the edge of the bed and gave him a heated look.

"I guess they won't really worry about us right away. Will they?" he agreed.

Katie gave a throaty chuckle as she realized her victory and she pulled off her shift in eager anticipation of his coming. Christopher quickly undressed himself and joined her on the soft mattress.

"You know, beds are nice, but there was something so special about our night together on the beach . . ."

"Ummmm," Katie agreed pulling his head down for a kiss. "Maybe we should forget about going west and find ourselves a desert island somewhere."

"I think I've had my fill of islands for a while," he told her wryly.

"I can't imagine why," she teased.

"I think it was the weather," he murmured before kissing her again.

Christopher took her quickly then in a rush of unexpected passion that swept them both along like wildfire and left them breathless and sated in its aftermath.

George had arranged for dinner to be served in his suite and he was waiting with Mark, Dee and Jebediah when Katie and Christopher finally made their appearance.

"Glad you could make it," Mark teased Katie in a low voice and she blushed guiltily. Then turning to Christopher he said, "I've been trying to come up with the best idea of what to do with Greenwood's slaves."

"Have you hit upon anything yet?"

"Father has made a sensible offer that sounds good to me, but I wanted to know what you think about it."

"What?"

"He's offered to give any freed man a job with the railroad if they are willing to work for wages."

"Good. Present the offer to them, and then make arrangements for the ones who are interested to be shipped to the camp."

"I'll take care of it as soon as I get back."

"Well, that's one major problem solved." Christopher was relieved that they had figured out a workable solution so easily. "And, George?"

"Yes?"

"I think Katie's got something she wants to tell you."

"Katie?" he looked at his daughter.

"Christopher and I have decided to go with you. Christopher will take the job with the railroad."

George beamed his pleasure. "That's wonderful! I hate to admit it, but it's been damned lonely in camp since you two left."

"I've missed you too, Papa. But I have to admit in the beginning I was really angry with you for making me go . . . And then when Mark got into the fight on the boat . . ."

"Mark? You didn't tell me about any fight."

"That happened a long time ago and . . ."

"And, besides, he lost!" Katie teased.

"To whom?"

"Christopher," Katie answered, laughing.

George looked at Christopher with open admiration, but Mark took advantage of Katie's omission.

"Just ask Katie what happened next!" Mark egged him on.

"Katie?" George raised an eyebrow and Katie blushed. "What did you do?"

"Well," she hedged. "Well, I defended my poor little brother from this big bully," Katie gave Christopher a smiling glance.

"She hit me, George. She blackened my eye," Christopher added cheerfully.

"Katie! I thought I told you to behave yourself on this trip," he scolded lovingly.

"I was, but when I saw Mark get knocked out, I lost

444

my temper," she defended her own actions.

"Besides, George, if she'd behaved herself, we would never have met," Christopher put in candidly.

"That's true," he agreed. "I suppose everything always does work out for the best." Looking over at Dee, he drew her into the conversation. "Will you have any objections to living in a camp, Dee? I know it will be a little rough with Jebediah, but I think you'll do well."

"Ah'm lookin' forward to it," she said enthusiastically. "Ah'm beginning a whole new life."

"And it'll be a better one, I assure you," Christopher told her earnestly.

"Ah know. For me and my baby . . ."

When the supper had ended, everyone retired for the night, exhausted from the long excitement of the day.

Hours later, Christopher and Katie lay close together, enjoying the peace after having shared passion's delight.

"Do you know that the whole time you were missing, I was jealous of Dee?" Katie confided.

"Why?"

"Because she had Jebediah. I wanted your baby so badly . . ."

"You'd like to have a child so soon?" He was surprised.

"A baby would be the most perfect gift I could give you."

"Give us," he corrected, liking the idea of starting a family.

"Us," she smiled and her eyes were luminous with her love for him.

Lifting herself over him, she kissed him deeply.

445

"I've heard," he grinned mischievously, when the kiss ended. "That it takes a lot of practice to get it right."

"What?" Katie was confused by his statement.

"Making babies, of course," he replied, gazing at her warmly. "Would you like to start?"

"I'd love to," she told him and met him in a wanton embrace, eager to share in the wonder of his love once again.

A NOTE TO MY READERS:

In December of last year we lost our home to a fire. Luckily no one was injured, but that was only because we had a working smoke alarm. Please, if you don't have one, get one. If you do have one, check your batteries. It's a matter of life and death.

Thanks,
Bobbi